LUX DOMINI

ALEX THOMAS

LUX DOMINI

♀

Thriller

Lux Domini by Alex Thomas

Text copyright © 2018 by Alex Thomas.
Translation copyright © 2018 by Christine Louise Hohlbaum
All rights reserved.

Previously published as Lux Domini by Blanvalet — an imprint of Verlagsgruppe Random House GmbH, Munich — in Germany in 2011. Translated from German by Christine Louise Hohlbaum. First published in English by Alex Thomas in 2018.

www.alex-thomas.london

Cover design by Anke Koopmann — www.designomicon.de.

ISBN: 9781983058714

For Gene

You will be the Thirteenth.
You will be cursed by the other generations,
and you will come to rule over them.
(Gospel of Judas)

Prologue

Judas Iscariot had chosen suicide.

The barren tree from which his corpse hung appeared to be encircled by a sinister veil. The surrounding field seemed diseased like the skin of a leper. Not a single breeze stirred the air, as if the earth around the dying tree along with the dead had given its last breath. Not even the crows wanted to sit upon the tormented branches to have a go at the corpse.

Joseph of Arimathea shielded his eyes from the brightness of the sun. He shivered then, and despite its power, the sun's light couldn't seem to warm this place.

»Take this man down!« he commanded to both young men he had brought with him to bury the dead man.

Joseph owned a burial place near Golgotha. It was there that he had brought the body of Jesus and where he would have Judas brought, to a small grave nearby.

The sky turned black, as if a torrential downpour would happen at any moment over Jerusalem. But Joseph doubted that even a single raindrop would make its way to this field. Both boys severed the noose and let the dead fall to the ground. Joseph thought he could almost hear the barren tree breathe a sigh of relief.

»It's not what you think,« Maria Magdalene had said, looking at him with her ageless eyes. »His fate is also our own. We have to search for him and find him.«

Joseph set about on his way and finally came to this place. A seemingly God-forsaken place about which not even the scavengers wanted to know. He sighed. Maria, Bartholomew, Philip and he should have been on their way to Alexandria by now.

Joseph watched as the two young men rolled the corpse into a strong, grey cloth. Oddly the dead body didn't give off an odour. Decay had barely set in. Neither of the boys said a word, but Joseph knew that they wished nothing more than to get out of there as fast as possible.

Suddenly, one of the boys paused and carefully bent over Judas.

»What is it?« asked Joseph in alarm.

»I see something hidden here,« the young man said, carefully pulling out two scrolls wrapped around one another from the dead man's robe.

In that very moment, Joseph could feel a tiny breeze blow over the field. A soft rain fell across his face and body and over the entire wretched ground. As he took both leather scrolls in his hands, he couldn't help but shiver. Was this perhaps Judas' justification for his betrayal?

Tiny raindrops began to form on the backside of the outer scroll. For some inexplicable reason, Joseph peered over the tree and into the sky, only to see an enormous rainbow. A sign?

For a brief moment, Joseph toyed with the idea of reading the scrolls, but something deep within him warned him not to, told him that he had no right to do so. He recalled Maria's words once again: »His fate is also our own. We have to search for him and find him.« In that moment, he knew to whom he should hand over the scrolls.

THE SECRET

1

September 29, 1978, Rome, Vatican City

»Have you discovered anything, Doctor?« Kleier heard the youthful and impatient voice of his assistant behind him. He felt the dust and grime on his sweaty face and tasted the dirt on his tongue. This inept bungler, who had only gotten the job due to his family ties, pushed him over the edge. The researcher, who had gotten his doctoral degree in archaeology, slowly approached the new dig site, pushed his glasses and the spotlight resting on his helmet back in place, bowed down and began to carefully free the earth from the debris with a trowel until he came up against something. Specks of dust danced in the rays of light. The outline of a square stone shone forth beneath the dust, along with the hint of a door handle that looked like it was a part of a trap door. Trap doors were commonplace down here.

»Looks like it, Sebastiano.«

With his strong hands that were accustomed to hard work, Kleier swept away the dust and the stone until he had freed up the handle. Three months prior he had worked at an archaeological site in Old Jerusalem – in Golgotha – when His Holiness John Paul I. had unexpectedly called him to Rome. They had come upon an unknown and completely atypical tunnel system in the depths of the Vatican's grottos, a type of labyrinth that wasn't even recorded on Antonio Bosio's layout maps. Bosio had been considered the early seventeenth century Columbus of the Roman catacombs.

»May I help you?« Sebastiano had maneuvered himself a few centimetres closer through the tight shaft. His face was covered with dust.

»No, there's not enough room,« explained Kleier. »The brush please.« The assistant handed him the brush, which was more like a sturdy hand-held brush, and tried to steal a fascinated look over the doctor's shoulder onto the site. Even Sebastiano seemed to sense that something extraordinary awaited his discovery deep down beneath the base of St. Peter's Basilica.

The researcher carefully brushed away the remaining dust in the crevices of the ornamentation and slowly noticed the symbol of a coat of arms on the stone — a papal coat of arms! Although a part of it was really the handle. In that moment, Kleier realised what stood before him. It was the coat of arms from Pope Pius XII, the head of the Church who, as the highest moral authority of the Catholic Church, had kept a stony silence during the Holocaust.

Sebastiano stretched his neck to come a few centimetres closer. Kleier grabbed the handle and tried to pull open the iron trap door. He managed to open it with little effort as the door was supported by invisible mechanics. Now the rectangular iron trap door stood in his way of the tiny space and he couldn't see inside the opening. He peered over the open trap door. Sebastiano did as well. Unfortunately, by doing so, the assistant pushed the archaeologist in such a way that the stone fell forward through the opening, breaking away part of the solid ground and falling with a bang to unimagined depths below. For a millisecond Kleier imagined wrapping his hands around Sebastiano's neck and slowly squeezing the life out of him, but in the next they both lay paralysed on the ground and waited until the noise subsided. All they could do now is pray. The hollow space beneath their feet seemed to be enormous and the ground beneath their bodies could give at any moment if they didn't distribute their body weight evenly. The researcher asked for a larger spotlight, crawled to the opening, leaned himself over the edge and held the light against the endless darkness.

»Good God!«

The iron trap door had fallen down a broad set of stairs without a railing and had ended in pieces at the bottom of the steep descending steps. Judging from the size of the stairs, the room that lay beneath him and Sebastiano must be enormous.

Kleier signalled to his assistant not to move, then crawled forward a bit. Yes, he even crawled a tad toward the stairs covered in debris while Sebastiano, who lay flat on the ground, held watch. He circled the beam of light until it finally reached the wall. Using the light as his guide, he began to search the large room as he slowly and carefully moved down the naked stairs. He gave a start and almost cried out when he thought he had come across a monster with his light beam.

No, it was just a painting he had never seen before. There was nothing human about the painting. It was too perfect to be human. Somehow the section that was now illuminated by his spotlight reminded him of an old Jewish writing that was not found in the Bible. The passage with Michael, the supreme angel, to be exact. On Mount Carmel he had proclaimed to the prophet Elias the end of the world.

The beam of light travelled further along the same wall. Kleier saw how fire and sulphur streamed down from heaven upon the godless people on the wall painting. Lamentations in the eternal underworld. It was a disturbing sight. But he kept going, allowing the light to wander further until he came upon a row of slender, spiral-life columns. In the distance he saw something that looked quite like...he held his breath.

A library!

Pius' secret private archive? Could that be the library that Pius had brought to safety and hidden from the Nazis?

Kleier could hear Sebastiano calling from above as to whether everything was all right. Of course everything was all right. More than all right! He collected himself and approached the first shelf as he looked about and hoped that his eyes would quickly adjust to the darkness. He finally reached one of the wall shelves. There were a lot fewer rows than he had hoped. In fact, there were only three. He looked over the old volumes, randomly took out a few and discovered that they had been prepared for storage down here.

All of the works were written in Latin; all of them were organised according to their content and chronology. It appeared that they were all copies and translations of much older works. After several more samples, Kleier realised that these were unknown Christian works — apocryphal books from the Bible. The archaeologist looked about him for a volume that he could take up to the surface as evidence of his findings.

A slender scarlet red binder jumped out at him. It was the only red one on the shelf. Besides it had a good size for carrying back up. He opened it. A story of the apostles? In apocryphal book form? That could be very interesting!

After readjusting the spotlight, Kleier began to scan the text, letting Sebastiano know periodically that he was still alive so as to keep him calm. In less than fifteen minutes the researcher knew he was holding a revolution — or better yet — a bomb in his hands. After reading this apocryphal text, he began to view the Pius' pontificate, the history of the papacy and, yes, even the history of the entire Catholic Church in a new light.

Shaking with excitement, Kleier forced himself to remain calm and hid the volume under his work clothes. This was enough for starters.

Slowly, but surely he made his way back to the entrance and pulled the light away from the dark-as-night opening. In response to his assistant's questioning look, he gave him a quick and impatient wave.

They crawled back to the wider and higher main tunnel in silence. Dr. Kleier had received strict instructions from His Eminence Cardinal deRossi, should he come across anything unusual during his work. And this was certainly something extraordinarily extraordinary!

***

About an hour later Kleier hurriedly entered the Palace of the Holy Office and ran up the centuries-old, well-worn stairs. The Roman worldwide Inquisition still held watch here.

As he reached the antechamber of the prefect's office of the Congregation for the Doctrine of the Faith, he sensed the secretary's unusual inner tension. Monsignor Merlo remained loyal to his superior and had even rejected retirement in order to continue his work under deRossi. Word had it that the old secretary knew just about as many secrets as the cardinal himself.

»What may I do for you, Doctor?« asked Merlo. His superficial ease may have convinced Kleier, if he hadn't known the old man any better.

»I must speak to His Eminence, Monsignor. Urgently.«

Merlo shook his head apologetically as he tactfully scanned the archaeologist from head to toe in his dirty work clothes. »I'm afraid it's not possible, Doctor. His Eminence is currently in a very important meeting.«

Kleier had to contain himself. What could be more important than his unbelievable discovery beneath the base of the Vatican?

»It is incredibly urgent,« he said with great effort. »It is about the foundation of Roman Catholicism.«

Merlo did not look impressed. Too many enemies and challenges had already attempted to shake the Catholic faith. Unsuccessfully up to this point. He gave him a mild, yet tired smile.

»I must ask for your patience, Doctor. The meeting of His Eminence cannot be disturbed.«

»It has to do with archaeological excavations,« Kleier added for emphasis. He nearly stomped with his right foot. Luckily at the last minute he remembered that Merlo was no idiot and that he naturally knew it was about archaeological excavations. He must have remembered deRossi's instructions about Kleier's mission. Something outrageous must have happened that he was now not allowed immediate access to the prefect.

»What has happened, Monsignor?«

Merlo seemed torn, but since he trusted Kleier and he knew he couldn't prevent that the media would catch wind of it and broadcast it to the world, he decided to tell him.

»His Holiness is dead.«

LIGHT AND DARKNESS

2

Catherine shyly looked about her in Dr. Beverly Florena's office on the first floor. It was small, simple and — unlike a lot of the other rooms in the school — well ventilated. To the left of the door stood a shelf full of books against the wall. From the window, one could see the top part of the schoolyard where the older children enjoyed a break. But at the moment the courtyard was empty, even though it was lunchtime. Catherine was the cause for the break's abrupt ending.

»What's your name again?« Dr. Florena asked as if she didn't know. She curiously peered above the eggshell coloured file that lay before her on her desk.

The girl carefully shifted her small frame on the overly wide chair. »Catherine. Catherine Bell.«

It appeared her behaviour had set the entire school off kilter. Even still, she would do it again if she had to.

»How old are you, Catherine?« asked the teacher.

»Nine. Almost ten.«

With her long blonde hair and blue eyes, Dr. Florena looked like an angel to the schoolgirl. The woman in her mid-fifties had no idea how attractive her unpretentious appearance was.

»You know why you are here, my child?« asked Dr. Florena

softly. Catherine nodded hesitantly.

»Yes.«

The teacher took a deep breath, but her face remained open and friendly.

»You said Mr. Eliot was a bad man. You approached him in the schoolyard in front of all the other children and teachers and told him he was a murderer.«

Catherine nodded and remained silent.

»You know what a lie is, my child?«

»A lie is an untruth,« replied Catherine without moving in her chair.

The teacher looked pensively at the girl.

»To tell one is a very bad thing, Catherine.«

»I know.«

»What made you call Mr. Eliot a murderer then?«

»I could see his dark thoughts.«

Several seconds went by in silence. In the background Catherine could see the old hunched over janitor walking across the schoolyard with his bucket and broom.

Dr. Florena finally broke the silence: »It is a terrible thing to accuse an innocent person of murder. You will apologise to Mr. Eliot.«

Catherine shook her head vigorously with a look of panic on her face.

»No, I won't! Mr. Eliot is not innocent. I could see his thoughts.«

Dr. Florena gave the schoolgirl a concerned look and waited a moment.

»Catherine, even if that were true, I mean, that you could truly read Mr. Eliot's thoughts…all of us sometimes have dark thoughts. That doesn't mean we do bad things. Right?«

The girl shook her head in resignation.

»No.« Then added with conviction: »But Mr. Eliot did do something bad. He carries a kind of evil around with him all the time. A dark veil encircles him.«

Dr. Florena stared at her in astonishment. »He is surrounded by a dark veil?«

Catherine nodded to which the teacher replied:

»Mr. Eliot is not only an excellent educator, but also a very distinguished individual. He has always protected this school«

Catherine considered Dr. Florena's words for a moment.

»But if he has always protected this school, how come he didn't protect the boy? Why did he hurt the boy with the scar on his back and all the other kids too?«

The teacher faltered and stared wide-eyed at Catherine. »The boy with the scar on his back?«

Catherine nodded. »The boy on the telly that the police are searching for.«

»How do you know the boy has a scar on his back?«

»I saw the scar in Mr. Eliot's thoughts. It's the same scar that the other boys have. A cross.«

Dr. Florena couldn't stop staring at the girl. She reached for the phone and asked for a man named Father Darius. She seemed to know him well.

3

Present-Day, Upper Bavaria, Mountain above Abbey Rottach

Pater Darius looked out at the monastery that rested deep in the valley with its centuries-old spiritual tradition. The red tiled roofs and the white facades shone in the sun like fresh blood against the purest snow. He was meditating upon his life, the gruelling years at the Institute and the fact that his best student, Sister Catherine Bell, stood before the Congregation for the Doctrine of the Faith for an informal conversation when a male voice interrupted his thoughts.

»Father Darius?«

The priest turned slowly around and blinked. Whoever had interrupted his meditation on this mountain stood in the glistening sunlight. Darius could only make out a silhouette.

»Yes. That's me. What can I do for you?«

»Apologies, Father. I didn't want to disturb your prayer. But…« The visitor hesitated briefly.

»His Eminence Cardinal Ciban has sent me. I am coming from Rome with an urgent matter.«

»It must be if Cardinal Ciban has forced you to make such a long journey just to search me out.«

Rome. Darius had retired several years prior, but Rome and the Order couldn't quite let him go. Was the stranger here because of Catherine? Did the strict Grand Inquisitor Ciban need his council? Darius turned toward the man and attempted to get a look at his face. The sun stood directly behind the man and gave off a halo-like glow.

»Pardon me, but I didn't catch your name.«

»Monsignor Nicola deRossi.«

»Then you are related to Cardinal deRossi?«

»He was my great-uncle, Father.«

»I see.«

Darius nodded thoughtfully.

»Show me your ring please.«

DeRossi took off his ring and handed it to the priest so that he could survey its interior. The man did seem to work for Ciban. But just in case, he had to undergo one more test.

»Intellige, ut credas, verbum meum; crede, ut intelligas, verbum Dei.« [1]

»Per fidem operationis Dei.« [2]

Darius' lips curled into a tiny, ironic smile.

»You really are a member of Lux Domini. What a change in generations. As Grand Inquisitor the cardinal was a man of Opus Dei.« The progressive Lux Domini under which the Institute had stood for several years was quite the opposite to the ultraconservative Opus Dei. The behind-the-scenes battles between both orders had increased massively since Pope Leo had introduced his reforms.

»My great-uncle was a learned and passionless man with a cold, ruthless character.«

»And quite successful,« Darius retorted in earnest. The air was filled with the scent of spring, but there was something else in the

---

[1] Know in order to believe, that is my word; believe in order to know, that is God's word. Augustinus

[2] Your faith in the power of God. New Testament 1, Colossians 2,12

air that the priest couldn't quite name. He ignored the feeling
that accompanied that certain something.

»Why has Cardinal Ciban sent you to me?«

»It is about the Congregation of His Holiness. As a member of
the council, your life is in serious danger, Father.«

Darius grew irritated.

»Even if my life were in danger and even if you do belong to
Lux, how could you possibly know whether I were a member of
the Congregation of His Holiness, Monsignor? Cardinal Ciban
certainly did not tell you.«

DeRossi moved out of the blinding light. He was large and
strong and had the devil's good looks. Even the badly healed scar
above his left eye did nothing to detract from his appearance.
Quite the contrary.

»You speak like an Inquisitor. Unfortunately, I have little time.
My job is to bring you to safety.«

»No matter what your job may be, I won't budge until I have
spoken with Cardinal Ciban.«

DeRossi's eyes suddenly appeared amused as he added in
Latin: »Qui credit in me, etiam si mortuus fuerit, vivet.«[3]

Darius took a step backward. Whoever this stranger was and
wherever he had received his information, one thing was clear:
Cardinal Ciban never would have sent him.

»What are you really here for?«

»As I said, I have a job to do.«

Darius could feel a wave of nausea wash over his body. Up on
this mountain he was trapped like an animal. In that very moment in which Darius realised what was happening, deRossi
grabbed the priest with extreme speed and precision, lifted him
high above his head and tossed him over the cliff like a rag doll.

---

[3] The one who believes in me will live, even though they die. John 11,25.

As Darius hit against the rocks the first time and the air pressed out of his lungs, he could hear nothing other than the cracking of his bones as his entire life flashed before him. He finally returned to his childhood in which he discovered his gift one cold winter. Within milliseconds he relived all the pain that his gift had given him in his lifetime. All the hate. And finally, the study, the understanding and acceptance…the wisdom, the insights that he was able to pass on to his students.

He wouldn't be able to stand by Catherine any more…The air smelled of springtime. Then, one second before Darius shattered to the ground, he finally knew what else the air smelled like.

It smelled like death.

June 17, 1984, Chicago, Catholic Primary School for the Gifted

In the following days, the entire school was abuzz with nothing other than Catherine's accusation, Mr. Eliot's arrest by the FBI and the rescue of his seventh victim from that church crypt. The schoolgirl heard from the older children that Mr. Eliot had been responsible for the disappearance of a total of seven boys in the Greater Chicago area. After a two-hour cross-examination, he finally revealed the location of the seventh child who was luckily still alive. Catherine had not only seen the boy in Mr. Eliot's thoughts, but also in a sort of dream. She could feel his fear. Sometimes it felt as if he had called her for help via her own thoughts.

A week later the girl would then meet the man whom Dr. Florena had so quickly called on the phone after she disclosed what she knew.

»Catherine, allow me to introduce Father Darius. He belongs to an organisation that deals with cases of extrasensory perception.«

With a slightly nervous smile, Dr. Beverly Florena pointed to the slender man standing next to her. The priest wore a simple black robe and had short grey hair and eyes that told her he was not a bad man. »Father, this is Catherine.«

Father Darius bowed before the schoolgirl and she shook his hand to greet him. »You are an unusual priest.«

»Yes, you are right, my child.« He laughed a laugh that the girl liked and, most definitely, the teacher too. »I am just a simple priest.«

»No, you're not.« Catherine pointed to the ring on his left hand.

»I have seen a ring like that before on another Monsignor.«

Father Darius looked rather awkward, exchanging a quick glance with Dr. Florena. »You know a lot for a nine-year-old.«

»I'm almost ten.« Catherine turned to the teacher. »How is the boy?«

A few seconds passed in silence as the teacher searched for the right words. »Ben is still very afraid. But Father Darius is taking good care of him. He will be better soon.«

The girl nodded in relief.

»Catherine, have you always seen such things?« asked the priest softly. She shook her head in fear. It was the worst she had ever seen thus far.

»I mean have you always been able to perceive other people's thoughts?« he corrected himself.

»I can make out colours and pictures.«

»Colours and pictures?«

Catherine nodded hesitantly. She didn't like these questions.

»What do these colours and pictures look like?«

»It depends. Red, blue, green, black or white…sometimes the pictures emerge from the colours. Sometimes it is the other way around.«

»Do you always have these pictures in your mind's eye? Or just every now and then?« asked Father Darius. The schoolgirl raised her eyebrows and thought about it for a moment. »Always every now and then.«

The priest laughed, but then became serious again. »You saved Ben's life with your gift, my child. Tell me more about it.«

Catherine looked uncertainly over at Dr. Florena. »Your mum is waiting outside,« said the teacher. »She can come in if you'd like.«

»No. Please don't.« The girl shook her head vigorously. »She doesn't like me to talk about it. Mum is…afraid.«

»Afraid?« Father Darius squatted down so he was at eye level with Catherine.

»Afraid of me.«

A few seconds passed. Then the father said: »Believe me. She will lose her fear with time.« Catherine remained silent as he continued with an encouraging smile: »Look at me. I too have a gift. And look what has become of me…!« He pointed to himself.

The schoolgirl smiled. »A simple priest…« She pointed to the ring. »And you work for this organisation.«

Father Darius nodded. »The people there are very nice and very smart. They've helped me live with my gift.«

»I don't understand,« said Catherine pensively.

»You will when you meet these people. Would you like to accompany me there?«

»No,« said Catherine spontaneously.

»Why not?« asked the priest. He wasn't at all annoyed, but he seemed rather disappointed.

»You have light thoughts. And if all of the people there have light thoughts, I will seem dark.«

Present-Day, Upper Bavaria, Abbey Rottach

The heavy rainfall started as Monsignor Benjamin Hawlett had nearly reached the Abbey. The grey-on-grey sky above the rocky mountainous landscape filled with evergreens and pine trees matched his mood precisely. The late autumnal atmosphere of this surreal place mirrored his state of mind. The Abbey was so far away from the rest of the world that he had to rent an SUV to get there. Upon further reflection it was no wonder his former mentor chose this place as his final refuge. Father Darius…Ben took a deep breath. He had known the priest for over a quarter of a century and had not seen him in over a decade. The first time he met Darius was as a child in the CIPG, the Catholic Institute for the Psychically Gifted in Chicago. From the very beginning he was fascinated by the man's peculiar blue eyes that seemed to see the future along with his humorous and earnest way in which Darius dealt with other people. Later he met the priest every now and again in Rome, in the Vatican. Their meetings were always filled with warmth, as if no time had gone by in the interim. And now…Ben took another deep breath. He simply couldn't believe that fate brought both of these two people back into his life who had once been like family to him. Now one of them was dead, most likely murdered, and the other suffered under the prejudice of the modern Inquisition.

You have to calm down, he warned himself as he navigated the SUV over the rocky uneven surface. He was here as an investigator and not a grieving family member, which is why he couldn't afford to be sentimental. He had to keep a clear mind during the investigation so as not to overlook anything important.

As Ben reached the Abbey and stepped out of the SUV into the inner courtyard, a biting wind blew across his face. Not even the high walls and mountains surrounding Rottach could reduce the effects of the whipping, swirling wind. It was mid-morning, but judging by the dim light, it could have easily been late afternoon.

The abbot himself greeted Ben, accompanied by one of his brothers whose umbrella the wind was close to ripping apart. Ben knew that Abbot Dominikus had at least two questions running through his mind. How could Rome have learned so quickly about Father Darius' accident? And what was so special about it that a Vatican investigator would be sent to such a remote abbey as Rottach?

»Apologies that we couldn't offer you better weather upon your arrival,« explained the abbot. »Yesterday we had the loveliest sunshine.«

Ben agreed. »What would the loveliest sunshine be without such a contrast!« In truth he didn't want to think about his departure.

Dominikus nodded gracefully, then said in a serious tone: »We have prepared everything for you. The corpse has been laid in the vestry.«

»Thank you, Father. As I was told, the death certificate has already been issued?«

The abbot cleared his throat.

»The doctor was here yesterday evening and examined him.«

»What was the diagnosis?«

»He fell to his death,« explained Dominikus simply.

They entered the cloister, which protected them from the elements and bordered the abbey's church. Ben was impressed by the simple atmosphere of the archway and columns. He followed Dominikus in silence and tried to absorb the peacefulness that the cloister exuded.

»We're here,« said the abbot, who opened the heavy door and switched on the light.

Ben approached the bier with both monks. How tiny and plain Darius seemed to look underneath the cloth. There were no traces of dirt and blood to be seen on it. Naturally, they had prepared and cleaned his body and had washed away any trace that the investigator could have used.

Ben wasn't certain what to expect. Never in his life had he seen a tattered body before. He pulled back the cloth and feared that he would have to mobilise all his strength not to groan at the sight of him. But the lifeless body just lay there peacefully, not nearly as battered as Ben had imagined he would be. The monks had done an amazing job.

»What do you hope to find?« asked Dominikus directly.

»I'm not quite sure.«

He turned toward the abbot.

»What about his clothing?«

»We burned them.«

The investigator suppressed a sigh and said: »Would you please leave me alone with the body?«

Dominikus seemed disappointed, but he nodded, signalled to his brother and retreated.

When Ben heard the door click in the frame, he turned his attention back to the dead body. Upon a second look the body did not look as peaceful as by the first. Controlling all his personal thoughts and feelings, the investigator slowly began his examination.

The back of his head had been shattered by the collision against the rocks, but his weather-beaten face was astonishingly intact apart from two lacerations. His arms and legs looked like wooden pieces of an incredibly limber marionette.

»You will most likely not find a single usable trace on the corpse,« his superior Cardinal Ciban had predicted as he told Ben of the death of his mentor, thereby assigning him the task of travelling to Rottach.

»But we must be certain as to whether Father Darius' death was an accident – or murder.«

Murder? Ben couldn't believe his ears. Who would want to murder Darius? The priest most certainly had no enemies who wished him dead. But then again…something wasn't right here.

»Is there anything else that might help me with my investigation, Eminence?« he had asked. Ciban had looked up from his desk and neither nodded nor shook his head. Ben's superior was a tall and very slender man with ice-grey eyes and short silver-grey hair. His classic well-formed face with its high brow and sharp nose reminded the investigator much more of the image of an ancient military commander than that of a contemporary church dignitary. Every word he spoke and every gesture he made was accompanied by something menacing. It had taken Ben years to learn how to deal with the cardinal's ominous aura.

»Not at the moment. Be careful, Ben.«

»I'll leave right away then,« he had answered in the hopes that Ciban wouldn't notice how much his mentor's death had rattled him. But the prefect knew very well the heavy burden he had laid on Ben with this journey because he had then nodded and in his otherwise distant cold eyes, Ben could see a transient flicker of compassion.

Ben continued his examination of the corpse in the quiet of the former vestry. The body was so full of bruises, contusions and hematomas that he had zero chance of finding traces of violence anywhere. Ciban had been right.

Upon completion of his examination, he returned the corpse to its peaceful position, took a deep breath and covered Darius back up. He still found it hard to accept that here in this remote abbey church lay the dead body of the man who had given his life direction, a goal and a purpose. Ben would have never recovered from the incident in that church without the help of Darius' and Catherine's friendship. He had barely escaped death and not even his gift that he had had as a child could have warned him against Mr. Eliot's insanity.

Ben's gaze rested on the corpse. Outside a storm raged, but he didn't care. He would ask Abbot Dominikus for an experienced local guide. He would seek out the alleged crime scene and the place where they found the body. Then he would not only find out if Darius had been murdered, if it was a murder at all. He would also find out who the murderer was!

12. October 12, 1984, Chicago, Catholic Primary School for the Gifted

The first time Catherine ever entered the Institute was a rainy, grey and dark October day. A cold storm blew from the North and whipped the rain across the forests. It rumbled and flashed streaks of lightning as if the Institute rested near the gates of Hell. The building was nothing Catherine had ever seen before either on the telly or in books. The tower, that was still under construction, rested atop a hill and stood at the centre of the property. It looked like a gigantic wagging index finger giving warning to the city below. The black limousine with which Father Darius picked her up from school took an entire fifteen minutes to move from the entrance gate to the tower and its surrounding buildings.

»No worries,« said the priest as if he could read her mind. »You will meet quite a few very interesting people here. You will certainly make friends. If it becomes too much for you, simply give me the word and I'll bring you back home.«

Catherine nodded in relief as her quickening pulse slowly returned to normal. She could tell by seeing his thoughts that he meant what he said. Darius showed her the premises – or at least the weather-proof part. She then explored the living quarters, which were surprisingly bright, airy and comfortable. Thereafter she went to the study room, the canteen, the gymnasium, the swimming pool, the library and much more. They all seemed filled with scampering, happy children.

Catherine had just started to warm up a bit to the new environment when Darius showed her the building complex that he called the spiritual area. Despite the impressive winter garden and covered courtyard, she didn't like this area at all. It felt like a combination of renovated monastery, train station waiting room and medical laboratory. No, she wouldn't stay here for a single day.

They then turned the next corner and Catherine saw the gallery for the first time…dozens, hundreds, thousands of pictures. They were photographs of people, animals and plants. But the pictures didn't show the actual subjects themselves, but rather their – thoughts!

Father Darius walked up next to her and laid a friendly hand upon her shoulder.

»In this department we ask ourselves: 'do we recognise the world as it truly is?' We differentiate between superhuman and supernatural. The gallery's name is Corona.«

Corona. Catherine stared at the photos as if she were hypnotised as one of the doors opened and a woman in a white lab coat walked along the corridor with a young boy. The schoolgirl thought there was something vulnerable about the boy. She had seen his face somewhere.

Father Darius beckoned to him. »Ben! – Ben, come here. There is someone I'd like you to meet.«

The boy came hesitantly closer and stopped before the girl and Darius.

»Ben, this is Catherine. Catherine, this is Ben.«

»Nice to meet you, Ben.« Catherine extended her hand.

Ben simply stared at her until Darius finally gave him a shoulder slap and said with a grin: »She may look like an angel with her blonde hair and sky-blue eyes, but believe me, she can be quite the devil.«

The girl realised something else in that moment. »You are the boy with the cross on his back.«

Ben nodded without saying a word. He was standing in front of the girl who had saved his life.

Present-Day, Upper Bavaria, Mountain above Abbey Rottach

The rain had relented somewhat, but not the wind that continuously swept across Ben's face. The weather seemed to have no effect on his companion, Brother Andreas. The monk stomped along before him as if he had been accustomed to this type of weather since he was a child.

Ben glanced back at the abbey that appeared to him more like a threat than a work of beauty. How many years had Darius had lived here? Three? If the investigator really thought about it, he couldn't image that his mentor had wanted to spend the rest of his life here. Far away from any type of academic research, the Vatican and Rome. Was there a reason for his retreating to this place? Is that why Ciban surmised that Darius' death was no accident?

»We found Brother Darius over there.« Andreas pointed to a broader rock spur far below the summit. »He lay exactly here amongst the rubble. If it weren't for the crows, I wouldn't have even seen him.«

Ben carefully climbed to the location where the body was found to take a closer look. It was improbable that he would find a trace after all the rain, but he might find a clue after viewing the location as to whether the priest had died by accident or if it was murder. After closely examining the location and point of contact where he fell, he looked up toward the place from which Darius allegedly had fallen. Slightly above that place was another rock spur. Ben stared at it for nearly a minute.

How high could the crash site be above this other rock spur? Fifty or sixty metres? Ben was certain if it had been an accident that Darius could have never fallen past that point without hitting this rock spur.

The sun broke through the cloud coverage and Ben felt as if he saw the first ray of sun after weeks of rain. Oh God! He was simply no longer used to such inhospitable weather.

Andreas and he climbed further up the mountain, stomping through mud and rubble to the summit just as an impressive view emerged from the sky. A large white cross with an equally impressive concrete pedestal as its base. Ben estimated the entire thing to be fifteen metres high.

»Brother Darius meditated here often,« explained Andreas with a touch of reverent nostalgia. »I think he never quite felt comfortable amongst other people.«

Ben said nothing. He knew the monk couldn't be more wrong. Darius had loved people, even the bad ones. He had been through hell and back for more than his share of them. Including for Catherine and himself. In the end, every gift had its price.

He carefully approached the place where the crash site must have been, peered over the valley and then up to the cloud coverage. For a moment he had the feeling he was floating away. He began to understand why the priest found this place high above the world to be so fascinating.

»Be careful,« warned Andreas. »Brother Darius was an experienced hiker – and now...« The monk stopped himself.

But that's just it, thought Ben, without telling his companion. Darius was healthy and fit. He was an experienced hiker and climber – and now he was dead. It made no sense at all.

He walked to a safe point on the edge and peered directly into the abyss, all the while thanking God that he wasn't afraid of heights.

The first rock spur really did cover the view of the second one. Ben took a thick, heavy and stubby branch he had brought with him from far below and tossed it into the abyss. After an impressive areal dance through the sky, the branch landed on the next rock spur. Ben was now convinced that Darius had not simply slipped from the edge of the rocks. If that had been the case, he would have landed on the first rock spur and most likely would have survived the fall.

But his mentor had landed on the second rock spur, a deadly fall that had only one explanation: someone much larger and stronger than the old priest had grabbed him and tossed him well beyond the first rock spur.

8

Present-Day Rome, Apostolic Palace

On some days His Holiness Leo XIV wanted to tell the apostolic constitution and all living cardinals of the Roman Curia to go to hell. On others he wished, with all due humility and respect toward the true believers and upstanding doubters, that he had rejected the elected office as Pontifex maximus, the representative of Jesus Christ on Earth as the head of the Catholic Church.

But he hadn't. He had stood in the Sistine Chapel beneath Michelangelo's ceiling frescos and had answered the Camerlengo's question with »Yes, I accept the conclave's decision,« just as one of his closest friends had predicted.

Leo naturally sensed what his conservative predecessor Pope Innocence had meant during their rare visits to the Vatican palace as he spoke of the impotence of power and the nightmarish helplessness he had experienced. It was only after he took on the position as Pope behind the Vatican walls that he remembered the wise saying that there is a clear difference between believing you know something and actually knowing it. The past Popes had left behind a heavy legacy. Leo was the head of an enormous bureaucracy that called on God and the truth, but whose sincerity only seemed to be a pesky detail to most of his brothers.

Leo lifted himself from the pew and bowed before the cross. The traditional morning reflection, Mass, praising God and the first hour of prayer had never lost their spiritual meaning for him. He enjoyed using the early hours of the morning to think and meditate. He left the little private chapel, went to his bedroom and glanced at the latest report from his security chief and Grand Inquisitor Cardinal Ciban. As always his report was short and to the point, wasted no time and simply stated that the ongoing investigations in the multiple murder case were at a standstill, which meant that His Holiness was the only one who could change the situation.

Leo knew it. Ciban never minced matters. Ever. Not even with the Pope Himself. Leo took a deep breath. Should Father Darius truly have been assassinated, that would mean they were now dealing with three murders. They thought the first one was an accident. Sister Isabella Rodik from Koblenz, a skilled driver, lost control of her VW Beetle whilst on a tour through the Swiss Alps and fell hundreds of metres to her death. Three months later, Father Sylvester André, a long-distance swimmer, was washed ashore off the cost of Southwestern France on the Cote d'Argent, dead. Both nun and priest had belonged to a secret society: the Congregation of His Holiness.

Leo was taken aback by Cardinal Ciban's question as to whether the dead were two of his council members. On the one hand he had sensed his slacking mental capacity for some time now. On the other he had suppressed the feeling and had continued working as if nothing were wrong. But now, in retrospect, he knew why it had been so difficult in the past few months to absorb and manage all the information that had collected on his desk in various languages. It was hard to make decisions. Two of his mental supporters were dead! And now Father Darius...

At the same time, Leo kept asking himself how Ciban could

make the connection so quickly between these two simple religious people and the secret congregation. Neither Sister Isabella's nor Father Sylvester's profile contained a single clue about their extraordinary personalities. Although the secret was passed down from Grand Inquisitor to Grand Inquisitor, the identities of the papal congregation were only known to the community and to the head of the Church itself.

Just as his predecessors had done, Leo made a sacral oath to never reveal the anonymous members of the congregation. That is, unless one of the members was dead. The oath was an essential part of the contract. Several dark chapters in the Church's history told of what could happen if the covenant were broken. Then the highest of all heavens would no longer be godly light, but rather enshrouded in a penetrating darkness.

The first thing Cardinal Ciban asked for were the names as he connected the deaths of Sister Isabella and Father Sylvester with the secret society. »Holiness, I desperately need the names and locations of the living if I am to prevent further murders. The names of the dead are useless!«

»Sorry, Marc, but the names of the dead are the only thing I can give you.«

Leo refused to pass along any information. It was one of the hardest tests. As much as he would have liked to help the man, he simply could not. But Ciban wouldn't be Ciban if he had given up that easily. In the midst of their hapless conversation Leo had yet another dizzy spell. He would never forget the look on the face of the otherwise stoic cardinal as he forbade him to call the doctor.

A half-day later the news of Darius' death arrived. Ciban had immediately sent one of his best employees to Rottach, an abbey in Southern Germany. The young American with Irish lineage went by the name of Benjamin Hawlett.

Leo now awaited the result of his investigations.

He sighed, took Ciban's report and stored it in a small wall safe. He left his bedroom and headed to the nearby dining room. Typically, Leo would have breakfast with both of his secretaries, Corrado Massini and Karl Ritter, who was presently spending his holiday in Scotland. On Sundays, he would eat breakfast with some of the nuns who served in the papal household day in and day out. Today the large dining room table sported two further settings for Marc Abott Cardinal Ciban and Monsignor Ben Hawlett. But Hawlett had not yet returned from Germany. As the Pope entered the room, Ciban stood at the other end of the table and read an article in the International Herald Tribune, one of the local and international morning papers to which Leo had subscribed to remain informed about the happenings in the media. The article seemed to preoccupy the Cardinal. Massini interrupted his chat with one of the nuns and greeted the Pope. Ciban carefully placed the paper back with the others, greeted the Pope as well and joined Leo at the table. They bowed their heads in prayer until one of the sisters entered the room with tea and coffee.

»I hope you had a pleasant night, Holiness.« The cardinal's voice revealed no scorn or ridicule. It seemed as though he had fully accepted Leo's refusal to reveal the names. He withdrew a pen-like apparatus reinforced with tiny sensors from his jacket pocket and placed it in the middle of the table. The interfering transmitter assured that not a single syllable of conversation could leave the room electronically.

»I imagine none of us slept well last night,« answered Leo, knowing full well that a man like Ciban, with all those inquisitorial and criminal cases swimming around his head, never really slept well. He passed around the overflowing breadbasket. He tried to smile, then glanced at the small sensor device whose technological functions were a complete mystery to him. »Always the wary one, right Marc?« Leo had at least found out in the past few months that Ciban thawed out a little when he called him by his first name.

»Wariness is a part of my job description, Holiness,« replied the cardinal with a relaxed look in his grey eyes as they rested on the sensor device. The Pope often asked himself what his predecessor Innocence had seen in such a strict, cold and imperious soul as Ciban that he would invite him into the inner circle of his most trusted allies. After almost two years, countless meetings and mutually shared meals, Leo barely knew this man at all. Even now in his simple priest's cassock, he seemed intimidating, even threatening, as if he possessed the ability to carry the insignia of his noble birth, his eminence and the power associated with it like an invisible, yet perceptible torch. Leo wished his predecessor had told him more about Ciban or at least acquainted them with one another better before Innocence's death. At the beginning of his office, Leo was only left with the official personal files in order to get familiar with the cardinal. But what was a personal file anyway? What did it say about the true essence of another person? Ciban was in his early fifties and thereby the youngest and most ambitious cardinal in the council. He was born on February 7 in Rome, had grey-blue eyes, was 194 centimetres tall and weighed 86 kilograms. Thereafter, the societal status of the family – or the name of the orphanage – followed. The Ciban clan belonged to one of the richest families in Europe. Schooling, university and career path were next on the list. He had studied in Rome, Paris, Tübingen and London. PhD in theology along with a postdoctoral thesis. In addition, Leo marvelled that he had a degree in astrophysics. He completed everything with »summa cum laude,« of course.

The psychological profile included in the file was a total joke in the eyes of the Pope. Either it was completely outdated or patched together from various psychological platitudes and dossiers or Ciban had simply outwitted the psychologists. According to Leo's impression, obedience was listed as one of Ciban's virtues only if he considered it of value to the Church. His career path had a few spots on it, which were noted merely as »business trips«. Leo now knew that it really meant that in Ciban's case he was actively employed in the Vatican's secret service. Under Innocence's reign and even before that during the time in the Congregation for the Doctrine of Faith, the Cardinal had often been found to be on such »business trips«.

Leo cast Ciban a sideways glance. Wariness was not only a part of his job, but it also had something to do with him as a person. They ate fresh buns, ham and eggs, sipping their coffee and freshly squeezed orange juice while chatting about current events in the world and their meaning for the Catholic Church. They came upon Sister Catherine Bell whose latest book, which was very critical of the Church, had recently been released. Leo learned that it had been given a full-blown positive review in the International Herald Tribune along with an accompanying article about the prominent Catholic author.

The article included a photo of Sister Catherine standing in front of a historic building in Jerusalem. She wore a long black robe and looked directly into the camera with a disarmingly warm smile.

»Her books might be less popular if she weren't so attractive,« one of the elderly Cardinals had once complacently said to Ciban in front of Leo. Ciban remained silent, but the look on his face nipped any further comments from the elderly cardinal in the bud.

Legal proceedings against Sister Catherine had been running for years. They began under Pope Innocence and Ciban's predecessor Monti. When he was still Cardinal, Leo had shown more sympathy for the smart, courageous nun than Innocence, Monti and the courts of the Inquisition. For that reason, Catherine stood as well as she could under his protection since the latest papal election. Admittedly, it didn't make his relationship to Ciban any easier, but it appeared that the prefect was professional enough not to let it affect their working relationship.

Massini finally asked: »Any more news about the death of Father Darius?« As Leo's confidant, he knew about the murders.

»No,« the cardinal said tightly.

Leo found it rather discomforting how Ciban distanced himself inappropriately from Massini. Leo had taken on Massini as his private secretary upon Innocence's suggestion and he saw no reason for Ciban's cool demeanour toward him. The man was not only kind, but he also did excellent work and treated Ciban with the utmost respect without being subservient.

»No clues? Not a single one?« pressed Massini further as if he didn't notice Ciban's reserve. Ciban stared at the younger man. Just as Leo wanted to intervene, Ciban said: »Well then, the usual suspects can be eliminated. Extremists, the Mafia, our friends the Free Masons, the directorate, the council, the league, the syndicate, the alliance, Opus Dei…there isn't a shred of evidence pointing to any of these groups' involvement in the murders.«

The words »Opus Dei« echoed in Leo's brain. At the beginning of his papacy, he thought Ciban might just be a member of the ultraconservative Catholic federation. But then he had learned from a significant prelate in the Papal State that the cardinal and the Opus were not exactly on friendly terms. Although the Opus had tried to woo Ciban to become a member for years, the cardinal began an investigation against the order and started a fight with his predecessor instead. The old, power-hungry cardinal of the Roman Curia Sergio Monti, an incurable archconservative, had the reputation of eating his opponents alive. Leo liked the fact that Ciban defied Monti and even triumphed over him. As fate would have it, the elderly cardinal, who was the Grand Inquisitor during Innocence's papacy for nearly two decades, was one of Leo's worst enemies.

Because he noticed the Pope's doubts, the significant prelate went one step further in his comments about Ciban. »Cardinal Ciban and I are not the best of friends, Holiness, but I would trust him with my life. And I can't say that about many of my other colleagues. You may view him as an extremely conservative and closed off man, but you must know that he is quite capable of seeing the big picture and to do what's necessary. That's what several cardinals, including Signore Monti, realised too late.«

Not only Cardinal Monti, but also Steffano Cardinal Gasperetti exhibited veiled hostility since the last conclave. He was the chairman of the congregation for the bishops, which stood under the watchful eye of the Congregation for the Doctrine of the Faith. He was also the chairman of Lux Domini. Gasperetti was much more subtle than Monti. Lux Domini believed in the youthful spirit of the progressive Pope Leo and hoped for an appropriate church reform for the third millennium. Leo would have loved to cast a glance at the order's membership list. But Lux kept its list just as private as Opus did. In any case, the order had fine-tuned the Catholic community during its nearly fifteen years in existence. As a result, its members had moved up the ranks to the highest levels of the clergy as well as in the Catholic community outside the Church. In other words, due to their opposing political views, both organisations were enemies, especially since the founder of Lux had been a religious figurehead with a talent for channelling who founded the very first Catholic Institute for the Psychically Gifted. At any rate, Leo decided that due to their powerful positions both Lux and Opus were to be handled with caution.

»Well then, if the usual suspects can be eliminated,« said Massini, »we'll just have to wait for the results of Monsignor Hawlett's investigation.«

Ciban nodded. »Looks like it.«

Leo knew that it didn't look like it at all. Hawlett's mission was important, but it was only a small part of Ciban's entire investigation. The prefect had already put out his feelers in every possible direction and had exhausted sources that the Pope would rather not know about. Lux Domini might just be one of his main sources. Even though Leo doubted that the cardinal was an active member of Lux, the order under Gasperetti's command still stood beneath the Congregation for the Doctrine of the Faith and thereby beneath Ciban himself. There was a list of names spanning from the last five Inquisitors, anonymous Lux members to the last six Popes. Not only Ciban, but also Cardinals Sarcina, Castelli, Leone, deRossi and Monti as Grand Inquisitor knew of its secret.

Regarding the Popes that knew not only of the secret but also of the identities of the congregation members... »You're researching all the way back to Pius?« Leo had asked with disbelief during one of their last private conversations.

»There could have been a leak as far back as Pius. But to be honest, what interests me more in this case is John Paul's papacy.«

»John Paul? His papacy lasted only thirty-three days.«

Ciban nodded and began to talk about a certain Dr. Thomas Kleier who, along with his assistant Sebastiano Luca, made an amazing discovery in the grottos beneath St. Peter's Basilica. On behalf of John Paul. The cave was clearly marked by archaeological digs and soon thereafter partly collapsed. Upon Cardinal deRossi's instruction, further digs came to a halt, but not before the scientist was able to save a book about the secret and bring it to the surface. It is said that the book is preserved in a strongbox in a secret archive somewhere.

»Do you think Kleier read the document?«

An amused smile, quick as lightning, passed over Ciban's lips. »Before deRossi could prohibit him to do so. Although Kleier took a sacral oath to keep the knowledge to himself, I am not so certain he is as strong-willed as you are, Holiness.« A mild side blow that, despite its gentleness, did not go unnoticed.

»What happened to the assistant?«

»He doesn't seem to know anything about the contents of the book. But we are still checking into that. He works and lives in Milan.«

»And Kleier?«

»Been retired for the past eight years and has returned home to an idyllic city by the name of Saarbrücken, the capital of Saarland, a Catholic stronghold in Germany, Holiness.«

»I cannot imagine that the archaeologist or his assistant could have anything to do with the murders.«

»Maybe not with the murder, but they may have unwittingly served as a source of information…«

Ciban briefly paused, shifted his slim, stately figure in the large chair across from Leo's desk and casually pointed to the list of numbered names that sat on the massive table between them. There were actually more numbers than names, at least those names pertaining to the papal congregation. Behind each of the three murdered people was a simple cross.

»Out with it, Marc. What are you thinking?« Leo had never seen the cardinal be this hesitant.

»I was wondering whether you have noticed any suspicious activity of late. This spiritual connection between you and…«

»Yes?«

»Could it be that one of your special advisors…how should I

say…is emitting dark energy?« Leo shook his head. »I don't sense anything like that. Like most of the Popes before me, I am not a medium. That is why this covenant is so important for us.«

»Could Sister Isabella, Father Sylvester or Father Darius have noticed anything?«

»Possibly. They were all talented mediums. What are you getting at, Marc?«

»Unlike me, every single member of the community knows both the secret as well as the names and locations of the others… knowledge that the murderer must have had.«

»A traitor? Please!«

Ciban's eyes rested as calmly on him as they had on the sensor device at breakfast. »I'm afraid so.«

»I don't believe it,« Leo barked. »I know you don't think much of Lux Domini. But why would one of the congregation members do such a thing?«

»Why did Judas betray Jesus, Holiness?« Ciban said dryly. »What if the covenant wasn't broken by the papacy this time?«

Leo swallowed hard and had to admit that the idea was much more plausible than he had hoped. Sometimes he wished Ciban weren't so pragmatic. On the other hand, what use was a overly trusting man at the head of the Vatican's security to him after all?

»Another cup of coffee, Holiness?« asked Massini, thereby pulling Leo back to the present in the papal dining room.

»No, thanks, Corrado.«

Leo thought about the possible consequences of all those decisions he had made based on his personal congregation's advice. The most secretive and loneliest decision he had ever made was entrusted only to his journal. He didn't want to even think about what would happen if the traditionalists such as cardinals Gasperetti or Monti came across it prematurely…

Oh Lord! What if Ciban were right? What if there was a

traitor lurking within the congregation? Then Leo could forget trusting any of his advisors ever again.

9

Present-Day, Munich Airport

Even if he would never admit it, Ben hated to fly. He felt a great level of unease when several kilometres of air and nothing else lay between his feet and Mother Earth. Unfortunately, it was also the fastest method to get from one point to another in the world. From Munich to Rome, for instance.

At the Munich airport, he had treated himself to a Bavaria specialty while he waited to board his flight. Two Munich white sausages with a pretzel and sweet mustard. As an Irishman whose family had emigrated to the United States, he loved foreign cuisine. No matter where his job took him, he would eat at least one traditional dish. Admittedly, Munich white sausages, sauerbraten and fried potatoes were among his favourites in Germany. They tasted better than the customary airport fare. He certainly couldn't deny how much he enjoyed the wheat beer that went along with it.

Upon his return to Rottach after viewing the crime scene with brother Andreas, Ben had looked through Darius' personal belongings. He had sat along in the priest's cell, allowing the coolness and peacefulness of the small, sparsely furnished room to sink in. He had searched the room systematically until he came upon a small, unlocked oak chest in Darius' wardrobe.

The chest didn't contain much. A few letters, several photos, an old pocketknife, an old watch...and an old leather-bound Bible. Darius had received the Bible from his parents as a young man after his ordination. As a young boy, Ben had admired the black, supple leather-bound volume with its golden edges so much that his mentor had even promised to give it to him one day. Ben reverently opened up the well-worn book and flipped through the pages.

The priest never spoke of his parents. Sometimes Ben had the feeling that Darius feared he would endanger them both if he even mentioned them. He slowly flipped through the Bible. The pages were wafer-thin. He discovered a photograph between the Old and New Testament. The image showed him as a twelve-year-old, earnest young boy along with Darius, who smiled lightly into the camera and a joyful Catherine Bell. Ben remembered every detail of that day. They had made an excursion to Sears Tower. Catherine had enjoyed the breath-taking view over Chicago from the one hundred third floor while he fought against his revolting stomach. Looking closely at the photo, he could see that his face was rather greenish.

Ben wondered if there was more to the priest's research work at the Institute than he had suspected. But why had Darius spent so much time in Rome over the last decade?

He carefully closed the Bible and pocketed it. It was the only keepsake, other than his memories, that he had of Darius. After leaving the cell, he had posed a few questions at the abbey. Questions that were not unsettling to the abbot. No, none of the monks had seen a stranger on the day of the accident, neither the day prior nor the day thereafter, although...Dominikus faltered slightly. Hadn't Brother Johannes complained about a fresh patch of oil near the monastery on the day of the accident?

It turned out that on that day Brother Johannes had indeed

seen a suspicious patch of oil in the forest along with two tyre tracks. Johannes stated further that due to the size of the tyres they must have belonged to an SUV, much like the one Ben had rented.

Ben could hardly believe his ears. The first trace!

Two hours later back in Munich, he had put together a list of all SUVs that had been rented in Munich on the day of the accident with the help of the German Federal Intelligence Service staff member Ralf Porter, one of Cardinal Ciban's sources. With just five automobiles on the list, Porter's search quickly led him to discover that one of the renter's identification had been forged.

»We need to look at the surveillance video,« demanded Porter from the airport car rental employee. With his neatly combed blonde hair, square glasses and black suit, the man looked like an FBI agent straight from the 60s.

Impressed by Porter's agent ID and overall appearance, the car rental clerk asked one of his colleagues to take over for him at the reception desk and brought Ben and Porter to a tiny, windowless side room. Not only was the technical core of the electric monitors and surveillance equipment housed here, but also multiple DVDs. The entire place looked like an unmanned control room. The clerk took out two of the chronologically stored tapes from the shelf and placed one of them in the DVD player.

»It must be these two. One from reception and the other recording from outdoor camera two on the parking deck.«

»The car has yet to be returned?«

The clerk shook his head. »It was rented for an entire week.«

»What about the GPS?«

»Our SUVs don't have them yet.«

»Thanks,« said Porter. »We don't want to keep you any longer.«

»No problem. I have time,« said the man calmly and waited expectantly to see what the tapes might reveal.

»If you might leave us alone,« asked Porter politely, yet firmly.

The clerk got it, exchanging glances briefly with Ben and clearing his throat awkwardly. »Oh yes. Of course. If you have any questions…you know where to find me.«

Ben started the first of the two recorders. The image was crystal clear. Finally a company that invested in high-quality recording equipment and didn't just bank on the deterrent effect of its cameras. He fast-forwarded to the moment in which the SUV was rented. Shortly thereafter it showed the man with the forged papers as he entered the office, approached the reception and exchanged a few words with the clerk to finish his business. Suddenly, the image quality grew fuzzy.

»How annoying! He is using an interceptor,« said Porter.

But that wasn't the only problem. Ben sighed. The stranger wore glasses and a baseball cap pulled so far down over his face that identifying him was simply impossible. The tape showed no other identifying markers such as a conspicuous ring on his finger or a wristwatch.

»Perhaps we will have more luck with the second tape,« said Porter. He didn't think they would. »At least we now know he may not be right-handed. Note how he signed the papers with his right hand, but placed them in his right interior pocket of his jacket and also pushed up his glasses with his left hand.«

»He's left-handed?«

»Looks like it.«

Ben played the second video. It showed a part of the parking deck in which the SUVs stood at the ready. The stranger kept his hat on as he got in the car and drove away. He knew exactly what he was doing.

»I'll take the tapes with me to the lab,« claimed Porter.

»Should I find anything, I will let you and your boss know right away. I will also question the clerk on the tape. It appears he is not here today.«

»His Eminence will be most obliged.«

Porter's blue eyes lit up with amusement. »I am the one who owes him something, Father.«

They left the tiny side room and walked down the hallway to the reception area where Porter asked about the clerk who was on duty the day of the accident.

»Eric Zander?« asked the clerk. »Sorry. I haven't seen him since the day before yesterday. He hasn't even called in sick.«

»That doesn't sound good,« said Porter as he strolled toward his company car.

»Do you think the perpetrator killed the man from the rental car company?«

»If he discovered something that could be of use to us?«

Ben remained silent. If Darius' murderer eliminated the young clerk as well, then he didn't have much regard for human life in general. Words such as conscience and compassion were not a part of his vocabulary. As a child, Ben once looked into the soul of such a murderer. He would never forget it for as long as he lived. Mr. Eliot haunted him to this day.

»I'll look into it,« said Porter finally. »I'll call you as soon as I know anything. Tell His Eminence 'hello' for me…«

The boarding announcement over the airport intercom pulled Ben back to the present. He grabbed his bag and Vatican papers. A part of his consciousness thought about the pending flight altitude and with every step toward the aircraft, his knees grew weaker and weaker. But then he remembered with some degree of happiness that he would see Catherine again once he landed in Rome, even if her visit was at the request of the Congregation for the Doctrine of the Faith and would be anything but joyful.

He had had to postpone the meal they had planned to share a few days prior due to the investigation in Rottach. They would certainly make up for it now. In the midst of his pleasurable feelings about their reunion, he felt a twinge of unease because Catherine thought Darius was still alive. The old priest had meant at least as much to her as to him, yet Ben wasn't allowed to tell her about his death just yet.

Before storing his hand luggage in the overhead bin, he pulled out the priest's Bible. He needed a way to distract himself during the flight. As the aircraft took off, he once again flipped through the Bible, looking at the old, faded photograph of himself, Darius and Catherine for a second time. That excursion to Sears Tower was half a lifetime ago. So much had happened since then.

Acts 4:20 – »For we cannot but speak of what we have seen and heard.«

Acts 8:37 – »If you believe with all your heart, you may.«

Acts 17:28 – »For in him we live and move and have our being'; as even some of your own poets have said, For we are indeed his offspring.«

Acts 26:31 – »This man is doing nothing to deserve death or imprisonment.«

Ben continued reading, nearly forgetting about the flight altogether. Darius had a soft spot for Bible verses and aphorisms. He had highlighted the passages that fascinated him most.

10

Rome, The Vatican

After experiencing the past few days in Rome with the various meetings in the palace of the Roman Inquisition, not much else could surprise Sister Catherine Bell at this point. The heart-warming email from one of the employees at the Internet office, a Franciscan nun by the name of Thea asking for a personal meeting, surprised and moved her:

Dearest Sister Catherine:

Not everyone in Rome misunderstands or despises your writings. Real church reform needs someone like you. I myself do not possess the same courage or quick-wittedness as you do, but I should like to offer you my friendship and support along the rocky path you have chosen. I would be thrilled to have the opportunity to meet you in person before you leave and to chat with you directly. No matter what the Congregation's decision will be, their interrogation of you will alter the thinking of many. You are doing the Church a favour, even if they don't see it that way just yet. If you should like, I would ask that you visit me next Thursday for the evening. I would be very pleased should you agree to our meeting.

Your Sister in Jesus Christ
Thea

Catherine had answered the email straight away and had asked if she might be allowed to visit the Vatican's Internet office. At the moment she found herself on the way there through hectic centuries old Rome in which nothing went according to plan and yet as if by magic everything seemed to work out anyway.

She had decided on a dark, comfortable pantsuit and a blue blouse. Without realising it, her outfit, combined with her blonde ponytail, high cheekbones and light eyes, made her look rather athletic and energetic.

Pausing in the middle of the bridge looking over the brown flow of the Tiber, she reminded herself that just a few days ago she had already pushed her way into the innermost part of the Vatican.

She had entered past the walls and gates that kept customary visitors at bay, thanks also to the guards in their historic garb or the Vatican police. After entering the Saint Anna gate, she stopped by the Vatican pharmacy for some ointment and then later at an ATM with instructions in Latin – which made her smile every time – in order to pick up some money for groceries at a nearby supermarket.

And then she had seen Benjamin Hawlett again. Ben!

Father Darius and he had become more and more like family to her ever since she had started living at the Institute and her mother had begun to distance herself from her and her inexplicable gift. Sometimes Catherine thought her mother had hated her gift as much as she had hated Catherine's father about whom she never spoke. Since the beginning of time, her father had been a big mystery, a taboo topic never to be mentioned. But then Father Darius and Ben had entered her life like a father and brother. And there stood Ben before her once again.

After all these years, the sadness remained in his dark eyes. He had gotten older, just as she had, but the past decade had made him more mature and even more interesting than before. The tiny wrinkles around his eyes and mouth revealed that, despite his melancholy tendency, he had not lost his sense of humour. Then in a moment of emotional adoration in which she briefly lost control over her gift, she was able to see his aura for a few moments. It was still filled with the heavenly white and blue she had known when he was a child. Every now and again a few red-orange sparks flickered through it, showing that behind his cool exterior lay a flame of excitement. It took all she could not to hug him right then and there in the middle of the chaste church state and plant a kiss on his cheek for the sheer joy of seeing him once again.

As he accompanied her along the marble corridors, she admired the paintings and sculptures in the Secretariat of State's office along with the extraordinary view of the Damasus Courtyard and St. Peter's Square through the high glass windowpanes. It was breath taking. Finally, they had visited the Sistine Chapel, Catherine's declared favourite spot in the Vatican. It was simply incredible how colourfully the frescos from Perugino, Botticelli or Signorelli glowed on the sidewalls after their restoration, not to mention Michelangelo's altar fresco, »The Last Judgement«.

»You're glowing like a child beneath a Christmas tree,« said Ben with amusement. »Perhaps you should come to Rome more often.«

»For a less formal occasion, anytime!« She added with a wink: »I question however how much I can trust an employee of the Palazzo del Sant'Uffizio.«

»Well, I'm not a spy, and I'm also not Ben the Avenger.«

Catherine laughed softly. »I beg your pardon. That was a dumb thing I said.« She knew all too well that Ben's aura was without trickery or evil.

He shook his head. »Not after all you've been through.« After a brief pause, he added: »What do you say we leave all this behind us for a few hours. What would you think of a city tour? Just the two of us? Of course, so that I can thoroughly spy on you.«

Despite their noble surroundings, she couldn't help but grin. A city tour that would help her forget the past few days was just the thing. They spent the afternoon in the city with its domes, towers and old facades, allowing themselves to wander through the Roman chaos with its cars and lightning fast Vespas, passing white-cuffed policemen with their gauntlet gloves who tried all the while and quite unsuccessfully to manage the uncontrollable tangle of traffic.

They made plans to meet for dinner the following evening at a cosy rustic restaurant called Matricianella close to the Palazzo Borghese. Catherine could nearly taste the fried porcini mushrooms, sardines, vegetables and mozzarella melting on her tongue when Ben had to cancel last-minute. An urgent business matter called him away to another country. He wasn't able to say more than that. But the young nun knew that his superior Cardinal Ciban was behind the sudden assignment.

Ciban…

As Catherine entered the Vatican now, she stayed away from the cold office building of the Holy Inquisition that stood to the left of St. Peter's Square in front of the papal audience hall.

In the past few weeks, she had defended her position as a woman and theologian during the multiple meetings with the smartest minds of the Inquisition along with the guardians of the faith including the exigent head guardian, Marc Abott Cardinal Ciban. Even though they no longer burned people at the stake in the twenty-first century, these men could turn their victims' souls to ashes.

In the first series of meetings, they had checked off every point

Catherine had ever made about contraception, celibacy, euthanasia, abortion, papal infallibility or marriage and divorce. She herself was rather surprised that she had raised her voice on so many different issues. Then the tribunal had moved on to her opinions regarding the gospels, in which Catherine's doubt about the virgin birth of Jesus Christ was the most welcomed point of criticism. Maria had one of the must unbelievable biographies in world history. An illiterate Jewish woman became the mother of God's child and remained a virgin forevermore!

Not even the Congregation of the Doctrine of Faith's prefect seemed to be bothered by it. Cardinal Ciban had even written in his book Christianity that Jesus' divinity would not be altered even if he had been the product of normal marital intercourse between husband and wife. According to Ciban, God's sonship was not a biological, but rather an ontological reality, an occurrence in God's eternal grace. Catherine had selected this exact passage from Ciban's book to support her point. And it was exactly her daring quote from the book that altered the course of the entire interrogation.

To her surprise, the tribunal that had questioned the young nun was suddenly absolved of its duties and replaced with a new one. Cardinal Ciban, who had up to this point not participated in a single meeting, suddenly sat before her. Catherine expected that he would explain to her in his cold, distant way that she had no right to proclaim his opinion in the name of the Church and that she quite obviously misunderstood his position entirely, but nothing of the sort happened at all. Instead, Ciban introduced her to a new jury, placed her current book The Disenchanted God on the table and opened up the book to a page with a highlighted passage. As he did so, he cast her a look that was so inhuman that, for a moment, she had to ask herself if he were on drugs.

»In your book you make the distinction between internal psychic experiences and objective facts, Sister Catherine. Please explain the difference to the commission.«

The »commission« as Ciban called the jury was made up of just four representatives of the Congregation of the Doctrine of Faith and sat on an elevated platform behind the judge's bench whilst Catherine sat alone at her table. She tried to read the faces of the newly appointed jurors. The only focal point she had was Father Michael Sorti from Lux Domini, a tiny, mouse-faced man whom she thought looked as though he awaited a revolutionary revelation – or perhaps a desecration – from her.

»We human beings like to project an internal psychic perception onto the outside world,« she explained. »Let's take the Marian apparition as an example. A religious experience takes shape in the material world as a type of ghostly appearance which gives warning and predicts the future.«

Father Sorti cleared his throat and sat up straight in his chair. »You speak of an error, Sister Catherine. But isn't Christianity a religion of revelations in which God reveals himself to share his will with humanity? Thousands experienced the Maria apparition in Fatima. An appearance of light that majestically soared through the room. Not to mention the miracle of the sun there. How can you speak of an experience that can be traced back solely to the brain's metabolic processes? That is not at all compatible with the Biblical image of God.«

Catherine knew very well that the canonical process that was documented and declared credible in 1917 was completed in 1930. Fatima became – just like Lourdes – a Catholic pilgrimage site to which millions of people made a pilgrimage. Fatima and Lourdes only strengthened the Catholic position.

»Why not, Father? God is not material from which hopeless promises should be made, seemingly realised dreams in the world. Apostle Paul once said: 'The Spirit itself beareth witness with our spirit, that we are the children of God.' To me that means nothing other than that God reveals himself in the deepest parts of man. And that is very well compatible with the truth of God and the truth of man.«

The young nun could literally see how Sorti followed her internally. The fact that she claimed God wanted to reveal himself inside each and every human being made her sound like a Protestant even though she was a Catholic. But it wasn't Sorti who spoke next.

»Then you do not see the work of God in the real world through the wonders of Fatima or Lourdes?« The question came from Ciban, in passing as he flipped through several papers, almost as if they were irrelevant to the conversation.

Catherine recognised the sinister nature of his question nonetheless: »Is your confession of faith a lie, Sister?«

»I believe in the power of the Holy Ghost. I believe that we must have faith, that we are downright predestined to be spiritual. It is written in the Holy Word and it is written in our genetic code. We are the image of God. We are God's children. As man and woman.«

Ciban took hold of the book, got up and walked down from the platform to Catherine's table. In that moment, only the young woman could see his steel-grey eyes. The unnatural silence reflected in his eyes made her shiver inside and gave her cause to be even more alert than before. It was her very first direct confrontation with the General Inquisitor and most likely not her last. She instinctively moved back in her chair. The cardinal stood directly in front of her table and placed the book before her.

»What about those children of God who have neither such vivid imaginations nor this genetic code, Sister?«

Catherine couldn't interpret his tone of voice. »As I said, our consciousness is formed according to His likeness. In order to deny him, we must first confirm that he exists.«

In that moment, Catherine realised something was awry with the nature of this meeting. None of the jurors recorded the minutes. Or was there a recording device hidden somewhere?

Father Sorti spoke once again. »You are a Christian woman, Sister Catherine. In addition, you are a Catholic nun and have made an oath. But when I read the thoughts you've recorded in your book, you believe in any old religion.«

Catherine nodded as she noticed how her mouth suddenly ran dry. »I cannot imagine that God would exclude a person simply because he is not baptised.« It was equally ridiculous to claim that the Roman Catholic Church was the custodian of absolute religious truth. Why should a person of faith not be able to practice his belief the way he should like? God had so many faces.

Ciban, who had glanced at Sorti, turned his back to the committee to confront Catherine once again with his eyes' spooky silence. She felt as if an icy shadow was cast upon her soul.

»What do you really think, Sister?« he asked forcefully. »You live the Catholic faith, you are a part of the Church, you made a vow, but you manifest an entirely different faith in your books. What do you know? What do you believe? What do you believe to know?«

Catherine reached for the book without opening it. She didn't break the cardinal's gaze, but she needed something to hold onto, even if it was Ciban's copy of her book.

»If matter is nothing more than condensed energy, Eminence, then differentiating between an imaginary and material world makes no sense, right? It makes equally no sense then to differentiate between God's human world in Catholic and non-Catholic.

We are all in the same boat. Is that really heresy?«

Catherine knew that her words were like throwing steak into a lion pit, but none of the black-robed men behind the judge's bench took the bait. Not even Ciban. What was going on here?

»As this committee knows, you have the ability to see the world in a way that other people cannot,« continued Ciban as if the prior moment had not taken place. »How would you classify your God-given 'privilege'? As a completely internal experience or as objective reality?«

Catherine gave the cardinal a stunned look. Was her gift on trial? Her departure from Lux Domini? The brainwashing of which they mercifully spared her? Or did they want to get to Darius through her?

»I view my gift as an objective fact. I can't simply explain away the reality of my expanded awareness.«

»No one expects that of you, Sister. What interests us more is whether or not your gift is a miracle?« Ciban stood in the middle of the hall, both measured and threatening at the same time.

Catherine tensely pushed herself forward in her chair as she peered at the group before her. She asked herself once again what was going on here. Was this a jury instigated by Lux Domini? But why would a conservative man such as Ciban want to actively cooperate with a progressive order such as Lux? Was Lux no longer under the Congregation of the Doctrine of Faith because the order had become too powerful within the Church? Or was the cardinal himself a medium?

The jury awaited her response.

»There are scientific studies and real world experiences that extend well beyond a fundamental hypothesis of pure metaphysics. It is true that my gift is no illusion.«

»You haven't answered the question,« said Ciban without flinching. »What is your gift? Just an evolutionary peculiarity, a coincidence, a mutation – or a part of God's plan?«

»I don't know what God's plan is, Eminence. But does the one have to exclude the other?«

Ciban gave her a nearly kind look. »Whether you know it or not, Sister, you are about to drift away from the truth, despite your gift.«

»Then you know God's plan, Eminence?« She looked straight into Ciban's unwavering eyes and thought for a moment that she might have seen a slight ironic flash in them. But a second later only his customary coldness and distance remained.

»Believe me. There are truths that not even you would wish to know.«

Later Catherine would feel an icy cold shiver run down her spine every time she recalled this meeting. What did Ciban mean by that? Was it a threat? She couldn't be certain. There was much more subtext to his words than she could decipher. She could feel it. But if the cardinal thought he could intimidate her that way, he was sadly mistaken. Catherine's strength lay in that fact that as an author and soon-to-be ex-nun she was a very prominent victim of the modern Inquisition and that the global press paid great attention to her case. The time when the Church could completely suppress thoughts and ideas was long over.

As she walked through the Saint Anna gate to the Vatican, she pushed aside her thoughts about the trial and Ciban as best she could. She dug through her pocket for her entrance permit and walked past both Swiss guards and the sentinels of the Vigilanza. Up until yesterday, she had had no idea that the Internet office was located directly in the Apostolic Palace. Life was full of surprises. She was intrigued to meet Sister Thea. Given her current situation, it took a lot of courage to extend Catherine an official invitation.

11

Rome, The Vatican, Apostolic Palace, Internet Office

The Vatican's Internet office was located three floors down from the papal chambers. Glistening neon lights fell upon a half dozen desks and three times as many computers. The quiet whirring of the air conditioner sounded to Catherine like the humming of a swarm of insects. A tiny figure got up from one of the computers and walked through a tight passageway to approach the visitor. The woman wore a brown habit and a black veil, much like Catherine had worn up until recently. The Franciscan nun was the only woman in the entire Internet office.

»Sister Catherine, I am Sister Thea. I am so glad you've come.«

Catherine shook the nun's hand. »Thank you for your kind invitation. Your email, well, let's just say it surprised me.«

A smile swept across Sister Thea's face.

»Well, I have read all of your books and writings and definitely wanted to meet the author before she left Rome. Tea or coffee?«

»Coffee, please, if it's not any trouble.«

Sister Thea turned to one of the young men, who quickly jumped up to fetch some fresh coffee. She then turned back to Catherine. »We can speak in my office undisturbed.«

The room was sparsely furnished. A portrait of the Pope as

well as an image of Jesus hung on the walls. A crucifix hung
about the door in such a way that the Franciscan nun could see it
at all times from her modern workspace. Catherine sat next to
Sister Thea on an old, extremely comfortable leather couch that
looked as though it had been around since the times of Pius XII.
The door opened and a young priest came in with a serving tray
carrying two simple office cups and a pot of hot coffee. He
placed the tray on a small table in front of the two women. Sister
Thea thanked him.

»Milk, sugar?« she asked.

»Just milk please,« Catherine took a look at the person next to
her. »You run the Internet office?«

Sister Thea poured them both a cup of coffee and nodded.
»The Curia has made progress, albeit somewhat hesitantly.
Thirteen years ago I was called to Rome. Ever since then I have
been responsible for spreading the word of the Catholic Church
throughout the Web. I have run the Internet office for the past
five years. By the way, I am not the only woman who has received
professional recognition here at the heart of the Catholic faith in
the past few years.« She placed the coffee pot back on the tray
and handed Catherine a cup. She then added outright: »I understand you are leaving the Franciscan order. Why?«

Catherine gave the older woman a look of surprise. Her decision couldn't possibly have been leaked to the outside world yet.
Only Mother Superior and a few close friends knew of it – and
of course, the Pope, who had invited her for a personal chat upon
her arrival to Rome. She lowered her cup. »I have my reasons,«
she simply said.

Sister Thea persisted. »I can imagine. But for which reasons?«

She inhaled deeply. »If the Congregation of the Doctrine of
Faith abolish my work – and they will most likely do that – then I
will be asked as a member of the order to remain silent at best.

In which case, I will leave so as not to harm the order any further.«

»Cardinal Bear in Chicago is on your side. Cardinal Weinstein in Vienna often stands between you and the Congregation of the Doctrine of Faith. Your Mother Superior supports you…«

»I know. That is one of the reasons why I must leave. By giving her oath, she has promised to honour the Church, but they are also my friends. I can just as easily remind the Church from the outside that reforms are necessary.« Catherine placed down her cup. »May I ask who told you of my decision?«

Without hesitation Sister Thea said: »A friend. He said you needn't worry. It won't come to a canonical process. Not as long as Leo is the Pope.«

Catherine contained her curiosity so as not to ask another question. Sister Thea had probably revealed more than she should have. »His Holiness is an extraordinary human being,« she said. »It is as if all the positive characteristics of the last few Popes have been united in him.«

Another smile ran across Sister Thea's face. She stood up, went to her desk and turned the flat screen computer monitor toward Catherine. The coat of arms of the Holy See that served as a screen saver was replaced by the image of an article. »I don't know the exact numbers, but thanks to the Pope the Church has won ground in Germany and the rest of Europe. The communities are no longer shrinking. The number of candidates for the priesthood is on the rise…Successes for which neither the traditionalists nor the conservatives can take credit.«

Catherine arose and stood next to Sister Thea at the monitor. The article was from the German weekly paper Die Zeit and referred to an interview with Cardinal Herzog from Cologne, the successor of Eminence Eugenio Cardinal Tore, the current Pontifex maximus.

Sister Thea said: »His Holiness is a humanist first, Pope second. A lot of the social, ideological, political, ethnic and intellectual barriers of yesteryear no longer exist. It is for that reason that your vision of the future, a vision of a modern, adaptable church impressed him so much. Nonetheless, he is a part of the system.«

She tapped a few keys and a flood of emails rushed across the screen. »These are all for you, Catherine. Thousands of emails – hundreds coming in anew each day. People are hoping and praying for you all over the world.«

»I had no idea…« Sure, she had received emails here and there that supported her work or even criticised it…but never in such numbers – directly sent to the Holy See? Catherine was speechless.

Both affection and determination streamed across Sister Thea's face. »No matter what happens, no matter how you decide, whether you stay or leave the order. You are not alone. I wanted you to know that.«

Catherine took a seat next to the Franciscan nun at the little table, drank coffee and ate cookies while chatting with her as if it were the most natural thing in the world to discuss inner-Vatican politics, the future of the Church and as to whether Leo's selection perhaps meant the dawning of a new era.

Finally, Sister Thea asked: »Do you have plans for tomorrow evening? Cardinal Benelli has invited a few of us to a little dinner. He would be thrilled to have you.« She added with a conspiratorial wink: »You'd have the unique opportunity to observe several intrigue-loving Curia members live. In action, so to speak.«

Catherine waved her off. »I'd better not. I am the enfant terrible of the ecclesiastical world. My presence could easily turn the His Eminence's celebration into an apocalyptic fiasco.«

»Or the chance to straighten things out once and for all.

They've written so much about you in the papers, Catherine. So much talk too. But not many truly know you. We would be delighted if you should come.«

»Thanks. But I…please understand that I must first think about it.«

Thea nodded. »Of course. Pardon me. I didn't want to coerce you. You've been through a lot in the past few days.«

So true. The past few days hadn't exactly been a bed of roses. But the audience with His Holiness, the personal conversation with Pope Leo, had brought her renewed hope for the future of the Church, along with her own. Leo hadn't pressured her in the least. He hadn't reprimanded her or in any way rebuked her. He had merely spoken to her about the concerns of humanity, about that which moved her, about what the men and women in the twenty-first century expect from their church and what the church instead provided them.

»The issue is really quite simple, Your Grace,« Catherine had said with a touch of irony. »The Holy Father has the top authority. And the Holy Father is you.«

Leo had looked at her and laughed. He then pointed to his heart and said: »The top authority resides with Him and He is in our hearts, Sister Catherine. I know He won't let you fall.«

His words had given her enormous strength during the darkest hours in the past few weeks. But even the fierce Joan of Arc had been burned at the stake.

»Come,« said Sister Thea and gave Catherine's arm a friendly pat. »Let me show you the Vatican's gardens. A little fresh air and some greenery will do us a world of good. You'll see. It works wonders.«

The Vatican's gardens were wonderful, a paradise with its numerous fountains, statues, buildings and grottos surrounded by unique vegetation. During their walk, they passed by Sister

Thea's favourite spot, the Grotta di Lourdes, a replication of the Lourdes grotto in the South of France where the Virgin Mary appeared to Saint Bernadette over fifty years ago.

After Catherine arrived at her room in the guesthouse Isa in the Vatican late that evening, she thought about Cardinal Benelli's invitation. She didn't know the man, but Sister Thea had assured her that he belonged to the most open-minded members of the Vatican and that he somehow managed to make friends with even the most bitter of opponents.

Catherine sat at the tiny hotel room desk, turned on her computer and called up her emails for the day. She was a foundered angel in God's court and parts of the world just awaited her fall. Could she even afford to reject the invitation? Just as she was about to finish with her electronic correspondence, she came upon a message sent by Albert Cardinal Benelli late that afternoon. His friendly tone revealed nothing of his high clerical rank. Without being hurtful, yet full of compassion and with a touch of encouragement, he asked her how she liked the »global village« that is the Vatican after the strict guardians of the faith had administered to her needs. In the next breath he invited her to a little dinner party that he was arranging for the following evening. He forwent all Vatican subtleties, which Catherine found quite refreshing.

She sat there for a while, then thanked him for the invitation, which she gracefully accepted. Should the party tomorrow turn out to be a battlefield, she would do her best to stand above it all. But she would fight back in her way. Benelli must know that, even if he wouldn't expect that from her.

Her mobile phone beeped once. A text message from Ben. He would return to Rome tonight.

12

Rome, The Vatican, Palace of the Holy Office

Ben had the feeling as if he had entered Cardinal Ciban's office a thousand times already even though he had only done so perhaps three dozen times. Once again the astounding combination of past, present and high-tech equipment made an impression on him. It was as if a highly skilled interior designer had taken the best from antiquity, the Middle Ages, the Renaissance and the modern era and artfully arranged it in this room as if it were the most natural thing in the world.

Ben sat in a comfortable Renaissance chair with high armrests and a dark leather seat cushion. To his left stood an old open bookshelf that looked as if it and the books inside had come from the Biblioteca Apostolica Vaticana. A flat screen monitor hung on the right wall while the remainder of the media station rested underneath the screen on an elegant iron and glass structure. Angelic figures armed with swords overlooked the room from ceiling level on another shelf.

Ciban had just returned from a meeting with His Holiness when Ben entered his office's antechamber. For a few days now rumours had been floating around that the Pope had suffered a stroke. The young investigator asked himself how much of it were true. Ciban hadn't said a word about it. He now stood at the window, staring at the cloudless sky, and appeared to pay no attention at all to Ben's report about Father Darius' murder, the Rottach Abbey and the Munich rental car company. It was only after he ended his stocktaking with a slight cough that Ciban turned back toward him.

In the past few years, Ben had learned how to read the cardinal's sparse gestures, but at this moment he couldn't tell in what type of mood his superior was. It was moments like these in which Ben wished he had Catherine's gift to see what she saw when she read a person's aura. Had she risked taking a look at the prefect's soul during her interrogation?

Ciban took a seat across from Ben at the large Renaissance desk and crossed his slender legs. Even though the cardinal was in his early fifties, the young Vatican agent knew Ciban could physically take him on at any time. The prefect was also known for his phenomenal memory. Quite a few of his Curia colleagues, including the old-school Cardinal Secretary of State His Eminence Sergio Cardinal Monti, had learned that painful lesson. A further consequence of his great memory was the well-organised desk of His Eminence. The sealed well-polished surface looked as if no one had worked there for even a single hour.

»Our German agent just called,« explained Ciban. His melodious voice would have most likely shot up the number of Radio Vatican listeners by several percentage points. »The young man from the rental car company, Eric Zander, is dead. Apparently, he died of an overdose.«

Ciban clicked on the flat screen monitor and Ben saw the bleak image of a drowned corpse. Ralf Porter from the German Federal Intelligence Service was right. Zander had seen someone who could have identified the stranger and that cost him his life.

»Where did they find the body, Eminence?«

»Zander's body was pulled from the Isar near Baierbrunn last night. He was already dead before someone tossed him into the river. That was about three and a half days ago.« Ciban switched off the monitor.

»Did the rental car company's surveillance videos show anything?« asked Ben.

»They're still at the lab. Porter will keep us posted.«

»To be honest, I don't understand it, Eminence. For heaven's sake, who would have a reason to murder Father Darius? What's the motive?«

The cardinal shook his head. »I'm sorry, Monsignor. I know Father Darius was your mentor and friend, but I am not authorised to speak about the details of this case with you.«

»Does it have something to do with Lux?« Ben persisted.

The order investigated and managed all secret knowledge surrounding all extraordinary phenomena both inside and outside the Church. Darius had worked for decades for the institutes in Chicago and Rome. Ben and Catherine had both received lessons and instruction in one of them. But Ben had left Chicago shortly before Lux had taken over the direction of the Institute for the Psychically Gifted. Nonetheless, Lux was under the control of the Congregation of the Doctrine of Faith, the modern Roman Inquisition. If anyone could answer the question, it would be the cardinal.

Ciban gave Ben an indulgent glance, leaned back in his comfortable desk chair and tapped his fingers together lightly. »I think you've understood what I said. I cannot speak of it. With no one. Except with His Holiness.«

What nonsense. Ben's gaze fell upon Ciban's left hand, the one with the tiny scar. This black-robed predator who had saved Innocence from an assassination like a bodyguard three years ago in Mexico was one of the most powerful men in the Vatican. No one could forbid him to speak about the case if he so desired.

Not even His Holiness.

»How is the Holy Father?« asked Ben carefully to at least feel out the measure of this rumour.

»Considering the circumstance he is well. Why?«

»I heard a few things.«

Ciban gave him an ominous, casual smile. »What would the Vatican be without rumours.« After a brief pause, he added: »I must ask you to put your investigation on hold.«

Put the investigation on hold? Ben stared at the prefect incredulously. He thought he may have heard incorrectly. To remain silent about a case was one thing. He wasn't even able to tell Catherine about Darius' murder. But to completely stop his investigation made no sense at all.

»Quite frankly, I am surprised, Eminence. I've only just gotten started.«

»I know. But I must ask you to let it rest for a while. Trust me.« Ciban looked into his counterpart's eyes in such a way that he had to ask himself if he shared Catherine's gift to read his soul.

»What about the lead in Germany?«

»We will look into it, of course.« Within seconds the prefect elegantly swung himself up and stood by the door. Ben was certainly not short, but his superior towered over him by at least ten centimetres. »I will get back to you immediately should anything come up.«

Ben had to admit that their conversation was over. He grabbed his briefcase and stood up. But if Ciban expected him to return to the depths of the archives and act as if nothing had happened, the cardinal had another thing coming to him.

»Before you go, I have one more question,« said Ciban, blocking his exit.

Ben had no choice but to stand there and wait to see what would happen next.

»When you went through Father Darius' belongings, did you come across anything…out of the ordinary?«

»Anything out of the ordinary?« Ben thought for a moment. Was the cardinal thinking about the little oak chest with the letters and papers? They must have arrived to the secret service in a sealed container by now. Ben had not discovered anything unusual in the chest. Nothing in the least that seemed suspicious or could have had anything to do with Darius' murder.

Regarding the old Bible with Darius' own highlights, Ben's only inheritance….he couldn't see anything suspicious there either. Many believers highlight Bible passages that help them with their meditation practice and offer them strength. Why should it be any different with Darius? »Not that I know of. What could it be?«

»I am asking you, Monsignor.« Ciban shrugged his shoulders casually, moved out of Ben's way and handed him the folder he had placed on the desk after giving his report. »Perhaps you will give it some thought.«

As Ben walked through the long antechamber toward the corridor, he could feel the cardinal's gaze piercing his back. He felt a sense of unease. Never before had Ciban held him back during an investigation. Never before had Ben felt so uneasy in the presence of his superior.

Good Lord! What had Darius gotten himself into that he was now dead and Ciban had halted all further investigations? Ben was certain it had something to do with Lux Domini. Lux now possessed a great deal of power due to its research. Its structure reminded Ben of a secret order like that of Opus Dei. On top of that, a great majority of the members were gifted mediums…

Suddenly, his mobile phone rang as he made his way back to the archives. It was Catherine.

At least there was one good thing about this day.

13

The master's flat was located in the north-western part of Rome and offered a breath-taking view of the city. At sunset Monsignor Nicola deRossi enjoyed the grand view of the dome of St. Peter's Basilica. The sparkling rooftops seemed to reach beyond eternity in the sunlight. The Roman emperors must have felt that way when they looked across the centre of their empire two thousand years ago. In a certain way the master seemed to deRossi to be a type of emperor, even if he remained uncrowned according to clerical standards. The master should have been the one on Petri's throne instead of the sentimental weakling Leo. The Church could achieve so much more under his reign.

The sun disappeared and the veranda's automatic lights switched on. DeRossi knew that the moment night fell, Rome would fill with a particular type of person: the night owl. He himself knew the nocturnal magic of Rome much better than its magic by day. He had promised some of those people heaven on Earth, then given them hell instead. The last nocturnal reveller he came across didn't survive the magic. The peace and quiet of the catacombs was quite ecstasising. The blood of the lamb was so sweet.

»A glorious evening,« said the master who sat next to deRossi on the veranda and followed his gaze. »I will never tire of this view, dear Nicola.«

»I believe you, Eminence,« agreed deRossi with a compassionate smile.

Just a few moments before they had enjoyed a delicious meal
and an excellent wine over conversation about the mission,
Rottach and Father Darius. DeRossi suppressed a pleasant shiver.
It was so tempting to recall the incredulous look on the priest's
face and the ensuing silent fall into the depths of his demise.
Rottach had been as successful as the two other missions in
Switzerland and France. DeRossi could be pleased with himself
and the world around him as he had done good work. Darius'
end meant another member of the foolish papal Lux congregation had left this world. Not a single trail could be made back to
Rome, not to mention to himself or the master.

The house servant came in with a new bottle of wine and filled
their glasses anew. This time it was a Châteauneuf-du-Pape 2002
from Belleville. Not nearly as fine as the wine they had enjoyed at
dinner, but a good one nonetheless with which to end the
evening.

»I envy you at this moment,« added deRossi with a tone of
sincerity.

»You have no reason to envy me, Nicola,« said the master with
a slightly paternal smile. Despite his advanced age, he sat in his
red-bordered black robe like a true church dignitary. »One day
this will all belong to you. Who knows? Perhaps you will be Pope
one day.«

DeRossi nodded with satisfaction. In truth he had no interest
in becoming Pope. It would only serve to restrict his freedom of
movement, especially his nocturnal prowlings around Rome.
Power and riches, well, that was something different altogether.
Ever since he began working with the master, he had filled his
personal foreign bank accounts royally.

»Has Cardinal Ciban heard anything from Rottach?« asked

deRossi calmly as he looked over the illuminated evening sky over Rome and took a sip of wine.

»He sent Hawlett on the road this time. If he hopes to help the young man out of his melancholy, that is certainly the wrong way to go about it.«

DeRossi grinned into his wine glass. During his studies in Rome, he had spent several semesters with Ben Hawlett. Ever since his childhood Reverend Hawlett had been fighting against an invisible internal demon, an inner darkness whose shadowy death swell would overtake him sooner or later. DeRossi unconsciously traced a finger over the badly healed scar above his left eye. He had had a similar experience over many years during his youth, but it had made him stronger. It made him the man he was today. In contrast to deRossi, it appeared to be slowly but surely killing Hawlett. Yet Ciban wouldn't give up on the weakling.

»Perhaps a meeting with Catherine would do him some good,« mocked deRossi.

The master gave him a conspiratorial look. »The two of them haven't seen each other in ages. It would be worth a try. That reminds me. Massini is ready to be included in our plans. Our handsome Aurelio has spent a further engaging night with him. We have recorded every word.«

'And certainly every position,' thought deRossi excitedly. Aurelio was one of the lowly workers in the master's Roman agent network. The prostitute hadn't a clue who his true lord and master was and what his objectives were, nor did he know Reverend deRossi. Should he find out, he would share the fate of many other Roman nocturnal revellers.

»When will you send a copy of the recording to Massini, Eminence?«

»Straight away tomorrow afternoon, right before his next

meeting with His Holiness, Ciban and Hawlett. That way he will have no time to recover from the shock when he sits across from the cardinal in the papal dining room.«

»Ciban?« DeRossi raised his brow, lending him a bizarre and dangerous appearance due to the scar above his left eye.

»Our ammunition is much more powerful than I thought, Nicola. In a moment of passion Massini admitted to our blessed Aurelio his weakness for our incumbent Grand Inquisitor.«

DeRossi whistled softly. He rarely smoked, but he now took a cigarette from the case sitting on the table and took a puff. The nicotine immediately calmed his severed nerves. »Miracles never cease.« Neither he nor the master could be certain as to whether Massini could be blackmailed when it came to Leo. It could have easily been that the fag admitted his transgressions to the Pope. Leo had a big heart. In contrast to Ciban.

»It's all well and good in Massini's case,« said the master as he observed his counterpart with pleasure. He had once been a heavy smoker until his doctor made him quit unless he wished to end his life early. »Benelli is causing problems. He's up to something. But I have yet to find out what it is.«

»What could His Eminence possibly have against us? He has nothing on us. But you have something on him. He not only renovated the Vatican bank, but himself as well.«

The master laughed. »And he did it so well.« He reached into his cassock, pulled out an envelope from an interior pocket and handed it to his protégé.

DeRossi opened the envelope and pulled out the impressive card. »An invitation to a reception at Benelli's villa?«

The master sighed. »It's not just a simple invitation, Nicola. It's also not just a simple reception. There's more to it. Believe me.«

»Do you know who else has been invited?«

»The usual suspects from the Curia. Including Massini. Aside from that a few of Benelli's friends from the order, including Sister Thea…«

»Sister Thea? Just what we needed.«

The master took a deep breath. »Indeed.« One thing he would never do again, and he meant never, ever again was to underestimate the director of the Internet office. »But before we turn our attention to the reception and Benelli's guests, we have another matter to discuss so that our mission will continue to be a success.« He wrote a short note on a small pad of paper, ripped off the top two pages so as not to leave a traceable mark and handed it to his counterpart so he could memorise the name and address.

DeRossi raised a brow. »Calcutta, the capital of West Bengal?«

The master nodded. »Sister Silvia is a kind of Mother Teresa. She has an immense godliness and compassion for humanity and, unfortunately, an equally immense psychic energy. Leo will immediately feel the loss of her support.«

»When should I depart?« asked the Monsignor slyly. He would certainly come across a few interesting nocturnal revellers in Calcutta.

»Day after tomorrow. The arrangements have already been made.«

»Good.« DeRossi took another drag from the cigarette and ignited the note with its burning tip.

Ashes to ashes.

Dust to dust.

TRAITOR

14

The black limousine with Vatican plates passed the old stone wall with its wrought-iron gate that separated Cardinal Benelli from the outside world. Catherine noted that there was neither a postbox nor a plaque indicating that a church dignitary lived there. She cast a timid glance at the winding road that lay before them.

The villa was located northeast from Rome and took about one-half hour by car from the Vatican during non-rush hour traffic in Rome. The limousine drove through a wooded area and about one mile uphill. Pushing up beyond the shady trees, the Renaissance-style villa was one of the most beautiful things Catherine had ever seen in her entire life. Benelli's refuge was a perfect symbiosis between art and nature, vegetation and light. It exuded pure joy and a kind of cosmopolitanism.

»The park is at its most beautiful with the water fountains in the summertime,« explained Ben.

He had taken Catherine because Sister Thea had been held up by her work at the Vatican. They had spent the afternoon in Di Marzio, a café with a view of the Piazza near the Basilica of Santa Maria in Trastevere where Fellini had filmed several scenes. Catherine could feel something was up with her friend, but she could also sense that he could or would not talk about it. She suppressed an urge to address it with him.

Afterward they had returned to the Vatican and left with the car in front of the building of the Congregation of the Doctrine of Faith. They had left Rome from the Via Flaminia Nuova and motored north. The landscape around Monterotondo was surrounded by thick chestnut, beech and oak forests that oscillated amongst the fields, vineyards and olive tree orchards. The sparsely populated area with just a few thousand residents was most known for the extraordinary healing powers of its spring water.

»Cardinal Benelli bought the villa from Cardinal Ciban,« said Ben. As Catherine looked at him with surprise, he explained further: »Benelli comes from a wealthy merchant family, you must know. The Cibans, well, their family tree extends back to the twelfth century. They are filthy rich. To balance things out, the clan is behind as many charity organisations as there are hairs on your head. Perhaps also as a way to offset the fact that their bloodline did not always stand for virtue and honesty all those centuries.«

»Where do you know all this?« In the same breath, Catherine shook her head. »Oh I see now. Your old tendency to snoop around hasn't died, has it?«

Ben laughed. »You know that people have always fascinated me. People and their stories.«

»Is that why you became an archivist?«

In her mind's eye, Catherine could see her friend all alone rushing along the shadows of the tall shelves, studying old tomes or losing himself in the secret files in one of the locked rooms of the Vatican's archives. Years ago she had been allowed access to one of the public areas of the archives and felt extremely ill-at-ease there. Without her guide she surely would have gotten lost in the building's many corridors.

»Someone has to care for the growing piles of papers.«

»And the archived treasures! Admit it.«

»His Holiness Pope Innocence once said: 'Go to the source.' I'm just following his lead. But honestly, Catherine, have you never asked yourself who the new man is who is so vehemently defending the faith of the Catholic Church against any and all reform?«

Catherine sighed. »Believe me when I say that I have gotten to know our acting Grand Inquisitor through his work in the Congregation of the Doctrine of Faith. His lineage made no difference to me.«

Ben parked the car in front of a large bubbling fountain. As they got out and took a deep breath of fresh air, Catherine looked one more time across the estate's dreamy panorama. She almost felt as if she were in an enchanted fairy tale like the ones she remembered from childhood.

They climbed the broad steps and walked through the tall door where a servant took their invitation. A chandelier as large as a planet hung from the entrance hall ceiling. Valuable old paintings decorated the walls, but the thing that impressed Catherine the most were the wall and ceiling frescos with scenes from classical mythology that, according to Ben, were said to have originated from the builder Baldassare Peruzzi himself.

Music streamed through the wide open side door into the hall, hypnotically pulling the visitors into its sway in the ballroom. A chamber orchestra played Corelli. To the right of the entrance way stood a two-tiered buffet that took up almost an entire wall. Tables decorated with flowers and candles stood like adjacent islands on which the guests could sit to chat, eat and drink. There was no seating arrangement.

Catherine discovered members of the various orders: Jesuits, Franciscans, Dominicans, Benedictines. Groups of the highest ecclesiastical dignitaries. So-called laypeople, men and women in ceremonious clothing and suits. She kept a lookout for Sister

Thea, but it appeared that the nun had not yet arrived. Neither had the Chicago Cardinal Bear, one of the few cardinals who dared publicly, if only tenuously, to lend her support.

She cleared her throat in irritation. »Didn't Sister Thea speak of a little get together?« Before Ben could respond, Cardinal Benelli had already excused himself from a little group of clergy- men and started to come at them in large strides. Benelli's poli- teness and hospitable warmth was so disarming that Catherine nearly forgot the breath-taking atmosphere that caused her a great deal of anxiety.

»Pardon me, Sister Catherine, I know it is more than what you had expected, but a tad bit of swindling was necessary to get you here.«

The young nun let the little portly man with his sparkling eyes stew in his own juices for a moment. He reminded her of the chubby angels often depicted during the Renaissance era. »I must admit that you've surprised me, Eminence, but I would love to know what you have planned for the rest of the evening.«

Benelli laughed and hooked his arm in hers as if they were father and daughter taking a mundane stroll through the city. »Come with me, my dear. Allow me to introduce you to some of my friends and acquaintances. Ben, I bet you'd like to join us?«

As he told Catherine some historical details about the Cibane- an villa, he led her from one group of clergymen and laypeople to the next. The reactions from the clergymen toward the church critic were mixed, but they remained friendly and polite at all times. No one would allow to lower himself to the level of provo- cation. Certainly not in the presence of Benelli and his exotic guest. No one except Curia Cardinal Sergio Monti who sat upon a high antique purple-covered chair from whence he directed a gathering swarm of listeners.

Catherine knew from various articles she had read that Monti's mind was still like a steel trap despite his advanced age. Long before Ciban had entered the scene, he had woven a web against Catherine under Innocence. Surely the younger cardinal had learned a great deal from the elderly shyster and former guardian of faith. The old frail-looking dwarf was also known for his biting sarcasm.

»I have heard that you intend to leave the Church, Sister Catherine?« He sounded more like a polite demand to do exactly that.

Some of the guests may have also detected the dispassionate conclusion that the author's excommunication was now just a mere formality.

»I hope not, Eminence, because the Church is in real trouble and I still have a few things to say to it.«

»Oh, I think you've said more than enough.« The old cardinal looked about the room with amusement as if he had just made a really good joke.

»You know, Eminence,« Catherine spoke emphatically and deliberately, »the Church is old and can only comprehend things slowly. But I won't give up on it for that reason. It is my home and I love it even when it isn't always loveable.«

Some of the listeners suppressed a smile. Others showed open indignation. Monti and Catherine stared at each other for several long seconds. The cardinal then smiled as if he had just enjoyed the bouquet of a high-quality wine or the first act of a very promising symphony.

»I will miss you, Sister Catherine. Oh yes, I will miss you, believe me. I wish you and your friends a lovely evening. Now if you will excuse me.«

Catherine nodded politely. »Eminence.«

When the old cardinal was out of earshot, Ben said without thinking about Benelli's presence: »Cardinal Monti has the ugliest character I have ever seen. How can the Church tolerate such a man in its midst?«

»I should like to say there are worse cases,« explained Benelli quietly. He turned to Catherine. »You put up an excellent fight.«

Catherine sighed. »I'm afraid it won't help me much in a war like this one, Eminence. And Cardinal Monti knows it.«

The host shook his head and said with an ironic tone: »Cardinal Monti knows one thing for certain: he cannot turn back the hands of time, but as you can see, he's trying anyway.« He pointed discreetly toward the old cardinal whose assistant was handing him a pill box in that moment. Monti swallowed the pills, then pulled himself painstakingly up out of his chair. A few moments later he moved toward the buffet as if he had suddenly grown younger by a decade.

»The blessings of modern medicine,« explained Benelli. »His Holiness Pope Innocence also benefited from it in the last few years of his papacy. Thank heavens! We would have had a whole range of other problems otherwise.«

Catherine gave Benelli a confused look. »Pardon me, Eminence, but I don't quite follow what you mean.«

The cardinal was about to respond when his telephone rang. He made an apologetic gesture as he reached into his cassock for his mobile phone.

»Yes?« He listened for a while in silence, said goodbye and turned off his mobile phone. He then turned back to Catherine and Ben.

»Sister Thea and Cardinal Bear are having car troubles. The tow truck company has been alerted, but I should like to send a car to collect them just in case.«

He waved to one of his employees, a stocky giant in a black suit and explained what had happened. The man immediately set off.

»Engine damage?« asked Ben.

»Not entirely,« explained the cardinal who looked about him to ensure no one was listening. He then said to Catherine and Ben: »Some crazy person tried to pass them on a narrow mountain road and pushed them to the side. Thank God nothing serious happened. But the car must be towed now.«

»I had better accompany the driver then,« said Ben.

»I didn't send Massimo off alone. You should know me better than that by now. We have taken all safety precautions so no need to worry now.«

Catherine looked at the two of them. Her face revealed her puzzlement. What on earth was going on here? But Benelli simply gave a friendly smile and said: »Later,« whilst introducing them the next group and the next one until Sister Thea and Cardinal Bear showed up on the scene, of which Cardinal Monti made note with an ungracious look. The host had explained to Catherine that Monti did not like the Americans. He despised Bear in particular. He found the Americans to be utterly corrupt and decadent.

In typical Benelli fashion, he greeted his new guests warmly. Cardinal Bear wasn't exactly reserved in his greeting either. As he gave Catherine a friendly hug, she couldn't help but glance over at His Eminence Cardinal Monti. He raised a glass of red wine to her, but the smile on his lips didn't reach his inscrutable eyes.

»What has happened,« asked Ben immediately.

Bear remained calm as if nothing had happened at all. »I'm afraid some crazy person tried to scare the wits out of us. If Sister Thea hadn't responded as quickly as she had, we may not have made it around the bend.«

Sister Thea? Catherine gave the Franciscan nun a curious look.

Thea explained: »In Australia I used to drive in rallies with my brother Toni. It's in my blood.«

»Thank God!« said Bear and gave his companion a grateful look. He was still white as a ghost. The experience had left its mark on him.

»What kind of car was it?« asked Ben. »Did you recognise the driver or the licence plate?«

The cardinal shook his head. »Everything happened so fast and we were in the midst of conversation…«

Thea said: »If I remember correctly, it was a green Lancia. But I didn't see it in the parking lot in front of the villa.«

Bear turned toward the young Monsignor with eyes as big as saucers. »You don't think it was a coincidence?«

Having heard from Sister Isabella's fatal car accident in the Swiss Alps, Ben replied: »I'll definitely keep an eye on the green Lancia.«

Benelli cleared his throat, acting as if they were speaking of nothing other than Thea's past as a rally driver or Bear's gruelling transcontinental flight as he said: »Careful. Let us speak of this later. At the moment, the chairman of the College of the Cardinals and his entourage are heading right toward us.«

His Eminence Steffano Cardinal Gasperetti! Catherine held her breath. The tiny elegant clergyman, with his weasel-like eyes who reminded her of a moustacheless novel-based version of Agatha Christie's Hercule Poirot, came right up to her. Apart from Gasperetti's high position, he was also considered one of the most conservative men in the Vatican. He had certainly not voted for Pope Leo during the last conclave; neither had Cardinal Monti in whose presence Gasperetti had often found himself. At the age of seventy-eight Gasperetti, like Monti himself, would most likely not participate in the next conclave.

All cardinals who had reached their eightieth birthday could no longer participate in the election of the new Pope. Officially, that is. Unofficially, it was an entirely different matter. Even if a cardinal could no longer vote for the Pope, there were plenty of ways to manipulate the election for the next pontiff if he were smart about it. Catherine wondered how well Leo, Monti and Gasperetti got along on the icy Vatican summit on which they all sat. It was no secret that Leo was tolerant. But Monti and Gasperetti? Not to mention Ciban.

They were given a formal welcome. When the cardinal shook the church critic's hand, his gaze turned stoic. »So, and here we have the young lady who has challenged the Catholic Church.«

»Just the conservative parts, Eminence,« corrected Catherine politely. She wanted in no way to provoke the cardinal, but at the same time she wanted to remind him that she certainly had supporters among his circle of men.

Gasperetti suppressed a crooked smile. »It takes a lot of courage, Sister, and certainly deep faith. His Holiness holds you in high regard and I cannot imagine you would disappoint him.«

»I vowed to dedicate my life to serve His Holiness and the Church. I would do the Church a disservice if I were to remain silent.«

The cardinal nodded pensively. »I see. I mean no irreverence when I say that you should be careful.«

Catherine couldn't quite believe her ears. Nonetheless, she decided not to take his words as a threat, but as well-meaning advice. »I shall do what is in my power, Eminence.«

Benelli said frankly: »If you are aware of something that Sister Catherine should know about, Steffano, then out with it.«

»That is the problem, Alberto,« replied Gasperetti as he shrugged his shoulders with regret. »I know nothing concrete. It's never concrete. But we all know one thing: the price of freedom is being on alert at all times.«

After he left, Thea said: »I never thought I would hear those words coming from Cardinal Gasperetti's mouth. Perhaps the spirit of His Holiness is rubbing off on him.«

Benelli shook his head. »I don't think so. His words were both a warning and a threat. He is the kind of person who wants something without being willing to pay for it.«

»That sounds very unchristian,« said Catherine.

»I believe his Eminence Cardinal Gasperetti is certainly capable in certain borderline situations to allow certain things to take an unchristian turn if it serves the Church in the end. Don't forget that although he is a conservative man, he is still running Lux even two years after Pope Innocence's death.«

Catherine was reminded of the Machiavellian phrase that her opponents ascribed to the Jesuits: »The end justifies the means.« His Eminence Steffano Cardinal Gasperetti certainly wasn't the first church dignitary to live and die by the phrase and he certainly wouldn't be the last. What amazed her even more was the fact that Benelli spoke of it so openly even though Gasperetti belonged to the opposition.

»Please excuse me for a moment, Catherine,« said Ben. »I don't think we should just let his inference go. I'm going to ask around.«

Catherine gave him a look of doubt. »Do you really think that is necessary?« She had received her share of warnings and threats in the last two years and had learned to live with them. Why should Gasperetti's words be any different?

Ben's response was both short and sobering. »Did you not originally want to go with Sister Thea to this reception?«

Just as Ben disappeared into the crowd, Benelli asked Thea and Bear to stay put whilst he took Catherine aside. »Come with me, Sister. The time is right. I have something urgent to tell you in private.«

15

They left the noisy chatter-filled reception hall and the sound of lively Baroque music behind them. Catherine looked around the high, lengthy corridors and was once again impressed with the villa's rich interior.

»I heard you bought the villa from Cardinal Ciban?«

Benelli smiled. »Well, that's not exactly true. The Cibans would never fully part with this estate. Let's just say it is on loan. Upon my death the estate will go back to the family and rented out by someone else. As beautiful as it is here, not even Cardinal Ciban would want to live here.«

»I don't really understand that,« said Catherine »This place is paradise.«

»Unfortunately, it is also a place of family tragedy,« explained Benelli with great emotion. »Cardinal Ciban's sister Sarah was found dead in the park at a young age. As far as I know the cause of her death is not known to this day. I imagine that is why he finally moved into the city to Rome.«

Catherine was shocked. She hadn't expected that.

The duo entered a small lively chapel with valuable stained glass windows, holy sculptures and an impressive altar. Benelli closed the door in front of which one of his employees was posted. He knew that to speak in private, one must be completely alone.

Catherine looked about. »This is all very mysterious, Eminence.« Up to this point she had not asked a single question about their pending conversation. But at this moment any further restraint seemed inappropriate even though she still refused to take a look at Benelli's aura. As a child she had read people's thoughts and auras without thinking that her gift was unique and that she could invade someone else's privacy by doing so. But now she controlled her gift like a well-practiced pianist did his instrument. Although to control it took much more out of her than allowing nature to take its course.

»It is going to seem even stranger to you now.« Benelli pointed for her to take a seat next to him. They sat near the altar in the soft candlelight as he reached into his cassock's interior pocket and pulled out a photograph. »I know about your gift, Catherine. Father Darius told me about it.«

The young woman looked at him inquisitively. She then looked at the photo showing Darius and Benelli standing on St. Peter's Square in mutual admiration. People were everywhere, including barriers. The picture must have been taken right before the last conclave. If Darius had confided in Benelli, they must both have a very trusting relationship. »Then you too are a member of Lux Domini?«

Benelli nodded and placed the photograph back in his pocket. »Let's just say I am a silent member. I have never been an official one. Truth be told I don't belong to any organisation or party within the church. You will discover the reason in just a moment.« The cardinal paused for a second as if to search for the right words. He finally spoke with as much compassion as possible: »I'm afraid I have bad news for you, Catherine. Father Darius is…dead.«

What did he just say? Catherine had heard the words, but she struggled with their meaning. The white-haired cardinal gave her a compassionate look and she suddenly had the feeling that the real revelation still stood before her.

Benelli continued: »They had been saying Darius had a fatal accident while hiking in the mountains, but we now know that is not true.«

She stared at the cardinal, summoning all her strength to control her reaction. She was speechless.

»It was murder,« explained Benelli. »And he is not the only victim we have to mourn.«

Murder?

The thoughts swirled in Catherine's mind.

Darius…

Hiking…

Accident…

Death…

Murder…

She had a vague feeling that she might faint. The priest had been like a father to her and Ben, a friend, a reference point, a safe haven without whom they might just have lost their minds. And now he had been murdered? What for?

As she tried to sort out her thoughts, Benelli told her of the other murder victims, of Sister Isabella and Father Sylvester. Both were also unofficial Lux members and members of a congregation that had a particular proximity with the Pope. The cardinal's voice suddenly seemed distant as he said to Catherine: »Isabella's, Sylvester's and Darius' murders are bad enough, but the actual attacks were meant for His Holiness.«

Catherine attempted to make sense of what Benelli had just revealed to her. Darius had been murdered, then he spoke of a secret congregation inside Lux and now the Pope was at risk! She closed her eyes, took a deep breath and tried to find a single thought that made any sense at all from the insanity she had just heard. But she had only one thought: Darius was dead and his murderer was still out there.

»Do they have any leads?« she asked with a voice even she didn't recognise.

»We have a vague lead. But given the circumstances it is no wonder. If we don't catch the murderer soon, it could be too late. One or two more murders and the Church would lose its balance.«

Balance? What does that mean? How could a church, an institution in existence for nearly two thousand years suddenly lose its balance? Then Catherine remembered what Benelli had said: »given the circumstances.« What in heaven's name could the circumstances be?

»I realise it is a lot to digest at once,« said the cardinal quietly. »It must sound completely absurd to you, but I haven't even scratched the surface of what you will need to know for your mission. I know Lux is history to you. You left active duty six years ago, but we need your help, Catherine.«

»If you will excuse me,« the young woman managed to say, »but I need to move around.«

She stood up and paced back and forth in front of the altar like a caged animal. Benelli remained calm, waited patiently and seemed to be the embodiment of patience itself. She finally stood still before him, gave him a scrutinising look and said: »Forgive me, Eminence, but why should I trust you? Just because you showed me this photograph and claim to have been friends with Father Darius?«

Benelli sighed. »Unfortunately, time is running out for lengthy explanations and even if we did have enough time, you most likely wouldn't believe me anyway, Catherine. We have to find another way. You will soon receive the necessary information you need.« He got up, walked toward her and handed her the photograph once again. »Keep the photo. I don't need it anymore. Regarding your trust in me…use your gift whenever you like. I'm not afraid of it.« Catherine stared at the cardinal. He seemed to be sincere in his offer.

»But now, my dear, let us pray for Darius, Sylvester, Isabella and the Pope before we have to return to the fray upstairs.«

The young woman moved her gaze from Benelli to the photograph in her hand. She couldn't explain why she had even accepted the picture or why she stood next to the cardinal and prayed together with him for Darius, Sylvester, Isabella and Leo, as if their conversation had never taken place. Perhaps it had to do with the old man's incredible calm and confidence that, with every passing minute of prayer, spilled over to Catherine. She had never felt such calm before. It felt as if their souls melted together during their prayer.

After they had finished praying, she felt both sad and relieved at the same time. Sad because the inner peace had disappeared slightly and relieved that she once again felt like herself.

With his winning smile Benelli accompanied her to the door. Oddly she felt no sense of distrust anymore toward the man, even though she had not used her gift. Everything seemed to be in alignment and harmonious even after their painful conversation with which the cardinal had so rigorously confronted her.

When the host opened the door, a figure dressed in a priest's cassock stood with its back to them in a long corridor and appeared to admire the wall paintings. Apparently, Benelli's employee had prevented the cleric from entering the chapel whilst they were there. As the stranger turned around, Catherine remembered having seen him in the reception hall in the group surrounding Cardinal Monti.

»Forgive me, Eminence. I did not wish to disturb you,« said the priest. »I only wanted to look at the house chapel that everyone has praised so highly.«

Benelli gave him a friendly nod. »Monsignor, allow me to introduce you to Sister Catherine Bell.« Despite his friendliness Catherine could sense a certain level of discord in the cardinal's voice, set off by the priest's presence. »Catherine, this is Monsignor deRossi, one of the most promising employees of the bishops' congregation.«

So one of Cardinal Gasperetti's people, Catherine immediately thought.

DeRossi offered her his hand and smiled, showing a row of perfect teeth. What fascinated Catherine far more was the visible scar above his eye. She wondered why the scar had healed so badly. Nevertheless, the Monsignor had a beautiful face. His black short haircut gave off an air of recklessness. But she could tell by his eyes that something wasn't quite right with him. From Catherine's perspective they seemed to lack all emotion, as if he had eyes like a shark.

»Your reputation precedes you, Sister Catherine,« said deRossi. »I hope you will enjoy the evening here nonetheless.« His voice sounded sincere even though his eyes revealed something different entirely.

»Thank you, Father.« Catherine managed to return his smile with as much sincerity as deRossi had shown. »You won't regret having seen the chapel. It is truly impressive.«

The Monsignor stared at both of them with equal measure before saying: »Of that I am certain.«

»If you would excuse us,« said Benelli with a relaxed smile.

Carefully but with determination he directed Catherine past deRossi. The young woman felt a certain tingling sensation that she normally only felt before important exams or appearances. For a second she felt as if she were walking through an invisible barrier, like a door from whence there was no turning back. She could feel how deRossi stared at the both of them as they turned the corner.

When they reached the lift, Catherine couldn't help but saying: »You didn't like the fact that Monsignor deRossi showed up down there, did you?«

»Everything is going according to plan,« the white-haired man said with amusement. He suddenly turned serious. »A few odd things are about to happen, Catherine. These things will seem even more absurd than our conversation. But no matter what happens next, have trust. Trust your gift in particular.«

16

The next two hours were almost peaceful for Catherine. The heads of the conservative Catholic stage had slowly but surely paid a courtesy visit to the revolutionary nun who in turn had parried with them. The conservative mob had exhibited restraint with the exception of a few smaller skirmishes here and there.

The young author even got to know a few of her email contacts personally at the reception. Martin Kreuz, a Jesuit priest and rector for the Roman college of priests Germanicum et Hungaricum and general secretary of the Jesuit order with whom she had enjoyed a very critical, yet constructive exchange turned out to be an extremely humorous man. He had not only locked both Sister Thea and Catherine into his enormous heart, but he had also shown an equally large appetite at the buffet which side he rarely left. No, he would only stop eating when the Church did exactly as Jesus had instructed.

They finally returned to the small group of clergy, which included Cardinal Bear, Sister Thea, Ben and now a certain Father Luigi Thomas. The latter worked for the archives as Ben did. He had clearly had a bit too much to drink.

»I heard that the investigation has been stopped.«

»I don't know anything about it,« said Ben, who was clearly uncomfortable with Catherine's witnessing Father Thomas' blunder. »I suppose it is more a police matter than anything else.«

The priest laughed as if he were suddenly very amused.

Ben remained calm. »You have had too much to drink, Luigi. Come with me. I'll get you a taxi to take you home.«

Father Thomas awkwardly freed himself of Ben's well-meaning grasp and whispered: »We both know you conducted investigations in Rottach. What did you find out that led to its abrupt ending?« He then turned to Catherine. »Perhaps you can write about it in your next book!«

A firm voice behind the priest said warningly: »Sister Catherine will certainly take your suggestion into consideration, Luigi. A taxi is waiting outside to take you home. You have had a few tough weeks. Get some rest.«

The priest froze as if someone had stabbed him from behind.

Catherine too almost lost control. She was all too familiar with that cool, sonorous voice from the meetings with the Congregation of the Doctrine of Faith that she had suffered through. Marc Abott Cardinal Ciban greeted the group with a bow and cast a sounding glance across them. His eyes rested a second longer on her. A young priest by the name of Rinaldo immediately ushered Father Thomas out of the reception hall.

The baroque music seemed to stop at once. In fact, it seemed as though the entire reception was frozen in time for a short moment, as if an icy veil lay in the air, signalling a pending catastrophe. Cardinal Ciban and Sister Catherine! Two arch enemies within the Catholic Church at a private reception with just one and a half metres between them!

Taking a deliberately formal tone so that only the small group surrounding the critical author could hear him, the cardinal said: »This room is filled with snakes waiting for us to reach for each other's throats, but we won't do them the favour, will we, Sister?«

Catherine nodded in agreement. »No, we will not, Eminence.«

Cardinal Benelli appeared from nowhere and greeted Ciban

by saying he was glad the prefect had found his way here. Light conversation followed, allowing for those present to relax in a more pleasant atmosphere. A certain tension remained, however, like the calm before the storm that would rise again in the form of Nature's thunder. It was inevitable when two such diametrically opposite weather fronts such as Ciban and Bell directly clashed.

But the storm remained at bay, at least for the moment, although some of the guests would have loved to have experienced the spectacular thunderous rainstorm. For what other reason could have Benelli invited both of these opponents to his villa? So they could reconcile their differences? Ridiculous! So they would wait as the night was still young. Someone would certainly know how to ignite the flame of indignation. Once the first shot was fired, the evening would become a historic event not only for the journalists present, but a free-for-all for everyone.

Undeterred, Benelli said to Catherine and Ciban: »As far as I can tell, some of my guests are a bit disappointed about your mutual meeting. The lion lies next to the lamb, making no motion to eat it.«

Catherine, whose heart was nearly at a standstill, managed to say between clenched teeth: »If you think I'm the lamb, you are quite wrong, Eminence. What kind of game are you playing? Isn't it a bit too late to tell us the rules now?« Benelli's side glance to Ciban told her that if it weren't for Benelli's guests, the prefect of the Congregation of the Doctrine of Faith would have torn him to pieces by now. Their host had a lot of explaining to do.

Benelli made a placating gesture. »Oh it is an old game. One of the oldest of all. It's called 'good versus evil'. Only the good is not always the lamb and the evil not always the lion.«

»What remains is the snake,« said Ciban, looking at his counterpart as if he were the embodiment of evil itself.

But Benelli only laughed. »A poet would say this reception is a meeting between the representatives of light and darkness. And you know what else? Most people here don't even know it.«

Ben said dryly: »The final question would be then who belongs to the darkness and who to the light. How is it with you, Eminence? Are you the good cloaked in evil or the evil cloaked in good?«

»Let's just say I am on your side, Ben. But I am also on the side of His Holiness and that of Sister Catherine. Just as I am on the side of His Eminence Cardinal Ciban.«

»Then it must be pretty damn hard for you to find anyone like you,« shot Ciban back.

Benelli's gaze went from Catherine to the cardinal as if he wished to create an invisible connection between the two of them. »After all, it isn't the mind, but rather the heart that connects equals, right?«

For a moment the tiny group looked at the white-haired cardinal as if he were mentally challenged. Then Ciban spoke with a surprising softness in his voice: »That is all well and good, Eminence. But what is the real reason behind your provocation, your performance?«

Catherine could sense that the prefect was referring to more than the tactlessness of having been brought together with her this evening.

»I won't survive the night, Marc,« said Benelli, shrugging his shoulders. As if the provocation of the evening had not yet reached its height, the cardinal took off his ring and placed it on the buffet table. »We will have an end to the powerlessness this evening, even if it means the end of my own earthly existence.« He turned to Catherine: »Remember the diabolical fire in your nunnery?«

The nun nodded. Of course she remembered. How could she

ever forget. Fire broke out about three years ago one night in one of the cells in the diocese. It took two of the nuns' lives and injured three others. »The fire was meant for you, my child. But luckily your cell was empty.«

»I…« Catherine faltered as the reality of his words sunk in. Someone hated her so much for her stirring up trouble in the Church that he was willing to kill her and would take into account taking the lives of others in the process.

»You received an anonymous phone call and were pulled away. That's the reason you survived.«

Catherine stood there paralysed.

The white-haired cardinal turned to Ciban. »I don't know who Father Darius' murderer is, but one thing I do know. He is here in this room. I want him to break out in a cold sweat and go through all levels of martyrdom. You've interpreted the hint correctly, Marc.«

Ciban stared at him. »So the anonymous hint, sanctioned by Brother Vasiariah, came from you?«

Benelli nodded. »Vasiariah, the helping angel of justice.«

The prefect appeared oddly moved. »You know that your words can lead me to only one conclusion, Eminence. For heaven's sake, tell me the names.«

»You know I cannot. The covenant doesn't work that way.«

Ciban's eyes were suddenly filled with a strange glow. Catherine couldn't tell whether it was displeasure, desperation or some form of realisation. The situation was turning more and more into an impenetrable riddle.

»Forgive me,« she said nearly inaudibly, »But what exactly are you talking about?« Then, she turned to Benelli: »And why exactly are you telling us about it?«

»Because the murderer knows you all are children of Lux. Each of them sympathises with the order one way or another.

Some of them are still members even today.«

»And that's all?« asked Ben.

»Oh no. You also sympathise with the archenemy of the murderer. With His Holiness.«

Ciban and Catherine both stared at Benelli for a few seconds as if they hadn't heard correctly. Catherine doubted that Ciban sympathised with Leo. Cardinals Monti and Gasperetti were more along his lines.

»You said you wouldn't survive the night?« repeated Catherine. »Why do you say that?«

»Because there is only one way to challenge our opponent to make a mistake. I think we will soon give these devils in priests' robes a rather large surprise.«

»By not surviving the night?« said Ben dryly. »By serving us all up on a silver platter?«

Benelli, who suddenly appeared oddly pale, pointed discreetly to the far-flung end of the reception hall to where Cardinal Monti's circle stood. At the moment, it consisted of the Chicago Cardinal Bear, Massini, the Pope's private secretary, Cardinal Orlando and Cardinal Gasperetti. »Take good note of the Christians on the other silver tablet, my friends.«

»Are you feeling ill?« Catherine grabbed Benelli by the arm and took an unexpected look at his aura. For a moment she felt paralysed.

The cardinal grabbed his chest and gasped for air. »The high dosage,« he squawked. »Oh Lord, it is working faster...than I thought. Marc...« Ciban jumped up to support Benelli, but the man fell to his knees. »Marc...look after Catherine...and speak...speak to...«

No more than three seconds later Alberto Cardinal Benelli was dead.

17

Catherine witnessed Benelli's body disappear into the ambulance. She couldn't stop thinking about his final words to Ciban, directing him to take good care of her. And with whom should Ciban speak? With the Pope, perhaps?

The emergency room doctor could only determine the cause of death, most likely heart failure. Catherine learned that Benelli had had a weak cardiovascular system for years and had been forced to go for regular visits to the Gemelli hospital in Rome. To be exact, his death was simply a matter of time because the cardinal refused a transplant. Catherine sighed. She would never know what Benelli had hoped to achieve with his premature death. She also doubted that there would be an official autopsy. Suicide was considered a mortal sin in the Catholic Church. A cardinal who committed suicide for whatever reason was an utter scandal.

The young woman could already read the headlines in tomorrow's paper: »Cardinal suffers cardiac death at reception« or »Did Cardinal Benelli party too much?«

Affected or in shock, most of the guests had already left the villa. Cardinal Monti and Father deRossi were among the last to leave. Perhaps the old cardinal wanted to be assured that Benelli wouldn't rise from the dead. Then again Catherine had seen concern and astonishment on Monti's face. Monti had even tried as best he could to help end the party while Ciban attempted to resuscitate Benelli with Ben's support until the ambulance arrived. Not a single doctor was present at the reception. Benelli had thought of everything.

Gasperetti, the chairman of the College of the Cardinals, hadn't left the party. Neither had Monsignor Massini, the private secretary to His Holiness whose utter horror was written all over his face. Along with Ben, Sister Thea and Cardinal Bear, they too had assisted in quietly ending the festivities. Massini now stood next to Gasperetti like a little boy who had just witnessed a bloody assassination.

As the rear doors of the ambulance fell shut and the vehicle pulled away, followed by Monti's limousine, Ben spoke softly: »Through his death Cardinal Benelli has officially declared war on the dark side. His gesture with the ring was crystal clear.«

The ring! Catherine noticed that the word made Ben flinch too. She was just about to turn around and run up the open staircase of the reception hall to look for the jewellery on the buffet table when Ciban gestured for her to stop. »It's safe.« The cardinal discreetly patted his chest to indicate it was in his cassock's upper interior pocket.

Cardinal Gasperetti along with Father deRossi approached them from the open staircase. »Not a pretty ending. For none of us,« he said as he peered down the villa's driveway as if he could still see the ambulance's tail lights through the thicket of trees. »Monsignor Benelli was the last living member of his family.« The old cardinal bade farewell and walked slowly with deRossi to his car. After a few metres, he turned around again. »Pardon me for my impoliteness. Can I give any of you a lift?«

»Thank you, Eminence,« said Ciban. His gratitude couldn't have sounded more sincere, but Catherine could still sense the discord lying beneath his words. »We all have cars.«

Gasperetti shrugged, smiling. »I should think so. Oh…I almost forgot.« He approached Catherine like an old wolf giving false assurance to his prey that he really means no harm. »You forgot something, Sister. It was lying on the buffet table.«

Before Catherine could respond, she held a small photograph in her hand. Cardinal Gasperetti was already on his way back to his car. She needed only a second to look at the photo to know what it was: the picture of Benelli and Darius standing on St. Peter's Square.

18

»What does all of this mean?« asked Catherine as she showed Ben the photograph.

He had suggested they drive the three cars back to Rome convoy-style. Cardinal Ciban was first, then Ben and Catherine and Cardinal Bear with Sister Thea in the rear. The green Lancia that Sister Thea had identified didn't show up again in the black of night.

Ben leaned forward in order to see the road better. It had started raining shortly after they began driving. Thick, heavy drops splashed weightily against the windscreen like juicy insects, making it hard to see. On top of that, the road was poorly marked. »I think Cardinal Ciban is asking himself the same question more than anyone else right now,« he said, checking the limousine's air conditioner again — a completely unnecessary check in such a modern car as this one.

»I think you know more than you are saying. And I think you owe me an explanation. What is going on?«

»Believe me, Catherine. The less involved you are, the better. For your own sake.«

Catherine pocketed the photo once again. »Listen. From what I could tell from this evening, someone has tried to kill me twice already. I was then graced with Cardinal Benelli's invitation. He spoke in riddles, then casually ended his own life while bringing

me together with the last man I would ever want to meet privately given my current situation. To top it all off, Cardinal Gasperetti handed me this photograph. Whether I like it or not, I'm right
in the middle of it all.«

»Ciban is not your enemy,« said Ben.

Catherine gave him a look as if he were crazy. Of course the
cardinal was one of the main representatives of the Catholic
camp that falsified Jesus' teachings and made certain that only
one single opinion and interpretation existed. He stands for
dogma, the enemy of all freethinking individuals! No matter
where she looked, the Congregation of the Doctrine of Faith had
blocked any and every attempt to modernise the Church. During
the entire interrogation process, Catherine had just waited for
Ciban to pose the question: »Are you even Catholic anymore,
Sister Catherine?« She had seen the question lurking in his eyes.
Of that she was certain. God only knows why the cardinal did
not openly ask her the question.

»You know what happens to the people who seek an open
dialogue in the Church. No authority, not even the Congregation
of the Doctrine of Faith, can make claim on the absolute truth,«
she said to Ben.

»I know,« he said sheepishly. He himself had had to remove
two entire chapters of his dissertation because they had contra-
dicted the Church's teachings. The Church's teachings and
traditions had moved well beyond the New Testament in the
Bible.

»And you are content with that?« asked Catherine.

Ben shrugged his shoulders and sighed. »Not everyone can be
like you and put up a fight against the dogma's superpower.«

»Against Ciban?«

»If you like.«

»So he is my enemy,« she noted.

Her companion shook his head. »Not in this war. Believe me.«

Catherine stared at him as if he had just told her he had turned into a Catholic fundamentalist. »Which war?«

»You heard Cardinal Benelli. The war between good and evil. The eternal war between the powers of light and those of darkness. It's not only being waged in the outside world, but in the Vatican as well.«

»Is that why Benelli…«

»…killed himself?« Ben slowed down. It had started to rain even harder, more aggressively and the wind had picked up. »I'm afraid the answer is 'yes'. Even though I have no idea what he wished to prove. But I know one thing for certain: he was a man of integrity. One of the few genuine souls.«

»I saw his aura, Ben,« said Catherine with a clipped tone.

»When?«

»A minute before his death. I have only ever seen such an aura once before. With Darius.«

Ben dared to quickly look over at her despite his hindered view of the road. »Then it must have been a damn good aura.«

»That too. But there was more to it…the auras were like – twins.«

»Twins?«

»Yes, somehow. It is hard to explain. Of course both Darius and Benelli are two completely different human beings, but still…I have never seen such a match before.« After a brief pause, she added in a puzzled tone: »Do you think Lux has something to do with his suicide?«

»Lux? Probably not. But if that were the case, we would at least know what we're up against.«

»If not Lux, who could it be then?« Catherine stuck to her guns. »Opus?«

»I have no idea.«

She looked at Ben sceptically. »You must have at least the tiniest of suspicions, given how you behaved at the reception.«

»I am an archivist, not a secret service agent, Catherine.«

She pushed herself back in her seat to give her legs more room. »The thing with Cardinal Bear and Sister Thea really affected you. Besides, the job as an archivist is the perfect cover if you work for the Vatican's secret service.«

Ben sighed. »You know as well as I that there is no secret service at the Vatican.«

»Not officially, yes. What case are you currently working on? As it appears, you knew about Darius' death!«

The pelting rain beat against the limousine with such force that the windshield wipers threatened to fly from their sockets. Ben drove even more slowly as he could barely see the road.

»Sorry, Catherine. You're asking the wrong man.«

As if on cue, they rounded the bend to find a hazard sign and seconds later the taillights of Ciban's heavy Mercedes that stood at a strange angle off the road. The headlights of Ben's car were as light as day, illuminating a massive oak that lay across the road and whose branches were like sharpened arrows pointing straight at them. Ciban's Mercedes Benz stood just metres from the tree. It was a miracle that the cardinal hadn't driven right into it given the poor visibility conditions.

Ben brought the car to a halt while Ciban hurried across the headlight's illumination like an eerie shadow coming toward them. As Ben rolled down the window, the rain whipped his face like a torrent. Catherine could feel Ciban looking at her. He turned his gaze away from her and said to Ben: »I need your hazard triangle.« They could barely make out the cardinal's voice. The young cleric made moves to get out of the car. »No. Leave well enough alone. Open the trunk. It's enough if one of us gets wet. You should rather call the fire department and the tow company.«

Ciban disappeared behind the car, came back with the bag in his hand and sunk into the darkness like an apparition to set up the hazard triangle for oncoming traffic. Just as he hurried back, taking a seat in the back of Ben's car, Bear and Thea came up upon them with their vehicle. Ciban must be wet to the bone. Catherine handed him a package of tissues so he could at least dry off his face and hair, which the cardinal gratefully accepted.

Ben's mobile phone rang. »Yes?« It was Bear. »No, no worries. Nothing's happened. The fire department and tow company have been notified. We will take a different route.«

Thea's car turned and both cars bade farewell with a honk before heading back toward Benelli's villa.

Ciban said: »Bring Sister Catherine back home, Ben. I will wait for the tow truck to arrive.«

The man resisted. »With all due respect, Eminence, I won't leave you here all by yourself. Not after what has happened. You bring Sister Catherine back. I'll wait here.«

»That wasn't a request, Ben.«

»Heavens,« said Catherine. »Do you gentlemen wish to argue as to who brings me home?« She took a deep breath. »To be clear. If it weren't for the heavy rainfall, it's the gospel truth that you would have run right into this tree after the bend, Eminence.«

In the rear view mirror, Ben could see Ciban's eyes sparkling. Without flinching the cardinal said: »There isn't a crime lurking behind every fallen tree, Sister.«

»After everything that has happened today, you think it's a coincidence?« Catherine pointed to the oak in the headlights, then turned to Ciban and coolly scrutinised him. »It's no coincidence and you know it!«

»Be that as it may,« replied the cardinal forcefully. »It is not necessary for you and Monsignor Hawlett to wait with me for the tow truck.« He grabbed the door handle with his slender, powerful hand, but before he could get out, Catherine yelled against the wind and rain: »Cardinal Benelli asked for my help!«

»What?« Ben asked.

Ciban fell back into the seat and closed the door so forcefully that one might think he was fending off intrusive demons. But before Catherine could say another word, he said: »Listen closely, Sister, as I will only say this once. Don't get involved in Cardinal Benelli's game-playing. He not only has an endless repertoire of exotic anecdotes from the Vatican, but he was also the master of disguise and confusion.« The cardinal paused for a moment as if what he was about to say took a lot to overcome. Nonetheless, he said it with urgency, sincerity, almost like a prayer. »I know you are a good person, Catherine and you want what is best for the Church, but believe me when I say this game is entirely out of your league.«

Silence filled the air for what felt like an eternity. Even the whipping rain outside that relentlessly drummed against the vehicle seemed to be torn away. Catherine tried to control her consternation. Ben stared into the rear view mirror as if he were hypnotised. In that moment Ciban's mobile phone rang. The sound made Ben flinch.

»Ciban.« The cardinal switched to his left ear before it could slip. In that moment, Catherine noticed he must have hurt his right hand. »No, Rinaldo. Nothing's happened.« A short pause. »Sister Thea called you. Um…no, everyone is alright.« He listened for a long while. Then he put his mobile phone back in his pocket. The cardinal acted as if he could hardly believe his ears as he said: »His Holiness has suffered a collapse. Dr. Lionello is with him now.«

19

It had hit Leo like a ton of bricks. He had been standing at his office window, puzzling over a file from the Cardinal Secretary of State when he suddenly must have fallen unconscious to the floor. Now he was dozing in his bed in the dim light, not really knowing how he had even gotten there. It was a miracle that he hadn't hurt himself during the fall.

There was no doubt that the murderer had struck again. Another member of Leo's congregation was dead. Since only he and the congregation itself knew the identities of its members, the murderer or at least the traitor must be one of them. Leo had no idea who had been murdered this time, but as macabre as it sounded, Isabella, Sylvester and Darius were no longer suspects. As it was with the fourth murdered congregation member now too.

The Pope felt shaken to the core. For the first time since he had learned of the murders, he felt more than fear. He felt panic. But no one, not even Ciban, was allowed to notice.

There was a knock at the door just loud enough that Leo could hear it. He had a feeling he knew who it was.

»Please come in, Corrado.«

His private secretary, Corrado Massini, entered his bedroom chamber along with Ciban. Leo searched the cardinal's face to detect any signs of »I told you so, Holiness,« but he saw nothing of the kind. In fact, the man seemed worried.

»How are you, Holiness?« asked Massini and approached the bed.

»I feel somewhat weak, but other than that, I am fine.«

That was the understatement of the century. In truth, Leo felt as if someone had ripped out his heart alive and it was now beating and thumping outside his body. Just as with his last collapse, Dr. Lionello had examined him head to toe in the tiny clinic in the Apostolic Palace, but he knew all too well that the cause for his collapse was not an organic one. In truth, a part of his soul, yes, a part of his spirit was missing that would allow him to do his job as head of the Catholic Church with no ifs, ands or buts. But he had grown weak. Perhaps too weak.

Massini seemed more worried than Ciban. It was no wonder. The young man could make no rhyme nor reason of Leo's fainting spells nor of the fact that even the most modern medical examination could offer no explanation for them.

»Corrado,« Ciban said softly and turned toward the young Monsignor, »would you please give His Holiness and me a few minutes alone.«

Massini didn't budge, but looked questioningly at Leo instead. Was the Pope imagining it or was his trusted secretary keeping a distance from Ciban like he never had before? Had they suffered an argument? Did the young man hold Ciban accountable for Leo's condition?

»It is alright, Corrado. Should I need anything, I will ring.«

»Alright then. I am just around the corner, Holiness.«

After Massini had left the room, Leo said: »Marc, you most likely know more than I, correct?«

As usual, Ciban got straight to the point. »There was an incident at the reception, Holiness. Cardinal Benelli is dead.«

»Benelli…« said Leo quietly with an inward gaze. The cardinal had actually won the election as Pope in the last conclave after it had appeared to be neck-and-neck between Cardinals Gasperetti and Monti. But when the Cardinal Chamberlain approached Benelli to ask if he accepted the vote as Pope, Benelli rejected the offer and exercised his right to appoint Leo, whose name was then Eugenio Tore. Benelli had certainly made more than just friends with his decision.

»He was my first spiritual counsellor after accepting the vote as Pope,« continued Leo quietly. »He taught me about the different meditative steps toward cleansing: Ablutions, Enlightenment and Unification.« Leo snapped out his daydream.

»Now that you see me just lying around here, I bet you think he was a member of the Congregation?«

Ciban silently took a seat next to the Pope.

»What can I say…you are right,« explained Leo.

»Your honesty venerates you, Holiness.«

»You couldn't help but jab me.«

Ciban shrugged. »To be honest, no. I couldn't.« He gave Leo a worried look. »How many more of these attacks can you handle?«

»Always the frank one.« Leo suppressed a smile. »To be honest, I don't know. Despite his heart disease, Cardinal Benelli was one of the strongest members of the Congregation. His sudden death literally bowled me over.«

»He committed suicide, Holiness.«

»Pardon me?« Leo stared at the elegantly dressed man on the chair next to his bed. According to Catholic doctrine, suicide was a cardinal sin against God. What made Benelli do such a crazy thing?

»He said he wanted to set a signal,« explained Ciban as if he could read Leo's mind. »But I am not certain if I understand which signal he meant. I was hoping you could tell me. What did his suicide prove other than risking your own health?«

Leo listened closely to the inner voice that had served him so well since becoming Pope. But at the moment, it was nothing more than a distant whisper, nothing more than a vague, indeterminable feeling.

»I don't know, Marc,« he said finally and shook his head. »I haven't a clue. But if there is a signal, we will certainly know more soon.«

20

Monsignor Corrado Massini waited in the antechamber for the Pope to finish his conversation with Cardinal Ciban and call him back in. Massini felt horrible, so horrible in fact that what he really wanted to do was make his way down the twisted pathways of the Vatican palace to the interior of St. Peter's Basilica to toss himself over the edge of the gallery at the foot of the dome drum. And he would do it in a heartbeat if he knew it wouldn't wreak such havoc for the Pope. But the Holy Father's current bodily condition wasn't the only reason for his horrible feeling.

The DVD had arrived in a business-sized envelope without a return address through the normal house mail. Massini thought nothing of it at first as he retired to his private chambers after a hard day's work and discovered the package. But then he had read the enclosed computer-written note: »The contents of this DVD will be of most interest to you. Watch it immediately. A well-meaning friend.«

For a moment, Massini had thought the whole thing was just one big joke, but he had a subtle feeling that he should watch the DVD right away anyway. He finally placed the silver disc into the player and turned on both the device and the plasma television set. The disc did not contain a text file, but rather a film as he discovered.

He flinched as he heard his own voice in the film and as he saw himself and Aurelio on the screen. They had just finished making love and Massini was quietly and calmly telling Aurelio about his weakness for…

The Monsignor had immediately turned off the player and stood with his entire body numbly shaking for several minutes as he stared at the plasma screen.

Until the phone rang. No caller ID.

»Yes.«

»I presume you liked our little film. Keeping it a secret comes with a price…« It wasn't Aurelio's voice, but Massini had heard voice-altering software before.

His fear mixed with anger. »Forget it.«

»Oh, I beg of you. I have here a second envelope that is, of course, addressed to His Eminence Cardinal Ciban. But if you're not interested…«

»You filthy pig.«

»You look pale. Well, that is to be expected under the circumstances.«

Massini looked around in shock. Had the blackmailer installed a hidden camera somewhere? Or was he just bluffing?

»So, what do you say,« said the foreign voice, »Are you interested in making a deal or not?«

»What's to guarantee that you won't send the second video after all? That it remains our deal?«

»No one,« said the voice coldly. »But I assure you that should you reject our offer, His Eminence will get to enjoy your little artwork first thing tomorrow morning.«

Massini's fear turned from anger to sheer desperation. »What do you want?«

»No worries. It isn't much. In fact, it should be as easy as pie for you.«

»Out with it.«

»His Holiness' journal.«

»What? Are you crazy? They will immediately suspect me!«

»Easy now. You aren't the only house employee with access to the private chambers of His Holiness. Perhaps it was the chamber servant. Or His Holiness misplaced the book. He has been rather…how should I say…forgetful of late. Be that as it may. You can do it.«

Someone behind him cleared his throat, bringing Massini back to the present. Monsignor Rinaldo suddenly stood before him. He hadn't heard him come in. A few months prior Massini had made friends with the younger Rinaldo. He was a nice guy, but a total archival mouse who didn't at all fit in with the rest of Cardinal Ciban's staff.

»Pardon me for being so direct, but you look as though you could use some bed rest and recovery time as well,« said Rinaldo. Massini knew all too well that he was right.

»I'm alright,« the Monsignor assured him quickly. »It has been an exhausting day. How may I assist you?«

»I have heard that His Eminence is still here. I have an extremely urgent message for him.«

Massini's gaze fell to the business-sized envelope in Rinaldo's hand. It took everything he could muster to not stare at the envelope in horror.

»I'm afraid it will take a while,« he said. »But since I am already here, I would be happy to take it for you.«

Rinaldo shook his head. »Thank you, but I would prefer to personally hand him the envelope.«

»Certainly. No problem.« Massini attempted a smile. Then he carefully asked: »Who is it from?«

»There has been an incident within Lux Domini,« explained Rinaldo hesitantly. »That is all I can say.«

Massini involuntarily gave an audible sigh of relief.

21

Catherine had just arrived at the hotel lobby when the night porter, a dwarf-like rotund man in his 60s, stopped her.

»Sister Catherine!«

She turned left, moved away from the lift and headed for reception. The incidents in Benelli's villa and thereafter were still swirling around in her mind. Ciban must have made it to His Holiness in the Apostolic Palace while Ben was on his way back home after having dropped her off at the hotel.

»This here,« the night porter quickly swung around to the mail slots next to the rows of keys and placed a small package onto the counter with his tiny, stumpy hands. »It was left for you this evening.«

The grey sealed cardboard box had neither a return address nor a recipient's address.

»Are you certain?« asked Catherine.

The little man nodded vigorously. »I had to swear to hand it to you personally.«

»Then you spoke with the sender?«

»With the messenger. I have never seen the young man in all my life. But he insisted that I give it to you personally as soon as you entered the hotel.«

Catherine looked at the package warily.

»Do you think it could contain anything…dangerous?« The

chubby porter took one step back from the reception desk.

»No. Of course not,« she quickly assured him with a smile. »Can you describe the messenger?«

The man didn't move. »Well…if you ask me…mid 20s, medium height, slender, short brown hair, eye colour uncertain…well, dark, I think. Jeans, red t-shirt. I would have to say he wasn't from the official postal agency. Oh yes! I remember now. On the backside, he shoved in a little card.«

Catherine flipped over the box and pulled out the card. In tiny letters she could read: 'If you believe with all your heart, you may. Apostles 8:37. Trust in your gift, Catherine.'

Benelli! This must be from Benelli! Good heavens, couldn't the white-haired cardinal leave her in peace even after his death? Catherine noticed that the night porter looked at both her and the package with even more astonishment than before. She quickly, perhaps too quickly, managed to bring a smile to her lips and kindly thanked him before approaching the lift.

It took all she had not to open the package in the lift. She had barely entered the room when she headed for the recliner and ripped open the paper. She carelessly threw the packing material to the ground, opened the box – and found another box inside. Then another. And another. It appeared that Cardinal Ciban had either forgotten Benelli's bizarre sense of humour or he had never received a package from him before. Catherine finally came to the innermost layer and came upon a sheet of finely folded paper. As she unfolded it, a key fell out. Not just any old key. It looked as though it belonged to a vault. A safe deposit box?

»Keep this in a safe place!« was written on the paper.

Catherine creased her forehead. Keep this in a safe place? Nothing else? She once again searched through all the boxes and bits of paper she could find, expertly kicking each examined piece to the side. When she was a child, she used to love playing football. Unfortunately, she found nothing. What in God's name could she do with a key without a single reference? As she looked around the piles of crumpled paper, she realised she still couldn't believe Benelli had taken his own life before her very eyes. During their conversation in the chapel, he had seemed so quiet, so reasonable, so determined. Not at all the kind of person who was about to stamp out his own existence or that one couldn't trust. Cardinal Ciban, on the other hand, saw it differently, thereby seeming to confirm Benelli's decision.

Catherine sighed. Once again the image of the dying Benelli appeared in her mind's eye. The amazing similarity between Darius' and his aura, not to mention the seconds in which he died.

She took the key and placed it together with the photograph in a small safety compartment in the desk. Then she took a hot shower, slipped into a comfortable nightgown and fell into bed utterly exhausted. By God, how tired she was. The sounds of the city pushed through the open window like the sounds of a distant waterfall. Rome's streets never slept.

She was truly exhausted, but only after she ran the events of the past few hours through her mind could she finally fall asleep.

Catherine slept like a rock. And she dreamed.

22

Ben drove through the nocturnal streets of Rome past arguing couples, groups of young people and adventurous tourists who just had to experience Rome's nightlife. The promising life of clubs, discos, restaurants, bars and plazas full of night revellers. None of it interested him anymore. He just didn't have the desire to go home just yet. Instead, he thought about Darius and Benelli and about how he might circumvent Ciban's stonewalling and continue his investigation. That's when he got an idea.

His gaze swept across a row of old apartment buildings near the Roman Forum. He knew that the buildings' facades were deceptive. Although they looked in disrepair from the outside, their interior was immaculate. His gaze stopped at one of the houses. A light burned in the second floor as he had hoped it would.

The priest he intended to visit had a soft spot for antique Rome, which is why he had chosen to live near the former government and commercial quarter of the city. Once upon a time the Roman Senate had held sessions and court proceedings in the Forum Romanum or had triumphal marches and religious processions starting at the Via Sacra that later moved toward the statehouse. Today the quarter was an archaeological park, a tourist attraction with its ruins from various epochs during the Roman Imperial Era. But for the young man who lived in the old apartment building and who loved to slip into the robes of Old Rome as a re-enacter to simulate life during antiquity, these ruins were the remnants of the Golden Age of world history.

Ben ran to the doorstep and rang the doorbell. No response. He pressed the bell again, this time somewhat longer. After about fifteen seconds, he heard a voice on the intercom. »Yes?«

»It's me. Ben. I need your help, Abel.«

»At this hour?«

He drew closer to the intercom, speaking with quiet urgency: »It's a matter of life and death.«

»Isn't that always the case with you?«

»Darius is dead.«

Seconds passed. »Come up.«

Abel's flat wasn't particularly large. It encompassed about sixty square metres, but it was filled with the craziest collection of high tech gadgets and historic museum relics that Ben had ever seen. Two-thousand-year-old clay fragments from the amphorae lay neatly in a row next to spearheads just as old. At least that's how they looked. A reproduced senator's robe hung over a chair. A gladiator's helmet lay on the desk next to one of the computer screens. Gladiators were professional warriors who fought to the death in public arenas.

Abel was not only a fan of antiquity, he was also a computer freak, which was the reason Ben was there to visit him. The priest was a former hacker. Truth be told, »former« was a loose definition. It wasn't official, but Ben was pretty sure that Abel worked for His Eminence Cardinal Ciban every now and then. And now he had to take the risk.

»Father Darius is dead?« Abel repeated in disbelief.

He had been the last student Darius had taught at the Roman Lux Domini headquarters before he retired. Ben had no idea what Abel's gift was. Lux didn't blare out the individual abilities of its members. Neither Ben nor Catherine knew what Darius' gift was even though he had instructed them over a course of many years. Abel's computer talent was most likely merely a marginal phenomenon of his actual abilities.

Ben nodded. »Yes. But that's just between us. If you say a word about it, I won't be worth a scrap.«

Abel continued as if he hadn't heard what he said: »How did he die?«

»Let's just say it wasn't from natural causes. I need your help.«

»I'd prefer if you took the official channels.«

»I don't have time for that.«

»But without Cardinal Ciban's backing, it won't only be your head on the platter. You know I am dependent on his grace.«

»And he on yours. It's about Darius,« replied Ben.

The priest sighed with resignation. »I sense it's not good. Okay. Tell me.«

»I want you to get your hands on a file for me. One from Darius.«

»I should hack into Lux Domini's computer system?« Abel turned pale. »That's like asking me to break into Cardinal Ciban's office while he's in there. I can't do it. Besides, he threw me out of the CIA thing.«

»Darius was murdered, Abel. I have to know why. I have to find his murderer.«

»I don't understand any of this. You are one of Ciban's agents. You need to ask him. He's the one to give you access to the files.«

»He has stopped the investigation.«

»What?«

»I'm out. He took the case away from me.«

»Then he must have good reason for it.«

»Perhaps. But what exactly?«

»Partiality. You know yourself that Darius was like a father to you. To us all.«

Ben took a deep breath. »He was murdered and that's why I need your help. Now!«

Abel's face revealed his deep sense of discomfort with Ben's request. The conversation made him turn another shade of pale anyway. The young man with the steel-rimmed glasses and closely shorn hair stood there as if Ben had just asked him to take out red hot coals from the oven with his bare hands.

»Please,« said Ben.

The priest sighed. »Alright, alright. But let's take it slowly. We'll need some time.«

Ben took the chair over which the senator's robe lay and sat next to his friend at the computer from which multiple cables hung. Abel's fingers danced on the keyboard as he made his way into the Lux' computer network, creating a chain to conceal his tracks as he went along. He connected his PC with hundreds of others through which he built a thick firewall for his opponent behind which he hid his own computer. He would only access the Lux Domini network through the very last computer with which he was connected.

»They are going to notice that we have crossed their defence line and send the dogs on us. I'll buy us as much time as possible under the current circumstances.«

Ben understood the principles behind it. At least in theory. The higher number of computers that Abel put between the Lux network and his own computer, the more time they had to research. It would also take Lux's defence programmes longer to trace back to Abel. When they were connected, each connected computer could only detect the name of its immediate predecessor. If Abel disrupted the connection before Lux's server could locate him through the chain, they would be out of danger. Should the dogs be faster, he still had the red emergency button that cut not only Abel's computer, but the entire flat from the Internet within milliseconds. Ben thought it was a bit over the top, but knowing that Lux would come out empty-handed if his friend pushed the button even if it was just one computer away from Abel's was somewhat comforting. He did ask himself why a programme couldn't just take over the job of the emergency button and monitor the pursuers. It took him quite some time to learn to accept Abel's slight schizophrenia in this regard.

Ben observed the world map on a neighbouring screen. More and more illuminated points distributed amongst all continents appeared. They represented the computers that Abel had used as springboards and that ran twenty-four hours a day as his connectivity log showed him. The list included both private computers as well as commercial ones from insurance companies, banks and law firms. The young priest worked tirelessly. After an hour of »building his firewall,« he finally said: »Okay. We're ready.«

»How much time do we have?« asked Ben.

»Two minutes before they discover us. Then Lux's security server will be notified and the dogs will be unleashed. We're in.«

A warning pop-up window showed up on the screen and an alarm went off. Abel turned off the acoustic signal. »That was easier than I thought. Let's go.«

The young priest entered the Lux's personal files and a list of names appeared. Thousands of entries. He punched in »Darius«. No dice. He filtered the names according to job title: researcher and lecturers, then priesthood. But Darius didn't show up there either.

»Try his birthdate,« said Ben and gave Abel the information, but once again they found nothing. It was as if Darius had never existed for Lux. A quick glance at the neighbouring screen revealed that the dogs had already raced through half of the chain concealing their tracks already. One spot of light went out after the other on the blue world map.

»I have something,« said Abel suddenly. »But I can't get direct access. At least not in the time we have left.«

»What is it?«

»Some kind of coded file that has to do with Darius. I don't know.«

Ben said spontaneously: »Punch in Benelli.«

»Cardinal Benelli?«

»Do it!«

Abel typed in the cardinal's name and his file magically appeared. But it only contained the typical biographical data: School. Studies. PhD. Further career moves until he was named cardinal. Not a word about what had made Benelli a Lux member.

»Look for a connection between him and Darius,« asked Ben. Perhaps the search would yield something, even though they had yet to find anything on the priest himself.

Abel did as he asked. Ben's adrenaline shot through the roof as he once again looked at the world map. The seconds raced by so quickly, eating away at the lights point by point.

»Darn. If there was indeed a connection between Benelli and Darius, I can't find it…or…wait a minute.«

Both stared at the screen.

LUKE.

LUKE? Who the hell was that?

But before Ben could even begin to think about the name, Abel pressed the panic button. The entire flat fell into darkness. It was pitch black. He could hear his friend's hectic breathing.

»That was close. They almost had us.«

23

DeRossi sat in the car and watched as the light in the second floor of the apartment building that Hawlett had entered suddenly went out in every window. He would have loved to know what the cause of the blackout in the flat was. One thing was for certain: Hawlett was with the little chicken with the glasses who had evoked a pretty heavy confrontation between the Vatican and the CIA with his hacking activities.

DeRossi waited, not letting the apartment building's entrance or the second-floor flat out of the his sight. Fifteen minutes later the lights went back on. His greatest virtue was patience. And he had an unmistakable instinct for when it was appropriate to use it. That Hawlett had spent over an hour with the young cleric meant one thing and one thing only: they were concocting something. The Monsignor was not at all interested in the young pimple-faced man. The secret truth was that Catherine Bell was too close to his heart for that.

Another fifteen minutes passed before Hawlett left Abel's flat. DeRossi carefully followed him with his eye as the young man got into his car and peeled away onto a side street. What interested deRossi most was what Hawlett had wanted from Abel. Did it have to do with illegal computer research? It could certainly explain the blackout in Abel's flat. And if that were so, was Cardinal Ciban behind it?

DeRossi sat motionless in his car for a minute or two and thought about it. It was a chance of a lifetime to find out what Hawlett had learned. He quite possibly could have learned something about Benelli's plan through his research. The only thing was little Abel wouldn't survive the interrogation.

DeRossi started his car and parked it a few streets down. He opened the glove compartment and pulled out a pair of latex gloves. When he returned to the apartment building, the street was dark and empty before him. Not a soul to be seen.

He entered the entranceway and pressed the doorbell. With vigour. It took almost a full minute before the young cleric answered.

»Yes,« deRossi could hear his voice of the intercom. Apparently, Abel had already fallen asleep.

»It's me, Ben,« deRossi imitated Hawlett's voice as best he could. If he wasn't quite on the mark, Abel would hardly notice given he was half-asleep and listening through an intercom. »I forgot my car keys at your place.«

»Great,« the priest yawned with annoyance.

The door buzzed open and deRossi entered the front lobby that led to the lift. He passed it and took the stairs instead. When he got to the top of the stairs, he saw that Abel had left his door open.

»Come in,« he could hear the young man call. »I can't find your bloody car keys anywhere. Help me look for them, for God's sake.«

With pleasure, thought deRossi as he locked the door.

24

Catherine awoke with a panic, gasping for breath like someone drowning. Her mouth was dry, her tongue wooden. Her body was feverish as if she had taken a stroll through Death Valley at midday. It took a while for the panic and paralysis to subside until she finally realised that she wasn't in some desert dying of thirst somewhere but rather on her hotel room bed in Rome.

Catherine's gaze swept across the room. She had no idea what she expected. Order? Chaos? Had she really looked behind the veil of death? She teetered into the bathroom and held her head beneath the shower's cool water stream. She dried her hair and fell back into bed exhausted.

She slowly remembered her dream as she put together the random pieces like those of a crazy puzzle. She had sat outdoors beneath a foreign radiant starlit sky. Dozens of fires were ablaze around her. Hundreds of people came to see and hear him. An old white-haired man sat next to her. He wore a grey cloak and was completely peaceful and concentrated. She thought she might know him, but couldn't remember where.

Then she heard a voice in the distance. His voice. It had the most unbelievably hypnotic power.

»You are the salt of the Earth. If it grows stale, what shall we use to salt it? It is only worth tossing out and being stomped on by people. You are the light of the world. A city that rests on the mountain cannot remain hidden. One does not ignite a lamp and place it under a bushel, but rather atop a lantern so that it can shine for everyone who is in the house...«

She looked carefully about her. More and more people flocked to hear the voice and its words. They listened with such intensity as if they were one knowledge-thirsty people.

»Do not think that I have come to revoke the law or the prophets. I have not come to revoke, but to fulfil. Verily I tell you that not a single iota or line of the law will vanish until heaven and Earth vanish, until everything has come to pass...«

»Are you surprised?« the old man asked Catherine.

She looked at him in bewilderment. Goodness, she did know this man, but she couldn't place him.

»They say he is the anointed,« he continued. »What do you think?«

What did he mean by that? There was no doubt. Not for her. Nor for any of the people there either. Not in this moment. Still she was afraid and she said it.

»Afraid? Of what?« asked the old man. »The cup that he was given will pass you by. You have not yet even been born.«

Catherine stared at the old man with his wide eyes and snow-white hair anew. »I know you. I have seen you somewhere before.«

The old man smiled. »Yes, but that is in the distant future.«

Catherine turned to him with confusion and listened once again to the words coming from the mountain.

»But I tell you, do not resist the one who is evil. But if anyone slaps you on the right cheek, turn to him the other also.«

The old man stated: »The priests call him a liar. But they fear nothing more than that he actually does speak in heaven's name. You know that John baptised him in heaven's name.«

Catherine somehow split her attention between the sermon

and the old man's words. »You speak as if you had already experienced all of it.«

The old man nodded knowingly. »Three crosses stood on Golgotha. One of the crosses held him. As his blood dripped from the cross, the rock shattered. Then came the earthquake.«

Catherine leaned over to the old man in the increasing darkness, but just as she was on the verge of recalling who he was, the scene around her changed.

She was suddenly looking at a church tower clock as she stood on the top step of a three centuries old fountain on the Piazza of the Basilica of Santa Maria in Trastevere, Rome. The heat and humidity were oppressive. Hordes of tourists rushed in and out of the medieval basilica armed with cameras and handy travel guides. The four papal statues that decorated the balustrade over the main entrance seemed to greet the masses of visitors.

Catherine knew that, according to legend, the basilica had been built by Pope Callixtus I. It had been erected over a place of worship where the early Christians persecuted by Emperor Nero had secretly gathered. But at this late afternoon hour she barely even noticed the medieval splendour of the sacred building with its twelfth-century belfry and its elaborate mosaic facades. She took a deep breath and pulled the straw hat she was using as sun protection down over her eyes. And now? What would happen now that the old man had placed her here? She sighed and cast a look at the basilica's clock. It was much too late for her liking.

Something pulled at her jeans. She turned around and asked herself if one of the young guys sitting on the steps of the octagonal pedestal was cheeky enough to try to get into her pants. A little boy about ten years old pressed a note in her hand and disappeared back into the crowd faster than she could realise.

Catherine unfolded the note. A floor plan. No, it was more than a floor plan. It was a detailed multidimensional plan of the

basilica with a single mark. A red cross. Cardinal Pietro Stefaneschi's tomb. The next meeting point?

She folded the plan in half, descended the fountain steps and
moved through the crowd of people from various countries. The
whole time she kept an eye on the entrance to make sure no
pickpockets would come too close. The papal statues seemed to
look down at her as if they knew exactly what was going on.

When Catherine entered the vestibule from outside, she had to
take a moment to adjust her eyes to the new light conditions. The
church's interior was pleasantly cool and the dimmer light felt
good. She made the sign of the cross with holy water, then glanced back at the plan more out of nervousness than out of necessity. Cardinal Stefaneschi's tomb was located at the back of the
church to the left of the semi-circular apse with its twelfth-century mosaic. The Virgin Mary sat there surrounded by saints to the
right of Christ.

Catherine got in line with the murmuring stream of people
that spilled over the magnificent mosaic on the ground, past the
granite columns of the main nave that was constructed from the
ruins of ancient Roman structures. Although she knew that this
place was extremely unusual even by Roman standards and that
its aura spread over other historic buildings and monuments, the
atmosphere left her feeling utterly indifferent at the moment.

The crowd kept moving forward painfully slowly, quietly chatting. Catherine made certain not to leave the flow of people. It
protected her, yet she still felt oddly vulnerable. She looked
upward across the valuable gold-leafed wooden ceiling and
stopped briefly to view one of the cameras that hung on the walls
high above the visitors' heads, keeping a watchful eye on the
basilica's interior.

Was the old man watching her?

Catherine stopped for a moment to the right beneath the semi-circular apse, directly in front of the Cavallini mosaic and took a close look at the details of the scenes from life of the Virgin Mary. Normally she felt how the awe-inspiring aura of the medieval art mysteriously reverberated through every air molecule. But at the moment she could have just as easily been studying circuitry sketches. Was the old man somewhere in the crowd?

She finally found herself standing on the small pedestal in front of the tomb that seemed to be made of crimson and marble and looked at the stony image of the church dignitary. His hands were folded over his chest and the insignias of his clerical standing were etched there: the robe and the cardinal's red hat. Catherine took a quick look at the Latin epigraph. As she once again peered at the cardinal's noble pale face, she suddenly had the feeling that she was no longer alone.

»Isn't this place magnificent?« The voice seemed to be coming from the tomb, just loud enough that the young woman could hear it above the din of the clicking cameras. »I love it. I was baptised here. And I always return to recharge my batteries.«

»Who are you?« Catherine looked around, but she couldn't see the old man anywhere. What was going on? Why was she here?

»We need your gift, Catherine. Your second gift.«

All at once she felt the old man's presence and sensed he had not come alone. There were suddenly other figures close to the tomb, shadows surrounded by a blinding circle of light.

»I don't have a second gift,« she explained.

»Oh yes, you do,« said the man. »You just aren't aware of it because it comes naturally to you. I am talking about your energy, or rather your ability to take on your environment's energy without harming anyone. I want to add mine to it.«

What was the old man talking about? She didn't have superhuman energy. Never did! His response sounded like laughter. She looked at him and suddenly recognised who he was...

Benelli!

»Your mission has begun, Catherine. Now let me tell you what to do next.«

25

LUKE...

Even before Ben had left Abel's flat, he was clear that there was only one direction in which he could investigate further. He had to go back to Benelli's villa. It was the only place in which he could find out what type of connection Darius and the cardinal had and what LUKE stood for.

Abel had searched the Internet for clues about LUKE, but he came up empty-handed, at least in terms of the connection between Darius, Benelli and Lux. Various companies came up during the search under that name including artists' paintings, a young professional football player, a publishing house, a comedy series and much more. They had finally come upon the name's original meaning. It came from the Latin and described a person who comes from Lucania. Ben realised the exact translation was more interesting: »To be born in the light,« stemming from the Latin word lux. Did LUKE have something to do with the CORONA project that Ben recalled from his childhood at Chicago's CIPG?

When he left Rome and cast a look in the rear view mirror, he noticed an unusual glimmer of light on the horizon coming from his direction. The rain had finally stopped and the moon shone through the clouds with a fiery red. Perhaps a bolt of lightning had struck somewhere? He took a detour to Benelli's estate as he doubted the rescue team had already removed the tree that had nearly meant his doom.

He finally reached the villa. It stood there like a fortress, but Ben knew from earlier visits with Cardinal Ciban that this building – at least for him – was hardly invincible. There were no watchdogs or watchmen, just a security system he was quite familiar with and the usual personnel. The villa was completely dark. Nothing pointed to the tragedy that had just transpired only a few hours before.

When Ben neared the house on a side path, he noticed that something was missing in the darkness. The security system's red diode on the aluminium panel next to the main entrance was not on. That meant the alarm had been turned off. Had the house staff forgotten in all its distress to turn it on?

He crept toward the entranceway to make certain the alarm was not activated. He noticed that the diode on one of the side entrances was also not on.

He glanced at his watch. He had an hour at most before the house staff began to stir. He had no time to lose.

Within thirty seconds he broke into the side entrance door and found himself standing in a dark, narrow corridor. The delivery service entrance. Ben needed to get to the other side of the villa where Benelli's library and office were located.

While his eyes adjusted to the dim light, he made a mental run through of all his personal notes surrounding the case. He was a Vatican agent, not a profiler. Nonetheless he had been able to think about the profiles of both perpetrator and victim in the past few days. He knew close to nothing about the perpetrator, but at least he was able to draw a picture of what he looked like thanks to the surveillance cameras. The victim was another story. He had known him personally.

The perpetrator was between thirty-five and forty-five years old, was more than 1.85 metres tall and weighed about ninety kilograms. He had a strong, athletic build with short, brown hair. He was also a cold-blooded liar who was both charming and extremely intelligent. He was no amateur. He had a lot of experience with murder, which led Ben to believe he himself had no personal motive to kill his victims. But did he have an individual advantage if the priest was dead? Did Darius know something that could endanger Lux Domini?

Ben wondered once again if it was possible that a part of the research department for which Darius worked might have been involved in some kind of criminal scheme. Is that why Ciban had blocked any further investigation? He had had no idea what kind of work the priest had done in the past few years. Abel hadn't known either and he had been the priest's last student. Could LUKE be the final research project on which Darius had worked? If yes, what part did His Eminence Cardinal Benelli play in it?

He thought about the victim's profile. Darius had been seventy-four years old, but he had the constitution of a man in his late 50s. Honest. Selfless. Darius loved people. Beyond that he was also a gifted medium even though Ben had never found out which gift his former mentor had possessed. Ben knew just as little about the type of research the priest had done. But LUKE was the only connection between Darius and Benelli, at least when it came to Lux Domini. And now both Darius and Benelli were dead.

As Ben made his way through the villa's silence, the dark corridors and chambers under which an enormous cellar must lie, he mentally put together the first profile regarding the cardinal, even though he was still missing some crucial information.

Benelli had been a small, chubby man, completely out of shape but somehow still very agile and intelligent. Like Darius he was charming and emotionally extremely intelligent. Ben didn't know how long he had been a Lux Domini member. At any rate, Benelli had been a somewhat influential cardinal of the Roman Curia. And as Catherine had said, he had an aura like Darius'!

Ben looked around in the darkness and tried to focus. A narrow elegant marble staircase at the end of the dark corridor led into the somewhat better lit ground floor of the villa. Hidden lamps cast indirect lighting on the room, creating a pleasantly dim atmosphere. He carefully slipped passed one of the Roman statues. He thought he must be walking through the stucco gallery depicting scenes from Ovid's Metamorphoses and select myths from antiquity. The arch showcased several paintings, including a representation of Narcissus as he self-absorbedly peered at his own reflection in the water.

After Ben had crossed the gallery and two more splendid rooms, he found himself very close to the library, which was located far beyond the large reception hall. He once again thought about what Catherine had said during the car ride. Darius' and the cardinal's auras were like twins, something she had never seen before. He then asked himself if Benelli's motive for killing himself had something to do with Darius' murder. Was there a connection?

For a moment, Ben stood there, not knowing what to do. Had he just heard a noise? He peered down the dim corridor. He couldn't see anyone, but that meant nothing given the number of niches, doors and side entrances the villa had. He held his breath for another moment, waited and listened before starting up again with a rising feeling of nausea in his stomach. No, there was no way out now. He had almost reached Benelli's office behind the library.

The door to the room stood open. He looked at the glass-protected shelves that were as high as two floors. For a second he thought he might have seen something out of the corner of his eye. A spark or a reflection. But when he looked directly at it, he realised they were only the gold-laced spines of the thick volumes.

He scurried forward as if on tiptoe and listened at the tilted office door. No light. No sound. Nothing. He then slipped through the small opening into the office without touching the door. The nausea in the pit of his stomach rose a notch further. No matter. He had made it.

Once again he had to wait a moment until his eyes adjusted to the poorer light conditions. He found the dimmer switch on the wall and regulated the light so he could see better. He headed for the desk, searching his jacket pocket for the small LED lamp that he kept in a secret compartment in the trunk of his car. Ten minutes later he had completely searched the desk and had come up with nothing. Oddly not one of the drawers had been locked. From what he could tell Benelli hadn't kept anything suspicious there. On the other hand…something didn't seem right. Something was…missing.

Ben moved his gaze from the desk to the adjacent shelves and filing cabinets. Just as he wanted to go to one of the sideboards, he noticed that the rolling drawer of one of the filing cabinets wasn't quite closed. It stood open about a centimetre. He quietly made his way to the filing cabinet, pulled the drawer open and shone his lamp inside.

Darn!

Someone must have hurriedly searched the drawer and ran out of time before being able to close it correctly. A part of the file was missing. The drawer under »L« was completely empty. »L« could stand for »Lux« and »Luke«.

The nausea in Ben's stomach returned immediately. He might not have imagined that sound in the corridor after all. Perhaps the person who had gone through the drawer was still there with him in this room?

Ben took a deep breath, closed the drawer and decided to act as if he had noticed nothing of the kind. But in that moment he looked at the desk and he suddenly realised what had irritated him in the first place. A cable hung from the side of the desktop, pointing to the heavy rug. But there was no computer to be seen.

In that precise moment as he made this realisation, he caught something in the corner of his eye. Someone was coming at him and hit him on the temple. He fell to the floor.

26

It was pitch black, musty, raw and damp. Ben had a droning sensation in his head as if he had been run over by a herd of buffalo. He tasted dried blood. Just as he wanted to raise his hands to his pounding temples, he realised he couldn't because his arms were tied together in a sling over his head. His feet were tied together as well. But it wasn't just the shackles. He had the dull feeling that maybe he was lying on a torture table.

The nausea in his stomach quickly turned to panic. He had a hard time quelling the sudden desire to vomit. Then he remembered…Benelli, the villa, Benelli's office…

Damn, he must still be in the villa. Most likely in the circuitous labyrinth-like cellar vaults and tunnels deep beneath the living area. The building had been built upon the foundation of a much older estate building. Ben had only searched out this area with Ciban once before during some research. He came upon some human remains as one would in an underground graveyard. By God, down here in many sections there wasn't even electric light, not to mention that even if he could call for help, no one could ever hear him.

At once he realised something else too. Down here in the pitch darkness and cold, he was not alone. He started to yank wildly at his chains.

»Senseless,« said a thin, icy male voice. A slip of light filled the room. »As you most likely know, the word 'torture' comes from the Latin. Originally, it pertained to a medical term, an expression for pain and suffering. The stretching rack is only one of the ways to get at the truth. In Europe, its use spanned from the Middle Ages to the beginning of the nineteenth century. This villa knows a thing or two about it.«

»What do you want from me?« Ben's heart pounded mercilessly, but somehow he managed to keep his voice steady.

The thin, ice-cold voice came closer, but not close enough to reveal the person's face. »What were you looking for in Cardinal Benelli's office, Monsignor?«

»What if I were to say, 'Nothing!'?« asked Ben. He didn't feel as nearly as heroic as he acted.

The stranger walked behind the torture table and slightly tightened the rope with the manual lever. Ben felt the stretch in his entire body immediately, especially in his arms. »I hate to repeat myself: What were you doing in Benelli's office?«

Ben decided to gain some time by countering with a question. »Why did you remove His Eminence's computer and the files?«

The stranger took some time in answering, if he intended on answering at all. But then he finally said: »Can't you answer the question yourself?«

»Either you are looking for something or you want to cover something up. Who are you?«

»Now you see. We have two answers at once. I'm only interested in one thing: What were you looking for in Benelli's office?«

»If I only knew. Perhaps his secret?«

The stranger let out an ominous laugh. »You have a sense of humour. Well, it might help you withstand the torture a bit better.«

He moved the lever once again and Ben's arms were pulled

even more brutally over his head. This time he felt real pain, groaned and suppressed the desire to scream.

»Did your boss never show you this part of the villa?« asked the stranger with avid interest.

Ben cursed silently. »I'm guessing this here is the secret dungeon.«

The stranger took a step forward, just far enough so he could see him like a shadow from his peripheral vision. »Many an unpleasant tale has been passed down about this place, woven with insanity and blood, the cross and the sword. But as the last male offspring in his family, your boss most certainly won't be interested in warming up old tales. The latest drama isn't even that long ago either.«

»Cardinal Ciban's family history doesn't interest me,« Ben coughed. The pain in his arms was becoming unbearable. »It is none of my business.« In reality he knew Ciban's past history quite well, at least the public parts. He didn't like working for people whose background he didn't know. But the stranger was right: where there is much light, there are many shadows too. The cross and the sword that the man mentioned stood for nothing less than the Vatican's secret service. Ben had heard the rumour that the Vatican's secret service had been responsible for the death of Ciban's only sister.

»A little bit,« said the voice calmly. »Don't trust your boss too much. Because trust is something he doesn't deserve. But let's get back to the topic at hand: What were you hoping to find in Cardinal Benelli's office?«

»I don't know,« Ben said, groaning from the pain. »But I bet you will find out when you search the files and the computer?«

The stranger pulled the rope a bit further. Sheer agony racked Ben's body. He felt as if he could hear a deafening cracking in his shoulder sockets.

»At this point you will still fight against the tension,« explained the voice with a coldness that ran shivers down Ben's back, »not only with your arm and leg muscles, but with your stomach muscles too. In the next stage the strength in your limbs will immediately give out. First you will lose strength in your arms, then in your legs. The ligaments will rip first, then your muscle tissue. In the stage thereafter your stomach muscles will burst. And when I happily continue the torture tomorrow morning, your limbs will be completely dislocated. Believe me when I say the pain of this torture will be unimaginable.«

Ben didn't answer. His body was sore and soaked in sweat. Every fibre of his being hurt as if he were on fire. The stranger waited a moment, then approached the torture table. He wore a hooded robe that completely covered him. But he was as tall as Ben.

»How do you feel?«

»Like shit. And you know what: You won't achieve anything by torturing me. Not a thing.«

»I hope you are clear how serious your situation is. This is not a joke.«

Ben looked around the dim room, then looked back at the stranger without saying a word. Damn! What kind of trouble were Darius and Benelli involved in? And what did Ciban know?

»You're tough. Tougher than I thought,« said the stranger quietly. »What can I say – we no longer live in the Middle Ages. And to be honest, I loathe violence.«

With these words he opened a bag standing next to the torture table and took out a syringe and a vile with a fluorescent liquid. He filled the syringe, pressed the plunger and let out some of the air pockets through the needle's tip.

Ben tugged at his chains. »What the devil…«

»The devil has nothing to do with it. But since you aren't

willing to cooperate, I have been forced to rely on a more appropriate instrument to get to the truth. No worries, it isn't sodium amytal. This is much more effective. After it has been administered, you will be most communicative and open with the slightest of inhibitions.«

The hooded figure came at Ben with the filled syringe. He stared at it and felt a cold shiver run down his spine. What kind of fluorescent infernal stuff was this? It looked like liquid fire. He had never seen anything like it before in his life. What he knew about amytal is that it not only made you talkative, but it could also lead to brain haemorrhages. The active ingredient could make you insane or even kill you. And this luminous infernal stuff could do that too.

The stranger administered the syringe. Shortly thereafter, Ben had the feeling he was swimming in fluorescent blood.

27

After taking her shower, Catherine lay completely exhausted across her bed and stared at the white ceiling. It was the middle of the night. Not quite. The morning hour was about to dawn and after her strange dream, she hadn't had a moment of shut-eye. She looked over at the digital clock on the nightstand, registered what time it was, then promptly forgot.

By God, what did her crazy series of dreams mean? Wasn't the whole thing simply ridiculous?

She snapped on the small ceiling light, sat up and leaned herself back in a cross-legged position with her back against the wall of pillows. The encounter with Benelli still felt so real that her actual surroundings in the guesthouse room felt like a dream. At that hour even the exotic two thousand year old starlit sky over Golgotha seemed to have greater substance than the lamp above her head. She closed her eyes tightly for a moment and took a deep breath.

What should she do? To whom could she speak about her dream? Who would even believe her? Even she did not believe her dream, not to mention Benelli's completely crazy plan. She, of all people, should be the one to protect the Pope?! And with nothing more than her spiritual energy?

Did it sound crazy? Somehow it did. But it didn't sound any crazier than all the bizarre things that had transpired in the past twelve hours. Catherine also had the sense that what she had seen was only the tip of the iceberg.

She glanced at the laptop. For a moment she thought she might check her emails to distract herself. Perhaps she should simply surf the Internet for a little while to calm her nerves? A walk would have been better. But a walk alone at night as a woman in Rome? She had better not.

A stroll through St. Peter's Basilica would have been lovely with a quick jaunt to the Sistine Chapel and the Vatican's gardens. That would have refreshed her mind and calmed her nerves in order to think clearly again.

Could she tell Ben about her dream? Hardly. On the other hand, whom else could she confront with it, if not him? Darius was dead. And Ciban? She didn't want to think about him. Ben and she had confided in one another about everything as children at the Institute.

The world outside her hotel room gradually started to fill with the typical early morning sounds. The first people to walk about, the first cars to start, most likely deliverymen slowly and almost thoughtfully drove through the streets.

Catherine decided to find out more about Cardinal Benelli. She sat at her laptop, opened the Internet programme and visited the Holy See website and its alphabetical list of cardinal lecturers.

Benelli's resume didn't reveal anything out of the ordinary. Born in Todi, Umbria, first school, then his priestly ordination, studies, PhD, episcopal consecration and finally his appointment as cardinal...But what else should Catherine have expected? The official short biographies of the living cardinals in the Catholic Church wouldn't contain any inconsistencies.

She decided to take a different approach. This time she tried to find information about Darius', Sylvester's and Isabella's murders. No dice. No accident report. Nothing aside from the obituary from the corresponding orders.

For a moment she entertained the thought of logging into the Lux Domini website, but then she remembered that after her resignation her password was no longer valid and she was certainly not a hacker. She would have to ask Ben. If at all.

She turned off the computer, lied back down in bed and tried to run everything through her mind one more time. Before she knew it, she succumbed to her exhaustion and fell back asleep.

28

Rom, Vatican, Apostolic Palace

Envelope in hand, Monsignor Rinaldo was still waiting with the Pope's private secretary for Cardinal Ciban to end his meeting with His Holiness and leave the private chambers. As he waited, Rinaldo attempted to start a conversation with Massini, but the secretary was rather mum and seemed even a bit glum.

The young priest gave an inward sigh. Perhaps he should have rather waited for the prefect at the Inquisitor's Palace rather than sitting here waiting all dressed up with nowhere to go. On the other hand the envelope's contents were of an extremely explosive nature.

Rinaldo had worked at the Inquisitor's Palace for five years, two for Ciban. Not a day went by without something unpleasant arising. The Palace oversaw not only the Vatican City State, but for the past five centuries the entire Roman Catholic world as well. Up to the 1960s a marble plate with an inscription had hung over the gates, which read:

This house was built to fight against heresy
and to support the Catholic religion.

In the same decade the plate was removed, never to be seen again, in the name of a more popular approach to publicity. It disappeared into one of the countless cellar vaults beneath the

Vatican's surface that served as the City State's junk rooms. The
effect the building had on people remained even in times when
the faith's protection was no longer assured through interrogation
and torture.

Since the twentieth century, the members of the Congregation
of the Doctrine of Faith, the name the Roman Inquisition gave
itself in 1965, has had to deal with a daily onslaught of suspicious reading material. It was mostly those young priests tem-
porarily deputised by the various diocese and religious orders
who sorted the incoming mail according to the gravity of the
accusation, sending it up the chain of command depending on
rank.

Even Rinaldo, who had gotten his PhD in ecclesiastical law,
had started out as a young priest working for the Congregation
of the Doctrine of Faith based on such a job assignment in the
Vatican. He had studied the works of suspicious theologians on
behalf of the Congregation, put together the most important
documents and given his assessment of the works in light of
Catholic doctrine.

In the interim, he had moved up the ranks to become Cardinal
Ciban's undersecretary and had taken over a great deal of the
tasks assigned to the ageing secretary His Excellence Archbishop
Tardini. There was no reason that Rinaldo himself wouldn't have
an impressive career inside the Vatican. There was just one catch:
he wasn't interested in advancing his career, a fact that Ciban,
the exigent Grand Inquisitor commented about once with surprisingly gentle irony: »You know, Rinaldo, this noble characteristic
didn't help priests such as Angelo Roncalli, Albino Luciani or our
acting pontiff. We serve the Church where it needs us and it is
seldom where we wish to be.«

Shortly thereafter, the head of the department for Catholic
doctrine promoted Rinaldo to be the Congregation's underse-

cretary. He could have cursed Ciban with all his might if the time spent repenting wouldn't have been so lengthy. Over time, however, he had grown to appreciate his superior as well as the responsibility of the new position and its accompanying tasks. Even in moments such as these in which he had the feeling he had to wait an eternity for His Eminence, costing him his very last nerve.

Rinaldo was about to give up any hope that his superior would end the meeting with His Holiness tonight and nearly placed the envelope with the Lux incident in his cassock's interior pocket when the door to the papal private chambers literally flew open. Ciban swept out of the room with his mobile phone to his ear as if the devil himself were chasing him.

Without paying any mind at all to Rinaldo – Ciban had nearly run over Massini – the cardinal hastened toward the corridor and the lift and left both baffled Monsignori alone in the antechamber.

Rinaldo was able to just make it to the lift in time before the doors closed. Ciban still had his mobile phone to his ear and seemed to be in the darkest of moods.

»I'm not interested in that. If your club can't keep a handle on its people, then I suggest you shut down shop entirely.«

There was something threatening in his voice and his icy-grey eyes that made Rinaldo retreat to the farthest corner of the lift possible. He realised that the envelope in his cassock's interior pocket played a subordinate role at the moment, even if the incident was questionable.

»Listen up. If he dies, I'll follow you. Have I made myself clear?«

With those words Ciban hung up and switched off the phone. He had glanced briefly at Rinaldo, but he was uncertain as to whether he had even registered his presence. They had barely made it to the ground floor when the doors opened just enough before Ciban shot out into the corridor. Both Swiss guards holding watch looked at him aghast.

When both guards were out of earshot and Rinaldo had nearly caught up to Ciban, the cardinal turned around so abruptly that the young priest nearly ran into him. Rinaldo wanted to apologise, but the prefect raised his hand and the priest fell silent.

»I could use your help, Monsignor. And your silence.«

»What is it about, Eminence?«

»Monsignor Hawlett's investigations have gotten him into a tangle with one of Cardinal Gasperetti's men.«

Gasperetti? It could mean a most dangerous confrontation with Lux Domini and that wasn't exactly the work he felt called to do. But it was just as unacceptable to leave Ciban in a lurch. He took a deep breath and nodded. »What can I do?«

»I'll tell you on the way. We have no time to spare. It's urgent.«

It truly was urgent. They ran onto the Damasus Courtyard where Ciban's car stood. Rinaldo had barely sat down in the passenger seat of the heavy limousine when the prefect stomped on the gas pedal. Every now and again Rinaldo had asked himself why the cardinal, unlike his colleagues, never took advantage of having a chauffeur. Now he knew why. It wasn't only because he had more freedom of movement, but he also seemed to be a passionate and fast driver.

When the car took on its highest speed around the bend, Rinaldo gave the Cardinal a brief side glance. His superior's dark facial expression bode no good. In moments such as these Ciban reminded him more of the prince of darkness than the prince of light.

When they left Rome on the Via Flaminia Nuova due north, the young priest finally realised where they were headed: They were going back to Benelli's villa.

29

When Massini returned to the papal sleeping chambers, Leo looked at him with reddened eyes. He looked both exhausted and astonished. Obviously, Ciban's sudden departure came to him as much of a surprise as it had to him and Rinaldo.

»How are you, Holiness?«

»I am somewhat tired, but other than that I am doing well under the circumstances. Did His Eminence say anything else?«

»No. At least not to me. I have never seen him in such a hurry before. What happened, if you don't mind my asking?«

»An unexpected phone call. I don't know more than that.« Leo leaned back into his pillows.

»Do you need anything else, Holiness?«

»No, thank you, Corrado. You may retire. Try to get some sleep.«

Massini nodded. »Yes, Holiness.«

He looked down at the little nightstand next to the bed. At Leo's journal. So close and yet so far. It lay open, showing a blank page. Even in his weakened condition, the Pope recorded his every thought. Massini asked himself where Leo kept his journal when he wasn't writing in it. Certainly not in the nightstand drawer.

»Shall I put away the book?« he asked completely innocently.

Leo shook his head. »Thanks, but that won't be necessary. I

want to write something in it. Not much. But at least I will have gotten it out of my head and I can sleep better.«

»Well then, good night, Holiness. Sleep well.«

»Good night, Corrado. Thanks again for all your help.«

Massini nodded with a smile. Then he left the room and quietly closed the door behind him.

On the other side of the door, he took a deep breath and leaned against it, trying to quiet his nerves.

He had tried to get in touch with Aurelio to find out who his blackmailer was. But his friend – if he could ever be considered that – had vanished from the face of the Earth. The boy hadn't answered any of his calls and the small flat in Monti, the Roman merchants' quarter, appeared to be vacant. Aurelio hadn't responded to Massini's knocking and banging at the door. The neighbour on the same floor, a massive bleach-blond Roman with a serious up-do had finally just given him a complacent smile and said the guy he was searching for would be gone for a while. Up north. Wherever that was.

Had Aurelio betrayed him?

Massini left the area of the papal private chambers and went to his living quarters in the Apostolic Palace. Fully clothed he plopped down onto his bed and asked himself how much time he had left before the blackmailer would contact him again. Despite the odd inferences from the massive Roman woman, he was worried about Aurelio.

He finally fell into a fitful sleep. A part of him still thought it would be a damn short, damn awful night. Another part of him saw the tiny wooden nightstand with the journal on it. And yet another part of him asked himself what had distraught Cardinal Ciban at this very late hour.

30

»Ben…?«

The young investigator could feel his eyelids being gently opened. He knew the voice. Oh yes, he knew that voice. It wasn't the stranger's. The direct, brightness of the room made his eyes tear up and blinded him. He had lost all sense of time. The darkness, the torture and the drug had swept him away. Then he had lost consciousness. He had tried to stay conscious, but his body shut down.

»Water.« By God, the only thing he could think about was water. He was incredibly thirsty.

As if the familiar person had read his mind, he carefully lifted his head and gave him a sip of water. »Not too fast and not too much,« he heard the voice say. His head was then gently placed back down.

Ben blinked at the ceiling light that continued to blind him and realised that he was no longer shackled, but he was still lying on the hard surface of the torture table. He felt out of it, strangely sleepy, but not as foggy-brained as he had felt after being given the luminous infernal liquid. Nevertheless, everything seemed to be fuzzy and distorted as if he were looking at the lively colour photography made of steel and acrylics by Katharina Sieverding.

At that moment he noticed the syringe in the man's hand; that is he saw the glistening needle. No, not another injection! In an act of desperation, he sat up, but was gently pushed back down. He thought maybe the syringe's plunger was already empty.

»Ben! Can you hear me?«

His muscles burned like fire. He carefully wiped his cheeks. They were wet. He must have cried very recently. »I…yes,« he said with heavy breath.

The hand that had been holding the syringe now felt his forehead. In that moment Ben felt as if a surge of energy flowed through his brain down to his entire body. He began to shake slightly and momentarily had the sense that he was unified with his entire surroundings, including the stony vault, the hard wood of the torture table and the hand on his forehead. The drug still worked. It was immensely powerful.

»Can you see me?« asked the voice calmly.

Ben blinked. He could see the outline of a face, fuzzy, indeterminate. »No…not really.«

»We have to bring him to the hospital, Eminence,« said another, younger voice. Ben knew that one too. But it was hazy.

»That won't be necessary. We made it just in time.«

Ben tried to get up once again, but someone gave him a patience nudge to lie back down. »Easy. Don't move around too much, otherwise it will make you dizzy and you'll have to vomit again.«

Vomit again?

The younger voice said lightly: »You would just spit up bile.«

As if on cue, the feeling overcame him. He couldn't hold back the nausea any longer, vomiting directly in front of the men. He felt a momentary sense of relief.

The man with the lower voice dabbed at his mouth with a fresh tissue. »Feel any better?«

Ben nodded carefully. He didn't want to spit up bile again. Certainly not in front of both of them. He touched his sweltering forehead, leaning himself back down. His eyes and ears weren't functioning properly, at least not the way they should. »Can I have the tissue please?«

»Most certainly.« As he was handed the tissue, he touched the fingertips of the older man. It was like an electric shock.

It took half an hour – or at least the voice claimed half an hour had transpired – for Ben's condition to normalise. First his hearing became less hypersensitive, then his eyes. In that moment, he realised who his rescuers were.

»How – did you find me, Eminence?«

»Later. Let's get you out of here first. Here's a fresh cassock.«

»But it is one of yours.« Ben knew that Ciban always carried a small packaged bag in his car in case of emergency. Sometimes the cardinal would disappear for a few days and no one knew where he went.

»Yes. I expect to get it back by tomorrow at the latest.« Did he detect a tad of humour in the prefect's voice?

Ben took the cassock from the cardinal. And there it was again, an unusual sensation of crackling energy around the fingers of his right hand even though their hands only touched one another through the material. He met Ciban's eyes, but he didn't seem to notice the sensation at all. That damn drug. Ben wondered when the effects of the infernal liquid would finally ease.

With Rinaldo's help he changed clothes and drank a sip of water. Later he barely remembered how he had gotten back to his tiny flat in Trastevere. Most likely, they carried him a great part of the way to the car before driving him back home. At any rate, when he awoke in the late afternoon, Monsignor Rinaldo was sitting on a chair next to his bed, reading one of his books, The Hero with a Thousand Faces by Joseph Campbell.

»I am sorry,« apologised Rinaldo with a crooked smile, »but I had to promise His Eminence not to let you out of my sight until you came to.« He handed Ben a glass of water. »How are you feeling?«

Ben emptied the glass in one draft. »Sh…aky.« His head pounded as if a beating heart lived inside it. »What time is it?«

»It is after five o'clock. You had lively dreams.«

»Oh. Should I be ashamed?«

Rinaldo blushed slightly. It had been a while since Ben had last seen a grown man blush. »No, no,« the young priest was quick to assure him. »A couple of times I had to prevent you from falling out of bed.«

»Oh, thanks. I probably would have broken a few bones. Did His Eminence say anything?«

»Not exactly. But my guess is he will wish to speak to you when you are feeling better.«

I bet, thought Ben. No matter how thoughtful Ciban was to him in the dungeon, he knew the conversation with him would be a hard one. The cardinal had taken him off the case for the time being, but he had continued to investigate. He had directly defied his command. His behaviour had bordered on high treason.

»Are you ready?« Rinaldo asked.

Ben cleared his throat. »To be honest, no. On the other hand, this chalice won't pass me by, right?«

»I'm afraid not, no. What were you doing in Cardinal Benelli's villa anyway?«

Ben sighed. »Further investigations.« The pain from his overstretched muscles and torn ligaments made his entire body throb. He clumsily fought his way out of bed, feeling like an old man with rheumatoid arthritis. »I'm going to take a shower now and put on some clean clothes. Let's see how I feel after that, okay?« For a moment he stood unsteadily on both legs, then fell back onto the bed. »Or maybe not. I'm afraid His Eminence will have to make his way here if he wants to interrogate me.«

»No problem,« said Rinaldo dryly and pulled out his mobile phone. »One call is all it takes.«

»You want to call him. Now?«

»What should stop me?« asked the younger man innocently. »It is just after five o'clock.«

The doorbell rang. Urgently.

Speak of the devil, thought Ben as he sank back into the wall of pillows. The young priest rushed to the door. Ben could hear Rinaldo speaking to someone, but he couldn't understand a word. It appeared he might receive a reprieve.

»You have a visitor,« said his caregiver and returned with a most beautiful woman by his side.

»Ben!«

He sat up with great pain. Catherine left Rinaldo standing there by himself and rushed to him.

»My God, what happened? The Monsignor suggested you had an accident.« She took his hand and held it tightly.

Ben and Rinaldo subtly exchanged glances. Then he said: »That's right. But nothing too serious. I was lucky.« He turned to the younger man. »Rinaldo, would you mind...«

He nodded. He knew that Ben and Catherine had been like brother and sister since they were kids. Nevertheless, he couldn't help but give Ben a warning look toward Catherine to be careful. Don't say too much! »I'll be in the living room watching the telly,« he said.

»Thank you.«

Catherine was still holding Ben's hand. He didn't feel very good about having to lie to her.

THE NEXT STEP

31

Rome, The Vatican, Apostolic Palace

It was after six o'clock when his Eminence Cardinal Gasperetti caught up with the prefect of the Congregation of the Doctrine of Faith in one of the less crowded corridors of the Apostolic Palace. Gasperetti knew that Ciban was on his way back to his office in the Palace of the Inquisition from the papal chambers where he had met with the Pope. The time for a chat couldn't have been more favourable for Gasperetti and the group of high-ranking cardinals whom he represented.

»We need to talk, Marc,« he said straightforwardly, looking up at the much taller prefect with his weasel eyes. »At the moment there are quite a few open questions for which we need answers.«

»We? Who is we, Eminence?« asked Ciban with great interest.

Of course, thought Gasperetti, his counterpart would very quickly deduce the 'why' from the 'we'. The younger man had amazed him more than once during various cardinal meetings. During the last conclave, for instance. By a certain measure the chairman of the Congregation for Bishops oscillated between sympathy and antipathy regarding Ciban. But at the moment – given the delicate goal Gasperetti was pursuing – aversion clearly took the upper hand. Moreover, after the incident with Ben Hawlett, Ciban didn't exactly hold him in high regard.

»Monti, Bear, Scipio, Delay and myself. Apologies that I have to confront you with this, but the matter is of too much importance to push it off any longer. I hope that you will be able to shed some light on the subject. His Eminence, Cardinal Monti has offered us his private office.« Ciban scrutinised him for a moment. Gasperetti thought he might just meet him with a rebuff, but the prefect agreed to the meeting.

When they entered Sergio Cardinal Monti's private office, the cardinals already present stood up to politely greet them before sitting back down onto their comfortable Renaissance chairs placed around the large rectangular table. Monti sat at the head. Gasperetti had an unpleasant feeling that the room's temperature dropped the moment he entered its space.

»Come, please sit down, Marc,« said Cardinal Secretary of State Monti who was Ciban's predecessor as the prefect of the Congregation of the Doctrine of Faith.

»Would you care for some coffee, tea…or something stronger? I could also offer you a scotch.«

»Thank you. A coffee, please.«

Cardinal Bear, who sat closest to the coffee machine, stood and poured Ciban a cup. Bear ran one of the wealthiest dioceses in the Catholic Church in Chicago. He was deemed the most influential cardinal in the US. Together with Benelli, he had cleaned up the Vatican bank in the 90s, which had been haunted with scandal since the 70s. »Milk? Sugar?«

»Just milk. Thank you.«

Ciban accepted the cup and placed it before him on the table. Every pair of eyes rested upon him. He got straight to the point. »What's on your mind, Your Eminences? What's this about?«

Gasperetti, who had taken a seat next to Monti and across from Ciban and had also take a cup of coffee, explained calmly: »It's about His Holiness' health. We need a statement. How is

His Holiness' physical and mental health? As your predecessor in the Grand Inquisitor's office, Sergio...« He pointed respectfully to Monti, the eldest cardinal in the group, »couldn't tell us much. But since we know that you have enjoyed the confidence of His Holiness for some time now and speak with him often, we thought you might be able to assist us further.«

»His Holiness is doing well. He is recovering nicely,« Ciban said with poise. »Dr. Lionello is hopeful that he will be able to resume his work day after tomorrow.«

Bear cleared his throat. »As far as I know, Dr. Lionello was called twice in the past few days to assist His Holiness due to a dizzy spell. Has he found out the cause of his collapse yet?«

Ciban took a sip of coffee, then said: »Let's grant His Holiness a little unofficial break, shall we? As you all well know, he has worked eighteen-hour days seven days a week since he entered office. It is a miracle that he has lasted this long. It would be premature to ask him to already draw up his resignation.«

Cardinal Monti laughed the croaking laugh of an old man. For a brief moment, the tension in the room eased somewhat. He then asked: »What happened last night?« The question sounded more like: What really happened last night?

Ciban returned Monti's gaze. For a second Gasperetti thought he might have seen sparks fly between both men.

»I don't quite understand the question, Eminence,« explained the younger cardinal politely.

Monti didn't avoid Ciban's gaze. »Might there be a connection between His Holiness' collapse and the incident in Benelli's villa?«

For a moment, the room went completely silent, then Ciban responded: »If a hammer falls to the floor here and five thousand kilometres away a cyclone hits, it doesn't mean that there is a... connection.«

»But perhaps the hammer is responsible for the cyclone,« retorted the old man.

»What do you want from me?« Ciban looked at the group with glowering deliberation, sweeping his gaze over Gasperetti and landing on Monti. »That I open your consciousness for the Holy Ghost's inspiration?« He kept staring at Monti. The old cardinal knew exactly what his successor was inferring.

»Calm down, Marc,« Gasperetti took on a placating tone. The old cardinal couldn't remember a single instance in which he had experienced such a moment while serving under Pope Innocence with whom he was close friends until the Pope's passing. But Innocence had also never had inexplicable dizzy spells.

»We have another problem altogether,« explained Bear, steering the group back on track. »The media haven't gotten their hands on the news about His Holiness' condition yet, but we all know it's just a matter of time before they do.«

Monti nodded, straightening his elderly frame in the chair. »Thank you, James. As we all know, according to the Apostolic constitution, the press office is subordinate to the Secretariat of State's office. Ultimately, it is I who carries the burden of deciding what we tell the world should it no longer be possible to keep His Holiness' health a secret – or should it worsen.«

When Ciban said nothing, Gasperetti carefully added: »We have to know what impact His Holiness' health condition will have on the Church. Will Pope Leo recover? Will he remain ill for some time? What should we tell the media should the worst case scenario come to fruition?«

After briefly exchanging glances with Gasperetti, Ciban turned his gaze back to Monti who, as Cardinal Secretary of State, controlled the press office. »His Holiness is most certainly able to both physically and mentally perform his papal duties. I also assume that you have enough influence to prevent any false reports from leaking out through the Vatican's press office.«

With that he stood up, took one last swig of his coffee, excused himself and left the room.

Gasperetti watched the tall, slender cardinal leave. As the heavy door slid shut, he gave an inward sigh. The incident caused by one of his agents in the Benelli villa hadn't improved his relationship with Ciban. Innocence had warned Marc about Ciban's stubbornness and tendency to be a lone wolf. But as far as Gasperetti knew, Leo and the prefect weren't exactly friends either. Not to mention Ciban's relationship to Monti. In any case, it wouldn't be smart to make enemies with this man.

32

After everything that Catherine told Ben, he thought he might still be under the drug's influence and was actually asleep. In a wakeful state her words sounded completely ludicrous, but under the influence of the numbing substance they would have made sense.

»How do you know that His Holiness is seriously ill?« he asked, trying not to sound sceptical. In any case he had heard the rumour that the Pope had suffered a collapse a few days ago.

»Not ill, just weakened,« corrected Catherine. »Benelli told me in the dream.«

»Have you had dreams like that before?«

She shook her head vigorously. »Of course not. Not that I know of anyway.«

Ben looked at her but said nothing. Catherine finally said: »Don't look at me like that, as if I were crazy or something.«

»You must forgive me, but your story sounds rather... confusing.«

Catherine let out a big sigh. »Benelli told me I have nearly three times the psychic power of the most gifted medium that Lux has ever had in the Institute's entire student body.«

»Who is the other most gifted medium next to you then?«

»He didn't say, but that doesn't mean anything. The cardinal also said that through his death he was able to unify his psychic energy with mine. Through his additional energy I would be strong enough to prevent His Holiness from a complete breakdown.«

»How does it work?«

»It's simple: I transfer Benelli's and my surplus energy onto His Holiness.«

Ben sat in bed, pale as a ghost, and remained silent. For the life of him he didn't know what else to say other than: Catherine, you're crazy!

»Please listen to me. You are the only person I can talk to about this without being sent immediately to the insane asylum. You have known me long enough. You know I'm not crazy and that I would never just think up something like this. I can barely believe it myself and I don't understand it either. But I swear to you if we don't set out to His Holiness soon so that I can do what Benelli has asked me to do, it might be too late.«

It was Ben's turn to sigh. »We can't just waltz into the Apostolic Palace and swing by to see the Pope, Catherine. They wouldn't even let us near the lift to the papal private chambers, much less offer us a private audience with him.«

»There has to be a way. Someone who can clear the way for us. What about Monsignor Massini?«

»Massini? Forget about it. He might allow the Cardinal Secretary of State a free pass without an appointment. But certainly not us. And certainly not with a story like ours!«

»The house is in flames, Ben. Ablaze. Think about the two murders that preceded Darius'. There will be more murders. Benelli is certain of that.«

»Which other murders are you referring to?« Ben stared at her from his wall of pillows as if in a trance.

»Sister Isabella and Father Sylvester. Both of the religious members that were killed in Switzerland and France. Did you not know about them?«

So as not to reveal that Ciban had hidden the information from him, he explained quickly: »I'm more interested in knowing how you learned of it?«

»Even if I have to repeat myself and feel idiotic doing so: from His Eminence Cardinal Benelli!«

Benelli, Benelli, Benelli raced through Ben's head. Time and again it was always Benelli! No matter which way he looked at it, all threads seemed to come from Benelli and lead back to him again. For a brief moment he toyed with the idea of asking Catherine whether Benelli had said anything to her about a project named »LUKE«, but he thought better of it.

»I know someone who might be able to help us.«

»You mean so we can be allowed to see the Pope tonight?«

Ben nodded. »Yes. But you have to explain the complete story again and you won't like it. I won't either, by the way.« He gave her a crooked smile. »Perhaps it is best if you left out the part about Golgotha.«

»Who are you talking about?«

»Cardinal Ciban.«

»Oh good heavens, no!« The words shot out of her like a cannonball. She let go of his hand and sat back down on her chair. »There must be another way.«

Ben leaned forward slightly. »If it is as urgent as you say it is, this is our only chance.«

»What makes you think he of all people would be willing to help us?«

Ben cleared his throat. »A rumour.«

»A rumour?« Catherine couldn't believe her ears. Since when did her friend trust in such things? »What kind of gossip is it that would make you trust it with our lives?«

»Benelli and Ciban are said to have worked together during

the last conclave.«

Catherine stared at her friend. »You're joking, right?«

»Not at all. I know you must be thinking that whoever started this rumour is either out of his mind or wishes to create confusion.«

»You are trying to tell me that this certain someone was a witness during the papal election.«

»It makes sense to me.«

She gave a deep sigh.

Ben could relate to her sighing. Catherine had access to neither the appropriate information from the Congregation nor from the archives. But if Pope Leo's life depended on Ciban learning of her mission as soon as possible, they might as well get it over with right away.

»And now?« he asked. »What shall we do?«

It seemed to take an eternity for Catherine to answer. But she finally did: »Alright then.«

He sat up halfway and turned his body to stand up, pushing his legs off the bed and groaning all the while. Catherine had already jumped to the ready to help him, but he waved her off.

»Heavens. No. That's all we need is for you to hurt yourself. Ask Monsignor Rinaldo to come in. He is more muscular than you are. He can help me get dressed and drive the car.«

Fifteen minutes later and after Rinaldo had phoned Ciban's secretary, they were on their way to the Palace of the Inquisition.

Catherine had never felt so relieved and wretched at the same time.

33

Cardinal Monti sat at his ornamental desk in the Secretariat of State's office with its view over the Damasus Courtyard, preparing various documents for His Holiness. He could no longer see the architectonic beauty that surrounded him. It had long become customary to him. His desk could just as easily be located in a gymnasium. Monti displayed the characteristics of a man who was accustomed to moving up the ranks, tossing around commands as if they were well-meaning requests. As he clawed his way to the very top of the ladder, his talents proved to be most useful. Most of them had nothing to do with humility and Christian brotherly love, both virtues that were entirely out of place in the Vatican, should you wish to achieve anything at all there.

Most of the men in the Curia thought of the new Cardinal Secretary of State as a driving force behind the Holy See just like during Pope Innocence's reign when Monti was prefect of the Congregation of the Doctrine of Faith. But to his dismay, it was far from the truth.

The cardinal let a file folder fall onto the large table. Of course, the new Pope once again had objections toward many of his suggestions. It was like that every time. By God, Leo was wreaking havoc in the Church with his immature, unrealistic ideas. One couldn't just turn a complex system such as the Catholic Church inside out overnight. It was best to leave well enough alone. The system should stay as it is. A collegial Church would mean its downfall. An imperial Church, on the other hand, like the one under Innocence, had a fighting chance in the future. People needed leadership much more than brotherhood.

»My dear Sergio, you still claim to be the keeper of fire,« Leo had said to him during their morning meeting. »You are still trying, like many of your colleagues, to maintain control. It is not my intention to destroy Innocence's life's work, or our Holy Mother Church. But I am going to listen to my inner voice. The words are clear! And you know full well that my predecessor's advisors are mine as well. What is making you so nervous?«

Since Leo had spoken so openly, Monti decided not to mince matters either. »Forgive me, Holiness, but it is the political undertone of your interpretation that give me cause for concern. You are the captain of a ship with nearly one billion passengers. There is no democracy on board for good reason.«

Leo responded with a tired, yet warm laugh as he gave Monti a friendly pat on the shoulder. Leo had no idea how repugnant his gesture was to Monti. »No worries. Whenever I catch too much wind, you will know when to pull the sails.«

Monti clenched his teeth and said: »I will do what I can, Holiness.«

The cardinal walked over to one of the large windows and looked down at the Damasus Courtyard. How he yearned for the times under Innocence. How claustrophobic he felt his new position as Cardinal Secretary of State under Leo was. As Grand Inquisitor under Innocence, he had enjoyed much more political influence in the Church than he did now. Even though Innocence and he looked very different on the outside, in the spirit of the imperial Popes they were very close in their strivings to ignore the ambitious goals of the second Vatican Council to deregulate the Church. But those times had changed with Leo's papacy.

Monti took a deep breath. Another church dignitary had long since taken over his old function. Naturally, his promotion to Secretary of State was an enormous leap in his career, but he was dissatisfied overall because he was now completely cut off from some of his important sources. At first Monti had felt honoured to have been named Cardinal Secretary of State, but he slowly started to realise that the prefect's office of the Congregation of the Doctrine of Faith had provided much more freedom and access to information he needed to pursue his goals and plans.

Of all people it was Marc Abott Ciban who now held the position, who had once been his most promising protégé. In the end he had disappointed Monti, even going behind his back politically. And what was worse was the fact that Ciban now knew about the secret.

Monti cleared his throat. He himself should have been the one to induct his much younger successor into the secret.

The prefect remembered the exact day of his consecration. He had met Ciban in the Sistine Chapel. After his humiliating defeat in the conclave, the chapel was his most favourite place in the Vatican. Monti had always considered the chapel with Michelangelo's breath-taking fresco of The Last Judgement to be a place for solitude and strength, a place for deeper inspiration.

Ciban and he had then silently left the Sistine Chapel north to the grottos through the long corridors of the Vatican's library. Monti wanted to show the younger man how fit he was for his age. The lights in the library automatically went on as the lights behind them automatically shut off. Two guards opened the massive bronze set of doors to the secret archives. They both stood there in the Vatican's secret archives, the world's largest library enshrouded with countless myths.

When they entered Bramante's corridor, passing some of the high, hand-carved wooden shelves with the countless documents and writings, Monti started to feel nauseous. He quickly reached for his pillbox and asthma spray. Ciban remained calm and collected, observing him occasionally as if the old cardinal hims-elf was a part of the archives' dark secrets from bygone-times. Monti was glad he didn't have to sound out whether the new Grand Inquisitor would even lift a finger, should he perish amidst the four-metre high wooden shelves.

After the wonders of modern medicine had taken effect, they continued to find their way through the maze of stack corridors, connecting hallways and lifts until they finally landed in a large cellar vault in the archives. It was divided into several rooms full of large, locked steel cabinets. Even down here in its remote sterility, the air somehow still smelled musty and dusty.

Monti approached one of the cabinets and broke the papal seal. Then he opened the steel door with a special key that he had pulled out of his frock. Several old, prepared documents along with a black leather-bound book lay in the cabinet. The counterpart to these scrolls and book was a red leather-bound copy that an archaeologist had discovered in the grottos beneath the Vatican. The copy had once belonged to Pius XII and now lay hidden in an armoured steel cabinet in the Tower of Winds.

»What do you know about Jesus and his twelve apostles?« Monti had asked his younger colleague.

Ciban gave him an irritated look. The new Grand Inquisitor began to outline the apostles' biographies. He started with John, Jesus' favourite follower, the only one who held out beneath the cross and ended with Judas Iscariot, the treasurer of the apostles that had betrayed Jesus and committed suicide. Ciban had to admit one didn't know anything about the lives of these twelve men.

Monti nodded, carefully taking the scrolls from the cabinet and spreading them out on the nearest table. He snapped on the reading lamp. The fact that the artefacts had remained in such good shape even before their restoration bordered on a miracle, just as many of the things that had to do with the apostles' stories and Jesus bordered on a miracle.

Ciban drew closer, taking in the scrolls that Monti presented. The prefect discovered in the younger man's eyes something he had never seen in them before: veneration.

»How old do you think these scrolls are?« asked Monti with pride as if he had been the one to have single-handedly unearthed and transported them under the greatest of sacrifice to Rome.

Ciban looked at the findings. He certainly couldn't understand the ancient language. »I have no idea, Eminence. But when I think about the Qumran scrolls, I would estimate anywhere between the first and third centuries after Christ.«

»Not bad, Marc,« said Monti in a conversational tone. »A C-fourteen analysis revealed that these scrolls come from the first century after Christ. A Bedouin shepherd discovered them in one of the Dead Sea's caves in the eighth century. But these scrolls have absolutely nothing to do with those found in Qumran.« Monti grabbed the black leather bound volume from the cabinet and placed it next to the vacant space next to the scrolls. »These texts actually belong in the New Testament.« He stepped aside so Ciban could take a better look at the book and open it. The leather-bound volume contained a Latin translation.

The old cardinal watched his colleague raise an eyebrow at the sight of the title. The Book of Acts? Of course Ciban knew the Gospel of Luke. Did these scrolls perhaps contain the original? He opened to the first page, then the second, flipping further while Monti silently took a seat on a nearby chair. Time lost all meaning. Ciban read and read, not looking up from the pages even once. When he finished studying the book for the time being, he kept his gaze lowered as if he were concentrating on something between the lines. When he finally looked over to Monti, his face was expressionless.

The old prefect arose from his chair, slowly returning to the reading table. He remembered exactly how he felt during his consecration. From one hour to the next a great part of his Christian worldview had toppled.

Ciban shook his head. »I beg your pardon, Eminence, but I don't believe it. This is nothing more than a bad joke.«

Before Monti could say a word, a quiet, relaxed voice coming from the entrance said: »It is no joke, Marc. And it is certainly not a bad one either.«

Both cardinals turned their heads. His Holiness Pope Leo had entered the dim room and walked slowly toward them.

»But I understand your momentary doubts,« Leo said further. »I didn't want to believe it myself.«

The Pope took off the papal signet ring, placing it next to the scrolls and the book on the table. Apostle Peter, the first Pope, was illustrated next to the current Pope and the fish.

The words »You are Peter and I want my church built on this rock,« were inscribed in Latin around the dome of St. Peter's Basilica.

The fisherman's ring had been used until the middle of the nineteenth century to seal papal letters. Leo's predecessor Innocence had reintroduced its traditional use during his papacy. The ring was then given to the new Pope after the conclave. Upon his death, the Cardinal Chamberlain would destroy it with a silver hammer before the eyes of all cardinals present. Before doing so, the Cardinal Chamberlain had searched out the papal chambers to seal the cabinet with the secret documents that no one but the new head of the Church was allowed to read. Each Pope received his own ring, his own seal to prevent anyone else during the sede vacante from reading the documents and resealing the cabinet or even circulating publications in the name of the dead Pope.

Ever since his consecration by Pope Innocence, Monti knew that this ring stood for something even much greater than that.

»How can I ease your doubts?« asked Leo.

Ciban got straight to the point. »By giving me the names of all the consecrated, Holiness.«

Monti had suppressed a hysterical laugh. Ciban could take them all at once to trial – Leo, himself, Leo's congregation. Monti's reaction after his consecration had been a similar one.

Leo shook his head and said: »You are standing before the original texts of the real Acts of the Apostles. You have read these lines and now know that I cannot tell you the names.«

Ciban stood stone still, saying nothing. Monti said instead: »What do you think would happen if the Curia learned of this? Not to mention all of Christianity when it is hard enough for even us to comprehend and accept it? We are literally damned to keep the secret.«

»We too are bound to a two thousand year old contract,« sighed Leo.

Monti could only image what Leo was thinking. The moment of truth was a tricky situation. Several of the Grand Inquisitors had left office afterward. And nothing would be more unpleasant for Leo than to lose Ciban.

The younger cardinal had then looked from one man to the other, cast another look at the scrolls and said tersely: »Pardon me, but I have to take a seat first…«

An audible cough pulled Cardinal Monti out of the dusty archives and back into the presence of his room in the Secretariat of State's office.

»Eminence,« he heard his assistant's voice say. »The car is

ready. You had wanted to swing by your house before meeting with His Eminence Cardinal Gasperetti.«

Gasperetti...

Monti could make as little sense of the old man as of Ciban and Benelli. All three of them were descendants of Lux Domini, an order that he completely distrusted as an old member of Opus Dei. If he weren't mistaken, it was Benelli who had prevented him from becoming Pope.

He took a deep breath. Some defeats could follow one like a curse to one's grave. But that belonged to the past now. If he kept his eyes and ears open and believed in his goal, he would always find a way to reach it.

34

Catherine, Ben and Rinaldo passed inspection through the Swiss guards and Vigilanza. The Monsignor parked the car in the parking lot near the Palace of the Inquisition right next to two limousines. He helped Ben out of the car.

»Here we are then,« he said. »I have no idea what could be so urgent, but I hope you have a good reason for your evening visit. It must not have to do with the accident.« Rinaldo gave Ben a compassionate look, supporting him as he walked. »Come with me. We'll take the lift.«

A few minutes later Ben and Catherine stood in Ciban's antechamber, taking a seat on two beautiful chairs at the wall. They had to wait because the cardinal, according to the secretary, was still in a meeting. Rinaldo sat across from them and read his Breviary. He had offered to wait until their conversation was over so he could accompany them safely home. Ben suspected that he perhaps wished to stay so as to partake in the aftermath of their heads being shorn by the cardinal.

Nearly half an hour went by before the door to Ciban's office opened. Out came the commander of the Swiss guard along with the Vigilanza commander. Both seemed quite focused and determined, as if they had just set up a plan that had to be fulfilled without delay. They wordlessly passed through the antechamber, disappearing into the hallway.

The secretary turned to Ben and Catherine. »You may go in now.«

Ben, who had momentarily forgotten the effect that Ciban's office could have on visitors, realised that Catherine was rather intimidated by the antique, mediaeval and modern splendour. How could he forget? She had never seen his office before.

Ciban switched off the flat screen, got up from his chair and signalled to them to take a seat across from his desk where both Vatican commanders had just sat.

»Apologies for making you wait. It was rather unavoidable. We had to eliminate certain ambiguities.«

Catherine nodded politely to show she accepted the apology and understood the reason quite well.

»I can imagine that your workload is huge at the moment.«

»It's alright. Would you both like some coffee or tea?«

Ciban's facial expressions didn't reveal what he was really thinking. But Catherine immediately noticed that he hadn't offered his hand to either Ben or herself. His opponent sat just one step away from his desk and Ben had brought her into his space.

»Water is good for me,« said Ben. Catherine asked for the same.

Ciban got three glasses and poured them some fresh water. Catherine noticed that the label said holy water from Monterotondo, a town with the population of a few thousand that lay between Rome and Benelli's villa.

The prefect turned first to Ben: »After phoning with Monsignor Rinaldo, I thought you'd be the last person I'd see. How do you feel?«

»Somewhat out of it, but I'm okay. I am certain Monsignor Rinaldo told you of the urgency of our...matter.«

Ciban placed the water bottle onto the table and passed

around the glasses. »I don't know the details, but it appears to have something to do with…« He turned to look at Catherine with his light, impenetrable eyes. »…your companion here. How may I be of assistance, Sister?«

Catherine hesitated. She suddenly had the feeling that what she had to say was completely absurd. Especially in the presence of this man. On top of it, she would offer even more ammunition to the prefect of the Congregation of the Doctrine of Faith by revealing what she knew. She could feel Ben getting nervous next to her. Ciban took a sip of water and waited. He was the epitome of patience. He finally handed them their water glasses. »Have a sip. If it can help me, perhaps it can help you too. Besides I would like to assure you that that which you are about to tell me will be handled in the strictest confidence.«

Catherine brought the glass to her lips and immediately felt a bit better. She took a deep breath. Then she let the cat out of the bag. »It has to do with a dream, Eminence.«

Ciban remained expressionless, but rather sat motionless and stared at her instead. »And?« he finally asked when Catherine remained silent.

»It was about His Eminence Cardinal Benelli,« she said slowly. She felt like a complete idiot. How could she explain to an outsider that she was practically an intermediary between this world and the after world? At the very latest when she started to speak of the »mission« that Benelli had given her, the prefect would strap her to a catapult and thrust her out of the Palace of the Inquisition.

Ciban remained motionless.

Catherine took a deep breath and took another sip of spring water. »Cardinal Benelli came to me last night in a very real dream. He told me how we could protect His Holiness from further attacks.«

For a while it remained very quiet in the room. Ben had appeared to stop breathing altogether and Ciban sat there like a Roman statue.

»Tell me about your dream,« the prefect encouraged her softly when she continued to say nothing. »Every detail. What exactly did Cardinal Benelli say to you in the dream?«

»You don't think I'm…crazy?« asked Catherine with surprise and a measure of caution.

»I have to admit I am a bit unsettled, but I also know that Father Darius trusted you wholeheartedly. So please. Tell me more.«

Again the room remained silent for a while.

»Take courage,« said Ben.

Catherine prodded herself along and started to explain. She felt a slight easing of the burden she had been carrying because she could finally share it with someone else.

Ciban leaned back in his chair, closed his eyes and seemed to absorb every single syllable she spoke. He never once interrupted her. It was only now that she noticed that during the trial against her the prefect had been harsh with her, but at the same time he had never cut her off. In essence he had sat there mostly, listening and allowing the arguments and Catherine's and the jury members' rebuttals to sink in. Even when he did speak, he had never once spoken out for or against her. Nevertheless, he was known for his dogmatism.

It was only after Catherine had finished – she had left out the part about Golgotha – that he opened his eyes again, sat in silence, started at the water bottle and gave it some thought.

A brief thought crossed Catherine's mind that she had never noticed up to this point how attractive the prefect actually was. Was that the reason the media took pictures of him so often? Before now she had always thought it was because of Ciban's cold-blooded mediaeval-like policies that had caused so much controversy in the Catholic world. Particularly because of her books.

She regretted having not learned more about the cardinal's biography like Ben had. Up to this moment Ciban had seemed to her to be a soulless guardian of the faith. But before her sat a man made of flesh and bones, even if he was primarily rather formal in his manner.

Had he ever been in love before?

She noticed just in time that she had begun to stare at him. She took a quick sip of water to avoid blushing. The fact that Ben gave her a questioning side glance didn't help matters.

Luckily, Ciban seemed to have come to a conclusion. He reached for the phone and dialled an internal Vatican number. Seconds later he had the Pope's private secretary, Monsignor Massini, on the line and asked for an immediate appointment with His Holiness. The secretary didn't think to even question the request. It appeared he had merely asked the prefect for a moment of patience. A moment that felt to Catherine like an eternity.

When Ciban put down the phone, she had the feeling she was witness to a historic moment. And not only that!

»In twenty minutes you have a private audience with His Holiness, Sister.« The prefect pointed to the glass that she was still holding in her hand. »It might be best for you to take another sip.«

35

Ciban led Catherine through a labyrinth of hallways, department corridors and past numerous offices to a lift. Catherine entered the centre of the Apostolic Palace through one of the interior doors. In the interim Rinaldo had brought Ben home. She was in the lift alone with Ciban as the door opened and closed again.

Her figure was reflected in the metal door. Her shoulder-length hair hung across her forehead and over her blue eyes in a rather unruly fashion. She wore a dark pantsuit, not the traditional costume as she had during the proceedings at the Inquisitor's Palace. Ciban's aristocratic appearance through his reflection – like a dark angel standing at the other end of the lift — had a calming effect on her although it should have had the opposite effect.

During her interrogation in front of the tribunal, Catherine had asked herself whether perhaps the cardinal too had extrasensory abilities. In psychic terms it was possible that he was manipulative. On the other hand, based on her schooling she should have felt immediately if he had tried to touch her psyche in any way. Right?

On the way there she had expected Ciban to instruct her before her private audience with the Pope, but that was not at all the case. Ever since they had left the office, he hadn't said a word. Instead, he had held open quite a few heavy gateways and doors

for her. Their eyes met briefly and Catherine had the feeling for a
second that she might turn into a pillar of salt like Lot's wife. But
that was just her imagination. The gleaming lift doors slid open
and they walked out onto the hallway to the papal private chambers. Never in a million years had Catherine dreamed of ever
being allowed to set foot into the holiest space of the Apostolic
Palace.

Monsignor Massini, the Pope's private secretary, approached
her with a warm greeting. »Eminence, Sister.« It was obvious that
the secretary was bursting with curiosity, most likely because he
knew that he wouldn't be participating in the last-minute meeting
with the Pope.

Massini knocked lightly on the door. It looked a lot different
than Catherine expected. The Pope's private office was one of
the plainest she had ever seen. No valuable paintings graced the
walls. No antique objects decorated the room. The ceiling-high
utilitarian book shelves and the messy modern desk looked a lot
more like a contemporary office than the private work space of
the Pope whose office represented two thousand years of history.

Leo looked up from the file he was studying. The white cassock
with its cincture and white zucchetto looked good on him. But
Catherine thought he looked tired. His dark eyes seemed to hold
a great deal of intelligence, but they weren't quite clear and his
body posture suggested that it was sheer willpower that kept him
working at his desk.

»Holy Father,« said Catherine after Massini's welcome ceremony was over and he had left the room.

»Our last meeting was not too long ago, Sister Catherine.«
The Pope looked at her with a smile. His voice sounded sincere.
»What has happened that His Eminence personally accompanied
you here to me?« They took a seat in a comfortable corner of the
room.

Catherine took a deep breath. »I think it is best if I start from the very beginning, Holy Father. It all started the evening of Cardinal Benelli's reception…«

The Pope listened to her in complete silence. Catherine talked about her meeting with Benelli in the villa's chapel and then about her crazy dream that wouldn't leave her alone and, once again the next morning, repeated itself with even more intensity than before. Even Ciban listened intently. He seemed to absorb every one of her words, observing her carefully all the while. When she had finished, the Pope didn't seem at all surprised, much to her own astonishment. He seemed in some way even relieved.

Leo looked her in the eye and thanked her. »Well done, Sister. It takes a lot of courage to come to the prefect of the Congregation of the Doctrine of Faith with such a story.«

»Monsignor Hawlett suggested that His Eminence could help us.«

»And now you are here. I thank you for it.« He turned to Ciban. »It is a much bigger sign than we had expected, Eminence. I will accept Sister Catherine's and Cardinal Benelli's offer to help. It would be insane to do otherwise. Too much is at stake.«

»After everything that I've learned about our deceased Cardinal Benelli, it would be advisable.« Ciban looked closely at Catherine. His eyes seemed to shine from the inside out. »Tell me, Sister, where should this spiritual energy transfer take place?«

Catherine noticed that the cardinal didn't even ask how the transfer worked. It appeared that he was quite familiar with the Lux scientists' theories that tried to bring the physics of the material world in alignment with that of the spiritual world. Beyond the material world, the spirit had enormous power. Not many people suspected that they were essentially energetic beings

surrounded by a real ocean of energies. Everything was connected with everything else and influenced by it too. Catherine had
the ability to tap into this energetic ocean. Benelli would strengthen her gift with his own.

She explained: »According to Cardinal Benelli, it's really quite
simple. He said he has already prepared everything. His Holiness
and I should simply pray together in the papal private chapel.
The rest would take care of itself as long as I remain close by to
His Holiness in the next few days.«

»That shouldn't be a problem,« said the Pope. »We will find
some accommodations for you on this floor.«

Ciban tapped his fingers on the armrest. »Did Cardinal Benelli
say why he didn't speak of his plans with His Holiness?«

Ah yes. There was the Grand Inquisitor again.

Catherine nodded, looking at the prefect, then at the Pope.
»Forgive me, Holiness, but because you are not a psychic person,
Cardinal Benelli was forced to come into contact with me first
before he sacrificed himself, breaking the band between you and
him. I...« she hesitated,»...asked myself what this band and the
attacks on Your Holiness were about.«

Before the Pope could answer, Ciban intervened: »His Eminence, Cardinal Benelli belonged to a committee that His Holiness advises. This committee thinks well beyond the twenty-first
century.«

Catherine was clear that she wouldn't learn anything else from
them for the moment.

»Do you think it would hurt if Cardinal Ciban accompanied
us to the chapel, Sister?« asked the Pope.

She understood immediately: Ciban shouldn't just guard the
Pope, but also help him to the church on his shaky legs.

»I don't see why not, Holiness.«

»Good.« The Pope got up from his leather chair and painfully moved his body past the high, rectangular table. »Then let us not lose a minute, Sister. Let us pray together in the chapel and hope that Cardinal Benelli's plan, at least what he told you, pans out.«

They left the office through a tiny antechamber, slowly passed along the long corridor at the end of which was the Pope's private lift and entered the papal private chapel directly to the right. Ciban helped Leo kneel in the first row. Catherine kneeled on a pew directly next to him. Then the cardinal returned to the furthest of the five rows and positioned himself in front of the locked door in front of which a guard held watch.

They began to pray. Soon Catherine began to have the same sensation she had in Benelli's villa: profound peace and strength. The walls and roof of the papal palace no longer existed to her mind's eye. She looked directly at the blue cloudless sky into a white tunnel of light from which a figure came forth: Benelli. He looked different than she had ever experienced him. His aura was overwhelming. She had never seen something so graceful before in her life. The shining light that was Benelli floated toward her and smiled. Then he touched both the Pope and herself on the forehead without saying a word. His gaze was so permeating, so omniscient. Catherine felt an intense yearning to become spiritually unified with this being. She clearly saw that the Pope felt the same way.

Finally the prayer ended and Catherine exhaled with disappointment as if she had held her breath the entire time. But this time the feeling of inner peace in her soul stayed with her.

Ciban hurried forward to help the Pope stand up and take a seat. Leo sat there for several long minutes as if he were in a trance. An amazing transformation spouted from within his soul. The Pope returned more and more to his original form. After a while he stood up and suddenly seemed years younger. Catherine recognised at once the strong and balanced philanthropist within

him that she had gotten to know through the media and her first
private audience with him.

Ciban looked at the head of the Church with amazement.

»Holiness,« she said quietly, »we are now like the positive and
negative poles of a strong battery. My energy will bring a certain
balance and be carried by Benelli's energy. Unfortunately, the
boost won't last forever.«

»How much time do we have left, Sister?«

»Cardinal Benelli didn't tell me. It depends on how quickly his
energy flows back to him and when the next murder occurs. The
cardinal can only do this sacrifice one time. The balance between
the committee and yourself has been reinstated at least energeti-
cally for the time being.

The Pope nodded. »I see.« He turned to Ciban. »It would be
best for me to return to my office.«

»Are you certain, Holiness?« asked the prefect with a hint of
concern. He creased his forehead.

»Not to worry, Eminence. I am quite certain. I need to use the
time I still have left. Please take care of Sister Catherine.«

»One more thing, Holiness,« said the prefect quietly as he
pointed to the young nun.

»Sister Catherine will most certainly stay in the palace,« explained Leo.

»I didn't mean that.«

»Really?«

»Whoever is behind the murders will find out that you are
feeling better. And he is going to want to know why, Holiness.«

The Pope looked startled. »Of course!« He looked at Catherine. »We have to find an appropriate disguise for you if you are to
stay here.« To Ciban: »Do you have an idea?«

»Well...« The cardinal turned to Catherine and said with a
hint of irony: »Given the current proceedings against you, we

can't introduce you as the Pope's biographer.«

The young woman thought for a moment, then said: »I was in the theatre during my time at the University of Chicago. How about a job in the Pope's private household? I could make myself useful in the kitchen and keep an eye on things. A costume, a pair of glasses, some theatre make-up and no one would recognise me.«

»Theatre?« Ciban raised a brow. He was truly astonished.

»Virginia Woolf.«

The prefect blinked. Then he said dryly: »It could work. But one more thing, Sister: Do you need anything from your hotel room?«

Her hotel room! Heavens! She had completely forgotten. Monsignor Rinaldo was keeping an eye on Ben and she couldn't return there. At least not yet. She would have to go by foot to the hotel. Or perhaps by taxi. On the other hand, she couldn't leave the Vatican for the next few days.

»It would be good if one of your guards could accompany me back to the hotel so I can pack a few essentials.« She thought in particular about her laptop.

Ciban shook his head. »I'm afraid I have to object, Sister. The fewer who know about this, the better.«

Catherine swallowed hard. »And that means?«

»I'll change quickly and drive you to your hotel in one of our unmarked cars. You can pack what you need, then we will return immediately. Tomorrow you will get your theatre make-up.«

36

Ben was certain now that Rinaldo wasn't keeping an eye on him because of his injuries, but because he wanted to monitor his every move. He would have liked to have resented the young priest a bit more, but too bad for him that he was one of the few people on this planet that was not only sincere, but also extremely likeable. It amazed Ben how Rinaldo had taken everything that had happened in the past few hours in such stride. He had barely blinked even when Ciban and Catherine hastily left the prefect's office.

Catherine…she must have already been to visit His Holiness and reported to him what had happened at the Benelli Villa and in her dream.

»Do you need anything else, Ben?« asked Rinaldo.

»Thank you, no. I am going to read a little bit and then sleep as best I can.«

The priest grinned. »Very well then. I will make myself as comfortable as I can on your couch.«

»Sorry for that. It's a dumb job for you. I know.«

»You mustn't be sorry. The main thing is that you get well again.«

»So that His Eminence can tear me to pieces again?«

Rinaldo laughed. »Never fear. Things are never as bad as they seem. He will put you back together piece by piece. Believe me.«

»Well, that's reassuring.«

»You're welcome.« With that the young priest disappeared into the living room with a blanket in hand and closed the door.

Rinaldo had barely left the room when Ben carefully moved toward his computer in agony. He had set up a small workstation in his bedroom. It wasn't much: just a desk, a simple, yet comfortable chair, a shelf and a high-tech computer. It was sufficient enough to get the work done that he took home with him. In addition, the private computer connected him with some of the few good friends he had who lived and worked all over the world. At least now he could conduct a little research about the three murders.

Thanks to Catherine, he now knew that Darius wasn't the murder's main target. Neither were the two preceding murder victims, Sister Isabella and Father Sylvester.

Ben closed his eyes for a moment out of sheer exhaustion, took a deep breath and opened them again.

What had Cardinal Benelli said to Catherine again? The assassination attempts had actually been meant for the Pope! And now, Ben thought, Catherine is with His Holiness to iron out that which the murders had caused with Benelli's help. Three religious members had been murdered. Benelli's suicide made it a fourth death and the Pope had been weakened...These were the new facts that Ben had, facts that Ciban had denied telling him.

He dialled into the Internet and fed into the search engine the names of the first two murder victims along with a few other search terms. It wasn't every day that religious members had an accident in France or Switzerland. Maybe he would come across a tiny news report or something along those lines. He only came up with an obituary on the orders' websites. It appeared that Isabella's and Sylvester's deaths were not even worth a side note in the regional media. Ben hadn't really thought he would find anything there anyway. But it couldn't hurt to look. He researched further, surfed from one link to the next. This time he typed in the names of the monk and the nun in connection with the term »LUKE«. As expected, he found nothing.

He thought about Abel. It probably just required the talents of a resourceful computer freak who could easily tap into the media's databases or take a deeper dive into both orders' computer systems. Ben doubted however that he could convince Abel again so quickly to invade Lux Domini's computer system.

He activated the Internet Relay Chat that Abel had once said was much more secure for chatting than other chat services where a multitude of users usually hung around. Ben sighed. Abel wasn't available on IRC. To be certain he grabbed his mobile phone and dialled Abel's number manually and waited. He hadn't saved the number on purpose. After multiple rings, the mailbox came on. Either Abel wasn't home or he didn't want to be disturbed. Most likely, it was the latter.

Ben sighed, placing the mobile phone next to the keyboard. He stared at the bright monitor. Darn. What should he do now?

He opened his word processing program and wrote down all the ideas he had already gathered about the perpetrator's profile and the profile from Darius and Benelli. Perhaps it would help him to order his thoughts. He had already gathered several data points and he had already seen the surveillance video. He began with the perpetrator.

Perp's profile
  Perp: unknown
  Perp's location: unknown (last seen in Munich)
  Age: 35 to 45 years old
  Height: more than 1.85 metres
  Weight: about 90 kilograms

Eye colour: unknown
Hair colour: brown
Description: strong, athletic build, intelligent

Behaviour:
  Charming with a high IQ,
  Cold-blooded liar,
  Lacking any feelings of regret or compassion,
  Rational behaviour and targeted action
  Criminal action as a means to an end (but what is the end?)
  No amateur, murders with precision
  No interaction with the corpse whatsoever (no personal motive for murder?)
  No interaction with the investigating authorities

Motivation:
  Not sexually motivated

Possible motivation:
  Revenge, hatred, jealousy,
  Personal advantage through Darius' death (Note: Darius left no wealth behind, and he had already shared the results of his research. He had left the Lux as the director several years ago.),
  Did Darius have access to information that might endanger Lux?
  Organisation that is hostile toward Lux – and thereby toward Darius (if yes, which organisation?),
  Material gain such as money (contract killer?).

Ben asked himself once again if a part of the research area for which Darius had worked may have been involved in criminal activities. Is that why Ciban had prevented his further investigations? Indeed, Ben had had no idea what Darius had been working in the past few years. Not even Abel had known, even though he had been one of the priest's last students. Was LUKE Darius' last research project? The chances were pretty high. And if yes, how did His Eminence Cardinal Benelli fit into it all?

Ben turned to the victims' profiles.

Victim profile 1
   Victim: Father Darius
   Last location: Abbey Rottach, Upper Bavaria, Germany
   Age: 74 years old
   Height: 1.76 metres
   Weight: 73 kilograms
   Eye colour: bluish-grey
   Hair colour: grey
   Description: in good shape, ascetic build, constitution of a man in his late 50s, intelligent

Behaviour:
   Charming with a high IQ,
   Sincere,
   High emotional intelligence,
   Rational behaviour and targeted action,
   Religious,
   Loved people,
   Ability for selflessness,

Special features:
   Psychically gifted (ability not known),
   Distinguished member of Lux Domini,
   Veteran employee at the Chicago CIPG (Catholic Institute for the Psychically Gifted)
   Veteran employee at the Roman CIPG (1994-2005),
   Left his official post in 2005.

Note: It is unknown what Father Darius was actually working on at the CIPG. One of his projects in the 70s and 80s was called CORONA. A later project may have been called LUKE. LUKE is the only connection between Father Darius and Cardinal Benelli regarding Lux Domini. Both Father Darius and Cardinal Benelli are dead.

Ben glanced at the words for a while, scrolling up and down. He then began to record his thoughts about Benelli, although he didn't have much to go on for his profile.

Victim profile 2
   Suicide victim: Cardinal Benelli
   Last location: Villa Benelli, near Rome
   Age: mid-70s
   Height: about 1.65 metres
   Weight at least 75 kilograms
   Eye colour: brown
   Hair colour: white
   Description: small and chubby, flabby build, yet agile, intelligent

Behaviour:
   Charming with a high IQ,
   Sincere, yet somewhat dodgy
   Above-average emotional intelligence,
   Rational behaviour and targeted action (even if his alleged suicide might seem to contradict it)
   Religious,
   Apparently a philanthropist.

Special features:
   Member of Lux Domini (since when?),

Curia cardinal with a certain level of influence
Similar aura to Father Darius'.

After he had finished taking notes about Darius and Benelli, he
rested his eyes on them for a bit. Catherine had said that both
men's auras were like twins. It was true that even their profiles
were similar. Ben started to think about Sister Isabella's and
Father Sylvester's profiles. Could it be that they too were the
same as Darius'?

He thought about it some more, until LUKE finally occurred
to him. He hadn't a clue what was behind the name. LUKE
could be anything – from a seemingly harmless file to a secret,
trailblazing research project. But one thing was for certain:
LUKE was somehow associated with Lux Domini. It also had
something to do with both Darius and Benelli, as Abel had
discovered. Quite possibly, Isabella and Sylvester had something
to do with LUKE, which would mean they both must have been
psychically gifted people as well. Darius, Benelli, Isabella and
Sylvester had one thing undeniably in common: they were all
dead.

Ben turned his thoughts to Catherine who was now at the
Apostolic Palace with His Holiness in order to lend strength to
the weakened Pope upon Benelli's instruction in order to…

He faltered.

…in order to balance out the energy that Pope Leo had lost
through the deaths of Sylvester, Isabella and Darius…

Was that perhaps an indication about LUKE? Does the Pope
have something like a mental protective community?

Ben opened up the communication programme once again,
sending out an urgent heavenward prayer at the same time. But
Abel was nowhere to be found on IRC.

He let out a sigh of disappointment, turned off his computer and sat in the dark. When his eyes had gotten used to the darkness, he trudged over to his bed. But he couldn't dream of sleeping just yet. He had too many things running through his mind.

His thoughts returned to the perpetrator's profile that he knew matched the Pope's assassin. In his mind's eye he circled the word »contract killer«. In this case he was nearly certain that the murderer knew nothing of the true reason for the job. With that the first perpetrator's profile was deemed invalid. He would have to create a new one. He shifted to the contractor, the mastermind, quite possibly a hostile organisation.

Ben frowned, knowing full well that most questions about possible masterminds were left unanswered, even if the assassins were captured. If Lux Domini brought forth such people as Darius, Isabella, Sylvester or Benelli to protect the Pope, then it was most unlikely that the order was behind the murders. Who could have such a motive to weaken or even kill the head of the Catholic Church in such a bizarre way? At any rate, it had to be someone who knew about LUKE in great detail, that is, if LUKE had anything to do with it at all. So maybe it was a Lux member after all?

Ben began to feel his exhaustion take hold. His thoughts became muddied, melting like bath salts in hot water. He desperately needed some rest. He needed sleep. But as he closed his eyes in an attempt to fall asleep, his brain kept working. He suddenly came back to the question about what the stranger who tortured him with the truth serum was looking for in Cardinal Benelli's villa.

In the end it seemed to Ben that the stranger was just as surprised as he was to have discovered that the files in the cabinet had gone missing and the computer had been stolen. Ben had learned from Ciban that he had told Gasperetti about his unfortunate situation in the villa's dungeon. Apparently, the entire thing had been a misunderstanding. They had mistaken him for a burglar. That the Lux agent himself was a burglar didn't seem to interest anyone in the least.

Ben kept his eyes shut, breathing with regular intervals and trying to relax. At some point he finally fell asleep with the thought that he should speak with Ciban as soon as possible. Guilty feelings or no. The prefect owned him an explanation or two.

37

West Bengal, Calcutta

The Order of Charitable Missionaries

Shanti Nagar

The fingerless hands of the mutilated man reached for Sister Silvia. Lepers made their way daily to the colony after having been left by their spouses or excluded from their villages. Even today many people in India believed that the illness came from a curse and therefore incurable. Leprosy was an infectious disease that could be stopped and healed with modern medicine as long as the immune system didn't react against it with leprosy antibodies that could arise decades after healing, causing nerve inflammation.

Sister Silvia came from the Irish suburb of Dublin called Rathfarnham that lay to the Southwest of the city where the mother house of the sisters from Loreto was located. It was there that Mother Teresa had been prepared for her mission to Calcutta. In the meantime Sister Silvia had been working for the past twenty-five years in »Shanti Nagar«, the »city of peace« as the leper colony was called.

Contrary to some of her other European sisters, her first encounter with India, with its noise, dirt, stench, suffering and chaos on the streets, didn't make her horrified or call forth mons-trous images. She had liked Calcutta and the uniqueness of the natives from the very beginning. She saw the pulsating life behind the suffering, its lack of complication, its joy.

Sister Silvia touched the mutilated man, carefully helping him up with an encouraging smile. He had most likely waited half the night at the colony's entrance. She carefully brought him to the ward where one of her colleagues took him in. The leper lied down on one of the cots, utterly exhausted and relieved. Sister Silvia returned to the entrance gate to help other patients in the colony.

As the Irishwoman knew too well, leprosy began rather harm-lessly at first. The skin grew discoloured with a numb spot. It was rare that those infected even noticed the first signs of the disease or they kept it a secret. Most of those affected came to the colony only after their bodies had become mutilated and filled with boils. Their village communities had long since ostracised them. Many of the patients in Shanti Nagar lived with leprosy-induced handi-caps.

The fact that Shanti Nagar, »the city of peace«, even existed was thanks to the courage and drive of a single person: Agnes Gonxhe Bojaxhiu, the later Mother Teresa for whom a prayer without accompanying action was merely a prayer. Active faith was love, and active love was service. Sister Silvia had worked side by side with Mother Teresa for many years. She had marvel-led at her incomparable dedication to caring for the ill and dying. The »angel of the poor,« as the wealthy Westerners called her to this day, even after her death.

Sister Silvia had often accompanied Mother Teresa on her way through the slums' tight and dirty alleys, equipped with the most basic medicines to help the ill. Without the elderly woman kno-wing, Silvia had long since known about the enormous crises of faith that plagued Mother Teresa, well before the public learned of the correspondence between the Catholic missionary and her spiritual guides.

In her correspondence Mother Teresa had spoken of an emptiness and darkness in the deepest parts of herself and that she had lost her faith, barely daring to even mention it. She felt God had abandoned her. Despite all her doubts and pain, her smile and extraordinary commitment to helping the poorest of the poor never left her.

»Should I ever reach sainthood,« said Teresa one time, »then I will most certainly be called 'the Saint of Darkness'. I will go missing in heaven forevermore so that I can ignite a light for all those who live in darkness here on Earth.«

Silvia gave an inward sigh. It was moments like these in which she was tempted to breach the holy oath she had made to the Pope and the committee. She would have loved to have »proven« to Teresa that God had not abandoned her, not for a second. Quite the contrary! He had placed Silvia and all the other helpers on Mother Teresa's side. The missionary was never abandoned by God and left to her own devices, even if she felt it in her heart of hearts. But Sister Silvia was all too familiar with her companion's dilemma. No matter how hard Teresa worked, not matter how much she fought for the poorest of the poor, the suffering on the streets of Calcutta saw no end. In fact, it just kept growing.

Sister Silvia walked through the colony's entrance gate and saw a thin, mutilated person, nearly still a child.

The girl was too weak to make it to the ward on her own. Relatives had left the sick girl in a desperate attempt to give her a chance at survival behind the colony's gates. She recognised their hope by the fact that they had given the girl a piece of bread and some water while she waited. Perhaps the little girl would have an even better life than her parents and siblings in the city. Unfortunately, they had waited until the girl was handicapped before seeking help. Sister Silvia touched the patient, stroking her hair and comforting her. She noticed a glimmer in the girl's dark eyes. Then she picked up the little girl who was light as a feather.

»What's your name, child?« she asked.

»Asira,« said the little girl with a measure of hesitation, looking back at the nun.

»Asira…what a beautiful name!«

Sister Silvia gave the sick girl a kiss without showing her surprise. As far as she knew, Asira was an Arabian name and meant »the chosen one.«

38

Rome, The Vatican, Apostolic Palace

The master followed the show from his midsize flat screen in his Vatican office. The show was being transmitted live from one of the Catholic television channels via the Internet. It showed something that was actually quite incredible: an energetic Pope full of life while praying with believers and pilgrims to Rome. Tens of thousands of people had found their way to St. Peter's Square with flags and banners. They looked up toward the window of the Pope's private office and prayed the traditional Angelus with him.

The master zoomed in to show only the pontiff on the monitor without the papal flag that hung from the windowsill and without the crowd standing below on St. Peter's Square. Unfortunately, the transmission quality was rather poor so he was unable to see Leo's face clearly. The master would have loved to look the Pope in the eye.

Leo spoke of the good and evil in this world, claiming that good would triumph over evil in the end. The master's lips curled into an awful grin at the sound of his words. The old lyre. What did Leo know about good and evil anyway? Evil had existed long before good. After saying the Angelus, the Pope mentioned the canonisation of one of the religious men. The master knew him.

In his mind, the monk hadn't deserved canonisation. Neither had Mother Teresa. The Pope then expressed his sorrow about the natural catastrophe in South America. He prayed for all the people who had been affected by the tragedy, the victims and the population. The large community of believers and pilgrims on St. Peter's Square waved their flags and prayed with the Holy Father. The master postponed his prayer for another time.

When the official papal visit was over and the window to the papal office had been closed, the master switched off the telly and leaned back in his red-backed chair, lost in thought. He hadn't let the Pope out of his sight for even a moment, observing his every move, gesture, word. During his entire appearance, Leo hadn't shown a single sign of weakening and that, even though three of his committee members had been obliterated, despite his latest severe collapse. The Pope had even stood there larger than life, cheering to the crowd of people and praying the Angelus with them. That wasn't a hallucination!

The master took a deep breath. For the moment, it appeared all his work had been for nothing. But then he allowed himself a little smile. In a way he owed the Pope and his committee a certain level of respect. Through this latest twist that he never thought Leo could pull off, the master now stood before a tiny dilemma. For a moment he even considered interrupting his mission in Calcutta until he could get to the bottom of Leo's sudden recovery. In the end he thought better of it. Things should simply take their course.

He made a mental list of the names of the papal committee. Sylvester, Isabella, Darius, Silvia, Thea…

There was always a way. There was always a solution.

39

Catherine sat with Cardinal Ciban and Monsignor Massini in the office of His Holiness. She was now wearing the costume of a nun employed as a domestic worker in the papal household with thick horn-rimmed glasses and a good portion of theatre make-up complete with a wart over her lip. The three waited until Leo, who was standing on the podium at the window, completed the traditional Angelus with the community standing below on St. Peter's Square.

Catherine had followed the Pope's entire public appearance via one of the two monitors in his private office. The people loved the Pope. That much was true because they listened to him with a great deal of rapture and devotion. They loved him at least as much as they had loved John XXIII or John Paul. Not even Leo's opponents could deny it. Unfortunately, the enemy now officially knew about the Holy Father's excellent health condition too.

Catherine had had a second dream about Benelli the night before. It had been as real and intoxicating as the first. She didn't have a good feeling about the cardinal's plan to challenge the opponent and bring him to make a grave mistake, especially since they only had a few days left to capture the murderer. That's how much time they had before Benelli's additional energy dried up and she stood there alone with only her own.

»I am so sorry,« Benelli had told her in the dream. »But I can do nothing more at the moment. Even the after world has its limits that we must obey. We also ask ourselves here: What is the meaning of life? What is the meaning of death? Evil has always had the ability to disguise itself.«

Catherine watched as the Pope got down from the podium with a dynamic step. Massini closed the window so that they could only hear crowd's cheers on the open piazza as a dampened murmur. She had told Leo first thing this morning about her second dream, but Benelli's revelation hadn't unsettled him in the least. The Holy Father seemed to be as solid as a rock.

She took a deep inward breath as the Pope approached her because she had kept something from him. Before the dream with Benelli, she had had another one that was just as real and utterly bizarre. In her pre-Benelli dream or whatever Catherine should call it, it was like a sequel to the first travelling dream through the history of the New Testament that she had experienced two nights before. But this sequence had not been recorded anywhere in the New Testament. Catherine had decided to keep the dream, along with her encounter with Benelli in Golgotha, to herself.

She didn't wish to provide any more ammunition that the Congregation of the Doctrine of Faith could use against her. Catherine, the visionary! Just the thing to add to the list of charges! How could she have gently told the Holy Father? Oh yes, by the way, Holiness, I had a chat with Maria Magdalene in Jerusalem right after our Lord ascended to heaven. No, she would prefer to keep those completely crazy appearances to herself.

As the Holy Father stood before her and Ciban, he took the opportunity to give Catherine a good look over. She now looked like a nun in her early forties, slightly chubby or, more politely put, with a solid build, a big nose and a thick pair of glasses. With the exception of her blue eyes, she was completely transformed.

Not even Massini recognised her and as the Pope's confidante, he was in the know about her disguise.

»You look great, Sister,« said the Pope with a wide grin, hooking his arm in hers as he guided her to the seating area. Her fake wart seemed to fascinate him in particular. »Even in this get-up, you still have style.«

»Thank you, Holiness. I gave it my all.«

In truth, Catherine felt like a bloated whale. She was out of practice playing theatre. It had taken her nearly an hour to apply her make-up to perfection and she had almost missed her first task of laying out the papal breakfast buffet. Ciban had remained expressionless at the breakfast table when he first saw her in her new outfit, but Catherine could have sworn she could hear his inward efforts to suppress the laugh of the century. Why else should he have hidden his face behind one of Leo's daily newspapers for so long?

When Monsignor Massini had left the office after the Angelus prayer in order to prepare an audience, Leo said: »That was Act One, Sister. Do you have any idea where this journey is headed?«

Catherine shook her head. »I'm afraid not, Holiness. His Eminence Cardinal Benelli has only shown me the tip of the iceberg. I'm in the dark on everything else.«

»Well, then,« said Leo, »it's the opponent's turn.«

»I'm afraid so,« she said. »Let us hope the murderer sees how senseless his efforts are.«

Ciban shook his head. »He's come this far. I doubt he'll give up now. Let us just hope he gives up his cover and makes a mistake.« The cardinal looked Catherine directly in the eye. »There's something else that puzzles me, Sister.«

»And that would be, Eminence?«

»It may sound odd, but should you choose to leave the papal palace or even the Vatican in the coming days, for whatever reason, please let me or His Holiness know.«

»I don't intend to leave the palace, much less the Vatican,« she said firmly. Ciban kept his gaze on her. »Alright. You have my word.«

»Thank you, Sister.« The prefect nodded with satisfaction.

The rest of the day remained unchallenging for Catherine. She insisted on helping the nuns with their housework in the papal household and got a sense of everyday life behind the scenes in the Apostolic Palace.

In the evening after chatting with the Holy Father, she returned to her room and was overcome with the sudden urge to sleep. An iron weight seeped into her bones, taking hold of every single cell in her body. She had never felt such a need for sleep before. She could hardly wait, just barely making it before falling into bed.

The world around her disappeared and took on new forms and colours. A blustery wind blew across her face. Before her was an enormous lake. Catherine knew immediately that she stood on the western shore of Lake Tiberias, also known as the Sea of Galilee. She saw fishing boats returning to shore.

A man in a white linen robe tied with a belt made of the finest gold stood next to her. His body was like chrysolite, his face like a flash of light. Catherine recognised him to be one of the four angels at God's side. The angel guarded over a little girl with chestnut-brown hair playing on the shore and whose father was helping unload one of the boats. Only the girl who was now playing amongst the stacked crates and Catherine seemed to see the man with the flaming face.

»Without her help, without her wisdom and testimony, there will be no change,« said the angel, turning part of his attention to Catherine. He pointed to the child. His eyes blazed like torches. The work depends on her.«

Catherine wondered what he meant by work. »Who is she?«

»The mirror through which the world will soon see itself, even if her words are announced through another. You have already met her once in your dream.«

One of the towering fish crates slipped, sliding toward the child. Catherine had barely noticed she was in danger when the man stopped the crate with a quick hand movement.

»I don't remember having met this girl before,« said Catherine, realising now that the child might have died if not for the help of the angel.

»You spoke with her. Last night. You spoke of darkness and of light. Of hope for that which is coming.«

»Maria?«

The man with the fiery eyes nodded. »Maria Magdalene.«

»But she is still a child!«

»In her heart she will always remain one. In the name of truth. In the name of unity between heaven and Earth. She is the first chapter of the New Testament.«

Catherine looked at the angel. She suddenly realised the being next to her had no gender. His fiery face encircled with golden hair was equally masculine and feminine. Most likely the child Maria had seen the angel like that from the beginning.

»What purpose do these dreams serve?« asked Catherine straight out. She knew all too well that a lot of human fears and desires, even mental illnesses, came to light in dreams. It was quite possible that she was slowly losing her mind.

The corners of the angel's mouth curled into a smile. »What do you think?«

»They are supposed to show me something. But what?«

»These dreams are more than just dreams, Catherine,« explained the angel calmly. »They are memories.«

»Memories? But what I see lies far in the past. How can I

remember something that I never experienced myself?«

»Who says that they are your memories?«

Catherine stared at the angel, nearly expecting him to turn into Cardinal Benelli at any moment. But it couldn't possibly be Benelli's memory. But whose then? One stemming from the cosmic memory in which all past, present and future events are held? There were theories, also within Lux, that psychically gifted people were able to tap into this cosmic memory. That is how esoterics, for instance, try to explain paranormal phenomena such as clairvoyance. Was it possible that Benelli's additional energy now allowed Catherine to participate in this memory?

The angel took her hand without burning her and they entered a new scene. Catherine suddenly found herself in a village where children were running around simple houses.

»Those boys are Jacob, John, Judas and Simon,« explained the angel, letting go of her hand.

»Jesus' disciples…« said Catherine reverently.

»Jesus' brothers,« explained the angel, walking toward the crowd of children.

It was only now that the young woman saw the halos that surrounded each child. Just like with little Maria. »And where is Jesus?« she asked.

The angel pointed to a somewhat isolated cottage. »He has a heavy heart. He has been tasked with the role as saviour. Besides he has seen a hint of his future. Not even Judas could console him.« The children danced around the angel except for one boy who stared at the angel and Catherine with curiosity.

»That is Judas,« explained her companion calmly. »He has been tasked with the role of traitor.« The angel stuck out his hand, making the boy come toward him as if in a trance, all the while looking at the young women with uncertainty in his eyes.

The angel made a gesture, a gleaming flash came down from

heaven and the child's sadness fell away.

Catherine, who had witnessed everything with great calm, returned to her question: »I still don't understand what these dreams are trying to tell me.«

Her companion looked at her with great affection. »You know the objective, but you don't know the true path. You will soon understand. Go now and get some rest. You have seen enough for today.«

The strange world around Catherine disappeared, as did the angel. But when she awoke from her dream, she could still smell the Sea of Galilee and feel the blustery wind in her face. She blinked, pulled herself together, sat up and looked at her surroundings. The expensive wallpaper, the antique wardrobe, the shelf, the table, the chair, the bed on which she lay, the crucifix on the adjacent wall...she was clearly back in her room at the Apostolic Palace and no longer in Palestine during the times of Maria Magdalene. Her gaze rested on the travel clock on the nightstand. Not a minute had passed or the clock had stood still.

For a moment she toyed with the idea of sending Ben an email or trying to chat with him. But then she remembered where she was. No, it was better not to have a long discussion over the Internet. A brief text message would have to do. Straight away the next morning she would send Ben a message. She knew exactly what to write: »Gabriel was here. Regards, Catherine.«

40

West Bengal, Calcutta

Monsignor Nicola deRossi left the half-empty passenger plane and walked down the docked metal stairs to the oily ground of the Calcutta airport. This time he was disguised as an Italian businessman and gourmet looking for unknown Indian spices that he wanted to sell to high-end restaurants in the rich Western world.

Apart from the smell of kerosene, he already had the impression on the tarmac that the odour of the mega-city was starting to waft over him. Because there were no direct flights from Rome to Calcutta, the master's agent arranged for deRossi to fly via Germany. That way he could fly as a wealthy businessman from Frankfurt to West Bengal with Lufthansa.

He didn't need any tips while traveling to Calcutta as he had been to the city several times in the past few years. The place satisfied certain urges he had quite well. Even the master profited considerably from the corruption the Moloch's poverty brought forth. The master had contacts worldwide. And so it was that one of his Indian agents stood waiting already at the exit.

DeRossi thought again about what he could have squeezed out of Abel. Despite his intensive interrogation, he got little information out of him. All that effort had been for naught really, except perhaps for the pleasure of killing him. On the other hand through his intervention he had learned that Hawlett had now included Benelli's death as a part of the investigation and that made deRossi most curious. Not to mention this »LUKE« thingy about which Abel could unfortunately tell him nothing. The master most certainly knew what was behind it.

DeRossi took a deep breath. He had yet to inform the master about his unauthorised nocturnal operation. If he really thought about it, he didn't intend to tell him any time soon. That wimp Hawlett should air the secret about LUKE for him.

The Monsignor got into the Indian agent's unmarked car. His plane had landed at an off-hour so the Chowringhee, the Calcutta's major traffic artery, wouldn't be too congested. He would be spared endless traffic jams with solid lines of cars beeping unnervingly and overflowing sidewalks filled with too many people. Even the unbearable heat and humidity were held at bay by the car's Russian made air conditioner until they reached the equally air conditioned hotel.

DeRossi had busied himself with Sister Silvia's biography during the flight. He studied the life of each of his victims with near pathological precision. In the end he imagined Sister Silvia's life in Calcutta to be like a cheap Hollywood film in which good triumphs over evil. The reality, however, was a lot different.

In the film Sister Silvia and Mother Teresa knew one another. DeRossi wondered how much truth there was to the story about Mother Teresa's exorcism in the exclusive interview that the Sicilian Salesian priest Rosario Stroscio gave the Italian newspaper Oggi. Had Sister Silvia been privy to the exorcism? After all, she had worked with the missionary for many years in the leper colony Shanti Nagar. It was said the two women had even been friends. Merely the thought of their friendship dripped on deRossi's soul like acid on living skin.

In his hotel room, deRossi took out the city map of Calcutta once again although he had already memorised the relevant streets and quarters during his Lufthansa flight. Shanti Nagar was located on the other side of the Hugli, an estuary in the western Ganges delta, surrounded by slums. He had even studied aerial images of the colony and its surroundings. Of course he wouldn't actually search for Sister Silvia in the leper colony. That would be too risky. Instead, he had memorised her habits, her highs and lows, her likes and dislikes and her fears.

Her habits were the best starting point for the Monsignor. She held on to one of the habits she had developed with Mother Teresa in particular: as reliable as a Swiss clock, she still paid regular visits to the poorhouses for the poorest of the poor located in the Slum Motijheel near Tangra and the Loreto school in order to help out with medicine and food. Motijheel now had its own school and a little church. It was there, amidst the deepest abyss of human vegetation, that deRossi would expect her.

41

Ben's day had begun slowly. He slept well past noon, then enjoyed a late, simple breakfast with Rinaldo consisting of white bread, butter, Roman cheese and strong coffee. Then he read Catherine's mysterious text message.

»Gabriel was here. Regards, Catherine.«

It appeared she had had another one of her weird dreams so he had called her on her mobile phone. But she didn't pick up so he left her a brief message on her mailbox instead. Then he tried to reach Abel. No luck there either. It seemed that perhaps Abel had gone to bed very late and was now sleeping in for the remainder of the day.

After showering and changing, Ben had asked Rinaldo to come to the living room where he came upon a small stack of daily newspapers that the priest had read and left there. As he briefly scanned the various politics and sports sections, he came upon a headline in the regional news that made his heart stop.

»Catholic Priest Dies in an Apartment House Fire!«

Ben read the report. With each passing line he became more and more nauseous. It was said that one of the apartment buildings near the Forum Romanum had partially burned down. The origin of the fire was allegedly a flat on the second floor. Four had been slightly injured, two severely and two had died, including one Catholic priest.

The newspaper fell from his hands. Lord above! Abel was dead! It was certainly no accident. Most likely the young priest had been murdered at the exact time that Ben had made his way to Benelli's villa to find out more about LUKE.

Ben gagged, got himself up and made it just in time to the bathroom where he completely lost his breakfast. When he had finally pulled himself together and returned in a haze to the living room, he found Rinaldo standing there with the paper open to the article in his hands.

»Do you know something about this?« asked the young priest.

Ben nodded. »I am afraid I do. It would be best if you were to bring me to Cardinal Ciban straight away.«

42

Leo's ashen face looked like a mask of paralysed pain. Despite the immense energy surge from Catherine and Benelli, it took all his mental energy and discipline to let the agonising moment of death wash over him. Hours seemed to drag on although he knew it only took a few moments before the deep pain of dying was followed by death's peace.

Another committee member had been murdered, but Leo had no idea who the latest victim was. He only felt the spear in his flesh and torture in his soul, but thanks to the energetic transfusion, he didn't experience another collapse. Besides, he was in his private chambers looking for the journal he must have misplaced so no one was witness to his attacks and confusion.

There was a knock at the door. »Holiness?«

The Pope recognised the voice immediately. Sister Catherine. It appeared she had noticed his attack through the band that Benelli had created between the two of them. If that were the case, then she must also know about his mental dependency on the committee members and about his physical and mental withdrawal that Benelli's and her energy had softened like a substitute drug.

Leo called out for the young woman to enter. He saw in her eyes that she was both worried and confused. Could it be that she not only felt his concern and weakness, but also the death process? He knew death in the material world was not the end, but his encounter with it shocked him every time. When Catherine saw that he was alright, her worry and confusion turned to relief.

»Another murder, Holiness?« She had closed the door and approached him.

Leo nodded. She seemed so poised despite everything. Although he exuded calm and experience on the outside, he himself felt an enormous level of chaos on the inside. »It seems as though our opponent wants to eradicate the entire committee.«

Catherine eyed the Pope discreetly. The entire committee? She recalled Benelli saying in the chapel that Sister Isabella and Father Sylvester had belonged to a society that was closely related to the Pope. She also remembered the conversation Leo and Ciban had had when she had reported to the Pope about the dead cardinal's instructions in the prefect's presence. But it seemed at the moment that the Pope wasn't going to go into any further detail about the committee.

Although a part of his soul was in upheaval, the Pope gave her the overall impression that he was stable. At the same time, she could feel the energy being sucked out of her in tiny, invisible waves. She wondered if she could see the energy maelstrom if she tapped into her gift, but she dared not to do it for fear she might irretrievably destroy its magic. Quite possibly the connection between Benelli, herself and the Pope could have brought about the fantastical day dream, a short, succinct vision that she had just had a few minutes before while sitting on the rooftop terrace with her lap top and working on her new book.

In her daydream she had been a part of a group of men, women and children who were approaching Old Jerusalem and the Mount of Olives from Bethany via the three kilometre-long Jericho Road. It had felt so real, so tangible – until Leo had his attacks that had abruptly pulled her out of her vision through the energy band.

»I will let Cardinal Ciban know,« said the Pope. He went to his desk, grabbed the telephone and speed-dialled the number for the Palace of the Inquisition.

The conversation didn't last two minutes before he hung up. »Now we wait, Sister. I have no idea who the latest murder victim is, but I fear we are about to find out.«

43

Calcutta, Church in Motijheel

As Father Sam Raj walked into the tiny church in Motijheel through the vestry behind the high altar as he did every morning, the first thing he noticed was the warm candlelight. The evening before there hadn't been nearly as many lit candles in the church as there were now. The entire front altar was bathed in a warm, tender light.

Father Raj walked around the area and saw an angelic figure lying on the stone floor surrounded by a sea of candles. The figure was cloaked in a blue and white sari from the community, the order's habit of charitable missionaries. He gasped in surprise and made a sign of the cross.

»Sister?«

The priest ran to the nun who lay prostate with her arms outstretched, but the candles prevented him from getting any closer without burning himself. He felt his way through the first row of candles and thought he might have heard something moving in the dim light of the church. Did he hear a groaning coming from somewhere in the darkness?

»Sister!«

The nun lay on the ground and looked up at the ceiling of the tiny church as if she had just had a divine vision. Father Raj was afraid of the strange sounds and the shadows that the candles cast onto the stone floor, but he continued to sweep away several rows of them. As he did so, he noticed that the missionary appeared to be no longer breathing. The visionary look on her face seemed to be frozen.

In the midst of his movement, he himself froze. He recognised the face of the woman lying there. It was Sister Silvia!

The altar's crucifix danced in its own shadow and light high above her.

When he had removed the final row of candles that stood between himself and the nun, he leaned over her to see if she was breathing. Nothing. He grabbed her arm and felt her pulse. Again nothing.

The horror was etched in Father Raj's face. He made a sign of the cross, took Sister Silvia's cool hand in his and began to pray while crying.

44

Calcutta Airport

Monsignor deRossi placed his hand luggage in the compartment above him and sat down at his window seat. Unfortunately the external glass was so smeared that he could only vaguely recognise the world beyond the plane. A spooky, pale light glistened on the tarmac. It was only dawn. But it still made him nervous.

He turned on all three reading lamps above him. The plane was two-thirds empty so no one was sitting next to him to complain. Beneath the lamps' beams he took a deep breath and tried to relax.

His body was pressed against the seat during take-off. As the plane took flight, the sensation promptly reminded him of the very moment Sister Silvia rebelled with her last agonising breath. Everything had gone according to plan, but the nun's passing gave deRossi a unique surprise.

He believed to have had a mystical experience.

The first real-life encounter with Silvia in that tiny church – she had been immersed in prayer after making her way through the slums – had left him enraptured. Never in his life had he seen someone pray with such sincerity. But then that priest had come and knelt next to her, ruining the entire holy scene. Finally, after her prayer, Silvia and the priest had spoken quietly with one another. Then deRossi had seen – of this he was certain! – a timid smile race across Silvia's face.

After a warm goodbye, the priest had disappeared, leaving Silvia and deRossi alone in the church. It was the moment he had been waiting for from his discreet hiding place. Only the candlelit statues of the saints should be witness to his necessary intervention.

DeRossi quietly approached the middle aisle from which he could see both the vestry's entrance as well as the main church entrance. It was so quiet in the church that he could hear a pin drop.

During his travels he had not only studied up on Silvia's biography, but also on the church's secret underground and the only access to it.

Silvia was once again immersed in deep prayer. He walked before the altar and made a sign of the cross. He then knelt next to the nun as if he wanted to start a dialogue with God. The rag soaked with chloroform, which would serve as an anaesthetic, was already in his hand. It didn't even take a minute. The tiny, slender Silvia didn't stand a chance.

Half an hour later the nun awoke in the church's secret underground. Her eyes revealed neither fear nor shock. She didn't even scream, perhaps knowing that no one could hear her down there anyway.

»No matter what you do in your own ignorance,« she said to him with complete calm, »you will not destroy the work. Triumph is not the door through which you will go.«

For the first time in his life, deRossi felt a certain level of unease. The feeling raced through his body like a disturbing tickle. »I am only the medium,« he shot back.

Silvia shook her head. »No, you are less than that.« Her eyes flashed with courage and determination. »Your life is a blind, random hustle without purpose or aim. You love the darkness more than the light. You have never felt the flame of faith within yourself and have never loved a single other human being other than yourself, and yet you wear this ring.«

DeRossi winced, but then instantly pulled himself back together. He had replaced his clothing with Indian robes. He had indeed completely forgotten the ring this time, perhaps because it had long since become a part of him. He had been a Lux member since he was young. »Whatever has brought my master against you must be far worse than anything I have ever experienced,« he said, returning her intense gaze. »Your work no longer has meaning.«

DeRossi's fake indignation didn't impress Silvia in the least. She simply sat there and waited without saying another word. He went to it before he could wimp out. Silvia accepted her fate like a sacrificial lamb. Her death actually made deRossi anxious.

He had felt, no seen, quite clearly the very moment the life had left her eyes. Something in Silvia's final breath swept toward him like a streak of fog, touching him on the forehead.

He knew he had felt it. Like a sibling's caress. Like a tender kiss.

Silvia had forgiven him!

At the thought DeRossi clawed the seat's armrest with his fingers and looked out through the dirty window at Calcutta, a city drenched in suffering and joy. In his mind's eye, however, he saw a very different scene: candles. A sea of candles. With Silvia in the midst of them all. He unconsciously reached for a pack of cigarettes that he kept with him. But then he remembered that it was prohibited to smoke on the airplane. For the duration of the flight from Calcutta to Frankfurt, the Monsignor tried to do just one thing: to banish the image of the candles and Sister Silvia from his memory.

LUKE

45

Mount of Olives near Jerusalem, 33 A.D.

Catherine was outdoors. The sky above her was full of bright, foreign stars. She sat in a circle of men and women around a warm campfire. Others lay in the grass, already asleep. Catherine on the other hand didn't feel like sleeping. She could feel that it was going to be a particularly special night.

One of the men knelt next to her, laying a warm cloak around her body. It was only now that she noticed she was pregnant.

»You should get some rest. Too much strain isn't good for you or the baby. You shouldn't be here at all.«

»I am pregnant, not ill,« countered Catherine with a tinge of humour. She realised it was not her speaking, but that this conversation had taken place nearly two thousand years in the past.

The man pointed to a group that was sitting a bit farther away around another fire. »It is they. The chosen ones.«

»Which one of them is the – anointed?«

Her companion pointed to a lonely figure who stood apart from the rest. A second, smaller and more slender person went to stand next to him. Both of them hugged, standing quietly next to one another as they looked out at the promised land of Jerusalem.

»This man awoke Lazarus in Bethany from the dead,« he said

reverently. »I saw it with my own eyes.«

»This man has created miracles,« said a voice behind them. »And every one of these miracles has its price.«

Catherine turned around. The man introduced himself as Judas Iscariot, but the young woman thought she recognised someone else in him. A red aura mixed with some blue and white surrounded him. It looked as if he were fighting some internal battle with himself. She saw the demise of the anointed in his pain-ridden eyes.

In that very moment Catherine awakened, her nightgown drenched in sweat. She switched off the alarm clock, taking her time to come to. She lay in a dark room by herself. A wet film covered her face as if she had a fever. Then she remembered where she was. She was in the Apostolic Palace as a part of the papal household and was protecting the Pope with her psychic energy. But her dream didn't want to release her. It felt like a real memory in her mind and in this room.

She still saw the people around the campfire, felt its warmth on the Mount of Olives, saw the fear and pain in Judas' eyes. Somehow Judas was Cardinal Benelli at the same time.

She had to escape this world. This insanity. Catherine jumped up, ran to the bathroom and took a shower. After standing beneath the hot stream of water for several minutes, she turned off the faucet, grabbed a large towel and dried herself off. The entire bathroom was enshrouded in fog, covered with steam. She looked in the mirror and froze.

A crooked line appeared on the fogged up mirror. It was a half ichthys symbol, the secret marking of the early Christians. One person would draw an arch in the sand. The other then completed the fish symbol with a reversed arch and claimed to be a brother or sister in Christ two thousand years ago. Had Benelli sent her this sign? To encourage her? To remind her of the deeper meaning behind her mission?

As if hypnotised Catherine walked toward the mirror and completed the symbol.

46

Ben remembered that the Apostolic Vicariate of Bengal was established in 1834. It was named Archdiocese Calcutta by Pope Leo XIII in 1886. Three suffragan bishops stood by the archbishop's side to support him in his work. The ecclesiastical province included the suffragan bishoprics of Asanol, Bagdogra, Baruipur, Darjeeling, Jalpaiguri, Krishnanagar and Raiganj. But for most of the people in the slums the Catholic Church started to existed mainly through the selfless work of Mother Teresa. Less than one per cent of the Indian population was Christian.

Ben had gotten one of the airport taxis to take him directly to Shanti Nagar. Sister Bernadette, one of the charitable missionaries greeted him at the main entrance at the heavy wrought-iron gate. He had been travelling for virtually an entire day from Rome to Calcutta and although he was dog-tired, he insisted on seeing Sister Silvia's corpse. The crazy encrypted crime scene photos that Cardinal Ciban had received in his office via the Internet continued to swirl around his head. The dead nun had looked like a prophetic statue of a saint surrounded by a sea of candles. One of the photographs had looked so peaceful, so spiritual, so promising – so much so that it almost looked brutal. Sister Bernadette was a tiny, rotund person with steel-rimmed glasses and a warm-hearted aura. She had often accompanied Sister Silvia on her tours through the slums as she told Ben on the way to the morgue. That was the reason Mother Superior had asked her to support the Monsignor during his investigations surrounding the death. Of all the order members, she was the one who best knew her way around the slums near Shanti Nagar and the little church where the body was found.

Sister Bernadette opened the door to the morgue. They passed a little lobby that led down a dark corridor. In contrast to the heat outdoors, the air-conditioned room felt so refreshing that he almost nearly froze.

»Why didn't you go with Sister Silvia into the church?« asked Ben.

»I was called to another patient,« explained the rotund nun quietly in the blue and white sari. »Sometimes we divide the labour in the slums among ourselves to be more efficient.« She talked about the patient she visited. A mortally ill man with cancer who died that very night. The poor thing had suffered terribly over the past year, but Bernadette had never once heard him yelp or complain. In the end he was just skin and bones because he could no longer eat solid foods.

»I see,« said Ben with concern. He was slowly starting to get a sense of the level of unspeakable suffering with which the missionaries were confronted on a daily basis.

They walked through long, dim corridors to the right of which came recesses in regular intervals that were either empty or filled with a corpse laid out on a stretcher. Sister Bernadette finally stood in front of one of them. The missionary looked at the recess and froze.

»What's wrong, Sister?« asked Ben, surprised by her reaction.

»She's gone!«

»Pardon me?« He came closer. The stretcher was empty indeed. »Perhaps she was moved?« Ben thought out loud although he didn't quite believe it himself.

Why would someone want to bring Sister Silvia's corpse from
one recess to another? The corner seemed just as well air-conditioned as the others. He also couldn't imagine that the Archdiocese Calcutta had given an order to move her. Besides, the archbishop had informed the Vatican of the death. If he had had the
corpse moved elsewhere, he certainly would have let the missionaries' Mother Superior know.

»It is most unlikely,« explained Sister Bernadette. It seemed the
same thoughts had crossed her mind as well.

They searched the rest of the stretchers, even those they had
already passed, but they couldn't find the dead body anywhere.
Ben and Sister Bernadette finally spoke with Mother Superior
who then immediately called the archbishop's office. No one
knew about moving any bodies. None of the missionaries or the
other colony residents could say anything about where the body
might be. Sister Silvia seemed to have vanished out of thin air.

»I have little hope, but perhaps Father Raj can tell us something,« said Sister Bernadette ultimately.

Ben had heard that the priest had discovered the body in the
little church. After he had recovered from the initial shock, he
had contacted the Archdiocese Calcutta for help. The archbishop's call had come in to Cardinal Ciban's office in exactly the
moment that Ben had discussed Abel's murder with him. In
response, the prefect had handed him a file that had been lying
on the desk and asked him to open it. The first thing Ben noticed
was the encrypted anonymous report of an intrusion into the
computer system. The second thing — he had held his breath –
was exactly the same headline that he had just read about the
house fire near the Forum Romanum.

Ciban had already made the connection between the nocturnal intrusion into the Lux Domini computer system and
Abel's murder. He had most likely added Ben's nocturnal break-

in into Benelli's villa to the equation as well.

Ben had looked up from the file, gathered all his courage and asked: »What is 'LUKE', Eminence?« Ciban had not answered right away. Instead, he had asked for the file back and allowed it to disappear into one of the heavy drawers in his enormous desk. But Ben didn't relent. »What do Sister Isabella, Father Darius, Father Sylvester and Cardinal Benelli have to do with it?«

»Do you think it a clever question?« the prefect had asked simply.

For a moment they sat in absolute silence. Then the phone had rung and held Ben back from a much too brash response. The archbishop from Calcutta himself was on the phone and had reported about a bizarre death in a tiny church in Motijheel.

Sister Bernadette had been right. Chances were slim that Father Raj could shed any light at all on the body's disappearance, but perhaps he could tell them something that might help them further. Besides, Ben had wanted to examine the crime scene right away anyway.

They made their way to the quarter where the little church was located. Ben had insisted that they take the exact route that Sister Bernadette and Sister Silvia had taken that day.

They walked through the slums in which thousands of people rented tiny, windowless cottages without running water, sanitation or even the ability to cook anything. Unfiltered water only flowed through the public pipes at certain times of the day. The rain and waste water from the cisterns that the people needed to use to wash their clothes and themselves was, out of bare necessity, used by the animals too.

Sister Bernadette told him about the fate of a rickshaw driver who could no longer pay his buggy's rent and therefore lost his job. He then had no money to pay for his sick wife's medical treatments. The rickshaw driver basically gave up, retreated to his

modest home and took his own life. Unfortunately, Sister Bernadette only learned of the man's fate after he had committed
suicide.

On the way through the slums, the missionary told him that
many people here lived mainly off the things they found in the
dump and sold to the factories. Fragments of leather, rubber,
junk, plastic, etc. Fewer than ten per cent of the slum dwellers
could read and write. A lot of men escaped through alcohol,
leaving the women to carry the entire burden of their children
and their husbands. The terrible living conditions and signs of
famine and malnutrition led to further diseases such as cholera,
malaria or tuberculosis. A real devil's circle.

During the taxi ride to Shanti Nagar, Ben had seen how many
people live on the streets. The driver had told him that power
outages of up to several hours were quite common in Calcutta.
The city could no longer manage its twelve million inhabitants
with thousands more arriving daily. The impact of the city's
overpopulation was overwhelming. More and more industries
were leaving Calcutta and, as Ben found out, fewer and fewer
airlines were landing here, which meant the city was losing its
international lifeline. Nonetheless, Calcutta was not a dying city
as many liked to claim. Life went on. Everywhere.

»We are almost there,« said Sister Bernadette, pointing straight
ahead. »You see. There it is!«

Ben recognised the tiny, simple church in front of them. They
crossed the overcrowded market with its abundant offerings that
stood in the front courtyard of the Lord's house. Ben had never
seen so many people in such a tiny space before.

47

Rome, The Vatican, Apostolic Palace

Catherine had once again withdrawn to the rooftop garden with her laptop in tow while the Pope met with His Eminence Cardinal Gasperetti and Monsignor Massini. As far as she knew, the head of the Curia was unsettled and the cardinal hoped to get answers to some of his more pressing questions in order to placate his colleagues.

Catherine didn't know what to make of Gasperetti. On the one hand he exuded such calm and optimism. On the other she thought she might sense a deep division within his soul. But he seemed to belong to the good side in the game for power. If Darius hadn't taught her to control her gift and not invade others' privacy, she might have risked taking a quick look at his aura.

She placed her laptop on a small garden table and opened it. It seemed crazy to her that, as a proclaimed heretic, she would be working on her latest book right in the heart of the Catholic world. Her current chapter was about the term hell and its holy purpose of intimidation. The high prefects before whom she had stood in the court would most likely suffer a heart attack if they got wind of it.

Catherine had just referred to the Germanic origins, the goddess Hel and her protected kingdom of the dead, when her surroundings changed dramatically. The garden table upon which her laptop had once stood was now replaced with a decorated table at which several men and women sat. At the same moment she realised it was the Passover meal from the Old Testament that was later replaced through the New Covenant by the Last Supper in the New Testament. It was here that Jesus had first introduced the Eucharist.

One of the men sat next to a beautiful woman. He took the bread, blessed it and spoke: »Take and eat, then this bread is like my body.« Then he grasped a cup of wine, spoke a blessing and passed it around. »This is my blood, the blood of the New Covenant that will be spilled for many.«

Catherine recognised the man who broke the bread and passed the cup. It was the anointed. The air was filled with tension. They barely said a word. Everyone ate and remained silent. She recognised the man among the twelve apostles who had introduced himself as Judas Iscariot. He looked at her and seemed to recognise her as well. Judas was noticeably tense. Catherine knew all too well why: he had drawn the lot of traitor and had accepted it, whether he liked it or not.

She examined the group and suddenly recognised two additional men at the table: Benelli and Darius! Both seemed as unhappy as Judas Iscariot. They too seemed to see Catherine. By God what did the cardinal and the priest have to do with the Last Supper?

The anointed took a piece of bread, dipped it in the wine and passed it to Judas as an agreed signal.

»Do what you must – and do it quickly.«

Judas took a bite of the wine-drenched bread, got up and left the room without looking back.

The anointed immediately began the Last Supper. But Catherine knew, because Judas was in truth not a traitor, the anointed had ensured that he too had drunk the blood of the New Covenant…

She felt someone shaking her gently. »Sister? Can you hear me?«

She blinked, opening her eyes to the outside world. She noticed with alarm that she was lying on the ground. Cardinal Ciban knelt before her and carefully helped her sit up. She blinked again, pulling herself together.

»I…I don't remember falling down.«

»Thank God you didn't hurt yourself.« The prefect helped her into a chair. The laptop was still sitting where she had left it, untouched. »It seems to me that your dreams are becoming more and more unpredictable.«

Catherine noticed that he was still holding her hand. She pulled it away, perhaps a tad too hastily. She glanced at his strong, slender hands. In that moment, she realised that Ciban didn't just sit at his desk all day.

»Thank you. I'm alright. I…everything's under control. I'm afraid my imagination has gotten the best of me lately.«

The prefect shook his head. »The situation is getting more and more dangerous. Not just for His Holiness, but also for you.«

»I'll get through it,« she said with determination. »I ask of you just one thing: Don't watch my every move.«

Ciban hesitated for a moment before saying: »Will you do me a favour, Sister?«

It was Catherine's turn to hesitate. »That depends, Eminence.«

The cardinal's lips curled into a brief smile of resignation as if he were thinking she is not just a nun, but also a pugnacious rebel. Catherine once again felt a strange, fluttering sensation in her stomach.

»Get some rest. It might be best to take a few days off. Listen to your inner voice. Take good care of yourself and His Holiness.«

Catherine nodded. »I will.« She gave herself a mental jolt. »Do you already know who the latest victim is?«

Ciban took a deep breath – and nodded. »Monsignor Hawlett is already in Calcutta to investigate the case.«

»Who is it?«

The prefect bent down and whispered in her ear.

»My God…« Catherine said quietly.

48

Calcutta, Church in Motijheel

Sister Bernadette rang the bell at the church's back entrance. A sign hung on the door that claimed the church was closed due to renovations. The noise of the market behind Ben raged on, making him wonder if Father Raj could even hear the doorbell. Then he heard several bolts being slid back and the door opened.

Father Raj was a small, haggard man even in Indian terms. He was about fifty, had grey hair and pitch black eyes. Sister Bernadette introduced the two men. The priest gave a friendly nod and asked them inside. The church's interior was rather dim and pleasantly cool.

»I presume you wish to examine the altar area where I found Sister Silvia,« said Father Raj with a wavering voice filled with grief and sorrow. Like Sister Bernadette he spoke English very well. He went ahead of them and brought them to the vestry.

»That is correct,« confirmed Ben. »But I think we have another problem entirely.«

The priest pricked his ears.

»Sister Silvia's body has disappeared from the morgue in Shanti Nagar. No one can tell us where it is. You haven't heard anything about its removal, have you?«

The priest shook his head with concern. »Perhaps His Eminence gave a specific order? You must know that Sister Silvia was treated like a saint here. She is Mother Teresa's unofficial successor.«

»The body's disappearance is as much a mystery to His Eminence as it is to Mother Superior.«

Priest Raj looked with dismay from Ben to Sister Bernadette back to Ben. »Does that mean the corpse was – stolen?«

»We don't know that yet. At the moment no one is able to tell us where it is right now.«

»We live in crazy times,« said Father Raj with a sigh, »in which one of our most loyal missionaries is murdered and then her body disappears into thin air.«

»I am certain we'll get to the bottom of it soon, Father,« Ben ensured him without believing it himself. »Should you hear anything at all, please let Mother Superior know right away.«

»Most certainly.«

»Where did you find the body, Father?«

Father Raj took a deep breath. »Come with me. Over here.«

They walked further through the vestry, entering the back area of the altar and went toward the scene of the crime. It was dark. Just a few candles illuminated the interior room. »Could you turn on the light?« asked Ben.

The priest shrugged his shoulders. »I beg your pardon, but we are having a power outage. I will light a few more candles for you. I can't do much more than that.« He disappeared briefly, returning with a few candles he then lit from the already burning ones and placed them amongst the others.

Ben reached into his suit jacket and retrieved a few photos. »As I understand it, you took these picture, Father?«

»Yes. I…« Father Raj stopped suddenly, his body wracked with the memory of it. »You see I don't much trust the local police and you can believe me when I say I have my reasons. Besides,

for the authorities the case is already closed shut. His Eminence
made sure of it.«

Ben compared the photographs with the cleared out altar area.
»She lay here then?« He pointed to a place at the end of a flat
step to the altar.

»Yes, exactly here.« The priest pointed to the place where the
murdered woman's head and feet had been found. »The entire
area was filled with candles. I've never seen anything like it. I first
had to clear a pathway to get to Sister Silvia.«

Ben exchanged a glance between the photos and the crime
scene. The blood analysis had shown Sister Silvia had been
anaesthetised with chloroform first, then most likely strangled.
The candle arrangement, however, made this crime scene stand
out completely from the others. Ben tried to find a sign in the
way the candles had been arranged. Father Raj had sent Ciban
an email with a sketch of the original arrangement. The rows of
candles had effectively given the deceased a massive halo. Or an
oversized aura.

»Did you notice anything suspicious?«

»No. Not that I know of at least. Sister Silvia and I had spoken
briefly that evening, right here...« He pointed to the first row
pew to the left of the altar. »We talked about a German charity
organisation that wanted to support Shanti Nagar, providing us
with new medications. When I left, Sister Silvia knelt back down
to pray.«

»And you didn't see anyone?« asked Ben further.

»Other than two women who left the church after their
prayers, no one else was here that evening.«

»After you and the two women had left, the murderer walked
through the front entrance, drugged Sister Silvia and took his
time killing her then?«

Father Raj gave him a horrified look. Even though it wasn't his fault about the nun's death, he was wracked with guilt. »I'm not sure, but I'm afraid it might have happened just as you said. I left the church once more to go shopping, you know.«

Ben nodded, gave it some thought and then looked down the middle aisle. »Is there another entrance to the church?«

»No. Just the main and back entrances through which we just entered.«

Ben took a few loud, echoing steps down the aisle, then returned to the missionary and the priest. »Are you certain?«

»Yes.«

Sister Bernadette thought out loud: »What about the old storage cellar? The underground entrance that runs beneath the market?«

Father Raj shook his head. »Impossible. One of the holy water basins stands over it. The entrance hasn't been used in years…«

»Show me the entrance please,« interrupted Ben.

Raj nodded and hurried ahead of them. They walked toward the entrance, then turned right where the holy water basin stood. The priest pointed to the floor – and faltered. The basin wasn't standing in the right place. Someone had moved it along with its base half a metre to the right. They could now clearly see the seams of a stone tile with an embedded handle. The entrance must have been used very recently.

Ben quickly exchanged glances with Sister Bernadette, then gave the handle a strong tug. It took him a second try before being able to move the tile off to the side.

The Monsignor, Sister Bernadette and Father Raj looked in surprise at a wide stone stairway leading into the dark depths below.

»Do you want to go down there now?« asked the priest uneasily.

»Why not? You don't happen to have a flashlight, do you?«

»No. But I can get you one of the candles.«

»Get two,« said Sister Bernadette. She turned to Ben: »I will go down there with you while Father Raj holds watch. Four eyes are better than two.«

49

For the rest of the afternoon Catherine stayed in her room, attempting to remain level headed and concentrate as much as possible on her book. Unfortunately, her encounter with Cardinal Ciban on the rooftop terrace kept her preoccupied. Despite her best efforts, she was unable to distance herself from the memory, not to mention completely forget about the entire matter. When he held her hand…well, she had never felt anything like it in her entire life!

She was in the process of telling herself to pull herself together because she was, after all, no longer a teenager, when another visionary daydream crept up on her.

She suddenly found herself at the foot of the Mount of Olives in Jerusalem in the Garden of Gethsemane in a circle of mostly sleeping male and female apostles while the anointed prayed alone under the olive trees. Several of the female apostles held watch near a fire.

After a while toward the middle of the night a troupe of soldiers armed with swords and clubs that the leading priests and the elders had sent arrived. Catherine recognised the head of the troupe: Judas Iscariot. Awoken by the troupe's loud arrival, the male apostles jumped to their feet. Peter courageously opposed the man. He took away one of the younger soldier's swords and wanted to start in on the other fighters when he heard the anointed's voice that reminded him of each person's fate and oath. He put down the sword.

The anointed turned to the soldiers and to Judas. »It is time. The darkness no longer holds power, although it is a dark hour now. We have drunk from the cup of the New Covenant and must now do what we must do. There is the man who will betray me.«

Catherine suddenly had the feeling that her body, even the entire region surrounding Gethsemane, was pulsating as if something deeper, something more timeless pervaded the place. It was an invisible force that somehow refrained from using its power. She could feel this power touching her consciousness. It was one of those moments in which one believes one is registering the order of things, the paper on which the entire history of the world is recorded.

The anointed walked calmly toward the troupe of soldiers, then remained standing in front of the captain and Judas Iscariot. Judas stepped forward and gave the anointed a brotherly kiss. Catherine could see how Judas and Jesus exchanged glances, along with the suffering in Judas' eyes. The words the anointed had just spoken weren't able to heal the traitor's pain.

»Are you Jesus of Nazareth?« asked the captain finally.

»Yes, I am,« replied the anointed with conviction.

50

Ben and Sister Bernadette descended the steps carefully. A cold, moist burst of wind slapped against them and it smelled like a tomb. At the foot of the stairs they reached a surprisingly large room with a vaulted ceiling. A corridor ran behind it. Old crates and pitchers stood along the walls and lay all around the dusty floor. Judging by their inherent patina, one could say they had been down here for a very long time and had survived many a monsoon. At some point, the objects were completely forgotten.

Ben carefully swung the candle around, looking at the ground. On the right side of the room he discovered multiple footprints in front of some boxes and four tiny round prints for which he didn't have an explanation quite yet. Upon examining their size, Ben thought the traces were most likely not from an Indian. Had Darius' murderer hung out down here?

»Look at this, Father,« said Sister Bernadette from the other side of the room. She held up an old, chair that had toppled over and had spilt its back near the boxes.

Ben slowly drew closer in order to take a better look in the poor light. The surface of the grubby chair had been wiped clean. Even the armrests and legs had been roughly wiped over. The chair appeared to have been in use rather recently.

»May I?« He grabbed the chair, returned to the footprints on the other side of the room and placed the legs directly on the place where the prints were. They fit perfectly. Next to the prints he noticed a second set of smaller footprints. He could feel his stomach hurl. It appeared that the murderer had anaesthetised Sister Silvia and dragged her down here. But why hadn't he simply cleared his tracks down here? Was he so certain that no one would remember the secret trap door? Or had he simply left the church after the act through the front entrance?

»I see candle remains on the floor here,« said the missionary. »I wonder where the perpetrator got all these candles.«

Ben nodded to her. Sister Bernadette had hit the nail on the head. They looked around, went to the boxes in the dim candle-light, but at first glance none appeared to be open. He approached one of the boxes lying on the ground and lifted the half-rotten wooden lid. He had barely touched the lid when the wood broke in two, allowing dozens of candles to roll out onto the floor.

»Well, that answers one question,« said Sister Bernadette, lighting several of them to provide more light.

They searched the room some more. After finding nothing, they walked along the back corridor.

»No footprints,« said Ben quietly as he led the way. A somewhat fresh, warm breeze blew passed them both. With every metre the air seemed less stuffy. The path was on a slight incline. Ben had to make sure the breeze didn't blow out his candles. Shortly thereafter, they reached a tall, heavy, locked wooden door that wasn't quite sealed.

»I can't be certain,« explained Sister Bernadette, »but my guess is we are on the other side of the marketplace in one of the rear courtyards. There is an old floor plan of the church. The corridor is most likely shown on it. Father Raj will certainly let us take a look at it.«

»Thank you, Sister. But it appears that the murderer didn't come through here. Do you see the cobwebs? This door hasn't been opened in years.«

They returned to the cellar vault and blew out the candles they had left there. Ben wanted to turn on his heel and go up the steps in disappointment when something caught his eye on the floor between two boxes. »I think I've found something, Sister.«

The missionary leaned forward with her candle, followed his vision and raised an eyebrow. »A cigarette butt...«

Ben nodded. »It doesn't look like the butt has been down here long.« He pushed one of the smaller boxes to the side, reached into the interior of his jacket, pulled out a plastic bag, knelt down and manoeuvred his findings into it without touching the butt itself.

Sister Bernadette gasped. »Do you think Sister Silvia's murderer had taken a cigarette break?«

»I hope so. Because if he did, we would have both his cigarette brand and most likely his DNA too.«

They ascended the stone steps and returned to the church's entrance area. It looked as though Father Raj hadn't budged the entire time they were gone.

»Well?« asked the priest.

Ben showed him the plastic bag. »Someone has been down there very recently. Besides there are a few boxes lying around whose contents you may wish to check out.«

Father Raj nodded. »I will ask one of my helpers to do so. I don't like tiny dark spaces very much.«

»I see. Sister Bernadette said there might be a floor plan of the church's underground?«

»From the secret trap door?«

»Yes.«

Father Raj seemed slightly ashamed because he hadn't thought of it himself already. »We did indeed have one. I'll see if I can go find it. If not...the archdioceses should have a copy of the floor plan. I'll let you know.«

»Very well, Father. We'll return to Shanti Nagar now. Perhaps there is news as to the corpse's whereabouts. Would you please call us a taxi?«

The cleric shrugged his shoulders apologetically. »We still have a power outage, I'm afraid. But I will send one of my helpers to fetch one for you.« He disappeared in the direction of the vestry.

Sister Bernadette sighed, saying to Ben: »Do you know what I just can't understand, Monsignor?«

He wasn't certain so he shook his head silently.

»The murderer's motive. Sister Silvia has never had a single enemy. The murderer must be insane.«

51

Catherine peered through her reddened eyes at the imposing marble-covered interior room of St. Peter's Basilica. She was looking for a distraction and a respite from the increasingly intense dreams that overcame her more and more. She had followed a winding path from the Apostolic Palace that led directly to the church. Cleaners were in the process of sweeping the Basilica after the daily throng of tourists. Catherine enjoyed the workers' activity in concert with the immense room's peacefulness.

She walked the Basilica's entire circuit. She paused beneath Michelangelo's weighty dome and read the two metre high letters from St. Matthew's Gospel: »Tu es Petrus et super hanc petram aedificabo ecclesiam meam et tibi dabo claves regni caelorum – You are Peter and on this rock I will build my church, and I will give you the keys to the kingdom of heaven.« Through her visions the true meaning of these words along with the anointed's crucifixion seemed to become clearer.

The crucifixion…just the thought of it filled her with outrage. She had once read during her studies that the nail through the wrist hit the Nervus medianus, the largest nerve that runs through the hand, thereby destroying it. The pain must have been indescribable. The Romans had even created a new word for it: excruciare, which literally meant »from the cross«.

Hollywood had shown the anointed's final breath in multiple monumental films: Jesus' head, falling onto his breast, followed by a gigantic lightning bolt that split the darkness and an ear-deafening thunderclap. Catherine still had this vision ahead of her as the last one had brought her to the mountain of Galilee upon which the risen Jesus had spoken to his disciples. The young woman had recognised Benelli and Darius and she was quite certain that Sylvester and Isabella were also present. Hadn't there also been a female figure in a blue and white sari?

»Peace be with you,« said the voice of the anointed on the mountain. »Our mission is not yet over. My journey on Earth has ended whilst yours has just begun. Forget not that the powers of heaven and Earth are with you. So go and create peace amongst the people. Teach them everything that the heavenly light has taught us and forget not that you are with the people all the days until the world's end, as are the shadows...«

»No shadows without light, no light without shadows. The seductive power of the apocalypse,« Catherine could suddenly hear Benelli's voice next to her. »You reminded us all of that in your last publication, Sister.«

The scene changed. Catherine was seamlessly witness to Judas Iscariot's desperate suicide. Joseph of Arimathea retrieved his body along with the anointed's. She saw the carefully rolled together scrolls that they had discovered in Judas' robe.

The scrolls...what did they mean?

Benelli motioned to her to follow him. Together they walked to the edge of the field of blood. In the middle of the landscape they passed through a door that led them to a room with mountains of files and documents and a large steel cabinet.

»We are in the Tower of the Winds,« explained the old cardinal as he pulled out a key from his robe and opened the heavy cabinet. Catherine knew that the Tower of the Winds was a part of the Vatican's secret archives. Only a few of the consecrated were even allowed to enter. Cardinal Ciban most definitely had permission. She most definitely did not. Pope Gregory XIII had built the tower as an observatory in the sixteenth century. The Gregorian calendar reform originated here.

»Here it is!« Benelli pulled out a little red book with gold letters from the cabinet and showed it to her. Catherine randomly noticed that although it was night outside the walls and there was no electric light in the Tower of the Winds, she could see as well as if it were daylight! The cardinal held the book up to her, but the vision began to dissolve in that very moment. Benelli, the files, the documents and the steel cabinet got blurry as if they were behind a moving wall of water. Before the dream completely disappeared, she was able to catch the title of the book: The Book of Acts.

Catherine turned her gaze back to the Basilica's interior and returned to the winding path to the Apostolic Palace. When she got to her room, the last dream sequence wouldn't let her be. The Book of Acts. That was the name of one of the Acts of the Apostle from the New Testament. But what had Benelli wanted to tell her about it?

52

Ben looked around Sister Silvia's tiny cell. Of course her corpse hadn't resurfaced and no one had a clue where it could have disappeared to. Not even Sister Bernadette or Mother Superior. Could the corpse have revealed something to Ben that would have led him to the murderer?

Ben sighed. He had heard about the corpse traders in Calcutta that collected all the human and animal corpses that lay about the streets in the entire city and did God knows what with them. A flourishing industry that partially replaced the vultures, rats and starving dogs, thereby keeping a few epidemics at bay. Should Sister Silvia have fallen into the hands of such a trader, there was most likely nothing left of her except her shroud. Most likely, however, the murdered body had already been burned somewhere.

Ben opened the wardrobe that contained nothing other than Sister Silvia's few pieces of clothing. Two neatly folded Saris, a second pair of sandals, the usual stuff. It was true what Sister Bernadette had said. The missionary had placed no value on material possessions. She had come to peace with all things worldly. Including her family. Ben had yet to find a single photo of Silvia's parents, siblings or even friends. Her possessions were even sparser than Darius' had been. The nun lived solely for the mission and for the poor.

He closed the wardrobe again, made a routine scan under the bed and lifted the simple mattress. Nothing. He finally opened the tiny drawer of the narrow table that stood together with an old chair at the window.

For a moment he stood there paralysed as if he had had a serious déjà vu. It wasn't the black soft leather-bound Bible from Darius that he discovered in the drawer, but rather its counterpart.

He removed the volume from the drawer and noticed how his hand shook slightly. Then he sat down and opened the old book. It was obvious that it had been used often. The pages of the New Testament were well worn, especially those of the Acts of the Apostles. Following an impulse, he carefully flipped through the respective pages and could hardly believe his eyes. Many lines had been highlighted with a ruler. He started to read the highlighted passages. It appeared to be the exact verses that Darius had emphasised.

Silvia and Darius? Had they known one another and discussed these Bible verses? And if that were true…had Father Sylvester and Sister Isabella also owned the same Bible version?

A light bulb suddenly went on in Ben's head: LUKE! The evangelist Luke! The Gospel of Luke who had written the Acts of the Apostles! But what did the Gospel of Luke have to do with the murders, Lux Domini and the secret file LUKE?

Ben took a deep breath in an attempt not to lose his cool. He had the feeling he was close to solving the case although he knew his impression was wrong. He had a new clue at best. Nothing more. And following this clue could be life-threatening.

He swept his eyes over the Bible pages once again. Two lines jumped out at him in particular:

Acts 4:20 – »For we cannot but speak of what we have seen and heard.«

Acts 8:37 – »If you believe with all your heart, you may.«

There was no longer any doubt. The underlined text passages were more than just the readers' contemplative mood. They suggested a type of commonality between them.

Ben snapped the book shut and pocketed it. Cardinal Ciban would most likely remain stubborn and reveal nothing of what he knew, but perhaps Catherine would be able to recognise the hidden meaning behind the highlighted passages.

53

The master sat back in his comfortable chair on the veranda and swept his gaze across nocturnal Rome. His hands, covered in snow-white paper-thin gloves, rested on Pope Leo's journal.

He couldn't find any further names of the papal congregation in Leo's private notes, which didn't surprise him, but they confirmed another one of his suspicious: this naïve idealist of a Pope, this daydreamer before God, actually planned a third Vatican Council.

The master thought with a great deal of unease about the harrowing consequences that the second Vatican Council had had on the Church. Although the cardinals of the Roman Curia, especially Popes such as Paul and Innocence, had been able to prevent the worst from happening, the post-Council crisis still had an effect to this day. There was no end in sight to the damage that these shockwaves had created. Clergy such as Catherine Bell were merely a product of this crisis. Leo's naivety was unfathomable. This Council had to be nipped in the bud! It was time that he, the master, take over behind the scenes.

He looked out over the stony edge of the veranda toward the seemingly close dome of St. Peter's Basilica. His expression grew dark. He still had yet to find out where Leo's sudden renewed energy came from. The success of his entire plan depended on finding the solution to this riddle. Time was running out!

For a brief moment he doubted his choice of murders, but he could absolutely trust Innocence on this one. The deceased pontiff and he had ruled the Church for two decades. They had been a nearly insurmountable stronghold against the modernists in their own ranks. Innocence had viewed the master as his successor. Everything had been arranged for the transfer of power. In part due to his powers of persuasion, Innocence had entrusted him on his deathbed with a few of the names in the secret congregation. Six names to be exact. He wasn't able to tell him the seventh. But for the master's plan, the six names that he did have were more than enough, at least for now. Their elimination had proven at first to be most effective. The reason for Leo's surprise recovery had to lie elsewhere. But where?

Were the murdered papal counsellors, these spirituals as his friend Innocence had always called them, been replaced? As far as the master knew, this had only happened a few times in the papacy in the past two thousand years. It usually took an additional conclave, a renewed covenant with the new Pope to release the necessary force for the papal congregation to regain its strength. The master had no concrete idea how it happened, but he knew that it did. It seemed to be as miraculous as the resurrection of Jesus Christ.

His house servant's subtle cough pulled him out of his dark thoughts. »Monsignor deRossi wishes to speak with you, Eminence.«

The master nodded and asked the house servant to accompany the priest to the veranda, carefully hiding Leo's journal and the paper-thin gloves in a side pocket of his comfortable chair. When deRossi entered, the master ordered a light meal and some good wine from the servant. His most capable student shouldn't submit his report on an empty stomach. Besides, it was easier to think more clearly, to chat and strategise over a good meal.

»Good evening, Eminence,« greeted deRossi.

The master pointed to a chair across from him. Strange. He thought he heard deRossi's heartbeat. Was there an issue? Did the mission in Calcutta fail? But as the Monsignor took a seat across from him, it was as if his protégé's accelerated heartbeat had never existed. In effect he was as cold as Ciban, but he had at least chosen the right master. He took a deep breath. The memory of such a deep disappointment that Marc Ciban had inflicted upon him rose up again like bile from his stomach. One could even say that what he had done was close to treason. The prefect had responsibilities first and foremost to the Church, not to some Pope who had lost all grip on reality.

»The mission is complete,« said deRossi calmly.

»Were there any…issues?« asked the master tactfully.

DeRossi looked around for the house servant. When he couldn't find him anywhere, he leaned in closer and whispered: »No. Not a single difficulty. But the corpse has disappeared and I have no idea where it is.«

The master hid his amazement.

»Are you certain?«

»Our agent in the archdiocese told me right before my flight.«

»Then Monsignor Hawlett stands before the exact same problem,« said the master calmly.

»I thought you might have an explanation for it, Eminence,« said deRossi in a whisper, leaning back once again in his chair. »Up to now, we have never had a missing body.«

The house servant returned with fresh white bread, cheese and wine. When he had left and closed the veranda door, the master explained: »You mustn't worry about a thing, Nicola. The corpse trade has a long history in Calcutta.«

»But a Catholic missionary?«

»We are all the same in death. Most certainly one of the colony residents sold the corpse in secret. There isn't a soul outside the quarter around Shanti Nagar who knows who the woman really was. Let us enjoy our meal and talk of the future.«

They ate in silence, each lost in his own thoughts. Every now and then the house servant came to check on them and would disappear again. When they had finished their meal, the master finally said: »Your next mission is going to be a challenge, Nicola.« DeRossi didn't blink an eye, appearing to be his normal self. »Your next operation is in the heart of the Catholic Church.« As if it were an ancient ritual, the master made a short note on a sketchpad, ripped off the top pages to prevent a carbon copy and handed it to his loyal protégé.

DeRossi stared at the page as if in a trance. This time it was none other than the director of the Vatican's Internet office: Sister Thea. »What is the timing?« he asked softly as if speaking to himself.

»Within the next thirty-six hours. You have free reign. Tomorrow I will be lunching with His Holiness and three other cardinals of the Roman Curia.«

The master didn't reveal the deeper meaning behind his meeting with the Pope. He himself had initiated the meeting to get behind the secret of Leo's miraculous recovery. It was quite possible that Benelli had pulled a few strings before his death.

Besides it was time to grill Cardinal Ciban. He still couldn't believe that, of all people, the prefect of the Congregation of the Doctrine of Faith had placed himself on the Pope's side. What did the man hope to achieve? Innocence had promoted Ciban, whose potential he had readily recognised, had made him the youngest member of the College of the Cardinals to strengthen the conservatives' fraction and now Ciban was striking back at the conservatives' power. And all because the Vatican's secret service had shut up a few overeager loudmouths in Italy, France

and Germany on the progressive side. And now the prefect had
to prove himself to be a moraliser as if he hadn't worked for the
secret service under Innocence, as if he didn't know what this
crusade was really about.

But what was even more interesting to the master was the fact
that Ciban knew about the secret as well as the running investigations. That could be most useful, if the younger cardinal were to
make a mistake.

The master poured himself and deRossi another glass of wine.
The sun had long since disappeared behind Rome's rooftops and
the city lights glimmered like a sea of stars weighing mightily on
the ground. The master would not allow Leo and his devilish
congregation to destroy the Church's centuries-old power.

54

Ben arrived to Rome in the middle of the night. The fifty-minute taxi ride from the Leonardo di Vinci airport to his flat was a dreary infinite loop past a monotonous, empty wasteland until they reached the edges of the city. When he got home, he placed his luggage down and fell straight into bed. He was dead asleep within seconds. Four hours later the alarm clock rang, tearing him out of a deep sleep. In order to clear his head, he made an extra strong coffee, took a cold shower and put on a fresh cassock. He burned his tongue on the coffee. He swore in a most non-Christlike manner, but at the moment he could care less, although he crossed himself automatically when doing so.

Then he sat down at his desk, opened the middle drawer and got out Darius' Bible to compare it to Silvia's. Both copies were indeed identical. They had even been published in the same year by an American publishing house.

Ben compared each highlighted section in the Gospel of Luke. He wasn't wrong: the underlines were exactly the same. He tried to recognise a code or a message in which he read each and every letter or word that appeared in specific intervals. No dice. He then wondered if the verses themselves had some kind of deeper meaning, independent of the text's regular context. He googled several of the highlighted verses. But even there he came up empty-handed aside from a number of cross references to the respective Bible verses and links to countless ominous forum posts.

Then he remembered that meeting with Ciban in which he forbade him to investigate the murder case any further. »Did you find anything unusual in Father Darius' belongings?« the cardinal had asked. Ben had denied it, but now he was certain that Ciban must have meant Darius' Bible. He had to speak with Catherine as soon as possible because if the prefect learned of both Bibles, he would once again take him off the case. Lux Domini was somehow behind this devilish matter even if it wasn't the original cause. And Ciban seemed to be covering for Lux.

Ben grabbed his briefcase with the report for the cardinal and made his way to the Vatican. Fifteen minutes later he entered the headquarters of the Congregation of the Doctrine of Faith, ran up the well-worn steps to Ciban's office and met Rinaldo in the antechamber.

»You are out of luck, Father,« said the young man, shaking his head. »His Eminence has been gone all morning. Right now he is sharing a meal with His Holiness.«

»When will he return?«

»He didn't say. It sounded like an unusual meeting.«

Ben looked at Rinaldo's right hand at the envelope he was holding. »Now don't tell me this is the same envelope that you were carrying around with you just a few days ago.«

The young priest gave him a slanted grin. »If that were the case, my esteemed colleague, then His Eminence would have long since fired me. Did someone order you here?«

»As a matter of fact, yes. I will try again later.«

Rinaldo nodded. »I must return to the archive. Good luck.«

When Ben entered his own office, he first opened all the windows. He had the feeling he might suffocate at any moment if he didn't let in a little fresh air, even if Rome's air quality was really quite poor. He placed the briefcase behind the desk and switched on the computer to check his emails.

There wasn't a single message from Ciban. Not even an encrypted one. The modern Inquisition had a special encryption programme for special messages that were absolutely not hackable. After Ben had read and answered the most important emails, he quickly ran through his archived private messages on his Internet provider. Catherine had written him a message only a few hours ago. She had had some more »dreams«. At the end she told Ben about something that made him gasp for air. Cardinal Benelli had shown her The Book of Acts.

It suddenly made sense in Ben's head. Darius' Bible! In addition to the Gospel of Luke there was an apostle's story of Luke, also known as The Book of Acts!

He looked at the clock. Darn! He wouldn't have a chance to chat with Catherine at the Apostolic Palace at this hour. He went through a series of possible meeting points in his mind that were not outside the Vatican walls. The best thing would be to meet tonight at St. Peter's tomb. He sent her a text message. He would now have to wait until he spoke with Catherine. Anything else would be too risky. He didn't even know if he could still trust Ciban.

55

Catherine had hardly slept all night. The dreams had barely given her two hours of peace. It appeared that the recollections in Benelli's mind that had somehow passed on to her through their energy transmission were fighting their way through her subconscious. She had once again had fragmented dreams about the anointed and his twelve disciples, mostly in a wakeful state. Whatever the dead cardinal had done to her to ensure she could strengthen the Pope, it now made her see things that she couldn't understand and utterly confused her. The disciples in her visions were other powers than those she knew from the Bible. What did this red book in the cabinet that Benelli had already shown her three times have to do with her mission?

In the wee morning hours she had met Sister Thea, dressed in a black hooded robe, in the Vatican gardens. When she began her duties in the papal household, she learned, thanks to one of her nun colleagues, about a sudden meeting between Pope Leo and several of the Cardinals of the Curia in the papal dining room. Several of the nuns had prepared a rich French meal in the morning and arranged for the respective drink selection at the table. Just as Catherine had finished her duties and wanted to leave, Leo asked her to be present at the meeting, disguised as one of the serving nuns that brought the food and saw to it that the light and somewhat stronger drinks didn't run out. The Pope was certain her presence would help at the pending meeting. He was still suffering from shock after his last collapse. As the head of the Church he couldn't afford to show the slightest sign of weakness.

Cardinal Ricardo, the head of the Vatican bank, was the first to appear in the papal living area. Then came Cardinals Gasperetti and Monti whom Catherine had met during the reception at the Benelli villa. Right before the meal was served, Cardinal Ciban arrived. He gave Catherine a brief, inconspicuous look filled with a slight surprise, then took a seat with the other cardinals and Leo at the table.

It was the first – and most likely the last – time that Catherine was witness to such a secret consistory. She would most likely get to hear things that no outsider ever would. The situation must have made Ciban most unsettled. The other cardinals paid no attention to either her or the other serving nuns. No one seemed to recognise her in the heavy clothing and thick glasses.

After praying, the cardinals ate together with the Pope. Catherine noticed that the group had known each other a long time. During their conversation about top Vatican politics, no one felt the need to play games. Gasperetti and Monti in particular laid their political views as a counterweight to Leo's perspective politely, yet firmly on the table. From the outside, it appeared the group had no animosities toward one another, even if Catherine could sense a certain level of tension.

»In the interests of the Church, we should be careful with such claims,« said Gasperetti, turning to Ciban with a slightly scornful tone: »You haven't said much today, Marc. Or have we already risked our necks with careless talk in your eyes?«

»We shouldn't throw the baby out with the bathwater, Steffano. I am quite familiar with the list of evils against which our Church has to struggle, including old and many new tyrannies.«

»Do I sense a mutiny?« asked Cardinal Ricardo with a roguish grin. »That isn't like you.«

»In what way, Leonardo?«

»In every way, if you ask me.«

Ciban laughed. He had an extraordinarily pleasant laugh. »One to zero. Your point. Is there any way for me to escape your judgement?«

»Well then I have no doubt that you already see this possibility.«

Catherine went around the table, pouring more wine. When she refilled Monti's glass, he suddenly asked her: »What do you think of all this, Sister?«

She was just able to catch herself before spilling wine all over the cardinal's robe. Even at the reception she had found his presence to be extremely unpleasant. Bringing her voice down an octave, she replied: »I beg your pardon, Eminence, but I know nothing about politics. It is a completely foreign world to me.«

Monti accepted her response with a generous smile, but he wouldn't let her go so fast. »You must be new here, Sister. I don't remember having ever seen you in the papal household before. Where are you from?«

»From Maine,« said Catherine, moving on to Gasperetti's wine glass. She had spent some time with relatives in Maine as a child because her mother had needed to stay in hospital after a difficult operation. Back then she had known nothing about Darius or the Institute's existence.

Gasperetti said: »I spent my last holiday in Maine. A beautiful area.«

»Oh yes, it most definitely is, Eminence.« Although Gasperetti seemed relaxed and friendly, his presence made Catherine feel extremely ill at ease. Or was this uneasy feeling simply coming from the fact that he had unexpectedly responded to her comment? »Especially in the fall.«

Gasperetti nodded. »That's true. The Indian summer in New England is one of the most beautiful I've ever seen. And believe me when I say I've seen quite of few of them in my lifetime.«

Catherine shifted her weight from one foot to the other. It could very well be that Gasperetti didn't buy her story about Maine. On the other hand, what could make him doubt it? »If you would excuse me. The buffet…«

»But of course, Sister,« replied the cardinal calmly. »We wouldn't want to embarrass you. Please excuse our curiosity.«

Catherine accepted the apology with a silent nod and hurried back to the buffet with her heart racing. She acted as if she was helping one of the nuns by cleaning up and seeing that everything was in order. In reality she had to fight off an inexplicably strong feeling of anxiety just like the encounter with Monsignor deRossi in front of the chapel in Benelli's villa.

After she had completed her work at the buffet and turned back to the large dining table, she played with the idea of applying her gift to see the group's aura. But at the present moment it would have taken her too much energy afterwards to protect herself from their radiance. To let the mental shield fall was quite easy. It was like dropping water from a tall mountaintop. But to build the protective shield back up took enormous strength. Catherine hadn't let the shield fall since she had turned her back on Lux. And she had never regretted it for a single moment.

But perhaps she would be able to risk taking a quick, inconspicuous look through the shield?

She carefully felt her way through an entire series of protective veils surrounding her, step-by-step. With every veil she left behind, she came one step closer to the mental reality. Sometimes it seemed to her to be an inferno of both hot and cold, or no, more like a swirl of smoke made of darkness and light. Halfway

through she took pause. She could go here and no further if she
didn't want to lose control. From this distance she couldn't see
very well because there were still quite a few veils between her
and the auras, but it was better than nothing.

She looked at the table at which the Pope sat with his cardinals.
Everything appeared to be dipped in an oddly exaggerated
atmosphere as if looking through night vision goggles. Even the
furniture looked as if it were exuding slightly crackling radiation.
Catherine was reminded of the bizarre photo gallery of the
»Corona« project at the Institute that she had seen as a child.
Only this obscure exploration wasn't nearly as colourful.

Leo's aura was a mild blue and white as far as Catherine could
tell. Monti's body was covered in a red light with a bit of yellow
and orange-coloured bits. It was a very selfish, strong aura. A
smaller, flamboyant light storm containing all ranges of colour
raged around Ricardo while Gasperetti's aura looked like that of
a tiger, ready to pounce at any given moment. She wondered why
the cardinal sat ready to ambush. But perhaps that was what had
made her so fearful and she had thought it was all about her.

She looked over to Ciban's chair, only to discover to her dismay that it was empty.

»Retreat slowly, Sister, before Cardinal Gasperetti notices your
exploration.« Ciban's voice was barely a whisper in her ear, but
its powerful tone commanded respect. He had come up next to
her to serve himself at the buffet without her even noticing. »For
him life is about fighting. He is one of the Lux leaders. He knows
every detail of your file, not to mention your mental powers.«

Catherine held her breath for a moment. Had Ciban been able
to register her careful exploration? Did he have psychic powers
too? It seemed more and more likely that he too had been a
product of the Lux institutes.

Protected by the prefect, she retreated from her exploration veil for veil. When she had halfway collected herself and had the situation back under control, Ciban asked rather loudly and lively which type of fruit she might advise for dessert. She suggested the fruits from one of the Roman plantations as they had been freshly picked and tasted delicious. Ciban thanked her, gave her a warning, yet calming look and returned to his place at the Pope's table.

It was only later when Catherine was back in her room that she realised the cardinal had not only wanted to save her the embarrassment of being exposed, but that he too in his elegant manner wanted to evade her exploration. There was no doubt about it. He too was a psychic.

She realised something else in that moment too: Ciban knew virtually everything about her and she knew next to nothing about him. She couldn't say she liked it. Of course a lot of stories about the prefect shot through her mind, but they were only stories circulating all around Rome and the Vatican. You had to take what the media said with a grain of salt anyway.

All she knew for certain was that His Holiness trusted Ciban. But what was now more important to her was whether Benelli had trusted the prefect. What had the white-haired cardinal meant during the reception when he had told her and Ciban: »After all, it isn't the mind, but rather the heart that connects equals, right?«

She sighed because she had no idea anyway what she should think. She somehow had the feeling that fate was more than challenging her through Benelli's invention and that she hadn't stood a chance to do anything about it in the first place.

Catherine got up, went to her desk and grabbed her mobile phone to check if she had any messages.

To her delight she discovered a text message from Ben in her inbox.

56

DeRossi left the computer on, running out of his sick colleague's office into the hallway and back into his own around the corner. At the same time a troupe of Vigilanza appeared from the lift on the other side, storming the tiny room on the first floor of the Apostolic Palace.

The Monsignor immediately sat back down at his desk that was piled with so many files that it appeared as if he had been working hard the entire time and had not moved.

That was a close call. Too close. He hadn't even been able to find out anything anonymously that he had wanted to from his sick colleague's computer. What was behind this darn LUKE? Why had that wimp Hawlett asked the young priest to search for the term in the Lux database? Because the young priest had come across it during his investigations, LUKE must have something to do with deRossi's jobs. With the master's mission.

There was a knock at the door.

»Come in!« he said without allowing his inner turmoil to shine through.

»Pardon the interruption, Father,« said one of the Vatican policemen as he entered the room. »Have you noticed anything suspicious in the past few minutes?«

DeRossi looked up from his files with tired eyes. »Pardon? Why would you think I could have noticed anything suspicious here?«

»Did someone just run down the hallway?«

DeRossi shook his head. »I haven't left the room all morning.«

»Who usually works in the office on the other side of the hallway next to the lift?«

»Monsignor Bloch. Why?«

»Have you already seen the Monsignor today?«

»No.« DeRossi pointed to the mountain of papers in front of him. »If you would excuse me, please. I really have a lot of work to do. If you'd like, I can give Monsignor Bloch a message as soon as I see him.«

»Thank you, Father. That won't be necessary.«

The Vatican policemen left the Monsignor's office, closing the door behind him. DeRossi blew out the air in his lungs and leaned back in his chair. The Vigilanza had gotten there faster than he had anticipated. Lux obviously had very solid connections. Or the Vatican police had been alerted to Abel's breaking into the Lux database. He relaxed his expression. Now it would be Bloch's problem and then the spy's trail would dead end. Alright then. His attempt to find something out about LUKE had failed, but he ultimately had better things to do.

He fished out one of the files from the chaos on his desk that no one would ever have expected to be there if he hadn't know of its existence. The binder contained everything he needed to know about Sister Thea and her habits. The director of the Vatican's Internet office had a rather impressive résumé for a woman. Through his research deRossi had discovered she had an unusual hobby that she practiced under a pseudonym. Sister Thea loved to draw caricatures with ironic commentaries. She stopped at nothing even with the cardinals such as Gasperetti and Monti. Even Pope Innocence had come under fire in one of her most brilliant pieces of artwork. The caricature showed a heroic Pope standing on one of the seven hills of Rome, swinging an enormous banner with his papal coat of arms and screaming at the top of his lungs: »Follow me!« In truth only a handful of prelates followed him while the rest of the Congregation of the Doctrine of Faith walked in the opposite direction toward the future.

As predicted, deRossi had seen Sister Thea in the Vatican gardens this morning with that unholy rebel Sister Catherine over whom the Congregation sat in judgement. Both women remained in front of the Grotta di Lourdes as if they had seen a ghost. Well then, both Sister Thea and Sister Catherine had quite an imagination.

DeRossi looked at the clock. Half of his time was up and his plan to eliminate the Internet office director was still not fully in place. If only he had already discovered what LUKE meant.

57

Ben entered St. Peter's Basilica through one of the side gates. Tourists and pilgrims were milling around, impressed by the architectonic and spiritual splendour in the gigantic church. The apse and chapel of the Cattedra were blocked off for Mass. Some of the confessionals in which the usual languages were spoken were occupied by confessors.

Ben paid no attention to either the apse or the enormous papal tombstones. He knelt down briefly at the main altar. He stopped in front of the grottos' entrance somewhat away from the papal altar. He hadn't seen Cardinal Ciban for the rest of the day. Instead he had handed in his report for the prefect in a sealed envelope to the Secretariat and had made his way to meet Catherine.

Ben continued to look around the large church. No trace of Catherine. Just as he was about to give up the search, even though he could hardly believe she would ever blow him off, he noticed a chubby nun with horn-rimmed glasses near the confessionals. Holding a bouquet of flowers, she waddled toward him.

»Are you looking for Sister Catherine, Father?«

»Yes, Sister. Could you tell me where she is?«

The chubby nun scrunched her nose. Ben noticed the horrific wart on her face. Were there two hairs sprouting from it? It took all his strength to pull his attention away from it.

»I should tell you that Sister Catherine is already here.«

»And where might that be?« He looked around discreetly.

»Right in front of you,« replied Catherine quietly in her own voice.

»What?« He gave the disfigured nun the once over. »You?«

Catherine laughed softly. »Cardinal Ciban arranged for the costume so that my presence in the papal household wouldn't cause a stir.« She threw a telling look through the cathedral hall. »Interesting meeting place.«

»It's about to get even more interesting.« Ben opened the door to the grottos. »There is an entrance to the tomb of St. Peter that is not open to the public. We can talk privately in the underground chapel without being disturbed.«

The young woman knew that St. Peter's Basilica would never have existed without the tomb of St. Peter. The cathedral's dome and the high altar with Bernini's canopy towered directly over the necropolis with the tomb of St. Peter.

They descended many tight, stony and badly lit stairs into the depths until they entered a low tunnel with raw brick walls. Catherine carefully followed Ben past several heavy iron gates that secured corridors off the right and left. Most likely most of the side tunnels led to an old Roman cemetery that lay beneath St. Peter's Basilica. Ben finally stopped in front of one of the unofficial entrances, opened one of the iron doors and led his companion to a surprisingly large, cave-like room that looked like an underground chapel. A hidden light bathed the room in a surreal twilight-like atmosphere. Catherine could see two church pews at the edge of the semi-darkness.

»We are very close to the tomb of St. Peter,« explained Ben as he pointed to one of the naked, whitewashed walls. He placed the bag that he had brought with him onto the back pew.

»How's it going between you and the Pope?«

»It is going well. His Holiness is a very amiable human being. Only with every day that passes, I keep losing more and more of Benelli's energy and I'm not certain as to whether my own is enough to protect the Pope. What did you find out in Calcutta?«

»You know about it?«

Catherine nodded. »His Holiness suffered a collapse when Sister Silvia died. I felt it directly. Then I asked Cardinal Ciban about it.«

»Of course.« He understood. »The connection that Benelli created between you and His Holiness – What about your dreams? Are they still so…abstruse?«

»They couldn't be any crazier. Even your boss caught me daydreaming.« She told him about her visions, the encounter with Judas Iscariot on the Mount of Olives, her participation in the Last Supper, the betrayal of Jesus in the garden of Gethsemane, the crucifixion and resurrection and the fact that Sylvester, Isabella, Darius and Silvia had appeared to her in the form of the apostles in Jerusalem and Galilee. Up until now she had kept everything to herself, but now the words just spouted out of her as if a dam had been broken. After she was finished, Ben remained very quiet, so much so that she had to ask herself if he might question her sanity after all. She knew herself how crazy it all sounded, but she had truly experienced all of these visions and religious appearances as if they had been the most authentic of present realities.

»Have you made any notes about it?« Ben finally asked calmly.

»Heaven forbid, no.« Catherine nearly added, Do you think I'm crazy? »Why should I ever want to do that? To deliver the Roman Inquisition even more ammunition against me?«

»Your visions could be extremely important. Have you ever thought of that? You should document everything. Cardinal Benelli was everything but your average clergyman. Not to mention Darius and the others. Tell me about your dream about The Book of Acts.«

»There isn't much to tell really,« said Catherine, trying to regain a modicum of calm. »In effect it is always the same dream. Benelli is standing in the Tower of the Winds in front of a large cabinet, opens it and shows me this red book.« She had had this dream, more like a vision, three times now.

»Do you know its contents?«

Catherine shook her head. »All I get to see is the title. Nothing else. Shortly thereafter I hear a sound at the door and the dream ends.«

Ben thought for a moment, reached for his bag, pulled out a book and laid it next to Catherine on the pew. Her eyes grew big as saucers. Wasn't that Darius' Bible?

»Do you recognise this?« he asked.

»Of course,« she responded with a trembling voice. »Darius had promised to give it to you when you were still a boy.« She took the book in her hand, reverently caressing its surface. »I remember exactly how you used to stare at it.«

Ben reached inside his bag again and placed the identical copy of the Holy Scripture next to it. »This belonged to Sister Silvia,« he said breathlessly. He could literally feel Catherine holding her breath. »Wait for it.« He opened both Bibles to the Acts of the Apostles. »Take a closer look at both of these pages.«

She knelt down in front of the pew and placed both open books in front of her. She flipped through the Acts. After flipping back and forth, she realised that the highlighted passages were nearly identical. It started to dawn on her. Lost in thought, she said to Ben: »Do you think Father Sylvester and Sister Isabella owned a similar Bible?«

He nodded. »I'd bet my life on it. — Do you know what the Acts of the Apostles is also sometimes called?«

Catherine considered the question for a moment, then her eyes widened. »My God, The Book of Acts.«

Ben winked and nodded. »Cardinal Benelli most likely wanted you to take a closer look at this book.«

Catherine was prepared to study the Acts of the Apostles once again until she stopped after a few minutes to reconsider. »It makes no sense.«

Ben looked at her quizzically.

»Hardly anything that is in the Gospel of Luke,« she explained further, »has anything to do with my visions. To be more precise my visions aren't mentioned there at all.«

»And that means?« Ben pressed further as he witnessed her think further about the solution to the riddle.

Her answer came like a bolt from the blue.

»Cardinal Benelli didn't want us to examine this version of the Acts of the Apostles, but rather the one that is kept in the Tower of the Winds.«

»Do you think the version there is not identical to this one here?«

»I am most certain that both Bibles prove Silvia and Darius were somehow connected, but it is not only the highlighted passages that will show us the actual reason behind their connection.«

Ben could see how Catherine's eyes not only lit up, but were illuminated. What he couldn't see was that his companion now remembered the little package Benelli had gotten sent to her at the hotel directly after the reception in the villa. »This steel cabinet that I've seen in my dreams…«

»In which Benelli kept The Book of Acts?«

Catherine nodded tellingly. »I think I have the key to it!«

58

Monsignor deRossi looked over at the digital clock hanging on the wall in his office. Just a few minutes prior he had fed the final piece of paper from Sister Thea's files through the shredder.

In just half an hour he would catch the director of the Vatican's Internet office on her way to the Grotta di Lourdes as soon as she passed the Radio Vatican building toward the gardens. He hoped that the gentle rain that had since started wouldn't keep the nun from her regular walk. Habits, rituals…how much of our wellbeing depended on such things and how much easier such dependence made deRossi's work.

Because he had worked in the archives at one time, he wore the simple, black robe of an archivist. No one would pay him any mind as he slipped along the rain-drenched gardens with a hood over his head. Not even Sister Thea.

He checked the shredder's contents one last time to be certain nothing was left of the documents except confetti. He then started on his way, taking the seldom-used stairwell in the papal palace and rushing down to the underground parking garage. He followed one of the secret corridors that ran underneath the Vatican gardens. When he came above ground again near the helicopter pad, an almost surreal peace hung over the scenery. Even the constant noise of the Eternal City seemed to be off in the far distance, swaddled in a thick layer of cotton.

DeRossi pulled the hood over his head and walked toward the fake replica of the Lourdes cave where a statue of the Madonna took the place of the Marian apparition.

While he waited nearly invisibly near the Grotto, the encounter with Sister Silvia ran involuntarily through his mind. The image of her sleeping body, surrounded by a sea of candles. And once again he seemed to feel her ghostly touch.

Her forgiveness.

His breathing quickened, his heart began to pound like it did that night beneath the tiny, cursed church in Calcutta.

No. He simply couldn't allow Silvia to get between him and Sister Thea. She would do no more damage to him. She wouldn't prevent his mission!

He stared at the Madonna statue and crossed himself. Thea had forfeited her life and that long before he had entered his master's service. He would rid the Church of this woman!

59

It had been years since Catherine had been allowed to enter the Vatican's secret archives as a student. Of course back then she hadn't entered the areas that were truly off limits, but in those days she had forced her way into areas that most people would never have access to. Laws up to twelve hundred years old that were promulgated from the Holy See and the Vatican's diplomatic correspondence were housed in the secret archives along with files from the Inquisition. The archive encompassed up to eighty-five kilometres of shelf space with treasures such as Michelangelo's letters, the bull of excommunication from Martin Luther or the trial records during the court proceedings against Galileo Galilei.

The ancient shelves that Ben and she now passed reached the ceiling. Every now and then they would come across an archive worker, but since they knew Ben Hawlett and his close association with Ciban, they didn't think twice about him and his companion being there.

Catherine followed Ben through multiple long dark corridors whose shelves contained a gazillion volumes. As they passed the ceiling-high stacks, automatic lamps switched on and off. A slight musty smell wafting from the centuries old parchments, files and books filled her nose. Catherine recognised the red papal coat of arms on many of the bound books.

»You know your way around here,« she said to Ben.

He shrugged his shoulders. »Not as well as I'd like to. Father Dominico knows the archives very well. Cardinal Ciban also spends quite a bit of time here. I have learned a great deal from them both, but I'd like to learn more.«

He told her about the Tower of the Winds close to St. Peter's Basilica. Catherine already knew the five hundred year old story, but she was pleased to hear it again from him. The tower's history harks back to Pope Gregory XIII who needed a nearby observatory for his sky explorations and calendar reform. Thanks to Pope Gregory's stargazing and calculations, he introduced the Gregorian calendar that includes leap year and still applies today.

At the moment the tower housed centuries old political and spiritual secrets, to be exact that part of the Vatican's secret archives that had hardly been researched or even catalogued. Only the Pope and a select few cardinals had access to the archive, only reachable via a narrow staircase. Four months ago Ben was added to the chosen few as well because Ciban made certain he had access to help with certain secret investigative work.

Catherine seemed to remember hearing that the square tower contained information in particular that was only passed down from Pope to Pope. Darius had confided in her that in truth the tower contained mysteries that even many pontiffs had never heard of in the least. Some were only passed down from Grand Inquisitor to Grand Inquisitor.

After they had gone down several other long dark corridors along thousands of thick volumes resting on metal shelves, they entered a room that seemed more like a scholar's room than the office of prefect's deputy in the archives. The old priest who arose from his desk must be Dominico. He looked like the consummate archival mouse that Catherine knew from various Internet cartoons. She bet Domino's appearance served as the basis for such sketches. Many of the circulating Vatican cartoons were from Sister Thea's hand during her free time as Catherine had recently learned. She wondered if Ciban knew about it. If he did, he didn't let on that he did and took it in stride. Sister Thea had said at least that his good relationship with her had not suffered because of it. Whatever that meant.

Ben pulled out a letter from the prefect from his robe. It was a proxy that was based on a type of general papal proxy. Dominico glanced at it briefly as he was already familiar with the document and with Ben from his various visits. The old librarian returned to his desk with his index volume and two flashlights. At the sight of it, Catherine was reminded that there was no electric lighting in the Tower of the Winds.

»Thank you, Father,« said Ben, opening the guest book and signing in both Catherine and himself as visitors with the old archivist as witness.

Dominico handed them both flashlights and went before them. After walking through one of the dark corridors, passing once again countless shelves with files and index volumes, they entered the ground floor of the Tower of the Winds. A steep, narrow spiral staircase led them to the top regions of the most secret of all archives. Once again, Catherine could smell the musty, dusty damp smell of old parchment and files. Papal directives, trial records, prophecies, unofficially approved or recognised holy writings, centuries old ecclesiastic history lay sealed here since time immemorial.

Catherine, Ben and the priest came to a heavy old oak door. The most secret of all secrets were warehoused behind it on the top floor. The archivist unlocked the oak door and both visitors entered the room while the old librarian waited before it.

Two walls were decorated with frescoes. The winds were designed as godly figures in long flowing robes. A mosaic on the

floor showed all signs of the zodiac from Pisces to Aquarius. A
wind gauge hung from the centre of the ceiling, showing the air
streams. The device was connected to a weathervane installed on
the rooftop.

Ben walked along several shelf walls, then headed in the direction of two steel cabinets whose surfaces were so well-polished
and reflected the room's atmosphere so precisely that they appeared to be nearly invisible. Full of hope, he turned around to
Catherine. »Which one is it?«

The young woman shrugged her shoulders. »I have no idea. I
only ever saw one steel cabinet. We'll just have to try it out.« She
reached into her nun's habit and pulled out Benelli's key. She
went to the first cabinet, placed the key in the hole and tried to
open it. »Well, it's not this one. Next.« After trying the second
cabinet, they discovered with much surprise that it was neither of
the two.

»Odd,« said Catherine, scrunching her forehead. »Benelli's
instructions have never been wrong up to now.«

»They were visions. And visions are everything but precise
documentations. Perhaps you wrongly interpreted the location?
There are a lot of steel cabinets down here in the archives. Perhaps the cardinal had meant the archives in the Castel Sant'Angelo?«

Catherine shook her head. »No, Ben. It was here. In the Tower
of the Winds. Of that I am most certain. Give me a minute.« She
closed her eyes, recalled the vision and reflected for a long while
in silence. Ben didn't make a sound. »There's only one explanation,« she finally said.

»And that would be?«

»There is another steel cabinet down here somewhere.«

»Okay,« said Ben, thinking it was a hopeless case. »Let's go
take a look.«

They walked along the shelf walls, illuminating each aisle as they went. Catherine felt as if she were in the Grimm fairy tale Hansel and Gretel minus the breadcrumbs. Where could Benelli's steel cabinet be? And why didn't the Tower of the Winds have electric lighting? She asked Ben who told her it was with good reason that there was no lighting because a single ray of light would reveal if any unauthorised visitors were in the tower or if a fire broke out.

»There isn't another steel cabinet here,« said Ben finally. »But maybe a floor lower.«

They returned to the exit and knocked on the heavy oak door. Dominico opened it for them, accompanying them to the room beneath the Meridian room where he once again waited patiently for them. Catherine couldn't say exactly why, but the moment she entered the dim square-shaped room, she immediately knew they were in the right place.

They walked along an extremely narrow aisle between the stacks stuffed with thick tomes. The aisle ended in a sharp right. Suddenly they were standing in front of the steel cabinet that Catherine had seen in her vision.

She stepped forward, placed Benelli's key in the lock, and turned it. It clicked open.

Ben pulled open the heavy door. Various files were lying in it, but no red book. Instead they found a steel box on the otherwise empty middle shelf. »I'm afraid we need a second key,« he said.

Staring at the steel box herself, Catherine was torn between fascination and disappointment. Benelli hadn't shown her this. What should they do? Ask Father Dominico for a crowbar? How ridiculous! They now stood before the open steel cabinet and they couldn't get at the book!

She started to pace back and forth along the tiny, narrow aisle without noticing. In the darkness penetrated only by their flashlights, she could barely see what was stored on the shelves around them. But at the moment she could care less. Had the cardinal forgotten to mention the steel box in her vision? If only Benelli had been clearer.

Ben leaned patiently against one of the shelves and let her be. Somewhere deep down despite this setback he seemed to have a godly trust in their mission.

Catherine stopped in front of the steel cabinet. If Benelli had only given her this one key, it was most likely with good reason. But which? Was the book not even in the box? She began to scrutinise every single file and tome in the cabinet. She also looked to see if the red book was perhaps lying on one of the back shelves. Not a trace. Nothing. Clueless, she looked at the box. The book must be in there!

Ben said: »It isn't customary, but perhaps the thing isn't even locked.« He took the box out of the cabinet, place it on the ground and tried to open it. No dice. It was locked.

Wait – Catherine's eyes widened. What if they only needed one key? The key had belonged to Benelli. What if there were two keys in one?

She knelt before the box and stuck the key in the tiny lock. The lid jumped open with a dull click. Catherine gasped for air.

A letter! And beneath it…

Benelli's red book!

60

The master stood in the Sistine Chapel, the largest chapel of the Apostolic Palace, absorbing the spirituality that the walls, ceiling and floor exuded. In its dimensions the rectangular room with twenty metre high ceilings was inspired by the legendary historical temple of Solomon. The master's gaze rested for a while on Michelangelo's fresco The Last Judgement. It had taken the brilliant artist six years to finish. The fresco showed Christ and the Blessed Mother Maria surrounded by saints and angels. Just as God the Father had separated light from darkness, Christ separated good from evil. The work depicts the end of human history.

The master worshiped this place. He visited it in particular when he needed answers to nearly unanswerable questions. The Sistine had never once left him in a lurch in the matter. He walked peacefully along the northern wall of the Chapel until he reached the entrance wall with the scene of the resurrection. The resurrection…

It was almost as if Leo had arisen from the dead. During their shared meal the Pope showed no signs of physical or mental weakness. Quite the contrary. The master had carefully observed every one of the people present during the meal. None of the other cardinals he suspected seemed to have anything to do with Leo's recovery. Not even Ciban.

Where was the Pope receiving his newly acquired power?

The master thought once again about a premature, extraordinary revitalisation of the covenant of twelve. But it was impossible that after just a few weeks and months it could happen again so quickly. He couldn't recall a single instance in the covenant's two-thousand-year-old history that such an incident had ever been mentioned. For many years even Clemens VII had to make do with just seven spirituals after five of his advisors died during the plundering of Rome.

Alright then. If there had been no revitalisation of the covenant, what was the cause of the Holy Father's inexplicable recovery then?

The master changed sides, walking along the south wall of the Sistine with scenes from Moses' life while lost in thought.

Leo himself possessed no psychic powers. That much he knew to be true. Innocence had been just as clueless in that regard. The superhuman powers he needed for his difficult office as Pope came thanks to the covenant of twelve. Their spiritual energy expanded his consciousness. It was the basis for his strength of steel.

From the chronicles the master had quickly found out that the covenant led to a strong mental and physical dependency. Should one or more spirituals be eliminated such as through an unnatural, violent death without having passed on their energy to the rest of the covenant, the respective Pope would feel its loss in the most brutal and painful way that often led to disastrous consequences. It hadn't surprised the master when Leo was able to handle Sylvester's and Isabella's deaths without much trouble. There was after all a mental security zone. But as late as Darius' and Silvia's passing, the pontiff should not have been able to govern of his own accord, which meant in the best case he should have had to rely on his worldly advisors, especially himself, the master. But because it didn't happen that way, Leo must have found a new energy source. But who in God's name could the source be? Who would have the strength to replace four simultaneously eliminated members of the papal Congregation? Not even the master's erstwhile protégé Marc Ciban had such energy potential despite his extraordinary abilities. On the other hand the source, as strong as it may be, still had to be in the immediate vicinity of the Holy Father. But where?

The master did a mental run-through of all possible candidates without luck. He kept returning back to the prefect of the Congregation of the Doctrine of Faith. Even if Ciban weren't the source, he had something to do with it.

Then it suddenly occurred to the master what the single change in Leo's circle had been: the new wart-faced nun with the thick glasses in the papal household. She hadn't left Leo's side for the lunch's entire duration. As he stared up at the scene of the resurrection at the Sistine's entrance, he thought for a moment about the nun from Maine. He didn't even know her name. How could this simple nun help the Holy Father?

Well then, a quick investigation couldn't hurt. His thoughts jumped to Monsignor Massini who was so close to the action that he was able to swipe Leo's journal for two days without anyone noticing. Massini would certainly be able to report on the new nun at the papal court. With this thought the master passed the choir screen that separated the clergy from the laypeople in the Sistine Chapel. He was in good spirits. Even this time the Sistine had given him the answer to his question.

61

Ben had positioned the flashlights in such a way on the open steel cabinet and one of the side shelves so that they both had their hands free and could take their time examining the contents of the box.

Catherine took out the letter, opened it and withdrew three carefully folded bits of paper. When she unfolded them she recognised Benelli's buoyant handwriting. The letter was addressed to her. The old white-haired cardinal must have developed his plan that he shared with her in the villa's chapel and in her visions long before his death if he left Catherine a message even here.

Dear Catherine,

If you are reading this letter, then it means you are making great progress in your mission and my spiritual energy and message have reached you. The mental connection between you and His Holiness must also have worked.

I know I have expected a lot from you in the past few days. Your visions and dreams have confused you and sometimes brought you to the brink of despair. Please believe me I would have chosen another way if there had been one, but unfortunately the dark side has escalated the matter so much that I had no other choice.

You must be asking yourself about the book. Why I brought you here so you can get familiar with its contents. The answer is not simple, and I fear you won't understand it in its entirety until you are at the end of your mission.

What you are about to learn is only known to a few of the consecrated. Darius knew about the secret as well as Sylvester and Isabella. And now I think through your dreams and vision you have become one of the consecrated too and have earned the right to know about the true Book of Acts even if I can only give you access to this incomplete copy.

It is the Gospel of Judas Iscariot. He wrote it in his darkest hours and ensured that it wasn't lost to future generations. His testimony reached France with Maria Magdalene who as member of the council of twelve also knew about the secret. A replica of this copy was discovered nearly two thousand years later in four sealed hollow cylinders with parchment scrolls in a country church in Rennes-le-Château. The complete original had already been kept sealed in the Vatican's archives. Only the Popes, the Grand Inquisitors and the covenant of twelve knew back then and know today about this original.

Dear Catherine, the revelation of the secret will cost you a lot of energy and places the foundation of our faith in an entirely new light. It is a moving story as Judas Iscariot incarnate lived it ever since he was a little boy. For that reason the story is quite emotional at times. Judas had a much more sensitive heart that he would have ever admitted and so he pulled the lot as traitor amongst the twelve. But let me say straight away that it is not just the story of Judas Iscariot. It is also the story of the twelve. It is the history of those people that God sent out into the world with the New Testament to lead humanity out of the darkness.

Dear Catherine, as soon as you have studied this testimony, take it and my letter to His Holiness. He will understand the meaning of your consecration because he knows that that which is not seen is not an illusion. There are powers in this world that could not only destroy individual people, but all of humanity.

Please never forget: Good sometimes appears in the form of evil, and darkness appears none too little in the form of light.

Trust your heart.
  Trust your gift!

Your brother in Jesus Christ
  Antonio Benelli

Catherine handed Ben the final page without saying a word. When he had finished reading it, he handed her the entire letter and said with a note of scepticism: »The covenant of twelve? The Gospel of Judas Iscariot?«

Catherine met his look of doubt. She could understand his suspicion. He hadn't experienced these vivid, all-consuming and indescribable visions and dreams that had haunted her in the past few days. Catherine knew Benelli's energy had prevented her from being left completely exhausted after the dream sequences, not to mention being driven insane. She allowed the letter to disappear in her nun's habit and took the noble leather-bound book from the box.

»Let's have a look at what His Eminence has up his sleeve for us.«

She opened the first page and discovered a hand-written reference next to the seal that this book had once belonged to Pius XII.

Pius' lost secret library! Catherine had heard of the legend, but quite honestly she had never quite believe it. There were so many unbelievable myths that trailed through the Vatican like a maze and its secret archive. It was nearly impossible to separate the wheat from the chaff.

She noticed that Ben, who stood next to her and also recognised the seal, held his breath for a moment. The papal seal really could be proof that Benelli's announcement about the true Gospel of Judas was based on a foundation they should take seriously. An enormity that even Catherine, despite her visions, had to first digest.

She flipped to the next page and hastily scanned its lines.

You will be the Thirteenth.
You will be cursed by the other generations,
and you will come to rule over them.
(Gospel of Judas)

Catherine and Ben gave each other a brief look. Then they continued to flip to the next page. In the silence of the archives, they began to read.

62

Jerusalem, in the year 33 A.D.

From the Gospel of Judas

It was God's plan. And I, Judas Iscariot, liked His plan the least.

We walked the people's Earth and opened their eyes like newborns. Slowly at first. As we grew, we reminded ourselves of God's plan and the reason for our existence. So that light could come from darkness, we were cast from the light into the darkness. Gabriel was our only heavenly guide.

Maria Magdalene was the first to remember. She had the greatest insight into the will of God. She was our memory, our only crucial centre point. We have her to thank that we didn't fail in the end. Maria was always there where Gabriel couldn't be. Her light showed through. It showed me in particular the way through the deepest darkness.

The second one to remember was Jesus and the awareness of his fate filled him with anger and fury. One day he went through the village, full of rage and desperation, when a boy walking by grazed his shoulder. Full of bitterness, but also unintentionally, he spoke: »You should go no further on your way.« In that moment, the young boy fell down and died. It was the one and only time that one of us took someone's life. Up to that point none of us was aware of the power that ran through us. Jesus fell into such deep mourning over the boy that he forgot about his fear and wrath about his own fate for a while.

I was the third to remember. On that day when the boy died, I recognised my fate. I couldn't believe it. I had pulled the lot of traitor. Or did the traitor's lot pick me?

One after the other, all of us began to realise our tasks. Simon Peter was the fourth, followed by Andrew, Jacob and John. Finally Philip and Bartholomew joined us. Then the others. Just as rivers flow into the ocean, we flowed toward one another one by one to become that unity that brought the revelation to the people and fulfilled God's plan.

Maria often warned us: We are all God's instruments. We will all fulfil his plan. And so it shall be.

We did our duty after we had recognised our purpose and our gift. We left our homes and families. We went out and preached. People should do penance. We drove out many evil spirits, anointed the countless sick with oil and healed them. We fed Jesus, who had pulled the lot of the lamb, with our God given energy so that he could make the blind see again, the lame walk again and the dead live again. Then one thing was for certain: Words are not enough for people. They have to see deeds and miracles every now and again. At that time there were enough miracles to see. They helped spread the light.

We worked amongst the people for many years. We travelled and proclaimed the right way, healing people until that fateful day when I had to fulfil my lot in life, the lot of traitor.

Yes, it is true. I betrayed Jesus that night. I had to sacrifice the body that enshrouded his soul to fulfil God's plan. The salvation of humanity required a traitor.

Without betrayal, no crucifixion! Without crucifixion, no resurrection! Without resurrection, no salvation of mankind!

63

Catherine noticed how the reality surrounding her suddenly divided. She was still in the Tower of the Winds, watching Ben continue to read the Gospel of Judas, all the while looking over the shoulder of one very desperate Judas Iscariot as he hurriedly wrote down his testimony as if he had to finish that night. In effect she was experiencing the very thing her friend merely read in the old book.

She saw Judas Iscariot's aura too. A radiant blue-white laced with many fine blood red lines. She also saw how Judas walked at Jesus' side as the only person besides Maria and Jesus who understood the true meaning of God's will. Before her very eyes, Catherine saw how he preached, taught and healed and how he shared his energy, just like the other emissaries, with Jesus so that the entire covenant of twelve could perform their miracles.

The scene changed. Catherine now experienced how Judas went to the high priests and scribes who charged Jesus in order to incite the crowd. In the house of the high priest Caiaphas, Judas promised to help capture his own master for the price of thirty pieces of silver. Caiaphas and his companions had no idea that they were merely acting as God's instrument.

The setting changed once again. Catherine saw that Judas secretly witnessed Jesus' crucifixion. While the Passover lambs were slaughtered, they nailed the anointed to the cross. Just like

Maria, Judas never once left Jesus' side. Now Catherine perceived three simultaneous realities. She saw Ben as he read the Gospel of Judas, Judas as he wrote the Gospel and Judas as he witnessed Jesus' crucifixion as Maria shared his pain.

While Judas wrote down his testimony, a white-robed figure appeared out of nowhere.

»The people are saved,« said the angel softly. »For now.«

Judas looked up. »What does he want from us next, Gabriel? How are things to proceed from here?«

»Only God knows God's plan.«

»Then there won't be another flood?«

»The human sacrifice is complete. The new covenant between God and man exists through the sacrifice of the twelve.«

»You know God better than I…« Judas looked off into an imaginary distance, then returned his eyes to the archangel. »This new covenant…how valuable will it really be?«

»It appears you have lived among people much too long.«

»Perhaps I have. Perhaps we all have. You and I, we know God's wrath. How valuable is this sacrifice? How long will this new covenant hold?«

»It will hold until the beginning of the Last Judgement.«

Judas took a deep breath. As if to look into the far-distant future, he said: »From heaven through the world to hell. War, hunger, plague and death.« He paused briefly, then asked with a desperate voice: »What about Peter? You know he isn't the right one for his lot. What he sows will falsify the message.«

»You know darkness reigns and we have to break through it. The path is clear. Peter is the rock.«

Judas agreed with a heavy heart and looked at the nearly complete writing that lay before him.

Gabriel said: »I will make certain that neither Maria's nor your testimony will be lost in human history.«

»Then the connection to the source, the covenant of twelve, will remain a secret,« Judas realised with exhaustion.

Gabriel nodded. »For now, yes. We cannot risk that that which happens on Earth also happens in heaven. One devastating war is enough.« The angel took a step forward, carefully taking the pen out of Judas' hand. »It is time.« The pen fell to dust. »Which place have you selected for your earthly demise?«

Judas watched the dust fall to the ground. »A barren, leafless tree high above Jerusalem.«

Gabriel nodded. »I will be by your side. You will outdo them all and return to our midst. The darkness in our master must not triumph...«

The image changed abruptly and Catherine saw a gaunt tree tortured by the elements from which Judas Iscariot's corpse hung. The sky was grey and dark, like before a storm. Gabriel watched over the tree, peering down at the dead body and said: »He carried the heaviest lot of all.«

»Why all these sacrifices?« she blurted out with a sigh. »Why these martyrs' deaths?«

Gabriel lowered himself and stood next to her. »Because it is the language of man. Because they would otherwise not truly understand.«

»And what should I believe?«

The enormous wings of the angel fluttered briefly, strengthening the wind across the field. Judas' body swung back and forth from the branch. »God created man in his likeness. You know the Old Testament.«

»That's how it is written, yes.«

»It is true. I am an archangel. I know.«

Gabriel made a slight gesture and Catherine saw a gigantic luminous spiral, a galaxy in complete darkness in the middle of the Tower of the Winds. Gabriel demonstrated a bit of his power, offering her a brief look from his superhuman perspective. Catherine was reminded of Stephen Hawking's book The Universe in a Nutshell.

»If you question the sacrifice of the twelve, Catherine, then you not only question the new covenant, but also Benelli's sacrifice. Lucifer didn't like the twelve's commitment. He sensed where the whole thing was headed: toward a stronger connection between man and God.« Gabriel pointed to Judas Iscariot's corpse. »He is the true saviour. Just as Maria Magdalene was. But her time will come later.«

»What does Cardinal Benelli have to do with it? He, just like Judas, had also committed suicide. Should he have to burn in hell for it?« Catherine couldn't say for sure, but she thought she saw a smile run across the angel's face.

»God judges according to motive, Catherine. Benelli acted completely selflessly as an apostle.«

Apostle! That was a word she never would have dared thought about in this context. She wanted to ask more questions, but Gabriel interrupted her with a gesture, saying: »You have read Benelli's letter. Hold yourself to it.«

Catherine swallowed, then asked directly: »If you know everything as an angel, then you also can see the betrayal in the Vatican. – Who is the traitor?«

Gabriel's wings moved again, blowing a strong wind across the field. »I know that this traitor exists, but I cannot recognise him. Lucifer is hiding him behind his dark sway.« Gabriel suddenly perked up. Then he said: »I have to go now. I am needed elsewhere. You too must leave this place. Darkness is falling.« The angel unfolded his enormous wings and rose about the earthly world. At the same time, Catherine's vision dissolved, and she was back in the narrow, dim corridor in the Tower of the Winds.

Ben looked up from the Gospel of Judas speechless, stared at his friend, let the book fall and held her tightly. »Catherine? What is it?«

Catherine leaned against one of the heavy shelves filled with tomes behind her in a half sunken position. She had the feeling that the noose that had strangled Judas was closing tightly around her neck. Ben wanted to help her by sitting on the floor, but she stood back up in a haze. »Quick, close the cabinet and grab the book. We have to get out of here! We have to go straight to His Holiness!«

Without a word Ben put the volume in the inside pocket of his suit jacket and closed the cabinet. They hurried along the narrow aisle between the stacks. He knocked on the heavy wooden door so Dominico could open it from the outside. After a brief moment, they heard the key in the lock and saw the heavy door slowly open.

»You have finished your studies?« asked the old librarian calmly. He had sat on a chair next to the door the entire time.

»Not quite, Father,« explained Ben. »But it's enough for today.«

Dominico nodded and closed the door. He then led both visitors back down the dark path to his desk where he took back the flashlights and bid them farewell.

Catherine and Ben hurried along the high hand-carved wooden shelves next to the tower in which every possible original manuscript and document lay, dark secrets of centuries gone by. The archive's long dark corridors seemed to be endless.

»Out with it, Catherine,« said Ben finally. He pulled out the red book and placed it under her nose. »What did you see in the tower?«

»The history, the meaning of this book. That's why we have to get to His Holiness as soon as possible.«

Ben grabbed her by the robe and held her back. He held the

book up to her nose again. »Does that mean you believe what is written here?«

»Don't you?«

He seemed visibly remorseful. »I don't know what I should believe anymore, but I have to say it's all going too fast for me. Shouldn't we first take some time to talk about it?«

»Here?« Catherine shot back, pointing to the surrounding archive with a quick wave of her hand. »Gabriel said we have to get out here. Pronto!«

»Gabriel?«

»Ben, it's not just human powers at work here, but superhuman powers as well. I know it is all a pretty big shock, but at the moment we have no time for long explanations. Let's go. Please!«

Ben sighed, hesitating. »Alright. But I will want a rock solid explanation. I simply don't believe it.«

»You'll get one. Promise!«

Ben hurried through the semi-darkness of the archive with Catherine close on his tail. She had no idea how far the Apostolic Palace was where the papal private chambers were. She had long since forfeited any sense of direction in the mysterious, most secretive labyrinth in the world.

Just as Catherine turned the corner of a somewhat longer aisle behind Ben, he suddenly stopped without warning. She nearly ran into him. She wanted to ask him if he had lost his mind when her eyes grew wide. She saw both Swiss guards in their traditional uniforms, crossing their halberds so that they couldn't go through. A larger interior room was behind the watchmen, a reading room. They were still within the interior of the archives.

One of the two guards lowered his halberd and demanded that they enter the room. Catherine and Ben entered the dark room that was sparsely lit by a single island of light. The island was located directly above a standing podium over which a figure appeared to be engrossed in one of the old documents.

Catherine held her breath.

Cardinal Ciban raised his head, turning a cold eye to them both. »I see you have already completed your studies.«

64

Monsignor Massini answered the telephone in his private chambers and froze. There was no caller ID on the display, but he recognised his blackmailer's voice straight away. Oh how he regretted the day he followed Aurelio to his flat in the hopes for a little affection. The blackmailer was still in possession of the DVD.

»We have a new assignment for you, Father,« said the voice in a tone that was hard to distinguish, but that certainly didn't tolerate one thing: back talk. »What do you know about the new nun in the papal household?«

Massini could feel the blood literally shoot straight to his face. »Why would a simple nun be of interest to you?« he dared to ask.

»Let that be my worry. I ask again, what do you know about the new nun?«

»Nothing much really.« Massini struggled for composure and wished that Pope Leo had never let him in on it. He then ran through the disguised identity that Ciban had created together with Catherine. »Sister Bernadette has been in Rome for just a few weeks. She is from the US and works as a kitchen aide in the papal household. That's all.«

»Odd,« said the blackmailer. »We checked the facts. They appear to be correct and yet the quivering in your voice tells me there's foul play at work here.«

Massini was in shock. What should he say next? He took a deep breath without really feeling as if any air reached his lungs. »What do you want me to do? Spy on a kitchen aide?«

»You took the words right out of my mouth, Father. I expect an answer by tomorrow at noon. Keeping your secret just between us has its price after all.« The blackmailer hung up.

Massini's knees buckled. He barely made it to his bed. No matter how he looked at it, there was no way out. His gaze rested on the cross hanging on the wall across from him. For a moment he thought to pray out of sheer desperation. But he dared not.

65

Catherine was still staring in disbelief at the prefect of the Congregation of the Doctrine of Faith. The archive's atmosphere
alone transported the dark weight of past centuries, but the
young woman had the distinct feeling that Cardinal Ciban's
presence added a new dimension to it. The man standing at the
podium was not the Ciban she had gotten to know in the past
few days. This man reminded her in one fell swoop of the tor-
tuous inquisitorial meetings she had suffered over the last few
weeks without a possibility for escape.

There was no turning back now either.

The prefect sent the two Swiss guards away. He then pulled out
a tiny, pen-like contraption from his cassock, unfolded it into a
type of multiple armed antennae and placed it on the podium.
Although Catherine had never seen something like it before, she
had an idea what it was for. Not a single word or syllable that
Ciban, Ben or Catherine uttered would leave this room electronically.

»You have something that doesn't belong to you,« explained
the cardinal, turning to Ben and holding out his hand.

Ben made no effort to hand over the book. Instead he explained: »We are on our way to His Holiness, Eminence.«

»The book,« demanded Ciban with a warning tone. »I don't
want it to land in the wrong hands.«

»It won't, Eminence,« Catherine butted in. She ignored the horrible pressure in her stomach and managed to keep her voice steady. »As soon as we have spoken with His Holiness, it will be returned to its rightful place.« As Ciban's gaze met hers, she felt as if a stake had been driven through her heart. The cardinal's eyes shimmered like polished quartz. She tried not to lose composure beneath his piercing gaze.

»You don't understand, Sister. This book will not leave this archive under any circumstances. Not even for His Holiness.« He once again held out his hand. His body language suggested he wouldn't tolerate any back talk.

As if under a spell, Ben handed him over the book.

Ciban placed it carefully on the podium, opened it and flipped through it page for page. »As far as I can see, Pius reduced this copy to the bare minimum. He always did have a knack for the essential. It must run in his lawyerly family.«

Based on his tone of voice, it was obvious the cardinal didn't really like the deceased Pope with the expressionless eyes and a face like an eagle. Catherine and Ben knew Pius had kept quiet during the Holocaust when he was head of the Catholic Church. It had stigmatised his papacy.

»Now that you have the book, we'll be going now,« explained Catherine, gave Ben a sign and turned on her heel.

»Regretfully,« said the prefect.

It wasn't just his words, but something indescribable in his voice that made Catherine turn around again.

»I presume,« continued Ciban, »that you both have studied vast parts of this book. Why else would you be so agitated and on your way to His Holiness.« He looked up from the book and awaited a response.

Before Catherine could say anything, Ben jumped in: »What's behind LUKE? We know there is a connection between LUKE, the murder victims and this damn book.«

»So you did discover Darius' Bible,« Ciban said coldly. »You made your conclusions and remained silent.«

Ben shook his head. »On the contrary. I hadn't a clue until I found Sister Silvia's Bible. Only then did I realise there was a connection amongst the murder victims. What is LUKE, Eminence?«

The prefect remained unapproachable. »Any other questions?« His piercing eyes turned back to Catherine.

She observed how calm Ciban was. The kind of calm underneath which a great deal of danger lurked. »What are you planning to do?« she asked simply. »What is going to happen to us?«

»That depends on your answers. You had no right to invade this archive and read Pius' copy. How did you even find out about it?«

»Sometimes you have to risk something to get to the truth, Eminence,« Catherine shot back at him. »Especially when it has to do with protecting the Holy Father. We aren't here for personal reasons. We have a job to do.«

Ciban raised a brow. A mixture of scepticism and hope flickered in his narrow angular face, but it didn't reach his inscrutable eyes. »Alright then. Convince me, Sister. Convince me that I can continue to trust you and Monsignor Hawlett.«

Catherine was about to say something else, but thought better of it. She reached into the pocket of her nun's habit, pulled out the letter and handed it to Ciban. »If this won't help, Eminence, I don't know what will.«

The prefect returned with deliberate steps back to the podium, unfolded the letter and scanned its lines. Other than the podium and its immediate surroundings, the room remained in an eerie shadow. As he read, both Catherine and Ben watched him undergo an incredible metamorphosis. His hard facial features softened. The cold in his eyes gradually retreated. After Ciban had finished reading, there was a moment of tomb-like silence. He finally refolded the letter, took the book and returned both to Catherine.

»Then…then are we allowed to go to His Holiness now?« she asked completely baffled. She could hardly believe Benelli's letter had ended the nightmare so quickly. She had secretly envisioned both she and Ben rotting away in some secret dungeon in Castel Sant'Angelo.

Ciban gave her a look and nodded. She suddenly got that he knew a lot more about the secret than she had realised up to now.

»Betrayal and murder in connection with this book have done great damage to the church in history,« he explained. »I would never allow something like that to happen during my time in office.« He paused for a moment without letting Catherine out of his sight. »Why this game of hide and seek, Sister? Why didn't you just ask me?«

»Would you have let me enter the Tower of the Winds? Would you have let me in on the secret? I beg your pardon, Eminence, but I didn't want to take the risk.«

The prefect stared at her in silence for a moment. Then he nodded. »You are right. Please forgive me. Should we find oursel-ves in this position again, please remind me of this day. The same goes for you, Ben.« He signalled for both of them to follow him. »Come with me. I know a little shortcut.«

»A shortcut?« asked Ben in disbelief. »There is no such thing here.«

The hint of a smile danced on Ciban's lips as he turned off the antennae device and pocketed it. »There is always some shortcut in the Vatican.«

After the cardinal had assured himself that no one was around, he led Catherine and Ben through a narrow aisle to one of the wall shelves. He pulled out an old, heavy tome and touched a sensor on the wall that one only saw if one knew where it was. The shelf silently swung back and an opening the size of a door opened up.

»A...lift?« Catherine blurted. She stepped forward, examining the transport cabin that could hold up to three people.

»And an unusual one at that,« explained Ciban. He signalled Catherine and Ben to step into the lift. The door closed and the cabin started to move, first downward, then sideways. There was no recognisable display, just a red emergency switch. Just as Catherine was about to have an anxiety attack due to the claustrophobic size of the lift, both men appeared to have no trouble at all with it.

»Pope Innocence had this lift system built,« explained the tall cardinal. »There is a connection between Castel Sant'Angelo, the papal audience hall and a secret path to the grottos of St. Peter. There are others, of course, as you have seen such as the one to the secret archives. You may recall that the old buildings desperately need an overhaul of their ventilation and other systems. Innocence exploited this need and the associated confusion.«

Catherine tried to remain calm. »You can say that again. How much longer do we need?« In that very moment, the cabin made a slight jolt to the right, then left and finally moved upward once again. She had the feeling she was sloshing about in a fish bowl that was clearly too small. They had most likely left the archives already and were now beneath the Apostolic Palace.

Ciban gave her a look of concern. »Hang in there, Sister. We're almost there.«

The transport capsule finally stopped. The door opened and to Catherine's surprise they found themselves in the familiar corridor belonging to the papal private chambers.

»The letter please,« asked the prefect. Catherine retrieved the document and handed it to him. »Wait here a moment, please. I will be right back.« He hastily disappeared behind the door to Pope Leo's private living room.

Ciban had barely left when Catherine asked quietly: »What do you think he would have done to us if we had really been nothing other than two rotten thieves?«

Ben, who was still staring at the door to the lift as if in a trance, turned to her. »Let's hope we never find out.«

66

Time seemed to stand still. Catherine paced back and forth like a caged tiger in front of the door to the Pope's private living room. »What's taking them so long?«

Ben, who had sat himself down on a small bench in the corridor to relax, said: »We haven't been here for more than five minutes, Catherine. Why don't you just sit down next to me and wait and see in peace.«

The young nun paused, looking at her companion. Wait and see in peace? She finally sighed and sat herself down by his side.

»How do you think Ciban knew we were in the tower?«

»Dominico?« answered Ben simply.

»You think the old librarian told him?«

»It's conceivable. Right?«

»What about your proxy as an archive employee?«

Ben shrugged his shoulders. After the latest incident, it seemed nothing could make him lose his composure. Not even Judas' legacy.

»Paper doesn't blush, you know.«

»But your proxy has been authorised by the Holy Father.«

He looked at her. The dark circles under his eyes showed how tired he was. »It doesn't mean a thing to His Eminence. After all he was the one to get me the proxy. You know what they say: Trust is good. Control is better.«

Catherine thought for a moment about what Ben had said, especially when it came to her utterly confusing feelings about Ciban. She swept her gaze down the corridor, past the doors and paintings to the closed lift door. She then asked the question that meant the world to her: »Do you trust him, Ben?«

The archivist gave her a tired smile. »I am afraid he is an idealist.«

»You didn't answer my question.«

Ben shrugged his shoulders helplessly. »What about you? Do you trust him?«

Catherine leaned back, considering the question for two or three seconds. Goodness, she wasn't at all certain. In the past few days she had become clear that Leo trusted Ciban unconditionally. But for her there were only two states of mind whilst in the presence of the prefect: she was either dog-tired or she had these damned and completely inexplicable butterflies in her stomach.

Just as she wanted to give her response, the door opened and Ciban entered the corridor. Catherine looked at his pale face and into his penetrating alert eyes. The events over the past few days seemed to have taken little out of the prefect – or was he able to fake it? Did he possibly take stimulants? His clear eyes told her he did not. »You may go to him now,« said the cardinal, beckoning to Catherine.

Just as Ben wanted to get up to follow her, Ciban held him back. »A private conversation between him and her.«

Ben nodded and wanted to sit back down on the bench when the cardinal added: »You and I need to have a different conversation, Ben. Please follow me.«

67

The Pope was standing at the high window when Catherine entered the simple living room furnished with antiques. Hidden behind the curtain, Leo looked out onto St. Peter's Square and the restless city beyond it. He was still holding Benelli's letter in his hand. He seemed to be lost in thought, miles away from Rome and the room he was in.

»Holiness,« said Catherine, letting him know she had entered the living room.

The Pope turned toward her, came up to her and forwent any formalities as he had in the past few days. »Cardinal Benelli loved Rome. He would walk the streets and take action on behalf of the homeless. I never really understand why he moved into that Villa a few years ago. Please, take a seat, Catherine.«

»Thank you.« She sat herself down on the high, comfortable chair, pulled out Pius' book and placed it on the table. »Father Darius moved from Chicago to Rome, then from Rome to this remote monastery in Germany. Perhaps there is a parallel between them, Holiness.«

»Perhaps.« The Pope stopped in front of a large baroque globe and spun it carefully. »At any rate, you quite impressed Darius and Benelli with your gift, Catherine. Otherwise there would be no letter.«

»Quite honestly, I don't understand any of it. All I know is there is a truth behind the truth. But I simply don't know if I truly understand it.«

Leo smiled, allowing the globe to finish a turn on its axis. »That would make two of us. Ever since the last conclave I have lived with this truth and it is still a mystery to me. Most likely you know more than I do at this point.«

»I quite doubt that, Holiness. You are Peter's rightful successor. You are the rock.«

Pope Leo's smile grew wider as he watched the globe with its baroque symbols rotate. »Oh no, Catherine. I am just a figurehead. The next sacrificial lamb.« His voice revealed no resentment or hurt pride, but rather an unalterable fact. »You, on the other hand, are following Darius' and Benelli's footsteps, even if it's admittedly not of your own volition. Your years at the Institute prepared you well for it.«

Catherine could feel a pang at the mention of the Institute. Even though she appreciated its protection and care as a child, teenager and student, the final years were more like a living hell. After the old guard left, things had turned for the worst, or at least she had thought so. She had had no idea exactly how long Lux Domini had placed its finger in the pie, thereby subordinating the Institute to the Vatican's secret service. One thing had become crystal clear to her years ago: she could no longer be party to its cold, calculating advancements. Darius had finally ensured her unchecked departure from Lux. But it seemed even now that this part of her biography would continue to haunt her.

»Prepared for what, Holiness?« she asked. Darius had never once even suggested that she would be sitting here with the Pope one day discussing the Gospel of Judas Iscariot. The priest had also never told her anything about his friendship and connection with Antonio Cardinal Benelli either.

Leo left the baroque globe alone, sat himself down in the chair next to her and placed Benelli's letter next to Pius' book. »What do you see, when you look at me, Catherine?«

Catherine swallowed. »I don't know what you mean, Holiness?«

»My aura. What do you see?«

»I...I have never observed your aura,« she stuttered. »As a child I learned to respect people's privacy.«

»Why don't you forget what Darius taught you for a moment, Catherine. What do you see when you read my aura?«

»I can't just read your aura, Holiness. I would have to let my shield fall away completely. And to be honest, I am not willing to do that as long as I am responsible for your safety.«

Leo nodded in disappointment. »I see. It would make you vulnerable.«

»There are two sides to every coin.«

»Odd.« The Pope smiled. »His Eminence Cardinal Ciban said the exact same thing to me a few moments ago. – Catherine, where did you get your gift?«

»Science speaks of a genetic disposition that hasn't been thoroughly researched yet. According to the Church, however, my genetic aberration is not the cause of my gift. On the contrary, my spiritual ability shaped my genetics.«

»What do you think?«

»I always knew it was the latter.«

»I envy you in some way. I myself have zero psychic ability. Up until two years ago I had to rely on my faith alone.«

»Isn't faith a much greater gift?«

The Pope couldn't help but smile. »That's how it should be. But let's be frank. For many of us modern people, Genesis is nothing more than a metaphor with all its poetic embellishments. And now...« Leo hesitated for a moment, looking at the globe. »Ever since the consecration, I no longer just believe. I know. My spiritual and mental horizons were expanded for this office. It is the power of the covenant of twelve that makes me so strong. Unfortunately, it is also the source of my greatest weakness that the murderer who killed Darius, Sylvester, Isabella and Silvia knows all too well.«

»Were there such murder attempts in earlier times too?«

»Yes. Three times. One caused the witch hysteria, the hunt for alleged wizards and witches. It was a long, dark time in history.«

»Judas Iscariot spoke of God's plan,« said Catherine carefully. »If his betrayal was a part of the divine plan, then your consecration is too. With all its implications.«

The Pope creased his forehead. »Let's see: twelve emissaries for the world's salvation. Twelve apostles who foot the bill for mankind's and the Church's fallibilities and keep the institution alive. We humans have not developed the way God had wished. Only seven of the twelve in the covenant are still alive. Perhaps God's alternative plan is hidden in the murderer's actions.«

Catherine squinted. »If that were so, Holiness, how do I fit in to this plan? As an alternative plan to God's alternative plan?«

Leo returned her gaze. »As hope?«

Catherine remained silent as she didn't know what to say to that. Why did Benelli have to speak in riddles? What good were all these dreams and visions if she didn't have a clear understanding of what her task was?

When she didn't respond, the Pope continued: »One thing's for sure: without your help, Catherine, the tides would have turned against us long before.«

»In my vision…« Catherine faltered. »Gabriel said this tie between God and man would hold until the beginning of the Last Judgement.«

The Holy Father looked at the letter and book, although Catherine had the feeling he was staring through both of them.

»The night without day. The end of history. The apocalypse. Armageddon. Twelve emissaries are standing between the end of time and us...Gabriel told you that? Angels often appear as revelators of this version of the future,« he said dryly.

»You think the murderer wants to bring about the apocalypse?«

»I wish I knew what Benelli knew. I wish I understood his plan. My guess is he never would have made the gamble if not so much had been at stake and...« The Pope paused.

»And?« Catherine pressed.

Leo returned her gaze. »And he didn't have something up his sleeve.«

»He is playing chess with God to prevent the apocalypse?«

»Someone or something – let's call it the 'dark force' – wants to wreak havoc on the Catholic Church. I assure you, Catherine, it would have consequences for the entire world.«

»But if this dark force wants to weaken you by hunting down the apostles, why won't you protect the surviving emissaries inside the Vatican walls? Why don't they unite all their power? Why hasn't Vatican security taken the necessary measures?«

The Holy Father got up, returned to the baroque globe and began to rotate it slowly once again. He seemed to consider how much he should reveal to Catherine. He finally said: »Because as Pope I am the only one allowed to know the apostle's identity. We would otherwise risk exposing the remaining survivors.«

»That's it?«

»Remember Benelli's letter.« The Pope walked away from the globe, quoting: »Only the Popes, the Grand Inquisitors and the covenant of twelve know about the secret.« Then he said: »What Cardinal Benelli didn't tell you, Catherine: Only I and the emissaries are allowed to know their identities. That is a part of the covenant. Even His Eminence Cardinal Ciban is denied knowledge of the names and locations of the twelve – as long as they live.« The Pope surveyed the young nun, then added: »Except Benelli and one female apostle, all the rest are distributed around the world.«

There was a female apostle in Rome?

»Quite honestly, I don't understand that part of the covenant, even if I do know that the emissaries are messengers of God who are supposed to work all around the world.«

»Remember Lucifer. Remember the fallen angel, the Nephilim. Remember the attempt to be in God's image, the pride and some angels' refusal to give man respect. An important aspect of the covenant is none of that happens with the emissaries. For one the apostles are messengers on Earth; for another their energy and power would be too strong if they remained united over centuries. It is for this reason that the covenant of twelve is completely replaced with every third Pope. Think about what Ignaz von Döllinger suggested about power and what his famous student Lord Acton appropriately repeated in one of his dictums.«

Catherine's eyes widened: »Power tends to corrupt; and absolute power corrupts absolutely.«

The Pope nodded. »Not even heaven is immune to it. Take a look,« he made a sweeping gesture as if to include not only the Vatican, but the entire world, »at what the power has created even under 'controlled conditions'!«

Catherine took a deep breath and considered for a moment if she should leave a part of her visions unmentioned, but then she thought better of it, letting the cat out of the bag: »Judas never trusted God.«

»I know. Just as little as Lucifer did.« The Pope then scrutinised Catherine as if he were considering whether the young nun, who had just learned that she was to follow in Darius' and Benelli's footsteps, was ready for an additional truth. At the last minute he decided against it, saying: »The murderer knows the names of the emissaries. He even knows their power spots.«

»Power spots?«

»Their favourite places where apostles meditate to renew their energy reserves. The murders happened in each of these places. It appears that we may have a traitor amongst us.«

Catherine stared at him.

»That's Cardinal Ciban's theory at least. I know the identity of the living emissaries, but I am not psychic. I don't see even a sliver of a connection between God's messengers and myself.« He looked at the young woman with curiosity. »What about you, now that you are part of the connection in some way?«

»There isn't a traitor amongst the twelve,« Catherine determined.

»Are you...sure?« The Pope looked at her, full of hope.

»I may not know their identities, but I would have felt it ever since the connection with His Eminence Cardinal Benelli, Holiness. Besides, Benelli would have noticed if it were so. Whoever wishes to destroy the covenant by killing the emissaries didn't find out the names and locations from one of the twelve.«

Leo placed his shaking hands on the globe and appeared to be incredibly relieved. »That's what I had hoped, Catherine. Because if it had been different...good heavens, I am afraid we wouldn't stand a chance. Then we'd be...« He stopped in mid-sentence, staggered, fell against the globe and pulled it down with a crash to the floor.

Catherine, who had equally sensed death, fought against her own powerlessness, pulled herself over to Leo, raised a shaking hand, felt his face and opened his eyes to see if he was still alive despite his collapse.

He was still breathing!

She noticed how Cardinal Benelli's leftover energy flowed to him, revived him and brought him back to a conscious state. But she also knew that the Pope who was about to wake up would not be the same Leo with whom she had just spoken about the covenant of twelve. That Pope would be a lot weaker.

Just like herself.

68

Monsignor deRossi had left the Vatican through an underground secret passage that ran beneath the Passetto from the thirteenth century and also led to Castel Sant'Angelo. The master had given him this plan and had arranged for the appropriate keys to the old wooden and iron doors. After all, he knew the Vatican's underground better than the archaeologists.

Originally Castel Sant'Angelo had been used in the second century as a mausoleum under Emperor Hadrian. Later various Popes turned the massive structure into a castle.

The name Castel Sant'Angelo came thanks to a vision Pope Gregory I had in the year 590 as the plague raged in Rome. He saw archangel Michael appear over the mausoleum, announcing the end of the plague. The structure served primarily as a retreat for the Holy Father. Ever since then an eight hundred metre long escape route, the Passetto, connected Castel Sant'Angelo with the papal palace.

The walls of Castel Sant'Angelo contained completely different stories, however. At some point they acted as dungeon and torture chamber for the Inquisition. One of the most famous prisoners was once Galileo Galilei. The former tomb also had to act as a treasure chamber and even as an expansion of the secret archive.

After deRossi had left the Vatican and Castel San Angelo, he continued his way to the Ponte Sant'Angelo. No one stopped him. No one knew that he had just rid the world of yet another abomination. It had been so easy. Sister Thea hadn't even noticed his approach. She had been so engrossed in her prayer next to the Grotta di Lourdes as his strong hands wrapped around her throat and head, breaking her neck in a fraction of a second.

And now...now Thea sat peacefully in front of the grotto, dreaming with her eyes wide open. It had taken quite a bit of imagination and effort to arrange her head just so on its broken neck in the short time he had left.

That wimp Ben Hawlett would get excited about this one.

69

»How are you feeling, Holiness?« asked Cardinal Ciban with concern in his voice. He had picked up the Pope off the floor and placed him on the couch in the living room as if he were light as a feather.

Catherine had discovered both the prefect and Ben in the Pope's private chapel where they were having a rather serious, if not tense, discussion. But when Catherine entered the chapel to report on Leo's latest collapse, the derision between the two men seemed to wash away in seconds. Catherine had wanted to return to the corridor toward the living room when Ciban held her back and said: »Don't go through the corridor again, Sister.«

They ultimately returned to the living room through a connecting door in the chapel via the sleeping chambers and the private office. The Pope was lying on the couch like the severely injured.

»Holiness...?« repeated Ciban softly.

Leo opened his eyes, looked at the ceiling and seemed completely disoriented. But then he saw Catherine. »I...I think...I...had a...vision...Benelli was here...here in this room...and he wanted to let me know that Sister Thea is dead.«

»Thea?« Catherine could feel her knees getting weak. A moment later she realised Thea was the one Leo had spoken of when he had said that all other emissaries except Benelli and a female apostle were spread across the entire world! She barely noticed Ben helping her into a nearby chair.

Thea was dead...murdered! Brought to death by a madman who was hunting the apostles.

Although Catherine was strong, she suddenly had the urge to slump down. But she mustn't do that. Not now! She felt someone carefully take her hand in his. Through his touch she received new energy. Ben? But her friend was already standing next to the Pope.

Cardinal Ciban looked her straight in the eye with an unwavering expression. »I know you were friends with Sister Thea, Catherine. But don't allow your grief and anger about Thea's death to eat up your mind and vitality.«

Catherine would have loved to yell at the prefect due to his restraint, but as cool as his words sounded, she also sensed his sincerity and tremendous compassion. Thea, Darius, Benelli and all the other victims weren't lost on Ciban. Quite the contrary. But the prefect wouldn't let his anger about the murders affect his action. Fury made one blind. Blindness led to great danger. And great danger could mean death.

Catherine nodded, pulled her hand away and, in the very next second, missed his soft touch.

Good lord, what was wrong with her? She was a rebellious nun! And Ciban was her judge and executioner! Was she suffering from a type of Stockholm syndrome? Was that the thing that was confusing her feelings? It must indeed be the stress. She could only hope that the prefect didn't notice any of her completely irrational feelings for him.

»You are right, Eminence,« she said with great effort. »I won't allow my anger to consume me.« In her mind she added: Just as I did during the interrogations. Sadly both her memories of Thea and the grief and pain of her loss were not easily suppressed. Thea's lovely, courageous letter popped into Catherine's mind

again, then their first meeting in person in the Vatican's Internet
office and her encouraging words of consolation during their
walks through the Vatican's gardens…

She faltered.

What had the Holy Father said during their conversation just
before? »The murderer knows the names of the emissaries. He
even knows their power spots.«

She looked at Ciban who was still squatting in front of her and
said: »I think I know where we will find Sister Thea.«

»You know the crime scene?« Ben blurted.

»In the Grotta di Lourdes.«

The prefect gave her a doubtful look. »Are you sure, Sister?«

»She used to pray there often. It was her favourite place in the
Vatican.« She looked at Ciban, then the Pope who understood in
that moment what she meant. Apparently, the cardinal had never
heard about the power spots.

»You are right, Catherine,« said the Pope. »The emissaries
renew their energy reserves at their favourite places. Darius,
Silvia…they all died in their favourite places.«

Without questioning the matter, Ciban pulled out his mobile
phone from his robe and speed-dialled the commander of the
Vigilanza. After issuing his instructions, he explained: »Coelho
knows what to do. Should Sister Thea's body be found at the
grotto, he will notify us immediately.«

Catherine didn't doubt for a moment that the Vigilanza commander knew how to do his job. Especially one that requires a
cover-up. According to the official Vatican explanation, Thea will
most likely have been found dead due to a heart condition, just as
Darius officially died during a hiking tour. In the end the same
mechanism would kick in as it did in 1998 when the truth behind
the murders of the Swiss guard commander Alois Estermann
and his wife was prevented from ever being discovered. Appar-

ently a young soldier had killed them both in a fit of rage over not receiving an accolade. But there were too many contradictions. In truth no one believed this particular version of the story. On the other hand no one had been able to shed light on the case to this day.

Did Ciban know the real motive for the murders? As far as Catherine knew, Cardinal Monti had headed Vatican security as prefect of the Congregation of the Doctrine of Faith under Pope Innocence. A few years later Monti had made sure that Catherine fell under the scrutiny of the faith authorities. She presumed that her extraordinary gift was the only thing that had protected her from burning at the stake during Innocence's reign. Even after her departure from Lux Domini, the Congregation of the Doctrine of Faith had shown great restraint.

»Eminence,« Ben said cautiously. »While we're waiting for the commander to return your call, wouldn't now be a good time to talk about LUKE?«

Catherine heard Ciban give out a soul-deep sigh for the first time.

»I can't tell you anything more than I've already told you, Ben. Everyone in this room knows that the Church monitors its psychic members very closely. They didn't just start doing that the day before yesterday... since the 60s Pope John XXIII had tried to ensure that even the controllers were controlled. But unfortunately most of that which he had initiated was undermined after his death and the second Vatican Council.«

Perking her ears, Catherine asked: »And that means?«

»It means that such a progressive order as Lux Domini, a religious, scientific organisation that examines special people and phenomena and overshadows even the Jesuits' actions and should actually control the controllers, has unified too much power in and of itself.« Ciban returned her gaze. »You yourself belonged

to the Institute and the order, Catherine. You have since left the
order which is why I can presume you know of which I speak.«

»But you are the head of Vatican security.«

The prefect shrugged his shoulders. »I do what I can, but my
predecessor slacked off a bit too much. And His Eminence
Cardinal Gasperetti who, if you recall, presides over Lux
Domini, is extraordinarily careful in his goings-on since I've been
in office.

»How was Darius connected to LUKE?« Catherine wanted to
know.

Ciban creased his forehead. »You mean whether or not he was
active or passive? Sister, he was your mentor! He directed many
of the Institute's projects with great success.«

»LUKE as well then?« asked Ben.

»LUKE is top secret and extends well beyond the apostle
mystery.«

The young nun couldn't help but let out a short, painful snort.
»Pardon me, but after all that Ben and I have been through in the
past few days…what possibly could extend beyond the apostle
mystery?«

»Perhaps your visions will give you the answer one day,« said
Ciban earnestly. He then added: »As far as I know, LUKE conta-
ins the profiles and research results from those psychics whose
abilities go well beyond the measure of an average gifted psychic.
Darius' profile must be saved in its database, just like Cardinal
Benelli's. And most likely yours as well, Sister.«

Catherine stared at the cardinal. She had no words in response
to what he just told her.

Ben cleared his throat. »Another thing, Eminence. Could the
murderer have gotten the apostles' identity from LUKE?«

»Possibly. But it is not very likely.«

»Why not?«

»Lux does not know the apostles' identities. Nor do I. The list of names of all spirituals alone would be too complicated to derive the emissaries from it. An apostle could be behind any one of the names.«

The Pope, who seemed to be recovering more and more by the minute, said weakly: »Sister Catherine is convinced that there is no traitor among the apostles.«

Instead of showing relief, Ciban's face drew dark. He closed his eyes for a moment. When he opened them again, he turned to the young woman. »I should actually be relieved by your statement. But what we are now dealing with is a different, far more worldly problem and earlier as I'd like at that.«

A far more worldly problem? What did Ciban mean by that?

His mobile phone rang. He answered it. Coelho was on the other end of the line and confirmed Catherine's intuition. Thea's body had been hidden at the Grotta di Lourdes. The crime scene had been secured and documented.

»We have a lot of work to do, Ben,« said the prefect. Then he turned to Catherine and the Pope. »I will send Monsignor Rinaldo to you. Now, if you would excuse us.«

70

The day had turned out even better than the master had dared hope it would. The sixth apostle was dead. The Pope had experienced a recent collapse, even if it wasn't as strong as he had hoped. And now a messenger stood before him with a small gift revealing something about the new kitchen nun in the papal household. It had taken a certain emphasis before Monsignor Massini finally talked.

»Thank you. You may go now.«

After the messenger had left, the master opened the sealed envelope and took out the sealed file. When he opened it, his eyes fell onto the photograph, making him hold his breath for a moment.

Catherine Bell!

A small world indeed!

The master scanned the file, stopping at one point or the other: Chicago, primary school for the psychically gifted, Darius, Corona, the Institute, Georgetown University in Washington, Lux Domini. He then passed it on to his protégé Father deRossi. He didn't have to read every single detail of the file to know who this nun was. With Father Darius' help she had left Lux Domini and, in Gasperetti's eyes, had therefore betrayed the order. And now she stood before the Inquisition's court and not even Marc Ciban seemed to be able to control her.

The master well remembered a secret meeting between Darius and Gasperetti, two years before the priest had retired. One of his ambitious employees had taped the conversation in the grottos of St. Peter's Basilica. As he listened to the tapes in his living quarters, the master had been quite astonished.

»It is nice to see you have time for a meeting, Eminence,« Darius had greeted to Cardinal Gasperetti with great calm.

»You wanted to chat. So here I am,« said the cardinal with cool reserve. »What's it about, Father?«

»I just learned of Sister Catherine's intention to leave the order as soon as possible. The request has been sitting on your desk for over a year.«

»Oh, stop it, Father. You know full well that it is quite a complicated process. One can't just come and go as one pleases.«

»You have no right to deny her leaving.«

»I'm not doing that either. The investigation procedures are underway and...«

»Since when?«

»A month ago,« answered Gasperetti firmly. »Good Lord, Father. Don't be like that. You know quite well that Sister Catherine's case is an extraordinary one. Her unusual gift...« He interrupted himself briefly, then added with a regretful tone: »She is not willing to have the artificially induced amnesia.«

Darius' voice suddenly turned cold. »We have both experienced what that can mean for the delinquent. A life in the shadows.« When Gasperetti did not respond, the priest added: »I would not like it should you continue to place obstacles in her path.«

»Is that a threat?« asked Gasperetti with composure.

»You know I do not place threats. Never. Neither did His Holiness Pope Innocence.«

The master knew full well that Innocence was one of the

hardest men ever to enter the Vatican. Gasperetti knew even better what the hidden message was behind the priest's words.

For a moment both men sat in silence.

»You are asking a lot, Father. You are asking me to break the order's rule.«

»You needn't break it, Eminence, just bend it a little.«

Again they sat in silence until Gasperetti finally said with resignation: »I take it you have a plan?«

»A plan is saying a bit much, Eminence. But I see a possibility for a win-win situation. But we shouldn't discuss it here.«

Lost in the memory of his conversation with the priest, the master stared off into space while his protégé deRossi continued reading the file. Darius had indeed been willing to go through fire for Sister Catherine. Her provocative criticism of the Church even in Innocence's time had grabbed the attention of the faith authorities and had brought her before the court and that before Lux could do anything about it. A veritable sensational trial could have come of her interrogation, but the nun was smart enough not to allow the confrontation to escalate. Nothing that went on behind the scenes had leaked to the press, which actually provided rich soil for speculation and rumours to emerge.

DeRossi, who had studied the file quickly, yet intensely, looked up and said: »This woman has extraordinary psychic abilities.«

Indeed, thought the master, without letting his fury show. He had heard of Catherine's unusual gift years ago, but now he could hardly believe that this heretic, whom he would have loved to see burned at the stake under Innocence's reign, was a psychic who had managed to replace several apostles' energy simultaneously, thereby possibly thwarting his plans. It seemed she now stood in the Apostolic Palace under Ciban's protection, which explained why the trial was taking so long.

»Don't allow yourself to be impressed by it, Nicola. Sister

Thea and Father Darius had their share of amazing abilities as well.«

With an angry laugh, the master remembered his encounter with Catherine at Benelli's reception. He couldn't deny that the woman impressed him on some level. She was smart, attractive and arrogant. She hadn't taken his warning seriously and had caused him great concern several times in his life, just as Darius had. Wasn't it ironic that this heretic shared his preference for the Sistine Chapel? Darius had casually told him that once when they had met in the Sistine.

»She is your next target then?«

The master considered deRossi with a knowing smile. »From this point forward she is the ultimate target. As soon as we have eliminated her, the path will be clear. But we have to be prudent. Most prudent. As you have seen, she is currently living in the Apostolic Palace as Sister Bernadette and belongs to the papal household staff. It will be more than difficult to get to her.«

DeRossi thought for a moment, flipped through the file, then poured the master and himself more wine. »I think I have a solution.«

The master perked his ears. »And that would be?«

»There is one man in the Vatican that Sister Catherine trusts unconditionally.«

The master scrutinised his protégé with curiosity. He couldn't possible mean His Eminence Cardinal Ciban. But then it dawned on him what his counterpart meant: »Hawlett!«

DeRossi closed the file. »He will bring me to Catherine this very day without his even knowing it.«

»Today?«

»The moment of surprise.«

»How on Earth will you pull it off?«

The Monsignor explained his idea to the master. He developed a plan that was so brief and concise that, on the heels of the last mission, it sounded quite promising.

The servant entered, announcing a second messenger, much to the master's surprise. The young man had barely entered the room, handing him a small sealed envelope, before the servant led him out again.

The master broke the seal, pulling out an additional envelope. Only after he had broken its seal was he able to pull out a copy of a file and an old colour photograph. The file copy came from the archive of a Catholic orphanage. The photo showed a sleeping baby on a nun's arm. Next to it stood a priest who smiled pleasantly into the camera: Father Darius. The master stared at the picture as if in a trance. Then he turned it over and read the note that had been written in pen on the backside: February 11, 1977, Catherine.

What a revelation! What an opportunity!

This photo could serve as ammunition.

To deRossi's amazement, the master looked at the image that the second messenger had brought for several minutes. He seemed to be obsessed with it. Then he said: »My dear Nicola, I have a tiny adjustment to your plan.«

71

Ben and Ciban sat in the cardinal's office, strong coffee at hand, mulling through the files with the crime photos that Coelho had additionally provided for them. It was late afternoon. Neither had slept a wink the night before. After the incident in the Apostolic Palace they had watched a rather catastrophic video recording of the crime scene with Thea's body. In order to avoid a stir, they couldn't directly illuminate the location. They established a new profile of the perpetrator. Other than the dead body and the photos, they had zero evidence. That was all that they had at the moment. In the meantime, the Vatican had returned to life. Coelho had been able to secure the area surrounding the Grotta di Lourdes by pretending to start a renovation effort to block any errant gardeners and curious tourists' view. The remainder of the traces had most likely been wiped away.

»He must have gotten to Sister Thea through the underground parking garage entrance,« Ciban had explained to Ben and Coelho as he pointed to a floor plan. »Everything else would have been too risky.«

The commander bent over the maps on Ciban's conference table, thoroughly taking in the connected routes around the Grotta di Lourdes one more time. »Which would mean he knows the premises very well.« Compared to his extraordinary position, he was a rather average looking guy, shorter than Ben, mid-forties, had mousy blonde hair, brown eyes and wore a dark, plain suit. If Ben hadn't known the level of influence this man had in the Vatican, he would have never noticed his power should he have met him casually on the streets of Rome. The archivist also got the impression that day that despite his expectation, the working relationship between the prefect and the commander of the Vigilanza was very harmonious.

»Or someone on the inside gave him explicit instructions.« Ciban pointed to a worn underground floor plan. »You see right about here a secret underground passageway starts that is nowhere to be seen on any of the maps. We should definitely take a closer look at it. And please be as discreet as possible, otherwise one of our citizens or one of the tourists might think we're investigating a bomb threat.«

»Are there any other secret passageways that I should know about, Eminence?« asked the Vigilanza commander dryly. He knew full well that the Vatican's premises was chock full of secret paths in order to get inconspicuously from one place to the next. He himself often used a part of the invisible labyrinth behind the architectonic setting.

»Not that I know of,« answered Ciban just as dryly. »Should you unexpectedly run into another passageway, I would be most grateful if you would let me know.«

A slight smile flit across Coelho's face. »Most certainly, Eminence. We'll get to it then.«

»What's happening with the check on the entry tickets?«

»No luck yet. But we're working on it.«

Two men had been tirelessly studying external and new access passes for the Vatican in the past weeks and months. Two had been removed from the investigation: that of Sister Catherine and Sister Bernadette.

After Coelho left, Ben couldn't hold himself back any longer.

»Back there at His Holiness' office you had mentioned you were concerned. About what?«

Ciban left the conference table, approached the small sideboard and poured them both another coffee. »Since the Holy Father himself could hardly be the murderer and we know through Sister Catherine that none of the apostles is behind it, we should be able to tighten the circle of suspects. But I learned a while ago that someone else knows about the Gospel of Judas. It's that archaeologist who found Pius' book in the Vatican's underground cemeteries during one of the digs.«

»An archaeologist found the book?«

»In the summer of 1943 Mussolini was deposed and in the following September the Germans occupied Rome. In October an SS commando arrived with machine guns at the borders of our city-state. Of course, in order to protect the Holy Father. But Pius feared that the Nazis would occupy the Vatican so he brought a part of his private library to safety in the grottos beneath St. Peter's Basilica. Through a twist of fate, Dr. Kleier discovered this treasure in September 1978.«

»In September 1978...« said the investigator, lost in thought.

»On the exact day that Pope John Paul died.«

Ben stared at the cardinal. John Paul's date of death. The media had had a field day, speculating about how he died. But Ciban gave Ben a look that indicated John Paul's death had nothing to do with the Gospel of Judas.

The prefect continued: »Dr. Kleier said he hadn't broken his vow to the Church and had kept the secret to himself. I have to admit I tend to believe him. The problem is: I don't like the alternative.«

»Which alternative? Quite frankly I don't quite follow you, Eminence.« Ben knew what an honour it was that Ciban was willing to share with him some of his innermost thoughts.

The cardinal returned to the conference table, handed Ben a steaming cup of coffee and allowed his gaze to wander indifferently over the map.

»That Pope Innocence betrayed the apostles to one of his confidants.«

72

It was shortly after six o'clock when the messenger brought the package of books to Monsignor deRossi's tiny, elegant flat in Trastevere. Once again the master's network worked beautifully. DeRossi accepted the package with gratitude, gave him a big tip and unpacked the contents in the kitchen he rarely used. After he had removed the bubble wrap, he discovered that whoever had prepared the delivery had a rather inappropriate sense of humour. Inside he found an antique shrink-wrapped copy of Peyrefitte's The Keys of St. Peter.

DeRossi took the book into the living room and flipped on the television. While he followed the news, he removed the nearly tear proof wrapping and opened the book cover. At first glance there was nothing special about the volume. It was only after he flipped another one hundred pages that he noticed Peyrefitte's book was hollowed out in the middle as if it were an original cigar box. The work itself was of no interest to deRossi. He was much more fascinated by the well-packaged contents, the tiny technical device that hid within it.

He quickly pulled out the mobile phone, removed the shrink-wrap, and checked whether it was working by calling his landline. As he expected, the old cabled telephone in the tiny hallway rang once. When deRossi was satisfied that everything was working properly, he leaned back in his television recliner. He would only make one other call – it was the whole reason this tiny technical wonder had been designed in the first place.

Satisfied, he took a sip of the coffee he had prepared before the messenger had arrived. The fact that the coffee was now luke-warm didn't bother him in the least. He only cared about its effects. It was going to be a long night.

73

It was late in the evening. The nuns and Leo had long since retired to their rooms. Catherine had also retired to her remote chamber, had removed her disguise and had tried to work on her new book. But despite her very best efforts she couldn't concentrate on the material and so she switched off her laptop and took a walk along the papal rooftop terrace. Perhaps she would get into her writing a bit later, but for now, it was out of the question.

During her stroll the events of the past day ran through her mind again. Half an hour after Ben and Ciban had left, Monsignor Rinaldo appeared in the Pope's living room to keep them both company. The prefect had let him in on part of the deal and he appeared to have been well instructed because he did his job without comment. In the interim Leo had regained his strength. It was amazing how much Benelli's and Catherine's energy revived him. No outsider would have noticed that the Pope had actually been considerably weakened.

The next morning Catherine came across the Holy Father in his private chapel. When she had noticed his presence, she had wanted to quietly retreat, but he noticed she was there and had asked her to stay so he could speak with her.

»How well did you know Darius, Holiness?« asked Catherine finally. She wanted to learn more about her paternal mentor.

»Not as well as you, Catherine. I only met him twice. The first

time during my consecration at the Sistine Chapel. He led the
ceremony and created a connection between me and the apostles.
The second time we met at Castel Gandolfo where he spoke to
me about the dangers of my policies to the Church. As we strolled through the Castel Gandolfo gardens, he also spoke about
you, Catherine, and your trial. He asked me to keep an eye on
you. You were like a daughter to him. He would have done
anything to protect you.«

»Thanks to him I was able to leave Lux.«

Leo allowed himself to smile. »I remember. I had never seen
Cardinal Gasperetti sweat like that before. Back then as cardinal
I didn't make the connection between your case and Darius. My
God, it seems like ages ago.«

Catherine hesitated, then said: »Darius never spoke about his
family or his friendship with Cardinal Benelli. Now I understand
why.«

»It is not easy to be an apostle. It is not allowed to become
public knowledge. Not even your own family is allowed to know.«

»Was it a big shock to learn about the secret, Holiness?«

The Pope thought for a moment. »You know, Catherine, I
could have stepped down, but I didn't want to. I wanted to
continue and further the policies started by John XXIII and John
Paul no matter what. After all the damage Innocence did to the
Church. The emissaries promised me their support.«

»The same emissaries that had supported Pope Innocence
before? I beg your pardon, Holiness, but that makes no sense.«

»Apostles are human too. They die. During Innocence's long
papacy, two of his apostles died of natural causes. Their energy
wasn't lost right away, but rather absorbed by the other apostles.
It was only after my enthronement that both unoccupied apostle
seats were filled. It allows for a bit more flexibility.«

»But how could those apostles who had supported Innocence

suddenly support a totally different set of policies?«

»For the apostles, it is about maintaining the Church. I imagine they supported Innocence in managing the office, but at the same time they curbed his traditionalist ways. I can assure you the apostles guide my progressive approach just as much toward less destructive paths. But that doesn't seem to be enough for the murderer.«

»It doesn't sound exactly like free will.« On the other hand, Catherine thought, I never did have the impressions that Darius manipulated me. I would have felt that right away.

The Pope had shaken his head with a smile. »Through my connection with the twelve, I not only have a higher consciousness, but I also have gained a deeper insight into that which can destroy.« He had paused for a moment. »Believe me, Catherine, even in the will to do good lies an incredibly strong temptation...«

Power and temptation. A topic as old as man himself.

Catherine reached the rooftop garden, her thoughts returning from her meeting with Leo to the present. She sat down on a bench, allowing her eyes to wander along the magnificent, exotic plants when she noticed she wasn't alone. Monsignor Massini stood on the balcony, lost in thought as he looked across the Vatican premises. He looked tired, even haggard. The past few days and nights must have taken a lot out of him.

When he noticed her, he turned to her. »I had hoped to meet you here, Sister.« He approached her with dark rings under his eyes and a film of sweat on his face. He sat down next to her.

It appeared as if he carried a ton of bricks on his sunken shoulders. Catherine couldn't remember the last time she saw him so uncertain and feverish as if he were going through hell.

»Please forgive my frankness, Father, but you don't look well. You need rest, perhaps even medical help.«

Massini smiled. It was an oddly resigned smile. »Not now, Sister. Not as long as you and the Holy Father are in such danger.«

Catherine hadn't thought that Thea's murder could be such a terrible shock to the priest. On the other hand it was clear that the murders were no longer just happening in the outside world, but rather right here in the Vatican's midst.

»You shouldn't leave the Apostolic Palace for any reason in the coming days,« said Massini quietly. »Evil is among us.«

»Evil has always been among us, Father.«

A strange radiation emanated from Massini. He was pale as a ghost.

»That might be, but I fear your disguise won't protect you much longer.«

»What makes you say that?«

»One made enquiries about the new nun in the papal household.«

»Who is one?«

»I don't know. But I am certain it has something to do with the murders.«

»Have you spoken with Cardinal Ciban about this already?«

»No, not yet. I thought it was more important to tell you first. Listen. I am not familiar with the details of these murderous events and I don't want to be, but I can feel that you will be the next victim. The next few days will be critical. For you and His Holiness!« With that Massini got up and ran off without turning back.

Catherine didn't get it. The priest hadn't told her anything new, just the obvious. She returned to her room and switched on the laptop to work on her book some more. Aside from a few lifeless sentences that made utterly no sense at all she simply couldn't do it. My God, how she missed Darius and Thea. How lonely she felt.

Her mobile phone rang. It was Ben's number. With great joy she answered. »Yes?«

»It's me, Ben. Rinaldo says His Holiness is feeling better?«

»You could say that,« said Catherine. Her friend's voice sounded a little reserved. »His Holiness is working the entire day again.«

»And how have you been?«

»I just had the strangest conversation with Monsignor Massini. I think he's going a tad loopy regarding my safety and that of the Holy Father.«

»Would you like to speak with me and His Eminence about it? I am examining the crime scene at the moment and to be quite honest, I could use your help.«

»That would be great, Ben. Sure.«

»If you would like, I'll meet you halfway.«

»Thank you, but that won't be necessary.«

»See you in a bit!«

Catherine hung up, slipped into sturdier shoes, pulled on a hooded robe and rushed out into the corridor. It would do her some good to talk to Ben and Ciban about the odd encounter with Massini on the rooftop terrace. Something was definitely awry.

As she walked down the corridor toward the back stairwell, she saw that the light was still on in the Pope's office. She remembered her promise to Ciban to tell him or Leo every time she left the Apostolic Palace.

74

Ben expected nothing less. If he read Ciban's expression correctly, the cardinal didn't have high hopes either. The Vigilanza didn't find any traces regarding the murder in the underground parking garage or in the secret passageway that ran beneath the Apostolic Palace and was now under constant surveillance. It was as if a ghost had searched Sister Thea out at the Grotta di Lourdes, appearing from nowhere to quickly break her neck.

For the umpteenth time Ciban looked at the crime scene photos taken from every angle imaginable. The prefect also watched the video again that was so underexposed, it was a complete waste of time to even try to view it.

Ben took a deep breath and thought about Ciban's disclosure about the deceased Pope Innocence and how he could have betrayed his congregation to one of his comrades-in-arms so that his policy could live on well beyond his own papacy. At least the list of possible perpetrators was more manageable now. According to Ciban, there were only seven men who came into question, two of which were already deceased. Sadly there was still the possibility that none of these candidates was the perpetrator in the end. It was quite possible that the murderer belonged to Innocence's worldly circle of friends, perhaps even to Opus Dei.

In the end the prefect reduced the list of suspects to just three people, but before he knew anything for certain, he had refrained from telling Ben any of the names. It was one thing to have a hunch; it was quite another to say it out loud and possibly ruin the person's reputation. But as Ciban had assured Ben, he had been exploring these avenues for some time now.

Ben looked at one of the photos that lay at the top of the pile. How peaceful Sister Thea's face looked. Without any mistrust. Without even a hint of rancour. Without a slight bit of pain. The images reminded Ben of the pictures of Sister Silvia that Father Raj had shown him in the tiny church in Calcutta. How could a crime scene photo emanate such peace?

Ciban suddenly left the conference table and walked over to the computer on his desk. Ben hadn't even heard the computer ping.

The prefect gave him a look as he banged a few keys on the keyboard. »A message from Ralf Porter at the German Federal Intelligence Service!«

Ben dropped everything and hurried to Ciban to take a look at the computer screen himself. Ralf Porter summarised what he had discovered in his encrypted, concise email. The perpetrator's missing rental car had been found in an underground parking garage, but the traces of DNA they collected led nowhere. Porter had also examined the poorly taped surveillance video from the Munich rental car company and had created photos from it. The search through the Interpol database had also led nowhere, but perhaps the photos would be able to help Vatican security in its further investigations.

The cardinal opened the encrypted attachment. It took a moment for the individual images to form on the screen. When the material was shown completely on the monitor, both Ben and Ciban held their breath. Even though the images were rather blurry still, they both looked the murderer in the eye. They recognised him, despite his glasses and baseball cap. Ben would recognise that scar over the left eye anywhere. DeRossi!

For a moment both of them stared at the photo in disbelief, as if they were paralysed. Ciban quickly grabbed the phone and asked to be connected with Coelho. They had no time to lose.

75

Monsignor deRossi's flat was located in Trastevere, a historic quarter with picturesque lanes in the southwestern part of Rome, just a short walking distance from the Vatican. Coelho stood at the door of the flat with two of his Vatican policemen and rang the bell. It was the only flat on the floor and it had one of those old, classic entrance doors that in and of itself was an antique treasure.

The commander rang a second time. No one answered.

He took out a bundle of skeleton keys, opened the door lock within seconds and entered with his men, who raced through the corridor from room to room.

There really was no one there. Not even a mouse. Had deRossi caught wind of it? Or was he simply strolling through Rome and would be back soon?

While one of the men held watch in the hallway, the others combed through every single room without leaving a mark. In the living room Coelho came across a little library with about two hundred volumes, including specialist literature and non-fiction books, academic works and treatises as well as a series of art and photography books. To his amazement there was only one work of fiction, aside from the Holy Scripture and a few schoolbooks. The novel was called The Keys of St. Peter by Roger Peyrefitte.

They found nothing suspicious in the bedroom, bathroom,

kitchen, hallway or living room. It surprised Coelho greatly that deRossi didn't own a private computer, not even a laptop that he might have kept in one of the wardrobes or under the bed.

They searched through the trash, the flushing cistern over the toilet as well as the tiny broom closet without leaving a trace. Coelho didn't even find a key to a bank deposit box or a post office box in the drawers or beneath the rug. Nor did he find a tiny bit of correspondence. Even the post-box that the watch outside had quickly examined was empty.

If not for the cassocks, suits and remaining clothing in the cabinets or the dishes in the kitchen cupboards, the commander might have thought the flat was occupied by a ghost. The bed was so tightly made that it appeared as if no one had ever touched it.

Coelho's gaze fell on the library in the living room once again and on the antiquarian copy of Peyrefitte's The Keys of St. Peter. He pulled the book from the shelf and faltered. It was entirely too light for its size.

When he opened the book, something fell out. The body of the book had been neatly hollowed out. The commander of the Vigilanza looked with great amazement at a mobile phone whose brand he had never seen before.

He bent over, picked up the telephone and checked its cache. Nothing. With the exception of two numbers, it was empty. Coelho placed the mobile phone back in the book and pocketed his findings just as one of his employees entered the living room pale as a ghost, holding a flat tin can.

»I found this beneath one of the creaking floorboards in the hallway.«

Coelho took the tin can, opened it and found multiple finger bones.

»It looks as though someone thoroughly cooked them before

they landed in the tin box,« said the younger Vatican policeman with a muted voice.

The commander snapped the tin can shut once again, concealing his own revulsion. »Bring that and this book here to Cardinal Ciban, Viktor.« He placed both in a plastic bag and rang the cardinal briefly.

Viktor went about his way while Coelho kept an eye on deRossi's flat with the other Vigilanza policeman. The sky grew grey and dark. With any luck, Coelho thought, Viktor would reach the Palace of the Inquisition before the rain began to fall.

76

The master pulled on the precious cassock and looked out the window of his office. Dark clouds rumbled over Rome, casting shadows on the dome of St. Peter's Basilica. It was going to be a stormy, rainy night in more ways than one. It seemed that knave Benelli had indeed challenged him even after his death because he somehow thought he was morally superior to him. Well, that Catherine Bell would pay the price for it. To hell with Alberto Cardinal Benelli and his entire damned brood of heretics. If he thought he could somehow maintain Leo's ridiculous modernistic policies through them, he was sadly mistaken. The second council called by John XXII had done enough damage as it was.

The master cast a look at the clock. Only a few minutes left.

How close he had come to becoming Pope himself. But Benelli had placed himself massively against him in the conclave without the other cardinal electorates even noticing. The master was convinced that Benelli's secret campaign against him had also brought about his defeat. Naturally his nemesis must have had allies. The master bet on none other than Ciban.

The amazing thing was that there wasn't any proof at all that Benelli and the prefect were either friendly or politically aligned with one another and that he might have betrayed him. There wasn't a single shred of evidence to solidify the master's suspicion in any way. Even in the Domus Sanctae Marthae, the house on the Vatican premises in which the cardinals stayed during the conclave, nothing suspicious arose when Benelli and Ciban came into contact. Both men had gone about their business during the papal election as if they had nothing more to do with one another than with the other cardinals too. That in and of itself made the master suspicious in retrospect. In effect they were the only two men who dared defy him. Only through their alliance did their power represent an insurmountable obstacle for the master during the last conclave.

It had appeared to be going his way at the beginning of the election. During the first round of elections, he had received thirty-three of the one hundred fourteen votes. Benelli had received twenty-three votes while Leo whose name back then was still Eugenio Cardinal Tore, only had twelve. The rest had been distributed amongst eighteen other cardinals. Including Ciban. After the second round, the master had received thirty-eight votes. A vast improvement. Benelli got twenty-nine and Leo only fourteen. It appeared to be a neck-and-neck race between the master and Benelli. The former was certain he would walk away the victor.

But then everything came differently than he expected. The event was drawn out over an entire week and in the end, the master left the race. The election would be decided by a simple majority for Benelli. But what happened next was a story that never made a single paper, book, radio or television report. It never once reached the public. When the Cardinal Chamberlain approached Benelli to ask if he accepted the election results, the madman – the master still couldn't believe it! – rejected it, saying he'd prefer to exercise his right to crown Eugenio Tore, the present Pope Leo XIV.

The master had expected a lot of things at that moment, but not that. What insanity it had been, and yet what a clever move too. All because he wanted to prevent one thing: that the master, the best candidate of them all, become Pope.

When Tore finally accepted the election and the cardinals applauded him, Benelli wore a look of great satisfaction. Even Ciban's applause was sincere, coming straight from the heart. The master had never seen the slender, tall cardinal look so relaxed before.

Tore! Tore of all people!

It was as if the cardinals had elected a second John Paul or John XXIII. Yet another stab in the master's heart. Of all people why did they select that wannabe revolutionary? He had no tolerance for Tore. Absolutely none. The man was simply too unrealistic, too foolish. Way too naïve!

Then a few days later after the conclave the master's supposed promotion to Secretariat of State. At first he had felt honoured, if not somewhat mistrusting, but he had soon realised how much more freedom and information his previous office as prefect of the Congregation of the Doctrine of Faith had afforded him to further his goals and plans. Now his sources had been cut off, occupied by another cardinal. Through Marc Abbot Cardinal Ciban!

It had been a further setback for the master when Ciban of all people found out about the secret as future guardian of the faith. It was hard to take the fact that Ciban's consecration could mean the end of the master's plans. The traitor of all people!

The master noticed that his aggravation was making him shake slightly. His thoughts returned to the nun. To Catherine Bell, who was living a double life in the papal household. It appeared that Benelli had given her explicit instructions. She most likely knew the secret now too. How could she have protected Leo otherwise? But that was over now! The key to solving the problem was her death.

77

It had started to rain. Catherine stood with her jacket over her head in front of the Grotta di Lourdes and looked around. The rain had created flat puddles all about. Small pools of water had formed atop the black plastic tarps that they had placed over the imitation of the Lourdes grotto to protect it from the rain. Her gaze swept over the veiled crime scene and surrounding area. Ben was nowhere to be found.

»Ben?«

She slowly walked toward the supposed scaffolding and looked about. The jacket covering her head reduced her line of vision so much that she had to push it away to get a better view. The veiled Grotta seemed like a supernatural monster in the rainy darkness.

»Ben?«

No answer. Hopefully nothing had happened to him?

A vague feeling that she was being observed suddenly overcame her. She looked over her shoulder. The area in front of the Grotta was dark and empty.

Then she heard a quiet coughing – and steps.

»Catherine?«

Clearly Ben's voice, even if it sounded somewhat muted as if he had a cold. He wore a hooded robe due to the weather, which is why she could not recognise his face.

»Are you still being haunted by your visions?« he asked. His voice sounded friendly and yet somehow – insidious? Why would he ask that? Did it have something to do with Thea's murder?

»They aren't just prophecies, but also memories.« An inexplicable shiver ran across her skin. »How can I help you?«

Ben took a step closer and lifted the tarp over the Grotta. Catherine still couldn't see his face. »Thea left you a message.«

»A message – for me?« As she bent forward, she felt a needle stick into her neck. Then she saw the face beneath the hood. The scar above the one eye.

78

Cardinal Ciban pulled on a pair of latex gloves, opened the book that they found in deRossi's flat and took out the mobile phone. The crime scene photos and the DVD with the film still lay on the table. The prefect turned on the mobile phone and looked through its cache. The first number was deRossi's landline – the Vigilanza had found out at least that much – and they were still checking on the second.

Ben winced when he saw the second phone number in the deRossi's mobile phone cache. »Good Lord above! That's Catherine's number!« he blurted out.

»Are you certain?«

Was Ben imagining things or had he just heard outright concern about the Vatican employee in Ciban's voice?

He pulled out his own mobile phone and checked the cache to compare the numbers. No question whatsoever! The last phone call on deRossi's mobile phone had gone to Catherine. Ben speed-dialled her number, but no one answered.

»Damn it! I have to go to the Apostolic Palace at once!«

Ciban grabbed Ben's arm just as he wanted to leave. »Wait. Catherine and I had an agreement. She was not to leave the Palace without telling either myself or His Holiness.« The cardinal went to his desk, picked up the phone receiver and dialled an internal Vatican number.

»Holiness, I fear we have a problem.« He switched on the speakerphone so Ben could listen in.

»What is it, Eminence?«

»Sister Catherine. We couldn't reach her on her mobile.«

For a moment there was silence on the other end of the line. Then the Pope said carefully: »As far as I know, Sister Catherine had just rung with Monsignor Hawlett and was just on her way to him.«

»Monsignor Hawlett did not speak with Sister Catherine on the phone, Holiness.«

»I beg your pardon?«

»Where was she to meet him?«

The Pope hesitated. »If Sister Catherine didn't speak with Monsignor Hawlett, who says that I am really speaking with you, Eminence?«

»I have your secret number, Holiness.«

»So what? – The murderer had the names and addresses of the apostles. Finding out my secret number should be a trivial matter to him.«

Ciban sighed, then identified himself by a buzzword that, Ben supposed, came from a very personal confession.

»Sister Catherine told me she was to meet the Monsignor at the Grotta di Lourdes,« said the Pope finally.

»At the Grotta di Lourdes?« repeated Ciban in disbelief.

»That is what Sister Catherine told me. Good Lord, hurry up then!«

The prefect had barely put down the receiver when Ben raced out of the office. Ben could hear Ciban calling to him: »Damn it, Ben. She most certainly won't be there anymore!«

But he didn't care. He had to do something. He had to find Catherine. It was imperative. Before it was too late.

79

Ben ran as if his life depended on it. When he reached the Grotta di Lourdes, he was soaked to the bone. He stood before the large arched imitation of the cave with the Maria statue and looked around him as the rain whipped against the ground and the tarps. He looked beneath the tarps just in case, but there wasn't a trace of Catherine anywhere. He wasn't certain if he should feel relief or not. It could mean she was still alive if he didn't find her dead body here.

Ben reached for his mobile and dialled Catherine's number once again. Maybe he'd be in luck this time. After a few seconds, a sound directly behind him startled him. The ringtone came from a nearby bush.

Oh no, please don't let it be!, he thought.

He ran through the pelting rain, squatted down and combed through the shrubbery. He was relieved to find out that there was no dead body lying there. But he found Catherine's mobile phone, grabbed it and checked whether she might have left a message for him. No dice. Disappointed, he pocketed the phone just as his began to ring.

»Yes?«

»It's me. Ciban. Have you found Catherine?«

»No. But I found her mobile. It was lying in the bushes.«

»That's a good sign. At least it means that she is still alive.«

Ben thought he heard major relief in Ciban's voice. Or was he projecting his own immense hope onto the cardinal?

»But where is she?« he asked.

»I have been checking my past research once again. I am pretty certain I know who deRossi's backer and secret mentor is.«

»You know who the mastermind is?«

»Most likely, yes. Do you know Catherine's favourite place in the Vatican?«

»Of course. The Sistine.«

»If I'm not mistaken, Catherine was dragged from the Grotta to the Sistine. Be careful, Ben. I am most certain that deRossi and Catherine aren't alone. I am on my way to you.«

»Who is the backer?« Ben wanted to know.

»I'll tell you when I get there.« Ciban disconnected the call.

Darn, thought Ben, he couldn't just stand there and wait for the prefect. He had to go to the Sistine. Straight away.

He began to run.

80

Catherine stumbled in a haze alongside deRossi who held her firmly in his grip and wouldn't let her go for a second. Whatever he had injected into her neck made her have no will of her own and impaired her sense of balance. She staggered next to him as if in an absurd nightmare, as if she knew that she was dreaming without being able to break out of it. The dark walls surrounding her turned into oddly deformed grotesque tunnels as if they led to an ancient Egyptian tomb. She suddenly suffered a weakness attack, forcing her to stand still for a moment, but deRossi just held onto her even more tightly and pulled her ruthlessly alongside him.

Catherine attempted to suppress the lack of will that the drug created and at least to maintain a sense of clarity in some part of her brain, but the fog in her consciousness only allowed for her to stumble alongside the Monsignor.

DeRossi had taken her mobile phone away and had simply tossed it. So she didn't even stand a theoretical chance of alerting Ben or Ciban; that is, if she could rid herself of her kidnapper. She suddenly grew very tired and her knees nearly buckled under the exhaustion she felt. Where was deRossi taking her anyway?

»I need a quick rest, please,« she said.

»Out of the question, Sister. It is important that you keep moving, otherwise you really will fall asleep. What you are about to experience will be worth the effort. Believe me!«

To Catherine's dismay, deRossi took it up a notch. They passed another tunnel, another chamber. The further they went in the underground labyrinth, the further Catherine thought they were getting from the Vatican. Was he taking her to Castel Sant'Angelo?

She suddenly remembered something from her childhood. That day when she and Ben had left the Institute and had gotten lost in the deciduous and coniferous forests at the Southern edge of Lake Michigan. It had taken two days for the ranger team led by Darius to find them and only because Catherine had stuck to the rules. Always walk downstream. Downstream...

She somehow had the feeling that the tunnel she was stumbling down under deRossi's gruff command led upstream. Swaying unsteadily and losing strength by the minute, she pushed herself forward step by step until her legs gave out and she fell to the ground like a sack of potatoes. DeRossi had grabbed her by the arm, but her collapse had been so sudden that he too lost his balance. He knelt in front of her and slapped her hard in the face. When that didn't work, he gave her a second, then a third slap until she was halfway conscious again.

»You aren't going to break down now, Sister. Not when you're so close to your amazing performance.«

Although Catherine was a nun, she had a hankering to punch deRossi's lights out or at least to break his nose, which would fit so well to the scar above his eye. Unfortunately, she was so out of it that it affected her aim. Not to mention that she simply didn't have the necessary strength to slap him down. DeRossi dragged her up forcefully and pulled her behind him along the tiny limestone pathway, up a narrow set of stairs to a side door that led directly to the Sistine Chapel.

The Sistine. Catherine's favourite place. So it was after all...

She was to die here!

She numbly went through her options, or at least she tried. Her brain felt as if it were packed in oily cotton, barely able to put two and two together. DeRossi pushed her past two Swiss guards that lay left and right of the wide entrance door, unconscious or possibly even dead. He then led her through the antechamber like a life-sized doll, through the choir screen and finally pushed her into the larger area of the chapel reserved for the clergy on official occasions. At the other end of the Sistine, directly in front of the altar, stood a man in a black cassock with a scarlet red biretta. He was short and had his back to Catherine and deRossi. His entire focus seemed to rest on Michelangelo's Last Judgement as if he were searching for something he hadn't found yet.

»Eminence,« said deRossi respectfully. »Sister Catherine Bell.«

The cardinal turned slowly to her and her escort.

»Thank you, Nicola. Sister Catherine, it is nice to see you again. I enjoyed our last encounter at Benelli's very much.«

Although Catherine was extremely out of it, the shock raced through every fibre of her being, allowing her a moment of clarity. As if in a trance, she could do nothing else but to stare Cardinal Monti wide-eyed in the face.

81

Catherine looked spellbound at Cardinal Monti, then Michelangelo's Apocalypse and then back to the old prefect. He was an
old man, a tiny shrivelled twerp that wore a cardinal's robe, but
in this very moment, he seemed as dangerous and powerful as a
demon, like an inexplicable anachronism that had stepped straight out of Michelangelo's scenario of hell. Catherine wasn't sure
if it was the drugs that made the flood of images behind Monti
come to life. The amply naked figures were watching her, moving
about as if the old cardinal had a devilish power over them. Two
angels carried the large book of the damned that weighed a ton.

The old Monti walked toward Catherine with an astoundingly
firm stride and a smile that seemed to say he himself had staged
the end of the world in all its glory.

»The most significant chapel in the history of Christianity,« he
said. »The Popes are elected here. The Holy Father is inducted
into the final of all secrets and that although the secret is in
principle evident to everyone.«

He stood still, looked about the Sistine with a fiery gaze, observed the painting of Jesus' life and finally said with a cawing voice:
»The Jesus myth has indeed served us well. For the past two
thousand years it has distracted Christianity from the actual
truth. It is really rather simple: Man only sees what man wants to
see. He adheres irrefutably to the old truths of faith. He wants

old wine in new cups at best. If they wanted, everyone could actually be consecrated.« Monti paused for a moment, took a deep breath and asked with a knowing smile: »How have you handled your consecration, Catherine?«

The young women simply stared at him as the drug continued to have her believe the images on the Sistine walls were alive. At the same time the marble floor swayed beneath her feet. It took everything she had not to collapse from sheer exhaustion. Monti didn't notice any of it and deRossi, who was standing behind her, seemed to wait for her next moment of weakness. She was so dog-tired, so weak and yet something deep within her told her she had to buy some time. So she played dumb. What did Monti care about how Benelli had introduced her to the truth step by step and how she felt about it?

»I have no idea what you are talking about, Eminence. What do you mean?«

The cardinal surveyed her, curious, predatorily, distrusting, as if he expected a monstrosity to appear in her presence at any moment. But in the end he couldn't help but explain to her what he meant.

»Let's take the example of Apostle Andrew.« His old voice quivered with excitement. »He performed a lot of miracles before he was crucified. And what about Matthew, Judas' successor? He was a missionary in Judea, then Ethiopia where he performed many miracles as well. Or let's think about John, Jesus' favourite disciple. With a single word he destroyed the Temple of Ephesus, had its dead priest resurrected and survived a torturous bath of scalding oil in Rome. And Peter? He moved to Rome through Asia Minor and Greece, healed the sick and raised people from the dead. That is what I mean, Sister. Anyone can see it as long as he wants to and yet the apostolic mystery is a well-kept secret.«

He cast Catherine a mocking look. »On top of all that, the apostles had not only a hard life, but a hard death too.« He turned toward Michelangelo's altar painting and pointed to Bartholomew who held his own skin in his hands. »It must be very unpleasant to be skinned alive. Or to be crucified upside down as Peter was. Not to mention how Simon was split in two with a saw. You don't see much more torturous suffering and blood baths even in modern horror films.«

He turned back toward Catherine. This time his movements appeared to be in slow motion. »But you know what's really upsetting about the whole thing? That no one seems to care. Go to any pedestrian area and ask the people about the miracles the apostles performed or about the suffering they endured upon their deaths. You won't get a single suitable answer...«

Let him talk, Catherine thought, attempting to remain standing on her shaky legs. The radiant colours of the renovated chapel around them ran together, creating islands of light and darkness as if they wanted to form new heavenly and hellish images. When she noticed that Monti's flow of words threatened to dry up, she said foggily: »You haven't mentioned Judas Iscariot.«

The cardinal stared at her as if he hadn't heard correctly. »I beg your pardon?«

»Judas. You haven't mentioned Judas Iscariot. The apostle responsible for your consecration as former prefect of the Congregation of the Doctrine of Faith. The apostle who ruined his reputation as a respectable disciple of Jesus Christ in the name of the secret. Without whose sacrifice there never would have been a new covenant between man and God.«

»Hogwash. Any dummy knows Judas' official story,« said Monti with an oddly mild tone of voice. »Now to you, Sister. Have you never asked yourself who you truly are?« He took one step closer, but kept a certain distance as if she were a dangerous, highly poisonous snake. »Darius was your mentor all your life and vouched for you in front of Gasperetti. Benelli chose you as the only outsider to whom he revealed the secret. Innocence avoided your condemnation. Leo trusted you with his life. Even Ciban doesn't seem to be in any hurry with your trial.« He made a theatrical pause. »Who or what are you, Catherine? An angel? A demon? A sort of super-apostle?«

»It doesn't matter who I am. But who gave you the right as a Christian to murder all these people?«

»People?« Monti literally spewed out the word. »Those aren't people!« He pointed to the altar painting. »Haven't you ever asked yourself why the angels and demons in the Last Judgement don't have wings? Yes, they don't even have an aura. Who are they, the sovereign, unapproachable messengers of heaven? And why aren't you answering my question?«

Catherine would have loved to grab the old cardinal and toss him out of the chapel. With or without wings. The angels stood for all that is good. She had even seen winged beings in the auras of a few people. Or demons such as that teacher in her primary school who had murdered several boys. What did Monti know about such truths? He certainly hadn't seen an aura, not to mention a winged soul, in his entire life. She wasn't going to let him provoke her.

»I'm only interested in one thing…« she said stubbornly. Time. All she needed was a little more time. Something was happening to the chapel, but she wasn't sure what it was. Was the drug making her crazy? »Why did you have Darius, Thea and all the others killed?«

»It is quite obvious,« explained Monti like a judge for whom everything was already decided. »The apostles have a strong influence on weak Popes. It all began with John XXIII.« He paused for a moment. »Did you know John is the most common name among Popes?« Then he continued jauntily: »It got worse with John Paul, despite his short papacy. And it has taken on catastrophic proportions with Leo. He is going to destroy the Church with his obscure plans and reforms. Innocence prepared me for many years to bring the Church in the right direction. And that is exactly what I intend on doing.«

Catherine stared at the wizen old man through her brain's thick fog. The entire Sistine appeared to be in a continuous flow through time and space. Almost like in her visions. »You want to initiate the apocalypse for that reason? Is that your objective? Is that what you wanted to achieve with all those murders? That humanity be placed on trial? I can't imagine that Innocence wanted that!«

»You have no idea what is at stake here; otherwise you wouldn't stand in the way of the Church's survival. The whole thing was a collusion from the very beginning, a deal between heaven and hell. A deal that has suppressed humanity and the Church for two thousand years. The apostolic power must be broken once and for all!«

»Just like the times during the witch hunt?«

Monti let out a short, cawing laugh filled with contempt. »You don't understand, Catherine. You don't even want to! He set us up. The angels, the apostles, the martyrs, the damned, the blessed, yes even Our Saviour and the Holy Mary!«

»Who set us up?«

»God!« screamed Monti. His voice suddenly sounded as piercing as a siren to her ears. Full of hatred, full of insanity. »God!« he repeated. He then became automatically calm, examining her with his intelligent, ancient, crazy eyes as the people in the painting behind him went either to heaven or hell. »It is time that humanity grow up and stand on its own two feet. You have the choice, Catherine. Which way will you decide for yourself? For heaven or for hell?«

The young woman didn't even need to think of her response. »I am 'the rebel,' Eminence. Remember?«

»If I had forgotten, we wouldn't be standing here.« He dug in his cardinal's robe, pulled out an envelope and tossed it her way. »You have been lied to as well, Sister.«

Catherine carefully bent forward to retrieve the envelope, pulled out its contents and, after briefly glancing at the picture and file note, held her breath. She could feel her whole body and soul begin to shake as a stake was rammed into her heart. Through the thick fog in her consciousness, she became clear that this letter stole the very identity she had always known. The mother she had thought was her mother her entire life wasn't her mother at all. She, Catherine, was a foundling. And Darius had known it all those years!

For a moment, they stood in complete silence. Only the figures in the paintings moved as if to catch a glimpse at the photo. Movement everywhere and yet time stood still.

»Father Darius used you. You and your foster mother. From the very beginning!« stated Monti with contempt. »I am offering you the truth, Catherine, not a lie. I am not hiding a thing. I can help you to bring light into your past. Forget the priest and abandon this disastrous connection with Leo. Follow me instead.«

The young woman looked up from the photo in a daze and shook her head. »You bastard!« Monti wasn't right. He was trying to manipulate her to bring her over to his side. She had known Darius since childhood. She had known him better than any other person on the planet, her mother and Ben included. She had seen his soul and his soul was good. Darius never would have used her. If he had kept her in the dark about her heritage, then he had had good reason to do so. He was an apostle!

»Together we will conquer heaven,« said Monti in a serious tone.

»You are insane!«

The cardinal shook his head indulgently. »It is not I who is insane, but the world, Sister. But both you and I can break through this insanity together.«

Catherine could no longer hold back the tears. »Never!«

Monti scrutinised her with a look of disappointment. »Are you certain?«

Catherine gave no response.

»Well then, you have made your decision. A shame, really. Such a shame. I had hoped you would understand. I could have given you so much more.«

The old cardinal gave deRossi a sign.

82

Ben ran like hell over the Vatican garden's wet, slick grass until he came across one of the two-seater covered electric golf carts on the level of the Palazzo del Governatorato. The carts were used within the Vatican grounds instead of fuelled vehicles for fast daily transportation. So as not to create a stir, he kept the headlights off until he had reached one of the side entrances of the Sistine with the nearly silent golf cart. Inside the corridors and antechambers it was nearly pitch black.

As he entered the chapel's antechamber, he discovered that both Swiss guards who normally kept watch lay unconscious on the marble floor. One of them was still clutching his halberd. Somewhat farther away inside the chapel, Ben could hear voices without understanding what they were saying. But he was certain he heard Catherine's voice.

As his gaze travelled over the two unconscious men, he realised that although he was a Vatican agent, he wasn't carrying a weapon. What was he thinking going up against a murderer like deRossi unarmed? The Monsignor most likely was carrying a weapon. A knife. A pistol. Something.

He bent over one of the guards and started to search him. Customarily the Swiss guards carried not only the traditional weaponry such as the halberd and a sword, but also a SIG 75 that the Swiss Army has used as its service weapon since 1975.

Ben had often trained with members of the Swiss guards and the Vigilanza so he knew how to handle the SIG 75. For special situations the Swiss guards also carried a pepper spray. He immediately found the pepper spray on the first guard, but no SIG. So he scurried over to the other guard while he continued to hear voices coming from the Sistine. A man's voice, an older man's voice, he assumed. The man seemed to be rather excited.

Ben discovered the desired SIG on the second guard and retrieved it for himself. Armed with a pistol and pepper spray, he tiptoed into the chapel through the passageway of the choir screen as he heard Catherine say: »You bastard!«

»I am offering you the truth, Catherine, not a lie. I am not hiding a thing. I can help you to bring light into your past. Forget the priest and abandon this disastrous connection with Leo. Follow me instead. Together we will conquer heaven.«

Ben held his breath. Monti! Sergio Cardinal Monti! The former prefect of the Congregation of the Doctrine of Faith! He was the brains behind the operation about whom Ciban had talked. And the younger priest that stood behind Catherine must be Monsignor deRossi!

»You are insane!« Ben heard Catherine say. Her voice sounded determined, but she seemed to be under shock. She stood there as if Monti had robbed her of her entire life force.

»It is not I who is insane, but the world, Sister. But both you and I can break through this insanity together.«

»Never!«

»Are you certain?«

Ben couldn't tell whether Catherine gave an answer or not.

»Well then, you have made your decision. A shame, really. Such a shame. I had hoped you would understand. I could have given you so much more.«

The old cardinal gave deRossi a sign upon which he moved

closer to Catherine and was about to wrap his hands around her neck.

Heavens! Ben wasn't a second too soon!

»FREEZE!« he screamed, pulling out the SIG 75 and moving through the entrance of the artistic choir screen. His voice echoed throughout the entire room.

83

Catherine sat there numbly, holding the photo in one hand, utterly helpless as Monti gave the sign. Suddenly she heard Ben's voice like a thunderbolt out of the blue echoing off the walls of the chapel.

»FREEZE!« Ben had a pistol in his hand and pointed it toward deRossi. She had never seen him with a weapon before. »Let the sister go at once!«

But deRossi did the exact opposite. He grabbed Catherine within seconds, using her as a human shield and placing a pistol to her temple.

Damn! It must be the pistol from the other Swiss guard, Ben thought. That bastard had gotten the same idea as he had.

DeRossi laughed forcefully with contempt. »Why so upset, Father? Wrong place, wrong time?« In the very next moment, he pointed the gun at Ben and pulled the trigger.

Ben had often wondered what it might be like to be shot with a nine millimetre bullet. At the moment all he felt was a sharp brutal jolt. He fell to his knees, feeling the wound...to his stomach! The Monsignor looked at him with satisfaction as he fell over like a felled tree, lying there motionless.

»Ben!« Catherine wanted to wrench free of deRossi, but he held her firmly in his grip. As she pummelled and kicked him, allowing the photo to sail to the ground, Monti went to the

Monsignor covered in blood and applauded him with exaggerated superiority. Catherine boiled with anger. She could have
killed both deRossi and the old church dignitary at once! Her
heart cried out for revenge. But then she suddenly realised the
world around her began to change and that she perceived the
colours in the paintings and the auras of the three men – Ben,
Monti, deRossi – with a sudden intensity that was completely
new to her. Was it due to the drug or simply the extremely high
level of adrenaline in her bloodstream? Or both?

The images around her were alive. There was no doubt about
it. And the three men...

Monti's aura smouldered with a deep black and fiery red from
his ego, even though he was a man as old as the hills. Too old to
participate in the next papal election and to get at the apostles.
DeRossi's aura looked like an absurd uncontrollable ball of fire
made of red and red-orange colours. And Ben...his aura was
getting weaker by the minute. He was losing blood as it seeped on
the ground and glowed! Monti laughed maliciously. His despica-
ble laughter seemed even more intolerable in Catherine's exaggerated senses.

And then...oh no, please don't let it be. Not now!

Catherine's mind became clearer and sharper. As the reality
around her sunk into even more abstruse images, the room in the
chapel became more lively. A figure tore away from Michelangelo's Last Judgement, floated toward her and gently took her hand;
the very hand she had used to hold the photo just moments ago.

Darius!

Catherine felt his energy and pure presence. Within milliseconds she relived parts of her past. Her birth. But she couldn't
see her biological mother. Then the adoption by her foster mother who knew nothing about her gift. The first encounter with
Darius in the primary school in Dr. Beverly Florena's office

where she immediately looked up to Darius as a father figure. The years at the Institute, the time in Rome, her further mental training in Lux Domini. The priest was by her side the entire time and had taught her how to be a self-confident individual and to manage her gift.

Further figures appeared next to Darius: Cardinal Benelli, Thea, Silvia, Isabella and Sylvester. But they somehow looked different than during their lifetime. An indescribable light shone around them. Catherine felt an unbelievable affection that emanated from each one of them.

It was Benelli who finally said: »I am sorry that I created so much pain for you, Catherine. But I saw no other way to stop him. Lucifer's dark vibrations have permeated Monti's soul. It was only after he recognised who you were that he could move to the light. We can only defy him with your help. The unbelievable power of your gift has made you my successor. But it was much too dangerous to induct you from the beginning.«

Catherine understood at once what Benelli had meant back in the villa's chapel during the reception when he told her that Darius had revealed her gift to him and that the attacks had been meant for none other than Pope Leo. The cardinal had spoken about that special community with which the Pope was connected. Shortly thereafter he had sacrificed himself at the reception so she could directly take over his legacy and to make her strong for her mission.

She observed as Thea, who was next to Benelli and Darius, floated over to Ben and touched him to stop the bleeding. Catherine had the impression that she could soar over everything that was happening and see every hidden corner of the Sistine. Ben's aura began to regain its strength.

Thea returned to the other apostles and explained: »We can't wait any longer. It is time.«

Darius caressed Catherine's cheek one last time, then let go of her hand and retreated with the other spiritual beings back to the altar painting where they gathered around Jesus and the Holy Mary.

By now deRossi and Monti had started to notice that something extraordinary was happening. Catherine felt the Monsignor loosen his grip ever so slightly, audibly gasping for air just like old Monti. The chapel's atmosphere was as weighty as the air before a pending thunderstorm. It was as if the air was burning. As if they were inhaling fire.

Catherine could hear Darius' voice in her head: »Have no fear, my child. This is the moment of truth. This is the moment in which balance will be restored. I will always be with you!«

Heavenly light glided along the Sistine's ceiling, suddenly shooting out of the walls onto the apostles and Catherine. The apostles suddenly looked like beautiful angels of death whose auras blazed in black and gold.

A ray of energy as thick as her arm came loose from Catherine's aura and hit Monti right in the chest. The skin beneath his robe sizzled as if someone had taken a branding iron to it. The old cardinal howled, bent over in madness and fell to his knees with a hideous scream and bloody foam oozing from his mouth. He had bitten his tongue due to the pain. DeRossi, who stood next to him as if in a trance and didn't notice either the light or the apostles, only smelled his burnt flesh and saw how the eyes of his master turned black as oil, writhing on the ground like a madman and babbling crazily as he stared at the ceiling painting and lost his mind.

DeRossi let Catherine go for a moment, leaned over Monti and tried to help him. The young woman quickly ran over to Ben, who was lying on his side on the marble floor in a pool of blood. She carefully turned him over and examined his stomach wound. Ben was half-conscious and seemed to even recognise her. As if by a miracle, the bleeding had actually stopped.

Then something happened that she never thought possible. DeRossi had recovered from his shock and yelled at her with hatred: »What have you done to him, you devil!« He literally nailed her with his intense gaze, stood up, ran to her and pulled her up by the arm to fulfil his assignment once and for all.

Catherine grimaced in pain and looked about for the apostles, but no one else besides Ben, deRossi and herself was there. So she took her right leg and kicked the Monsignor with all her might between the legs.

Pale as a ghost, deRossi collapsed to the floor, grabbing his groin with both hands. He gasped for air as if the chapel stood in heavenly flames once again. Every single breath hurt. Catherine used the seconds left to run to Ben and search for his weapon. But she nearly slipped on the pool of blood and couldn't find the pistol. DeRossi suddenly stood over her, his ominous face purple with rage.

»I would say it is time for you to go.«

He grabbed her by the throat, pulled her up toward him as if she were a child and wanted to break her neck when his head suddenly turned to one side with an empty look and he collapsed to the floor like a marionette. Ciban had knocked deRossi's lights out with a single blow to the temple.

Catherine's knees buckled. The prefect caught her before she could fall to the ground. He held her close and pressed him to her.

»Have no fear. I won't let you go.«

84

The storm raged over Rome through the night and into the following day. Veritable stormy winds lashed over the city in the early morning hours and had made the waters of the Tiber swell. Catherine sat in the back of a black Vatican limousine and was on the way with Father Rinaldo to Benelli's villa. The rain pelted against the windows, streaming in hurried rows down the glass and darkening the entire world.

An hour before she had visited Ben in the Gemelli clinic. He had not yet awoken from his coma. But what the doctors did tell her was that his wound healed astonishingly quickly and well after the operation. It had healed so well and so quickly that the doctors were greatly puzzled. It was a mystery that Catherine certainly wasn't going to reveal. She gave Ben a kiss on the forehead and made her way with Rinaldo to an appointment with His Holiness and Ciban.

As Rinaldo steered the car through the wooded area that led up the long hill toward the villa, thoughts about last night's events ran through Catherine's mind. She didn't want to think about what would have happened if Benelli's plan had failed in the end. She and Ben would have most likely been dead and His Holiness would have become Sergio Cardinal Monti's compliant mario-nette. She still couldn't quite believe that the old Monti of all people had been behind it all.

As far as she knew, they had removed Monti – who was now more a sad heap of insanity than anything else – from the Vatican that same night and had brought him to a German monastery near Cologne that was more a psychiatric clinic for Catholic priests than a place of contemplation. A place for the worst cases. Officially, Monti had suffered an age-related stroke and was being given the best medical care possible.

DeRossi had also left the Vatican last night in the custody of the Vigilanza. Catherine didn't know where they had brought the Monsignor. Neither Ciban nor Coelho, the commander, had said a word about it.

However, the people she thought most about after waking up from her restless sleep were Darius and her foster mother. She still couldn't believe the priest had remained silent about her heritage all those years and that she had never noticed that her mother wasn't her mother at all.

Monti had been right about one thing: People only see what they want to see. Even Catherine wasn't immune to it. She had never once doubted that her foster mother had been her real biological one.

She brushed away a strand of hair from her face and had to smile when she thought of Darius. She couldn't have had a better mentor. Ever since she had met the priest, she no longer felt abandoned. From the very first time they had met, they had gotten along in the most wondrous way. The patient, wise and fatherly scholar who never forced anything and yet taught her so much. And she, the fearful, defiant child who first had to learn how to manage her gift in an appropriate manner.

Mentor and student. Father figure and daughter figure. Two soulmates. And yet...

Catherine took out the photo with which Monti had tried to bring her over to his side and looked at it. At first glance, Darius looked so young in the photograph. But upon further examination, she could see the tiny wrinkles around his eyes and forehead as well as the greying around his temples. His eyes shimmered like mercury. Catherine had noticed this type of shimmer before during the hearings in the Palace of the Inquisition and recently in the Vatican's secret archives when Ciban had confronted Ben and her with the Gospel of Judas in their hands. Finally, in the Sistine when Ciban slapped down deRossi. The cardinal had discovered the photograph that had fallen from her hands on the marble floor, wiped off Ben's blood from it and had returned it to her with the words: »I believe this photograph belongs to you, Sister.«

As if in a trance, Catherine had once again stared at the image. Then she had asked the prefect: »Did you know, Eminence?«

»No,« Ciban had said, shaking his head.

»My mother…the image I had created about my father…« She had then faltered. »I don't know who I am anymore.«

»Oh yes, you do, Catherine. Darius showed you. And now you are beginning to understand why Cardinal Benelli's plan could work no other way.«

Catherine emerged from her retrospective thoughts, looked through the car window at the trees that rushed passed and put the photo away with a quiet sigh. She would never know who her real parents were. And Darius was dead. Irrevocably. Yet she had had so many unanswered questions that she would have loved to ask her mentor. Knowing that she would never find the answers pained her. Why did one only realise such things after the people one loves are dead?

»We're almost there,« said Rinaldo, guiding the car around an extensive curve.

Catherine's thoughts returned to last night. Directly after Ben was transported to the hospital and Monti and deRossi had been brought away, a troupe of Vigilanza policemen had shown up to remove any trace of the incident in the Sistine. After Catherine had halfway recovered from the shock, Ciban had taken her back to her room in the Apostolic Palace. When they arrived, he kindly took her hand and said: »I know it sounds hollow and meaningless, Sister. You need time to digest everything…and yet…try to get some sleep.«

»What about you?«

»I have some work to do.« Ciban had shrugged his shoulders and had given her a brief smile. »Would you believe I have a comfortable cot in my office in case of emergency. I can't quite manage no sleep at all.« He paused for a moment as if to say something personal about what had happened, but then he let go of her hand and said instead: »Good night, Sister. Sleep well and sweet dreams.«

Ten minutes later Catherine had fallen into a deep sleep and had dreamed about God knows what. When she awoke from her deep sleep, she had felt miraculously recovered. Even now, hours later in the limousine on the way to Benelli's villa, she felt as good as new despite all the stress she had experienced.

Her gaze followed the edge of the woods. This time as the estate emerged among the high trees, it emanated something enigmatic and mysterious like an old castle from whose towers and battlements grotesque hallucinations emerged, but also a kind of hope and strength, aligning with a strange sense of melancholy. Catherine spontaneously thought of Shakespeare's undying words: »We are such stuff as dreams are made on, and our little life is rounded with a sleep.« This phrase described the villa's aura to a tee and it was exactly this phrase that Darius had once used when they had visited one of the ghostly monastery ruins in Ireland.

85

On the large parking lot in front of the open staircase multiple black limousines were waiting, most likely the cars for the Holy Father, Ciban and the Vatican police. The cars' number plates, however, were neutral. Catherine remembered that the Villa must have gone back to the Ciban clan after Benelli's death. Benelli had told her that the family had avoided the villa since the death of their family member, Cardinal Ciban's sister Sarah. She wondered why their meeting had to take here of all places instead of in the Vatican, at Castel Sant'Angelo or at Castel Gandolfo.

As Catherine ran up the open staircase – Rinaldo attempted to keep most of the rain away with a large umbrella – she had two déjà-vus. In the first she saw herself as she entered the building for the first time with Ben; in the second she watched as two paramedics carried Benelli's dead body on a stretcher down the steps to an ambulance. Both experiences seemed to be light years away, but in fact it had only happened a few days ago.

Rinaldo left the umbrella in the entrance hall and led Catherine beyond a large ballroom as they passed through several most magnificent hallways and rooms. As they walked by, Rinaldo explained, among other things, the stucco gallery with scenes from Ovid's Metamorphoses and select myths from antiquity. Various paintings graced the arch. In one of the representations

Catherine believed to recognise Narcissus, who looked at his own reflection with the utmost of love. As she further saw, a divine spiral staircase furnished with double pillars and connecting the first and second floors topped off the villa's centre. In the depths of the villa there was also a type of dungeon.

Finally, Rinaldo opened a tall, heavy, ornate door and signalled to Catherine to walk through it. As the young nun entered the room behind it, she held her breath. She was standing in one of the most impressive private libraries she had ever seen. The shelved walls with countless old and new books reached nearly to the colourful ceiling fresco with an abundant gallery interspersed amongst the stacks. Multiple lecterns stood in the middle of the room. Three gigantic globes adorned the corners while elegant spiral stairs led to the gallery in the fourth corner. On the one side ceiling-high window facades could be seen in regular intervals between the shelves that ensured sufficient light. The ceiling fresco showed an allegorical representation of science and faith in addition to the four cardinal virtues in the form of angels: wisdom, justice, strength and temperance.

As Catherine drew closer, she discovered a sumptuously and abundantly set table with festive burning candles. The Pope and his secretary, Monsignor Massini, who had both been standing by the window looking out of it, approached her with a warm greeting. Leo appeared completely at ease and relaxed as if the strain of the past few days never happened. One could sense the exhaustion in Massini, on the other hand. He quickly said his goodbyes so he could, as he put it, catch up on his beauty sleep. Catherine thought that it was more that the secretary was being driven by an inner demon.

»Holiness.«

The Pope looked her in the eye. »It is so thoughtful of you to have come, Catherine. Marc...I beg your pardon...Cardinal

Ciban will be slightly delayed. He is still meeting with Cardinal Gasperetti.« He pointed to the walls of books surrounding them. »Impressive, don't you agree?«

Catherine nodded. »To be honest, I'm rather speechless.«

Leo smiled. »You are most likely asking yourself why we have called you here of all places. To get straight to it there is a special reason for it. Come with me. I should like to show you something.«

She followed him up the spiral stairs to the gallery. Once at the top they passed various shelves whose treasures were hidden behind glass until the Pope finally stood still and pointed to the marble floor beneath them.

»I realise this presentation may seem a tad theatrical, but you can only see it from up here and it is best from this position.«

Catherine followed the Pope's gaze and her eyes widened. Her dreams! Her visions! The apostolic history was integrated into the marble floor as a mosaic. The entire mysterious secret in twelve wonderful images.

»This villa is a special place,« explained the Holy Father. »Darius, Benelli and Thea spent quite some time here. Cardinal Monti didn't know about the significance of this place inside the villa. And His Eminence Cardinal Ciban only first understood the deeper meaning behind this place after his consecration in the Vatican's secret archives where the original Gospel of Judas Iscariot is kept.« The Pope paused for a moment, hesitating before he said: »Sarah, Cardinal Ciban's sister was a psychic.«

»Sarah was an apostle?«

»Not directly. But her case was a bit similar to yours, Catherine.«

»Cardinal Benelli told me about her tragic death, a cold case.«

»True. But I know His Eminence is following a trace.«

»After all these years?«

»He won't rest until his sister's murderer is caught, even if he has to go through hell for it. And I mean that literally.« The Pope gave the apostolic images on the marble floor another look, then turned to Catherine. »You have gone through hell in the past few days for me, and I don't know how I can thank you enough for it.«

»Thank Cardinal Benelli, Holiness. Not me. It wasn't until the confrontation in the Sistine that I grasped his plan at all.«

That was true. It wasn't until the early morning hours that Catherine became aware of the true importance of the chapel in this fight. The Sistine was not only her favourite place in the Vatican, but also the place of such psychic energy that even non-psychic people could feel. The Popes were chosen in the Sistine in the face of Michelangelo's fresco of The Last Judgement. It could only be there that the Holy Father could renew the two thousand year old vow to the apostles in a spiritual manner. But that same unbelievable energy that constantly electrified the atmosphere amongst all the colourful art works could also be used against one. With Catherine's help Benelli made sure of it in the case of Cardinal Monti. In the end, the Sistine's magic literally burned Monti out within seconds. He was still alive, but he was nothing more than a pile of human wreckage.

»Your modesty honours you, Sister, but without your support, we would have been utterly powerless.«

»Do you remember Benelli's letter, Holiness?« She was referring to the letter that the cardinal had left for her, along with the Gospel of Judas, in the Tower of the Winds.

»Yes, I remember each and every word of it.«

»Cardinal Benelli most likely would not have written it to me if Father Darius hadn't told him about my gift.«

Leo nodded thoughtfully. »Benelli recognised your potential during the crisis.«

Catherine reached into the interior pocket of her nun's habit and handed him the old photograph that Monti had left her.

The Pope looked at the picture, greatly moved. Then he said: »Darius loved you like his own daughter. But neither he nor Benelli can expect you to inherit the position as apostle due to your extraordinary gift. Not even they have the right to do that. Monti has been put out of business, there won't be any more apostle murders and you have been freed of any further duties regarding my own person.«

»I thank you, Holiness. But what if it isn't a duty, but rather a gift?«

»A gift?«

»You know that all I stand for is modernising the Church. I know you can't affect that level of change within the Church. That is why you need all the support you can get.«

Six of the Pope's spiritual advisers were dead. Whether Leo admitted it or not, he needed Catherine's gift, her mental energy, if he wanted to reach his goal. At least until the murdered spirituals could be replaced. Well then, Catherine could write her books just as easily in Rome.

The Pope stared at her as if seeing her for the first time. He finally said with a voice filled with emotion: »Cardinal Benelli's plan extends beyond what I thought possible. But yes, Sister. I accept your offer.«

The library door swung open and Cardinal Ciban entered. When he didn't see anyone on the ground floor, he looked up toward the gallery. The Pope signalled to him that Catherine and he would come down.

»I see, Sister, that His Holiness has introduced you to the villa's secret.« Ciban pulled out a chair for Catherine and then took a seat himself at the festively set table. It seemed he must have had a few hours of sleep on his office cot last night. »You know that

Cardinal Benelli lived here in the past few years. I think toward
the end he knew the villa better than I.«

They ate from the delicious dishes, drank from the selected
wine and spoke about heaven and Earth until Leo finally returned to the events of the past few days with a single question.

»What I still don't quite understand is this: How did Cardinal
Monti get all those names?«

»Sister Catherine is right, Holiness,« explained Ciban. »None
of the apostles was a traitor. His Eminence Cardinal Monti
exploited his friendship with Pope Innocence to get to the list.«

»Innocence told him the names?«

The cardinal nodded. »Most likely, he learned of the names on
Innocence's deathbed. At the time they both assumed Monti
would be the next Pope...«

»Something that both Benelli and yourself knew to prevent,
much to Monti's disappointment.« The Pope gave Ciban a look.

The prefect let out a pretend sigh before looking at Catherine.
»Bringing us to the next secret you now know, Sister. When
Monti lost the papal election, he saw his final chance to gain
power through his knowledge about the apostolic myth and their
names because he would have been too old by the next election.«
Ciban lifted his glass in her direction. »Then you showed up,
ruining Monti's plans with your gift. All of those assassinations
were for naught.«

Catherine wrinkled her brow. »But couldn't he have simply
had the rest of the apostles killed?«

Ciban shook his head and put down his wine glass. »Once you
arrived on the scene, Monti's plans rose and fell with your presence. We found a list of names in his apartment. He had in fact
only had six of the twelve names. Therefore it is my guess that he
pulled it out of Pope Innocence on his deathbed. Innocence must
have died before he could mention all of them. Thank God

Benelli's name wasn't on the list.«

»He would have ruined the Church with his thirst for power,« said the Pope simply.

»At any rate he wanted to sway the balance of powers in his favour, Holiness,« explained Ciban. »For one, to continue Pope Innocence's political direction and for another to thwart your plans for the future. I am sorry, Holiness, but your path to bring the Church into the twenty-first century will be even harder to manage.«

»May I ask what these plans look like in the near future?« asked Catherine gently.

The Pope gave her a meaningful look and a wink. »Just you wait, Catherine. I can tell you this much: Your engagement within the Church will play a significant role in its evolution.«

Catherine couldn't help but give Ciban a questioning look. What did the prefect think about all this? Could the Pope speak so openly in his presence? »I always thought you were a conservative, or even a traditionalist, Eminence.«

»Compared to you, Sister, I am. But compared to Cardinal Monti or Cardinal Gasperetti, I am a progressive member of the clergy.«

»Then you sympathise with Lux?« she dared to ask.

»Don't think in such black and white categories of good and evil. Lux is an important antithesis to Opus. Slowly but surely the order has overshot the mark in terms of the balance between both orders, even with a conservative man such as Gasperetti at the helm. Simply put: power is seductive.«

Leo nodded. »I'm afraid you are right.«

»By the way, Cardinal Gasperetti...« Ciban pulled out a note from the inside pocket of his cassock and handed it to Catherine. Did she see a gleam in those steel grey eyes of his? »Memorise both of these passwords. Then burn this paper.« He pointed to the candle, pushing a decorative ashtray toward her.

»What are they for?«

»These codes are the key to Father Darius' biography and the monograph in the Lux database, LUKE. Of course these files aren't the last of the secrets, but they will help you better understand your own past and the legacy you may possibly inherit.«

Catherine raised an eyebrow. »Cardinal Gasperetti simply handed you these codes?«

Ciban answered her question with a mysterious smile. »Tell me, Sister, what do you think of this wine?«

Epilogue

Catherine didn't like the atmosphere, but less the smell of hospitals, but when Cardinal Ciban called her to let her know Ben had awoken from his coma, she dropped everything and went immediately to the Gemelli clinic. When she entered Ben's hospital room, she was happy to see he was no longer attached to an IV or any other cable for that matter. She hugged him hard, not wanting to ever let him go again until he protested with a crooked smile and a gentle indication that he might otherwise suffocate should she chose not to release him immediately.

»I had the strangest dream,« he said. »In the Sistine...I saw you, Darius, Benelli, Thea, Monti and all the others. I now know it wasn't just a dream. His Eminence told me everything. I still can't believe Cardinal Monti was the mastermind behind it all.«

»None of us did. Yes, Monti was a schemer, but a murderer?«

Ben sat up and looked at her. »I saw the photograph.«

Catherine blinked in disbelief. On the other hand, what did it matter? Ben was and would always be like a brother to her. »I am going to need your help,« she said with a sigh.

»You've got it. Unconditionally.«

He asked her to open the nightstand's drawer, in which she found a book: Darius' Bible. She pulled out the Bible to give it to Ben, but he refused. »You take it. Please.«

»But it belongs to you.« Darius had bequeathed it to Ben.

The archivist shook his head. »I now know it was always meant for you. Its true power can only unfold in your hands.« He looked at her in silence for a few seconds, then explained: »You have made quite an impression on Cardinal Ciban.«

»Perhaps the tribunal's verdict won't be as damning then.«

»I mean it, Catherine. You have gained a very influential friend amongst the cardinals in the Vatican.«

»A friend? I wouldn't go that far.«

Ben gave her a crooked smile. »I disagree. You should gradually get used to the idea.«

»If I find out you talked nonsense about me…«

Ben waved her off with an even broader grin. Then he yawned, covering his mouth with his hand. »I am dog-tired and desperately need some sleep. No worries. Take it easy. And don't forget your Bible.«

»You're throwing me out?«

»What else can I do to get rid of you? Being subtle isn't my strong suit.« He laughed and she agreed. But behind all that laughter was indeed an endless feeling of exhaustion. She got up and put the book in her bag. »Well then, sleep well and sweet dreams. See you!«

When she left the hospital, it was already afternoon. She took a taxi, had it drop her off in the middle of Rome and went to a café to reflect on Ben's words. She then examined Darius' Bible more closely until her gaze fell on the headlines of the daily paper that another guest had left on a neighbouring table:

THIRD VATICAN COUNCIL: Pope Leo Walks his Talk

That had been Leo's secret plan all along. Introducing a third Vatican council! And that was what Monti had wanted to prevent!

Catherine grabbed the paper, sat back down and read the entire article.

But the paper offered an additional Vatican press release on page two:

Last night at 9:27 p.m. Cardinal Secretariat of State Sergio Cardinal Monti died of a major brain haemorrhage. He fell into a deep coma and died seven hours later. The cardinal's body will be given to the Vatican this morning where he will lay in a closed coffin in St. Peter's Basilica so that worshippers and mourners can pay their respects.

Cardinal Monti's successor has not yet been named.

As Cardinal Ciban, the prefect for the Congregation for the Doctrine of Faith, explained, the Church has lost a tremendous benefactor, who had supported numerous organisations, with Cardinal Monti's passing.

Catherine allowed both articles to settle in her brain for a moment before closing the paper and placing it back on the table. The world around her seemed to stand still. She heard neither the crowds of people nor the sounds of the city's relentless street noises.

Odd. The news of Monti's death should somehow have calmed her. Good had triumphed in this battle. Instead, it possessed her with an indescribable agitation. Something Darius had once said to her shot through her mind: »Normally, we chase evil. But this time, evil is chasing us.«

Catherine carefully folded the paper and pocketed it. For what felt like an eternity, her gaze travelled in the direction of the Vatican. The gleaming dome of St. Peter's Basilica loomed ominously over the rest of the buildings.

Author's Notes

The story in this novel is purely fictional. The names, characters, organisations and events are either a figment of the authors' imaginations or the results of research that were then used and expanded upon for the purposes of fiction. The Abbey Rottach, the order of Lux Domini or the Catholic Institute for the Psychically Gifted do not exist in reality. Along with the term Congregation for the Doctrine of Faith that has been in use since 1965 in favour of a stronger association, the earlier characterisations Holy Office or Inquisition were also used. In the same fashion, the term Palace of the Holy Office was also called the Palace of the Inquisition.

In Lux Domini Sister Catherine Bell quotes from a book from Cardinal Ciban during her disciplinary hearing as a means of defending herself. As prefect of the Congregation of the Doctrine of Faith, Ciban is her claimed archenemy. The idea for this scene is indeed borrowed from an actual historical event. Uta Ranke-Heinemann referred to a passage in Cardinal Ratzinger's book Introduction to Christianity during a written exchange.

The idea for the fictitious secret library of Pope Pius XII beneath the Vatican is based on a historical event in the summer of 1943 when Mussolini was overthrown and the following September German troops occupied Rome, much to the Pope's outrage. When in October an SS commando took position on the

Vatican's borders – allegedly for the Pope's protection – the
Vatican feared they would be occupied by the National Socialists.
Many art objects and documents were brought to safety. In Lux
Domini we are referring to the fictitious secret library of Pius XII
whose valuable pieces were hidden from the Nazis beneath St.
Peter's Basilica.

Acknowledgements

Throughout our research journey for the Catherine Bell series, we experienced a lot and exchanged ideas with many smart and inspiring people along the way. In fact, Rome and London have become our home away from home. We have mastered the art of crossing the streets of Rome with its breakneck traffic that has become as familiar to us as the silence of the antique ruins and the breathtaking atmosphere of the St. Peter and St. Paul cathedrals. A heartfelt thanks goes to all of you who supported us on our journey, whether it was through your great suggestions, your feedback on the story or your relentless encouragement.

Our thanks also goes out to all the booksellers, librarians, book bloggers and last, but not least, the many faithful readers who have loved and further recommended our Catherine Bell series since Lux Domini was released. We are so happy that you have chosen Catherine Bell and Mark Ciban amidst the gigantic sea of books out there. You alone have made it possible for us to continue to tell their stories.

About the translator

With degrees in Political Science, German and American Literature from Smith College, Northampton, MA, USA and the University of Constance, Germany, Christine Louise Hohlbaum has spent her entire life telling stories. Having published multiple books herself, the bilingual US-born writer enjoys working as a public relations professional, blogger and translator from her home office in Freiburg, Germany where she lives with her two children.

"Translating is like dancing in the shadows between two worlds. What emerges is magic," she says.

Homepage: http://www.hohlbaum-pr.com/en

About the author

Alex Thomas is the alias of a married couple. She worked for more than two decades in the book and media sector as editor, writing coach and novelist. He researched and taught computer science and artificial intelligence at German universities, then later as a professor in London, UK.

Both love to explore the intersection of science, religion and human history. Secret labs, conspiratorial centres of power and the mystic appeal of old cathedrals attract them. Their series featuring the rebellious nun, Sister Catherine Bell, excites fans of Vatican and mystery thrillers alike.

Homepage: http://www.alex-thomas.london

Glossary

Angelus: A prayer that the Pope conducts every Sunday at midday from his flat window in commemoration of the incarnation of Christ.

Apocrypha: Texts that do not appear in the canon of the Bible for religious and political reasons.

Apostolic Constitution: Governs certain issues, mostly canon law, as a papal edict or announcement, but without the infallibility claim such as in dogma, for instance, which for Catholic Christians is mandatory doctrine.

Apse: Semi-circular or polygonal niche for the altar in Christian churches.

Breviary: Liturgical book that contains the texts for the Liturgy of the Hours in the Roman Catholic Church.

Camerlengo (Cardinal Chamberlain): Determines the Pope's death and takes over the Church's administration without judicial power as long as the papal office is not occupied.

Cardinal electors: Characterises those cardinals from the College of the Cardinals who participate in the papal election and have not yet reached their eightieth birthdays.

Cincture: A belt that nuns wear around their habits and priests around their cassocks. Cardinals' belts are made of a broad, noble piece of scarlet red cloth.

Conclave: Describes the gathering of cardinal electors for the

papal election but also the enclosed room in which the papal
election takes place.

Congregation of the Doctrine of Faith: Has the role of
protecting the Church from divergent moral and faith doctrines.
It was founded in the sixteenth century by Pope Paul II and once
named the »Holy Roman and Universal Inquisition«.

Congregation(s): Term for the authorities of the central
authority in Rome that are organised according to their areas of
responsibility.

Consistory: The gathering of cardinals under the Pope's
chairmanship.

Council: Ecclesiastical gathering to clarify church affairs.

Crypt: Accessible burial grounds beneath the choir (apse) or
altar.

Curia: Roman Catholic central authority in Rome.

Diocese (See): Ecclesiastical administrative district; a bishop's jurisdiction.

Fish: According to oral, then later written documented lore, a
secret Christian identifying symbol of Early Christianity.

Golgotha: The place where Jesus Christ was executed before
the gates of Jerusalem.

Grand Inquisitor: A medieval term for inquisitors whose
authority extends beyond that of a normal inquisitor. The head
of the Congregation of the Doctrine of Faith is quite often
referred to as the Grand Inquisitor by the media.

Heresy: False teachings that diverge from the official dogma
of a large church.

**Inquisition (from the Latin: Inquisito =
investigation):** Persecution of people who hold different religious or ideological beliefs with the help of investigative and
court proceedings that didn't shy away from torture either.

Lot: The nephew of Abraham who was allowed to survive the demise of Sodom, the city of sin, due to his righteousness; his wife turned into a pillar of salt after defying the angels' ban by turning around one last time toward the city.

Necropolis (City of Death): Larger burial grounds of antiquity and prehistoric times located outside of residential areas.

Nephilim: A mixed creature consisting of human females and God's sons (fallen angels) who are larger and stronger than man and extremely evil.

Prefect (Cardinal Prefect): Head of a particular office in the Roman central authority, for instance that of the State Secretariat or the Congregation of the Doctrine of Faith.

Prelate: Ecclesiastical dignitaries (abbot, bishop or cardinal).

Promulgated Law: A law that goes into effect with its first announcement (promulgate: to announce publicly).

Qumran Scrolls: Characterises the scrolls found in the fifties and sixties at the Dead Seas, including the oldest known handwritten scripts of the Bible.

Sede Vacante: Encompasses the time period that the papal office is not occupied.

Temple of Solomon: The first Israeli temple built under King Solomon's reign in the tenth century in which the ark of the covenant with the ten commandments that Moses received from God were kept.

Zucchetto: A skullcap that is part of the ecclesiastical clothing for clergy members (black), bishops (violet), cardinals (scarlet red) and the Pope (white).

Made in the USA
Coppell, TX
13 August 2020